About the Authors

Growing up near the beach, **Annie West** spent lots of time observing tall, burnished lifeguards—early research! Now she spends her days fantasising about gorgeous men and their love lives. Annie has been a reader all her life. She also loves travel, long walks, good company and great food. You can contact her at annie@annie-west.com.

Leanne Banks is a *New York Times* and *USA TODAY* bestselling author, who is surprised every time she realizes how many books she has written. Leanne loves chocolate, the beach and new adventures. To name a few, Leanne has ridden on an elephant, stood on an ostrich egg (no, it didn't break), gone parasailing and indoor skydiving. Leanne loves writing romance because she believes in the power and magic of love. She lives in Virginia with her family and four-and-a-half-pound Pomeranian named Bijou. Visit her website at www.leannebanks.com.

Kandy Shepherd swapped a career as a magazine editor for a life writing romance. She lives on a small farm in the Blue Mountains near Sydney, Australia, with her husband, daughter and lots of pets. She believes in love at first sight and real-life romance—they worked for her! Kandy loves to hear from her readers. Visit her at kandyshepherd.com.

The Royals

COLLECTION

Royal Weddings

ANNIE WEST

LEANNE BANKS

KANDY SHEPHERD

MILLS & BOON

First Published in Great Britain 2019
By Mills & Boon, an imprint of HarperCollins *Publishers*
1 London Bridge Street, London, SE1 9GF

ROYAL WEDDINGS © 2019 Harlequin Books S.A.

The Sheikh's Princess Bride © 2015 Annie West
The Doctor Takes a Princess © 2011 Leanne Banks
Crown Prince's Chosen Bride © 2016 Kandy Shepherd

ISBN: 978-0-263-27599-5

0619

MIX
Paper from
responsible sources
FSC™ C007454

This book is produced from independently certified FSC™ paper to ensure responsible forest management.

For more information visit: www.harpercollins.co.uk/green

Printed and bound in Spain
by CPI, Barcelona

THE SHEIKH'S PRINCESS BRIDE

ANNIE WEST

For Dr G,
the original and the best.
Thank you!

CHAPTER ONE

THE DARK-HAIRED TOTS playing on the far side of the sumptuous hotel lounge held Samira's gaze. They weren't loud or boisterous, the middle-aged woman with them saw to that. They were just a pair of ordinary toddlers.

Yet Samira couldn't drag her eyes away from them. She watched the progress of one little boy as he walked the length of a sofa, his fingers splayed on the silk upholstery for support. He gurgled his delight and grinned at his companion who wobbled along behind him.

Samira swallowed. That hollow feeling was back, worse now, turning into a twisting stab of hurt that knifed all the way from her womb up high under her ribs.

She tried to focus on Celeste's animated chatter about a new restaurant. Apparently it had unrivalled rooftop views of the Eiffel Tower as well as several Michelin stars and was *the* new place to eat and be seen.

Samira's stomach rebelled at the mention of food.

Or maybe it was something else that made her insides clench so hard.

The second toddler landed on his bottom, arms waving, and the woman—grandmother? Nanny?—gathered him up. Samira's arms twitched then fell, lax and empty, into her lap.

She blinked and turned away.

Empty. That was exactly how she felt.

She would never have a child of her own to hold. The doctor had made that clear.

She'd tried so hard to regroup these past four years, and she'd come so far, but nothing could erase that searing, hollow ache within.

'I'm so pleased you can attend tonight's charity auction in person.' Celeste leaned across their porcelain teacups and Samira swung her gaze back to the pretty Parisienne. 'Bidders will adore the chance to meet the talented princess behind the gorgeous fashions. Your donation to the auction is sure to fetch a huge price.'

Samira fixed on a practised smile and refused to cringe at yet another reference to her royal status.

As daughter of, and now sister to, the Sultan of Jazeer, she knew all too well that royal rank didn't guarantee happiness.

Her heart lurched but she kept her gaze on her companion, not letting it stray to the other side of the opulent room.

She reminded herself she was a pragmatist. Her successful design business benefited from the cachet of her aristocratic name. Designs by Samira had taken off these last few years. Her clientele, among the globe's ultrawealthy, appreciated working with someone who understood their world, who promised absolute exclusivity and confidentiality. She had far more than many women dreamed of: independence, success, wealth.

What right had she to yearn for more?

Yet still that bone-deep ache persisted, no matter how often she reminded herself how lucky she was. For what did the trappings of success mean when deep at the heart of you there was...nothing?

Samira bit her lip. She *would* conquer this. She would!

'I'm looking forward to it, Celeste.' Samira wrenched her thoughts back to tonight's gala. 'You and your team have done a marvellous job pulling it all together. How, exactly, will the auction work? What do you want me to do?'

Celeste launched into an explanation of the auction, the exclusive invitation list and the business opportunities tonight's event would present.

Yet, businesswoman though she was, Samira couldn't conjure answering enthusiasm. Perhaps because, having been born to status and privilege, mixing with the stratosphere of European society held no thrill for her.

Was this all there was? Long days of work followed by an endless round of society events where she'd mix business, pleasure and occasional philanthropy, and leave feeling alone and empty?

Samira blinked and gave herself a mental shake, refusing to linger on the maudlin thoughts that had edged her consciousness for so long.

She leaned back in her chair, nodding as Celeste emphasised a point, letting her weary body relax for the first time, it felt, in days.

That was it. She was exhausted. No wonder her attention strayed. She'd been in consultation with a new first lady in South America yesterday about a gown for an inauguration ball, then had stopped off in New York to see another client, only arriving in Paris an hour ago.

When she rested she'd be herself, eager to be caught up once more in the challenges of business, and especially the joy of designing.

Movement caught her eye. A tall figure in a dark suit moved through the perfectly arranged seating with a long, quick stride that made her think of her dressmaker's shears cutting through rich velvet.

She told herself it was a ridiculous comparison but when she turned to focus on him she realised it was apt. Though dressed with the formidable elegance of the best bespoke tailoring, some indefinable air proclaimed he didn't belong

in the luxury of Paris's finest hotel. He belonged somewhere more vital, where crystal chandeliers and dainty
side tables were unnecessary fripperies.

A good head taller than every other man in the vicin-
ity, his shoulders the broadest Samira had ever seen, he
nevertheless moved with a fluid, athletic grace that spoke
to her designer's eye.

A squeal of excitement froze her in the act of turning
back to Celeste. One of the little, chubby-cheeked boys
had spotted him and was scrambling across the sofa towards him.

A low, rumbling chuckle reached her ears as the man
bent and scooped up both children, one in each arm, as
easily as she'd pick up a couple of cushions. He lifted them
high, making them giggle with delight, and held them close
as he ducked his head and murmured to each of them in
turn. Tiny starfish hands planted on his shoulders and hair
in their eagerness to get close and she heard him laugh
again, the sound a ribbon of warmth channelling through
the chill emptiness inside her.

Just like that, without any fanfare or warning, Samira's
world contracted to the cold void of her barren body and
the devastating vignette of a happy family on the other
side of the room.

The dividing line excluding her from them had never
been more real, or more unbreakable.

Pain juddered through her, making her clench her jaw
and grab at the arms of her lounge chair.

There would be no family for her, no children. As for
finding a life partner to love… The air hissed between her
teeth at the impossibility of that particular fantasy.

'Samira. Is anything wrong?'

'Nothing at all.' Samira turned to Celeste with a dazzling smile that only years of practice in the public eye
could muster. Surreptitiously she breathed in through her

nose, filling lungs that seemed to have cramped shut. 'It sounds like tonight will be a huge success. With luck you'll attract far more than your fund-raising target.'

'Thanks to you.' At Samira's raised brow she shrugged and smiled. 'And to the rest of the donors.' She paused, glancing across the lounge. 'Speak of the devil, there's one of them now.' Celeste sat straighter, swiftly smoothing her short skirt and flicking her blonde hair from her face.

She leaned close to Samira and whispered, 'If only we could auction off a night in his bed we'd make a fortune. I'd bid for that myself and, believe me, I wouldn't let anyone outbid me.'

Surprised at the change in her companion, Samira turned. Yet she knew which man Celeste referred to. It could only be the hunky father of two who wore his elegant clothes with such casual panache that even her long-dormant libido sat up and slavered.

Yet she wasn't prepared for the shock that slammed into her solar plexus as she saw him again. For this time he'd turned and she saw his broad, high brow, defined cheekbones and the rough-cut jaw that looked dangerous and sexy at the same time. A long, harsh blade of a nose somehow melded those too-strong features into a whole that was boldly, outrageously attractive.

And familiar.

Samira's breath hissed sharply as she recognised the man she hadn't seen in years. The man who'd once been almost as dear to her as her brother, Asim.

A tumble of emotions bubbled inside. Excitement and pleasure, regret and pain, and finally a sharp tang of something that tasted like desire, raw and real for the first time in four years. Amazement at that instantaneous response spiralled through her.

'Oh, I'd forgotten you must know him, your country and

his being in the same neighbourhood.' Celeste sounded eager. 'Sexy Sheikh Tariq of Al Sarath.' She sighed gustily. 'I'd even consider taking on a couple of kids for the sake of a man like that. Not that I'll get the chance. They say he hasn't looked at another woman seriously since he lost his wife. They try but none of them last. Apparently he was devoted to her.'

With one final, lingering look at Tariq and his sons, Samira swung round, putting her back to them, letting Celeste's chatter wash over her.

She'd once thought Tariq her friend. She'd looked up to him and trusted him. He'd been as much a part of her life as her brother, Asim. But that friendship had been a mirage, as fragile as the shimmer of water on hot desert sands. He'd turned his back on her years ago with a suddenness that had mystified her, making her wonder what she'd done to alienate him or whether he'd just forgotten her in the press of responsibilities when he'd become Sheikh. When she'd been through hell four years previously she'd not heard a word from him.

Strange how much that still hurt.

Tariq had been in the crowded banqueting hall just three minutes when his sixth sense, the one that always twitched at a hint of trouble, switched into overdrive.

Casually he turned, keenly surveying the glamorous throng even as he returned greetings. He'd been plagued by a sense that something wasn't quite right all afternoon, since he returned to the hotel, but to his annoyance couldn't pinpoint any tangible reason. Just a disturbing sense that he'd missed something important.

It wasn't a sensation he liked. Tariq liked to be in control of his world.

The crowd shifted and through a gap he saw a sliver of deep scarlet. His gaze snagged. Another shift and the scarlet became a long dress, a beacon drawing his eyes to the sultry swell of feminine hips and a deliciously rounded bottom. The woman's skin, displayed by the low scoop of material at her back, was a soft gold, like the desert at first light. A drift of gleaming dark hair was caught up in an artfully casual arrangement that had probably taken hours to achieve. It was worth it, for it revealed the slender perfection of her elegant neck.

Tariq's body tightened, every tendon and muscle stiffening in a response that was profound, instinctive and utterly unexpected.

Light played on the sheen of her dress, lovingly detailing each curve.

He swallowed, realising suddenly that his mouth was dry. His blood flowed hot and fast, his heartbeat tripping to a new, urgent rhythm.

It was a rhythm he hadn't felt in years. Tariq frowned.

The woman turned and he took in the fitted dress that covered her from neck to toe. It enticed a man's imagination to wander over the slim frame and bounteous curves beneath the fabric.

He'd taken half a pace towards her when his eyes lifted to her face and he slammed to a stop, an invisible brick wall smashing into him, tearing the air from his lungs.

Samira.

Tariq heaved in a breath so deep it made his ribs ache. *Samira.*

He breathed out, almost tasting the memories on his tongue.

But this wasn't Samira as he'd last seen her. This was a different woman: confident, sexy and experienced. A woman who was making her mark on the world.

For a moment he paused, drawn despite himself. Then his brain kicked into gear as he remembered all the reasons she wasn't for him, despite the tight ache gripping his lower body. He turned to the pretty blonde at his right who was half-wearing a gold sequinned dress. She looked up with wide, hopeful eyes that brimmed with excitement when he smiled down at her.

Minutes later she was leaning into him, her pale hand clutching his sleeve possessively, her eyes issuing an invitation as old as time.

Tariq made himself smile again, wondering if she realised or cared that his attention was elsewhere.

Samira watched him from the back of the crowd. Tariq was the obvious choice of speaker for the children's charity. He was a natural leader, holding the audience in the palm of his hand. Confident, articulate and witty, he effortlessly drew all eyes. Around her men nodded and women salivated and Samira had to repress indignation as they ate him up hungrily.

He was all she remembered: thoughtful, capable and caring, using his speech to reinforce the plight of the children they were here to help, yet keeping the tone just right to loosen the wallets of wealthy patrons.

She remembered a lanky youth who'd always been gentle with her, his friend's little sister. This Tariq was charismatic, with an aura of assured authority that he'd no doubt acquired from ruling his sheikhdom. She couldn't drag her eyes from his tall frame and the way it filled out his tuxedo with solid muscle and bone.

Samira gulped, disorientated at the sudden blast of longing that swamped her.

She blinked and looked up at his bold, handsome face, the glint of humour in his eyes, and remembered the way he'd been with his boys: gentle, loving and patient.

In that moment recognition hit. Recognition of what she wanted.

What she *needed*.

The family she longed for. Children to nurture and love. A partner she could respect and trust to share her life.

Eyes fixed on Tariq, she realised there *was* a way she could become part of a family. It was the perfect solution to her untenable situation. A solution not just for her, but potentially a win-win for all concerned. If she had the courage to pursue it.

The idea was so sudden, so outrageous, she swayed on her delicate heels, her heart thumping high in her throat, her stomach twisting hard and sharp.

'Are you sure you're all right?' Celeste grabbed her elbow as if afraid she'd topple over. 'You weren't yourself this afternoon either.'

'I'm…' Samira gulped, swallowing shock at the revelation confronting her. 'I'm okay, thanks. Just a little tired.'

Celeste nodded and turned back to Tariq. 'He's a little overwhelming, isn't he? Especially in formal dress. I swear, if he wasn't a king someone would snap him up as a model.'

Samira pressed her hand against her churning stomach, only half-listening.

She stared at the powerful figure on the podium and the voice of self-doubt, the voice that had ruled the first twenty-five years of her life, told her she was crazy. Crazy to think about wanting what she could never have. After all, she and Tariq hadn't been friends for years. There was no guarantee he'd even listen to her.

But another part of her applauded. The part that had grown stronger in the last four years, nurtured by her family and her determination to drag herself out of the mire of despair and make something of her life. The voice of the survivor she'd become.

She knew what she wanted.

Why not go for it?

Yet instinctively she shied away from such an action.

That wasn't her style. It never had been. The only time she'd defied convention and upbringing and had reached for what she desired, it had turned to dust and ashes, ruin and grief. She still bore the scars.

Yet what had she to lose by trying? Nothing that mattered when weighed against the possibility of winning what she so desperately craved.

In the mirrored lift, Samira straightened her neat, cinnamon jacket and smoothed her clammy palms down the matching fitted skirt. Her cream blouse was businesslike rather than feminine but this, she reminded herself, was a business meeting.

The most important business meeting of her life.

If only she felt half as confident as at her meetings with clients.

The door hissed open and she stepped out. A few metres took her to the door of the presidential suite and a dark-suited security man.

'Your Highness.' He bowed smoothly and opened the door, admitting her into the suite's luxurious foyer.

Inside, another staff member greeted her.

'If you'd care to take a seat, Your Highness?' He led the way to a beautifully appointed sitting room furnished in shades of soft taupe and aubergine. Large windows offered an unrivalled view of Paris. 'Can I offer you something to eat or drink?'

'Nothing, thank you.' Samira couldn't swallow anything. Her insides felt like they'd been invaded by circling, swooping vultures.

The man excused himself and Samira darted a look at her watch. She was dead on time. It felt like a lifetime had passed since she'd stepped out of her suite downstairs.

Slowly she breathed out, trying to calm her rioting

nerves, but nothing could douse the realisation her whole future rested on this interview.

If she failed… No, she refused to imagine failure. She had to be positive and persuasive. This might be unconventional but Samira would *make* him see how sensible her idea was.

She swallowed hard, squashing the doubts that kept surfacing, and walked towards the windows. Automatically she stretched out a hand to the luxurious silk of the sofa as she passed. It was cool and soft, the lush fabric reassuringly familiar. If she closed her eyes perhaps she could imagine herself in the quiet sanctuary of her work room, surrounded by delicate silks, satins and crêpe de Chine; by damask, velvet and lace.

'Samira.'

She started and turned, her heart thumping out of kilter as her eyes snapped open. There he was, his powerful frame filling the doorway.

Her breath snared, just as it had time and again that last year. She'd been on the brink of womanhood and suddenly noticed her brother's best friend as a *man*. A man who'd evoked disturbing new responses in her awakening body…

Samira dragged in a calming breath, squashing shock at the way awareness prickled the tender flesh of her breasts and belly. She wasn't the untried girl she'd once been.

'Tariq.'

How could she have forgotten those eyes, their remarkable colour legacy of marauding ancestors who'd intermarried along the way? Under slashing dark brows those eyes gleamed with the pure, rich green of deep water and were just as unfathomable.

His expression made her hesitate.

Was she welcome or did the hard set of his jaw indicate displeasure? Was he annoyed she'd used their connection to inveigle a meeting at short notice? No doubt he had huge demands on his time but he could hardly reject her request, given the close links between their kingdoms.

Samira's brow puckered. The Tariq she recalled had been infallibly patient and friendly, even though she'd probably been a nuisance, tagging along behind him and Asim.

'How are you, Samira?' He stepped into the room and the air evaporated from her lungs. He seemed to fill the space even though he stood metres away, watching her with that penetrating stare as if he saw behind the practised façade to the nervous woman beneath.

'Excellent, thank you.' This time when he gestured for her to take a seat she accepted, grateful to relieve her suddenly shaky legs.

She'd known this would be challenging but Tariq was more unsettling than she'd imagined. Not simply because he had the power to grant or deny what she'd set her heart on. But because that useless, feminine part of her she'd thought long-dormant reacted to him in ways she didn't like to contemplate.

As if the lessons of four years ago had been completely forgotten. More, as if the years had peeled back further and she was seventeen again, sexually aware for the first time and fantasising over Tariq. Heat washed her.

'And you? Are you well? You seemed in fine form last night. The crowd responded so well to your speech.' She snapped her teeth shut before she could babble any more. The last thing she needed was for him to think her a brainless chatterbox.

'I am. The evening was a resounding success. Did you enjoy yourself?'

He strolled across the room, making her aware of the flex and bunch of taut muscle under the superb suit as he sat down opposite her, stretching out long, powerful legs that ate into the space between them. She wanted to tuck her feet back under her seat but kept them where they were, determined not to show nerves.

She fixed on her most charming smile, the one that worked no matter how stressed she felt. 'It was a bit of a crush but worth it for the end result.' Her donation—two gowns to be designed exclusively for the highest bidder—had garnered far more than even Celeste had dared hope.

'Are you staying long in Paris?' It was a simple question, a polite conversation starter, yet the keenness of Tariq's scrutiny invested it with extra significance.

Samira shivered. He could have no idea of her mission here. Suddenly panic hit at the thought of how he'd react when he found out. It would be easy enough to turn this instead into a brief, social catch-up. She could walk out the door with her head high and her secret safe.

But the black void of desolation would be waiting to consume her again. Surely she had the gumption to fight for what she craved, rather than admit defeat so easily?

She was the daughter of generations of warriors. It was time she remembered that.

'I'm not sure how long I'll stay.' She smoothed a damp hand over her fitted skirt, telling herself he couldn't see how her fingers trembled. 'It depends.'

He didn't ask the obvious question, giving her an opening, however tenuous, for her proposition. Nervously she shifted in her seat, then realised what she was doing and stilled.

'I was very sorry to hear about your wife.' She'd added her condolences to Asim's note when Tariq's wife had died giving birth to their twins, but this was the first time Samira had seen Tariq since it had happened.

It was the first time she'd seen him in twelve years. Since the winter she'd turned seventeen and his sudden departure had devastated her. He'd even missed Asim's wedding three years ago due to emergency surgery on his appendix.

Now he looked like a stranger, despite those familiar features.

He nodded, his eyes never leaving hers. 'Thank you.'

Silence fell.

'I saw your boys yesterday in the hotel.' It wasn't what she'd meant to say but her carefully rehearsed words disintegrated under his silent regard. 'They look like a happy pair.'

He nodded. 'They are.'

'And full of energy.'

Samira bit her lip. She was babbling again. She had to get a grip.

'They're never still, except when they sleep.' A hint of a smile lurked at the corner of Tariq's mouth and suddenly he wasn't a stern stranger but the friend she remembered from years ago.

Friends she could deal with. It was the potently masculine Tariq who unsettled her. The man whose deep laugh and imposing body awoke longings that had no place in her life.

'They must keep you very busy.' This time her smile was genuine.

'I wouldn't have it any other way.'

Samira nodded. The Tariq she knew would find time for the demands of his small sons, just as he'd found time for his best friend's kid sister. He took duty seriously but, more than that, he was kind. He was the sort of man you could *trust*.

That was why she couldn't shake the outrageous idea that had taken root as she'd watched him last night at the gala. The idea that he held the key to her future happiness.

Samira swallowed hard. She'd known only one trustworthy man, her brother, Asim. The other men in her life, even her father, had let her down terribly. Could she trust Tariq not to do that too?

'Samira.'

'Yes?' She looked up to see him lounging back in his chair, the picture of ease. Yet his eyes were intent.

'What's wrong?'

'Nothing's wrong.' Her laugh sounded woefully unconvincing and caught her up short. She was stronger than this. Here was her chance to reach out for the one thing she really wanted in life. Surely she wasn't coward enough to give up without trying?

'On the contrary.' She sat forward, projecting an air of certainty she'd mastered in her professional dealings. She could do this. 'I wanted to see you because I have a proposal to put to you.'

'Really?' Interest sparked in his eyes.

'A rather unusual proposal, but a sound one. I'm sure you'll see the benefits.'

'I'm sure I will.' He paused. 'When you tell me what it is.' Those slashing dark eyebrows angled up in query.

Samira leaned closer, suddenly urgent to get this done. She licked her dry lips, holding his keen gaze.

'I want to marry you.'

CHAPTER TWO

'MARRY YOU?' ANGER splintered through Tariq that Samira should make him the butt of some jest. He sat bolt upright, hands curling tight around the arms of his chair. 'What game is this?'

Marriage was an institution to be taken seriously, as he knew first-hand. Sharp talons dragged deep through his chest; claws clutched at what passed for his heart.

No, marriage wasn't something to joke about, even between old family friends.

Though Samira was more than an old friend, wasn't she?

At one point he'd wanted much more from her. Long-buried sensations bombarded him—lust, regret, weakness. Above all, guilt. For despite the years apart, even throughout his marriage, Tariq had never completely managed to forget her. His one consolation was that no one, least of all Samira, had known. It had been his secret shame.

'It's no game.' Her voice, uneven before, rang clear and proud. Her gaze, which previously had skittered around the room, meshed with his and Tariq breathed hard as fire heated his veins. Those soft sherry eyes had always been amazing. Now, fixed on him so earnestly, they might have melted a lesser man.

But Tariq's strength had been forged and tested well. He wouldn't be bowled over by a beauty's wide eyes. Even if the beauty was Samira, the most stunning woman he'd ever known, the woman he'd once craved body and soul.

'What is it, then?' he barked. 'If not a joke?' His initial instinct—to avoid this meeting—had been right.

'It's a proposal of marriage.' Her voice was crisp and even, as if she had no notion how bizarre her words were.

Slowly Tariq shook his head. He couldn't be hearing this. Asim's little sister proposing marriage! Didn't she know it was a man's place to choose a wife? A woman's to accept?

What sort of tame lapdog did she take him for? The years since they'd known each other yawned into a fathomless gulf. She didn't know him at all.

He shot to his feet and stalked across the room, staring blankly at the city beyond the sound-proofed glass. 'Whatever the game, I don't appreciate it, Samira.' He swung round. 'Does your brother know about this?'

'It has nothing to do with Asim.' She folded her hands in her lap, for all the world as if they were politely discussing the weather. As if she hadn't offered herself to him in marriage.

An image of her last night, svelte and flagrantly feminine in that dark-red dress, filled his head and his temperature soared, his body tightening in all the wrong places. His hands curled into fists as he fought to focus on her words, not her sensual allure. Anger bit deep that, even now, just one look could ignite the fire in his belly.

'What is this about?' Savagely he reined in his temper, drawing on years of practice at patient diplomacy.

'I want to marry you.'

Those brilliant eyes looked up at him and again shock punched him hard in the gut. She looked, and sounded, serious.

For one disquieting moment he felt a quickening in his body, the sharp clench of arousal in his groin, a welling of possessiveness as he took in the pale honey perfection of her features, the sheen of her lush, dark hair and the Cupid's bow of the sexiest mouth he'd ever known.

When she'd been seventeen that mouth, those eyes, the promise of incandescent beauty to come, had sent him back to his homeland, shocked and ashamed by the hot, hungry thoughts that stirred whenever he'd looked at Asim's little sister.

He'd known then that she'd be breath-stopping, just like her mother, who'd been one of the world's great beauties. But the sight of Samira in the flesh, after twelve years of seeing only photos, took his breath away.

He stiffened, forcibly rejecting his body's response.

She sat there with her ankles primly crossed, her hands folded in her lap, saying she wanted to marry him! It was enough to drive a man crazy.

Tariq cupped the back of his neck, tilting his head and rubbing his skin to ease the tightness there.

'I have no idea what foolishness prompted this, Samira.' He paused, telling himself it was impossible that he tasted pleasure at her name on his tongue. 'But you of all people know royal marriages are carefully arranged. You can't just come in here and—'

'Why not?' She cut across his words and it struck Tariq that no one, not even Jasmin when she'd been alive, interrupted him. As Sheikh, his word was law, his status respected. Except, it seemed, by the Princess of Jazeer.

She stood and his eyes lingered on her delectable body in that figure-hugging suit. 'Why can't I arrange my own marriage? My brother didn't wait for advisors to find him a wife. He found Jacqui by himself.'

'That was different.' Tariq gestured with one slashing hand. 'That was a love match. They're crazy for each other.'

Seeing his friend in the throes of love made Tariq uncomfortable. He'd thought Asim was like himself, too focused on the wellbeing of his nation to choose a partner because of emotion.

Tariq's lips flattened. He didn't do emotion. Not that sort. And especially not now. He had no interest in marrying for love.

The idea ate like acid in his belly.

'If you want to get married, ask your brother to find you a suitable husband. He'll do anything to make you happy.'

Tariq was one of the few who understood Asim's fierce protectiveness of his sister. Their childhood, at the mercy of their parents' volatile on-again, off-again relationship, had left them both reluctant to trust anyone.

Was that why Samira was still single at twenty-nine? Traditionally, Jazeeri princesses married much younger, but he suspected his friend Asim had been in no hurry to rush his sister into matrimony after those early experiences of a dysfunctional family.

'I don't want Asim to arrange a suitable match.' She jutted her chin. In a woman less gorgeous, he'd call her expression mulish. 'I know what I want. I want you.'

Again that sudden blast of blistering arousal low in his body. For an instant he was tempted to forget his duty, his dead wife and his self-control, and haul Samira close, teach her the danger of trifling with him.

Only for an instant.

Tariq reminded himself she wasn't talking about sex. If she had been she'd have used a different approach— soft blandishments and seductive caresses. And she'd have worn something slinky and provocative. His nostrils flared as he sucked in air to tight lungs, imagining that soft mouth on him. Arousal weighted his lower body.

'And you're used to getting what you want?'

Abruptly she laughed, shaking her head, and his pulse faltered at the radiance of her smile. 'Only sometimes.'

'Yet you think you can have me for the asking?' Indignation at her presumption clashed with raw, disconcerting lust at the thought of them together and shame at how easily she got under his skin.

She sobered. 'I thought it couldn't hurt to ask.' She hesitated. 'I know this is unconventional. But we're old friends. I thought you'd at least hear me out.'

That was how she saw him? As an old friend? Why Tariq bridled at the idea, he refused to consider.

'Very well. I'll hear you out.' He folded his arms across his chest and waited.

Samira looked at the imposing man before her. He wasn't in a receptive mood. His crossed arms were all bunched muscles. The tendons in his neck were taut and his mouth a flat line. Even his eyes glittered a warning.

Yet still Tariq was the most breathtaking man she'd ever seen. Her stomach turned to treacle as the afternoon sun caught the solid plane of his jaw and the proud thrust of that impressive nose. She wondered how it would feel if, instead of shutting her out, he opened his arms and hauled her close into that broad chest. If he kissed her...

She blinked, suddenly light-headed.

That was *not* what she wanted. Sex had made a fool of her once. She refused to let that happen again. This, what she proposed now, was far more sensible.

Planting her feet more solidly, wishing she weren't quite so dwarfed by him, Samira cleared her throat, mentally flicking through the arguments she'd prepared.

'It's an excellent match,' she began, gathering herself. 'Our countries already have so much in common. I understand your customs and history. I'm not a complete outsider. And by marrying me you'd strengthen your ties with Jazeer.'

'Our ties with Jazeer are already strong.'

Refusing to be deflated, she kept her chin up. 'My background speaks for itself. I was born and bred to royal rank and responsibility. I understand what's expected of a queen and I've got a lifetime's experience of public functions and diplomacy. I understand royal duty and I won't shirk it.'

Expectantly she looked at him. Finally he nodded. 'All useful attributes.' He paused. 'But others could say the same. Your own sister-in-law has adapted well to her new role, and she wasn't born royal.'

Samira exhaled slowly. Had she really expected Tariq to agree instantly? She told herself his wariness was to be expected. He'd adored his first wife and his choice of second wife would affect not only himself but his precious boys and his country. Of course he needed to consider this from all angles.

Yet a small part of her wailed in disappointment that he viewed her so sternly, almost disapprovingly, when her own wayward impulse urged her to close the gap between them. Her very skin felt sensitised, as if longing for his touch.

Did she want him to look at her and *want* her? Not for her pedigree or her social attributes but for *herself*? Her wayward body betrayed her. Her flesh tingled as his gaze raked her and a slow, telling spiral of heat eddied low in her belly.

Samira sucked in a stunned breath, sensing danger.

She told herself it was nerves. The shock of seeing him again after all this time. The disconcerting discovery of how very…male he was.

Once the novelty wore off he'd be just as he'd always been—a friend, someone she could trust. Without trust she couldn't bind herself to any man. Trust had been so lacking in her life, she understood how rare and valuable it was.

The thought gave her renewed energy.

'I'll make a good queen,' she said firmly, locking her

hands together. 'Building my business has given me a chance to step beyond royal boundaries and mix with a range of people, not just wealthy clients. It's broadened my understanding of the world and improved my people skills.' Now she was as at home buying a bagel on the streets of New York as she'd been at last night's A-list gala.

Tariq didn't say anything so she kept talking, the thread of tension wrapping tighter around her insides. 'I'd like to continue working on a small scale, not enough to interfere with any royal duties.' When he remained silent she angled her head higher. 'I believe it would be a positive thing for people to see their queen with responsibilities and successes of her own.'

'You see yourself as a role model, then?'

Samira flinched at the steely glint in his eyes and the sharp pang of shame in her belly. Tariq knew as well as she that her past was tainted by that one, awful mistake she'd made. A mistake that would haunt her all her life.

'No one is perfect, Tariq. Young women in your country could do worse than a queen who's human enough to have made mistakes, yet has learned from them and built something positive for herself.'

Slowly he nodded and a feather of hope brushed her skin, making her shiver with excitement. She leaned closer.

'I'll be a loyal wife and a devoted mother, Tariq. You needn't worry that I'll embarrass you by falling for another man after we're married.' Bile swirled in her stomach and she tasted its bitterness on her tongue. 'I'm not my mother, for ever pining for romantic love. I learned from her mistakes, and my own.'

'You don't want love?' His words were sharp, his gaze intense as he leaned forward. His raised eyebrows signalled surprise, perhaps disapproval. She guessed he was used to women falling at his feet.

Samira's lips twisted. 'Would I be here if I did? If my

mother's example weren't enough, my experience with Jackson Brent cured me of any romantic ideas.'

Jackson Brent. The name no one spoke around her. The man who'd taken her dreams and her innocence and had smashed them in the cruellest way.

She read understanding in Tariq's expression. The whole world knew the story. Samira looked away, pressing her palms to her churning stomach.

Jackson Brent, the sexy film star, had taken one look at Samira, the ridiculously inexperienced princess living away from home for the first time, and decided to have her. Samira, swept off her feet and dazzled by what she thought was love, had believed it a fairy-tale romance come true.

They'd been feted and adored by the press and the public. Until the day Jackson had been found in bed with his beautiful co-star by her vengeful husband.

Samira's cosy world had blown apart, her dreams shattered as she'd been forced to see Jackson as he really was. Not Mr Right, but a feckless, selfish opportunist who'd played on her longing for love to get himself cheap sex and great publicity.

Guessing at her anguish, the press had hounded Samira to the verge of a breakdown—intruding on her privacy, rummaging through her trash, interviewing her friends and turning her heartbreak into fodder for the masses. Till her brother and the woman who'd later become her sister-in-law had helped her get back on her feet, stronger and determined to put the past behind her.

Was it any wonder, after the misery of a childhood watching her parents' marriage teeter from one crisis to another, that she'd finally come to her senses and seen she wasn't cut out for romance? Like her mother, she couldn't trust herself to make the right choice when her heart was involved.

'Samira?'

She turned back, her hands falling to her sides as she registered the concern on Tariq's features.

Instantly she shored up her resolve, locking her knees and straightening her shoulders. She was no longer a victim. She'd dragged herself out of the dark hole of loss and grief that had almost destroyed her.

Tariq didn't need to know those details. About the baby she'd lost before it had even been born. About the grief she carried in her very pores and always would.

Samira blinked and forced herself to concentrate.

'If you're worried about me doing anything scandalous to harm you or your family, don't. My one brush with notoriety was enough.' She might have been the innocent party in the Hollywood scandal but it didn't feel like it, with the press ravenous for every detail.

'You regret the relationship with Brent? You would change the past if you could?'

Samira caught her breath, her fingers threading tightly together. Tariq's directness pulled her up short. Everyone else tiptoed around that episode in her life.

'Oh, yes. I'd change the past if I could. Though...' she paused, remembering that all-too-short period when she'd carried her precious baby '...I can't regret all of it.'

She set her jaw, reminding herself to move on. 'I wouldn't suggest marriage if you were looking for a first wife. But you already have two sons. You can consider taking on a wife who doesn't quite meet all the traditional requirements.'

'Who isn't a virgin, you mean?'

Samira blinked. She couldn't recall Tariq being quite so blunt. The young man she'd known half a lifetime ago had changed since becoming monarch.

Yet she appreciated his frankness. Honesty was the best policy between them. They didn't need misunderstandings.

'All the world knows I once had a lover.' She swallowed over the tight knot in her throat. 'Just as it knows you have lovers.'

Tariq had never been short of female companionship. Since his wife had died he'd been again dubbed one of the world's most eligible men and, according to the whispers Samira heard, there was no shortage of women on hand to ease his broken heart.

'You're very direct.' His eyebrows bunched and she shrugged, refusing to apologise.

'I thought you'd appreciate my honesty, as I appreciate yours. That's what I'd expect in a marriage.'

'Honesty?'

Samira took a half-step forward, drawn by the intensity of his stare.

'Honesty and respect.' She licked her dry lips before continuing. 'I assumed you'd want something similar. That you wouldn't look for love in a second wife. I thought you'd want someone capable, loyal and committed. Someone who could help raise your sons.' Samira paused. 'Was I wrong? Are you looking for romance?'

'Who said I was looking for anything?' His stare was enigmatic, giving nothing away.

Samira spread her hands. 'You have two children under two and a country to run. Your schedule must be manic. But I know you well enough to understand you'll want the best for your boys.' She looked straight into his eyes and was rewarded with the slightest of nods.

'I'm sure you've hired the best staff available to help with them.' Again that infinitesimal nod. 'But no nanny can replace a caring mother. A mother who's committed to being there for them all their lives.'

She drew in a quick breath, knowing her breathing was too shallow, her heart racing, now they came to the crux of it all: the reason she'd braved this almost-stranger and proposed marriage.

'I've always loved children; you know that, Tariq.'
Even in her teens she'd taken every opportunity to be with
youngsters, getting into trouble for spending too much time
playing with the servants' babies in parts of the palace
princesses weren't supposed to know existed. 'I'd make a
good mother. You can rely on me.'

Tariq wondered if Samira had any idea how appealing
she looked, her dark-honey gaze earnest, her expression
serious, her hands clasped in unconscious supplication
before her.

Unconscious?

Could any woman so beautiful not be aware of her allure?

Yet Samira wore a conservative suit, not a low-cut dress.
Her make-up was barely there, her hair neatly up at the
back of her head.

And he knew an overwhelming urge to see her panting
and flushed, her rich, dark hair in lush abandon around
her shoulders, her body bare and inviting.

Desire hammered him, turning muscle and soft tissue
into beaten metal, hard and uncompromising. His lungs
bellowed as he hauled in oxygen, fighting for control.

The casual way she'd spoken of his lovers, about her
own, tugged at something primitive and deep-seated inside
him. Tariq knew if ever he possessed Samira he wouldn't
share her with anyone else.

And her wistful expression when she'd spoken of her
ex-lover, admitting she didn't regret the relationship, even
after he'd betrayed her so brutally… Tariq wanted to twist
the guy's neck in his bare hands! Brent hadn't deserved her.

He shoved his hands in his trouser pockets. What was
he thinking?

Shame smote him, the knowledge that Samira had always been his weakness, even when his loyalties had lain

elsewhere. The last thing he needed was to give in to this ancient folly. Besides, saddling himself with a wife was one complication he didn't need.

Yet she was right. A roster of nannies was no long-term solution for his boys. He wanted the best for them. Jasmin had wanted that too and he'd promised her before she'd died...

He scraped the back of his neck with one hand, feeling the iron tension there. Hell! He'd imagined this was some simple social visit from Samira since they were in Paris for the same event. He hadn't expected her to trawl every one of his 'no go' subjects.

'You've spoken about what I'd get out of marriage. But you haven't mentioned why you're so eager for it. Why do you want this?' Tariq didn't know why he was asking. It wasn't going to happen.

But as he surveyed her delicately flushed cheeks, her sinuous body and the long, taut outline of her thighs be-neath that pencil skirt, he realised why he kept the conver-sation going. Because, once conjured, he couldn't erase the image of Samira, abandoned and sexy, in his bed.

Years ago he'd walked away from the teenage Samira because she'd been far too young and he'd been too hon-ourable to act on his desire. That decision had haunted him. The fantasy perfection of 'if only' had overshadowed too many relationships.

But that Samira was gone. She was an experienced woman now, sensual and provocative in ways that spoke directly to his libido.

For long moments Samira said nothing. Her very still-ness conveyed tension, heightening his curiosity. Finally she spoke, her gaze settling on a point near his collarbone.

'I want a family.'

'You have family. Your brother and his wife.' But, even as the words emerged, he realised his mistake.

'My *own* family.' Her words confirmed it.

Tariq frowned. 'But why me? Why us?'

He had no false modesty. Acquiring lovers had never been a difficulty. His wealth and status, not to mention his power, attracted many women. But Samira hadn't seemed interested in his royal position, except to prove she was up to the task of being his queen. And as for her being smitten... He narrowed his eyes, watching her steadfastly staring at his collar. She gave no evidence of it.

Annoyance twisted sharply in his belly. He'd grown used to fending off women, not being ignored by them.

He watched her open her lips and found himself wondering if they were as petal-soft as he imagined. The direction of his thoughts sharpened his voice.

'There must be plenty of eligible men. Why not find one you fancy and start a family together? Why come to me?'

Her mouth tightened and she raised her eyes. For an instant he could swear he read pain in that shimmering, gold-flecked gaze. No, not pain. Anguish. Then she blinked, banishing the illusion.

'I told you, I'm not going to be swept off my feet again. I don't want romance.'

Looking down at Samira's beautiful, earnest face, Tariq suddenly felt ancient, like a greybeard surveying an innocent. Was she really too young to understand that was what women did? They fell in love, even if they then lived to regret it. It was in their nature. The heavy thud of his heart against his ribs tolled out the sum of such regrets. He'd grown intimately acquainted with them.

'But taking on someone who already has children—' The expression on her face stopped him midsentence. 'Samira?'

She looked down at her hands. They were clenched together so hard the knuckles whitened. When she met his eyes again, her own looked desolate.

'I want children. I've always wanted them.' She breathed deep. 'But I can't have any of my own.'

Something lodged in Tariq's chest. Something heavy that impaired his breathing. He couldn't imagine the world without his boys so he had some inkling of how bereft Samira felt.

He wanted to reach out and comfort her, pull her in to him and cuddle her, for there was no mistaking her pain. Despite the years since they'd been close, she was still the girl he'd cared for too much.

But he was older and wiser now. At thirty-seven he'd learned there were times when a woman needed her dignity rather than the comfort of an embrace. When nothing he could do would ease the pain.

Memory stabbed hard, slicing through his ribs, tearing at his conscience. Jasmin...

'You see now why I suggested marriage.'

Her quiet words dragged Tariq from a haze of memory and regret. He forced himself to focus.

'You proposed marriage because you want my boys?' Instantly his protective instincts were aroused.

'Don't sound so fierce, Tariq.' She even managed a tiny smile. The sight of it and the sadness in her eyes squeezed his chest. 'I don't want to take them from you.'

She took a step forward, then another, and a waft of light scent filled his nostrils: warm cinnamon and sugar, innocently sweet yet improbably alluring.

'I want to share them with you, look after them, grow to love them and support them.'

'You want to marry me for my *children*?' His mouth firmed. After a lifetime being chased by women, his pride smarted. Was anything designed to puncture a man's ego as much as that?

Did she have any idea of the insult she offered?

He might be a father but he was a red-blooded male

in his prime. A man, moreover, used to being the hunter, not the prey.

Samira stepped closer again, apparently unaware the movement brought her into his personal space. She was so close he felt the warmth of her body, saw the fine-grained perfection of her skin and the tiny shadows beneath her eyes that make-up didn't quite conceal.

'Not just the children, Tariq. I want a family. Someone to belong to. And I can't think of a man I'd rather trust myself with than you. You're decent and honourable.'

Competing emotions battled in Tariq's gut. Pleasure at her belief in him. Annoyance that she saw him as some sort of comforting protector who conveniently had the kids she wanted. And a shudder of carnal pleasure at the sound of his name on her lips, which inevitably led him to imagine her crying it out in the throes of passion.

But she was wrong. He sifted all she'd said, realising it wasn't really him she wanted, but some emasculated version of himself that existed only in her mind.

She didn't know him, had never really known him.

If she had any idea of the darkness within him, or of the urges he suppressed right now—none of them decent or honourable, all of them primitive and utterly indecent—she'd run a mile.

It was time to stop this.

Tariq looked into her eager, open face. 'You honour me with your offer, Samira. But the answer is no. I won't marry you.'

CHAPTER THREE

SAMIRA HAD STEELED herself for rejection but the reality was harder than she'd imagined.

The force of her disappointment threatened to take her out at the knees. Despite spending a lifetime projecting an image of calm, no matter how traumatic her reality, Samira felt her bottom lip begin to quiver.

She bit it. Hard.

She blinked and locked her knees, grateful her skirt hid her shaky legs.

Another second and she summoned up a semblance of a smile, ignoring the stagnant well of disappointment at the heart of her. She breathed deep, as if her lungs didn't feel brittle and papery, like they were about to tear apart.

'Thank you for hearing me out, Tariq.' There, her voice was even and admirably cool. Not the voice of a woman who felt her last hope of happiness had been snatched away.

It had been an outrageous idea. She'd known it from the start. Foolish of her to pursue it.

'I knew even as I asked that I wouldn't suit. You need a much more appropriate wife than I could ever be.'

She glanced around for her bag, only to realise she still wore it over her shoulder. She unclenched her hands and grabbed the thin leather strap for something to do.

'What do you mean, more *appropriate*?' Tariq's searing gaze pinned her to the spot.

'Let's not go there, Tariq. There's no point.' Samira stretched her smile wider and her taut facial muscles ached at the strain. 'It's time I left. I'll say goodbye and wish you and your family all the best for the future. Thank you again for making time to see me.'

She was turning away, desperate to be alone, when long fingers closed around her upper arm.

Instantly she stilled as shock waves ripped through her body.

It had been four years since any man, apart from her brother, had touched her. And this was different—as if a channel of fiery liquid coursed under her skin.

Samira frowned, trying to remember Jackson Brent's touch ever having inflamed such a reaction. But all she could remember were his charming smile, his easy lies and his insistence on kissing her in front of the paparazzi despite her protests.

'What did you mean, Samira?'

Experimentally she tugged her arm. His hold remained firm.

A glance at his face, now close, confirmed he had no intention of relenting.

She remembered that look of adamantine determination from her early teens. Tariq had been visiting Asim and had somehow found out about her one act of rebellion in an otherwise cloistered, well-behaved life. She'd secretly been slipping out, dune-driving without supervision or a crash helmet. He hadn't lectured her. It was as if he'd understood her need to escape her miserable home life, just for a few hours. He'd simply said he knew she had more sense than to risk her neck that way again and made her promise never to drive without him or Asim. He'd known her promise would bind her.

But she wasn't a teenager trying to cope with her parents' manipulation in their battle for supremacy. Why did he drag this out instead of letting her leave with some dignity intact?

She shrugged. 'No doubt your advisors wouldn't approve of you choosing a wife like me.' She took a step away, only to pull up short when he refused to release her.

'First, I make my own decisions, Samira, not my advisors; and second, I don't know what you're talking about.'

Samira whipped around, her eyebrows arching in disbelief. 'Don't be coy, Tariq. We both know I'm tainted.' When his face remained impassive she leaned closer, hurt turning to anger that he made her spell this out. '"Soiled goods", isn't that the phrase?' Her chin hiked up, but given his enormous height she couldn't look down her nose at him.

'In both our countries there are people who disapprove of me, a woman who's never been married but who had a lover.' She tugged in a swift breath. Her heart hammered and her chest rose and fell as if she'd just finished an hour's aerobic workout in the gym. But that was nothing to the distress curling deep inside.

'I thought that wouldn't matter to you since you'd already been married to a virtuous woman who gave you heirs. I'd assumed you weren't hung up on the old ways. But I see I was wrong.'

She'd told herself again and again she had nothing to be ashamed of, having chosen to be with the man she loved. Perhaps that would have been true if Jackson had proved himself worthy of her love. But he'd betrayed her brutally, proved her a fool, her judgement and her dream of love fatally flawed. Instead of the luxury of dealing with her pain and disillusionment privately, it had all been blasted across the press. Her loss of innocence had provided fodder for the voracious masses eager for the story of her heartbreak. She'd felt defiled.

Was it any wonder she refused to trust herself to romance again? No man could tempt her with talk of love. The very idea chilled her to the marrow.

This time she yanked her arm so hard in Tariq's grip it hurt. But still he didn't release her.

Instead he moved closer, dwarfing her with his height and his massive shoulders. But it was his eyes that held her.

'Don't tell me you believe that!' His brow pleated as he looked down at her.

'Why not?' She glared back. 'You're seen with a new woman at almost every social event but none of them last. So it's not as if you're in a relationship and I'm poaching on anyone's territory. I'm suitable, *more* than suitable, in every other way except for that.'

'Your virginity…' he paused on the word and the hairs on the back of her neck rose at his tone '…isn't an issue for me. That might have been relevant a generation or more ago but things have changed.'

'You think?' Samira's laugh was bitter. She surged forward into his personal space as unpleasant memories crowded. 'Tell that to the men who've offered to set me up as their mistress! Men who wouldn't dream of paying court to me as a possible wife. Men whose views haven't quite galloped ahead into the twenty-first century.' She paused, catching her breath, telling herself anger wouldn't change anything. 'Of course you don't want to rock the boat when there are so many who still think that way.'

Tariq's face turned to stone, but his eyes blazed with a heat that almost scared her.

'Who has insulted you like that?' His fingers dug into her arm.

'Tariq! Let me go. You're hurting.' Fear trickled through her insides at his fierce expression. She couldn't recall him ever looking this way. It was like staring into the face of a warrior intent on blood.

'My apologies.' The words were stilted but in an instant his hand was gone, the savage light in his eyes muted.

Yet Samira was still trapped. His big frame cornered her, blocking access to the door.

'*Who* was it?' He growled, the sound tracking across her skin and burrowing deep inside. 'Tell me.'

'Why? There's no point.' Restlessly her fingers slid along the slim strap of her bag. 'I'm not accepting their offers.' She shivered. Such an arrangement would destroy her.

'Does Asim know?'

Samira's lips twisted. 'You think I'd tell my *brother* about that? You have to be joking.'

She'd had enough trouble getting Asim to promise not to lay a hand on Jackson Brent all those years ago. Vengeance wouldn't help, only inflame the situation. Now here was Tariq, looking like he wanted to take somebody apart limb from limb.

A kernel of heat flared in the cold emptiness of her abdomen. He mightn't want her but he cared enough to be incensed on her behalf.

Samira sighed; his protectiveness was one of the attributes that would make him a wonderful husband and father.

She straightened to her full height, wishing she'd worn higher heels so she didn't feel so dwarfed. It wasn't just his size. He bristled with a furious energy that made her far too aware of the solid muscle and power in that long, strong body of his.

She dragged in oxygen, telling herself she wasn't overawed by this macho male. Wasn't her brother another of the same?

Her deep, sustaining breath drew in something new: sandalwood and spice and hot, male flesh. Her nostrils

flared eagerly and she stiffened, stunned as a swirl of reaction eddied within.

Samira stepped back, disturbed at the way her body
betrayed her.

'Not so fast.' Tariq paced with her, hemming her against
a sofa. 'I want to know—'

'No. You don't.' Finally Samira reasserted herself, projecting the composure she gathered about herself when
the going got tough. 'It's none of your business, Tariq.
You're not my keeper. In fact you've just passed up the
opportunity to be anything to me but an old friend. An
acquaintance.'

His mouth flattened and she sensed his keen brain sift-
ing her words. He didn't like them but there was nothing
he could do.

'So, once more, thank you for your time and goodbye.'

She didn't offer to shake hands. The imprint of his touch
still burned her upper arm. Not from pain but, she assured
herself, because she wasn't used to being so close to a man.
The tremulous little stirrings in her belly—the quickened
breathing, the reaction to his skin's aroma—were proof of
that. It wasn't anything personal.

'Wait.'

Samira hesitated, then slowly lifted her eyes to his.
There it was again, a twinge of something that felt far too
much like physical awareness.

'What is it?' The words shot out, crisp with challenge.

'Have you asked anyone else?'

Her eyes widened. 'To marry me?' Did he think she'd
lined up a list of candidates to interview by the hour?

What sort of woman did he think she was?

Desperate.

The word surfaced despite her efforts to suppress it.
And she was. But not desperate enough to do this more
than once. Today's humiliation was enough.

Besides, only Tariq had tempted her to think of marriage. There was no other man she trusted enough.

'Only you,' she said at last, daring him to preen at the compliment.

'And will you ask anyone else?' He leaned closer, looming over her as if to intimidate.

Except Samira was undaunted. She might have laid herself open to rejection but she had her pride. That and her determination never to give up were what kept her going. She didn't need his interference or his sympathy.

Anger spiked.

Deliberately she reached out and tweaked the precise knot in his silk tie, twitching it unnecessarily, then patting it in place, ignoring the heat of bone and solid muscle beneath his shirt.

'It's kind of you to be interested in my plans, Tariq, but what I do is none of your business. It ceased to be when you rejected my proposal.' She favoured him with a gracious smile that masked her desire to see him squirm. 'I'll give your regards to Asim and Jacqui when I see them, shall I?'

His hand clamped over hers as she made to withdraw it. He pressed her palm against the crisp, body-warmed cotton of his shirt so she caught the steady, strong beat of his heart beneath her touch. It felt too intimate.

She should have known not to play provocative games with Tariq. He had so much more experience than her.

'Not just yet.' He paused, his keen gaze roving her features. 'Come back tomorrow for my final answer.'

Samira stared back, hope and disbelief vying for supremacy, anticipation stirring. 'You seriously want time to consider?'

His thumb stroked hers in a long sweep, drawing a tiny, jittering reaction through her.

'You raised some persuasive points.' He murmured in

that dangerously deep voice. 'It would be premature to reject the idea out of hand.'

Did he hope to delay long enough to go behind her
back and contact Asim, hoping her brother would scotch
her plans?

As if it mattered. She wasn't in the market for just any
husband. If Tariq turned her down, that was it.

'You've changed your tune.' Samira narrowed her gaze
and pulled her hand from his before the tingling in her fingers spread up her arm.

He shrugged, the movement emphasising his superior
size and strength, but she refused to be intimidated. 'You
took me by surprise. I need to think about it.'

Slowly, Samira nodded. She'd give him the benefit of
the doubt. What other choice did she have? She smiled,
hope rising tentatively, and watched something flicker and
intensify in that deep gaze.

'I understand. It's not a decision to be taken lightly.'
She hesitated, searching for the right words. 'You needn't
worry, either, that I'd interfere with your...*personal* life.'
A flush warmed her cheeks but she ploughed on. It had
to be said and it might be a clinching argument in her fa-
vour. 'I know you have a lot of lovers and I don't expect...'
Samira paused, searching for words.

'You don't expect me to give them up? Is that it? You
give me carte blanche to play the field?' Tariq's tone was
harsh and for some reason she didn't understand why he
looked angry.

Samira frowned, wondering what she'd said to stir his
temper. Surely she was offering the sort of arrangement
any man would appreciate?

She understood his decency, his honour and strength, but
after so many years apart he was a stranger in many ways.

'I'm not looking for love or sex, Tariq.' Valiantly she
suppressed a shudder at the thought of deluding herself

with either, making herself vulnerable again. 'I don't expect you to pretend you feel for me what you did for your first wife.' She'd had her fill of pretence from a man. All she wanted was honesty. 'And it would be unfair to expect you to be celibate. I understand a man like you has needs.'

'Needs?' Tariq's gaze honed to shards of rough-cut emerald.

'Yes.' Samira swallowed, refusing to be daunted, reminding herself that she was worldly and experienced. 'Sexual needs. But it's companionship I want from you, Tariq. Respect and support. The shared bond of caring for your children. A purpose in life.'

She petered to a stop, feeling she'd revealed too much. 'I want to be a reasonable wife, Tariq.'

A reasonable wife.

The words echoed with a dull clang in the void where Tariq's heart supposedly lodged.

He couldn't believe he was hearing this.

Samira—gorgeous, seductive Samira—was offering herself in marriage and telling him in the same breath she didn't want to consummate the arrangement?

How did women come to have such twisted, unfathomable minds?

He'd never heard anything so preposterous.

Marriage to Samira but no sex.

Presumably no touching at all.

No kissing either.

His gaze lingered on the plump bow of her ripe lower lip and a groan rose in his throat, to be savagely repressed. The whole idea was a recipe for madness. He should squash it now before she got her hopes up.

But it was too late. Those stunning eyes shone brighter and she watched him expectantly.

As if at any moment he'd thank her for denying himself the one thing he really wanted. The one thing he'd

wanted since he'd seen her again. If he were truthful, that
he'd wanted for far too long. Samira. Samira up against
the wall of last night's venue, with her long skirt rucked
up around her waist as he pleasured her. Samira in his bed,
sharing his shower, or breathless beneath him on the long
couch just behind her. He'd pictured her on it since he'd
walked into the room and saw her caressing it. She was
so tactile, a true sensualist.

Samira any way he could get her.

Breathe. Deeper. Slowly.

How could any woman be so naive? Especially a woman
with such natural sensuality? It was there in her walk, her
love of texture, the way her eyes lingered with that hint
of longing that belied the words emerging from her lips.

How could she think of denying them such pleasure?

Yet she thought she was being reasonable, generous,
even.

In his years of marriage to Jasmin he'd never considered
straying. His word was his bond and he was traditional
enough to believe marriage was about loyalty.

'That's noble of you, Samira.' He paused, scarcely believing the words emerging from his mouth. 'I'll give you
my answer tomorrow.'

Twenty-six hours later Tariq halted in the doorway to the
twins' playroom in the luxury hotel suite. A crisis in Al
Sarath had disrupted his schedule and he'd missed his
meeting with Samira. She couldn't possibly have waited
this long for him.

He'd told himself it was just as well. Yesterday he'd
found himself arranging to meet her again, driven by the
need to prevent her propositioning someone else.

The thought of her with another man, offering to marry
him, even with that crazy 'no sex' stipulation, gouged a
chasm through his belly.

He wasn't her keeper.

He didn't want a wife. The thought of replacing Jasmin with Samira made him break out in a sweat. He might lust after her but how could he sign up to another marriage?

Yet for twenty-six hours he'd imagined little else. Her saner argument for marriage—to provide a loving, stable environment for his boys—made sense. Too much sense.

Tariq had put off for too long the need to find a mother for the twins. A warm, gentle woman who'd nurture them. A caring woman who'd love them as Jasmin would have.

A shiver scudded down his spine and the old blackness fringed his vision.

His boys deserved a mother. Already he realised he had to provide more than he could now with his taxing schedule. His wasn't a job he could set aside when family commitments demanded. His country, his people, relied on him.

Now, standing in the shadow of the half-open door, he confronted the most compelling reason yet for action— their happiness. He'd thought Samira had left hours before, but no, she was there, to the delight of his boys.

At the centre of the room his sons sat astride plush cushions filched from the lounge, enthusiastically jogging up and down to the rhythm of Samira's lilting voice. She had a clear contralto voice that tugged at long-forgotten memories of early childhood.

She sang a made-up song about Adil and Risay riding, one on a camel and one on a horse. Each time the boys heard their names they giggled and jogged faster, urging on their imaginary mounts, till at last the song ended.

With a sigh Samira sank back on the carpet, as if exhausted. Instantly the toddlers scrambled off their cushions and across to her. Adil snuggled up at her side and her arm automatically wrapped around him. Risay, more energetic, climbed onto her legs, ready for another ride. Instead of scolding, she laughed before scooping him close.

The three of them lay there. His boys and Samira.

She wore a dress the colour of amethyst that complemented the warm tone of her skin. The flaring skirt with its silky sheen looked indulgently feminine and expensive but there was a dark smear near the waist and a matching mark on her cheek. She'd kicked off her shoes. Her bare feet and legs looked tantalisingly sexy.

Something somersaulted in Tariq's chest as he took in the three of them, his precious sons and the woman who cared less for her expensive clothes than she did for them.

In the far corner of the room Sofia, the nanny, folded clothes, her back turned. The fact that the boys' fierce protector, who'd been with them since the day they'd lost their mother, was relaxed enough not to watch the newcomer like a hawk, told him everything he needed to know. Samira and the boys had clearly bonded.

All that remained was to decide how he felt about that.

For somehow in the last twenty-six hours, her proposal had turned from outrageous to possible.

Samira sighed and cuddled them close, breathing in the smell of baby powder and little boys.

Even if Tariq refused her, these couple of hours had been wonderful. The boys were a delight.

Her heart felt lighter, not just because she'd spent time with two such adorable toddlers but because she'd contributed, helping out while Sofia had packed, keeping the boys constructively amused.

Celeste would tell her she contributed with her fashion designs and charity donations. But there was something innately satisfying about the simple act of caring for this little family.

She breathed deep, knowing it was time to move. The

boys were ready for bed and the longer she stayed the harder it would be to leave. What had begun as a simple invitation to wait for Tariq and meet his boys in the meantime had turned into something far more complex, at least for her eager heart.

She opened her eyes to find Tariq standing over her. He didn't smile and his look was intent, as if he saw right inside her, to longings and regrets she kept strictly private. She felt caught out, at a disadvantage sprawled on the floor, her unguarded emotions too close to the surface.

Abruptly her heart leapt in her breast. Her pulse fluttered as he bent, his hands briefly brushing her as he scooped up Adil, now fast asleep, then left the room with the nanny following.

The gleam in Tariq's clear green gaze unravelled something within her. Something she didn't want to feel. It made her feel too vulnerable. She was still grappling with that, her breath coming too fast, when he returned, lifting a sleepy Risay and taking him to the bedroom.

Quickly she sat up, twisting up her hair into some semblance of order, frantically scanning the floor for her shoes.

'I'm sorry to keep you waiting so long.' Tariq's low voice came while she was on her hands and knees, peering under a settee.

Abruptly she sat back, feeling flushed and dishevelled, especially when Tariq looked just as debonair as ever. A lot of big men couldn't pull that off, appearing either too lean and lanky or so heavy-set you knew they'd run to fat with age. By contrast Tariq was perfectly proportioned and frighteningly attractive.

Samira's heartbeat skidded into a kick start. It was as well he hadn't agreed to marry her—that was clear from his carefully neutral expression. She didn't like the way her body behaved when he was around.

Samira scrambled to her feet, brushing down her dress,

noticing for the first time sticky patches where the boys had shared their food.

'No doubt you had more *important* business to attend to.' More important than declining her proposal. Her mouth tightened.

Only sheer doggedness had made her wait despite the lengthy delay. She was determined to make him say the words to her face, despite the temptation to avoid further embarrassment and slink away. She tilted her chin. She was a princess of Jazeer. She would see this through.

'You don't understand.'

'There's no need to explain.' He'd already made his position clear. 'I understand perfectly.'

'There's a crisis in Al Sarath. I've been dealing with it long-distance.'

Samira froze. 'A crisis?'

'One of the provinces has been hit by severe flash flooding in the mountain ravines. It's wiped away whole villages.'

Samira sucked in her breath, indignation fading as the import of his words hit. The mountain provinces were the poorest in his country. She remembered adobe houses perched in arid gullies so steep they became death traps on the rare occasions distant mountain rains brought unaccustomed water.

'I'm so sorry.' Guilt pierced at her petty indignation. No wonder he was late! 'You must be wishing you were there.'

He nodded, his expression sombre. 'We fly out soon. I need to be on the ground.'

'Then I won't keep you.' Relief filled her as she spied her shoes beneath a jumble of wooden blocks.

'You don't want to hear my decision?'

His voice stopped her as she bent, reaching for her discarded heels. Slowly she straightened. There was no chance Tariq would change his mind. He'd been dead set against the idea, even outraged. And now… She looked up into a penetrating stare that gave nothing away. He didn't look like a man about to grant her wish.

He was so stern, as if she represented a problem he had to tackle.

Again she wondered if Tariq would go behind her back to her brother, warning him she was going off the rails.

The idea almost made her smile. Asim had worried about her for too long—not because she was wildly kicking over the traces, but because she buried herself in her work instead of 'embracing life'. She knew he secretly feared she hadn't fully recovered from what had happened four years before. Surely propositioning his best friend counted as embracing life?

'Of course I want to hear. That's why I'm here.' But she refused to feel even a scintilla of hope. He'd given her no encouragement, not even a smile.

She almost began to be thankful. It had been a lunatic idea. Imagine her and Tariq…

He closed the space between them with one long stride, making her more aware than ever of their physical differences. Barefoot, she scarcely came up to his shoulder.

One large, warm hand closed around hers, lifting it high. Tariq bent his head, the light catching the blue-black sheen of his thick hair. Samira felt the press of surprisingly soft lips on the back of her hand as he made a courtly gesture that sent a shocking thrill right through her body.

Her breath was a sudden hiss, her lungs pumping like bellows as he lifted his eyes to hers. This time his expression wasn't grim or guarded. It was full of anticipation.

'You honour me greatly with your proposal, Princess Samira.' He smiled and the world tilted around them. 'I accept with pleasure. We'll be married as soon as it can be arranged.'

CHAPTER FOUR

'AT LAST! AFTER five days of celebrating we finally get to the wedding. These royal events are a real test of stamina.'

Samira looked at her sister-in-law, Jacqui, lounging on a couch, taking a glossy cherry from a silver bowl.

'How can you eat?' Samira's stomach was performing a nervous twist and dip that would have done an Olympic diver proud.

She had to call on all her years of training to sit still, rather than shift edgily and risk smearing the intricate henna patterns being painted on her hands and feet. Two ladies-in-waiting sat before her, creating the traditional designs.

Bridal designs.

For the first time, today, the wedding became real.

The official functions so far had been comfortingly familiar, like untold numbers of royal celebrations she'd attended in the past. Why that should be comforting, Samira didn't know. This marriage was her idea. It would be wonderful for all of them: her, Tariq and the boys.

Yet suddenly today she felt ridiculously wobbly.

Bridal nerves were normal, she assured herself. Even if she wasn't a bride in the usual sense.

Most brides looked forward to a night in their new husband's arms.

Her insides cramped and the skin at her nape prickled. Samira's brain seized at the thought of complicating this carefully planned arrangement with sex. Already she felt she walked a knife edge. Her unbidden physical awareness of Tariq was a constant undercurrent. As if there was a disconnect between her mind, that knew intimacy would be a mistake, and her body, that trembled at his touch.

'You think I should stop eating because of the upcoming banquet?' Jacqui shook her tawny head ruefully. 'I never used to have much of an appetite.' Her other hand slipped to the baby bump barely visible beneath her aquamarine top. 'But I've never been so hungry.'

'Except last time you were pregnant.'

'You're right. I was ravenous then too.' Jacqui laughed and Samira smiled. Jacqui distracted her from the anxiety that had somehow grown to a peak of apprehension.

'Pregnancy suits you. You really are glowing.' Samira smiled, feeling only the tiniest flicker of envy. She'd come to terms with her barrenness and couldn't begrudge another woman such happiness. Instead she basked in familiar warmth at the thought of her brother's family. Jacqui was the sister she'd never had, loving and supportive. She almost made Samira wish she could have what Jacqui had: a marriage based on love.

But that wasn't for her. She knew too well she wasn't cut out for that.

There was a bustle as her attendants rose and all four women admired the results. Samira's hands, wrists, feet and ankles were works of art, covered in ancient designs that proclaimed her royal lineage as well as talismans of good fortune, happiness and fertility.

She swallowed, ignoring a pang of regret. There was no sense pining over what could never be. She was the luckiest of women, about to acquire a wonderful husband she could respect and trust and two delightful sons. She could ask for nothing more.

Samira thanked the women warmly. When they'd left, Jacqui put aside the bowl of cherries and sat up.

'Now, do you want to tell me what's wrong?'

'Wrong?' Samira stared. 'Nothing. Tariq has done everything to make the celebrations a huge success. And the ceremony this afternoon—'

'The celebrations. The ceremony.' Jacqui waved her hand dismissively. 'They're spectacular and the whole country is enjoying them.' She leaned closer, her gaze appraising. 'But I look at you and I don't see a bride.'

'You don't?' Samira stared at the wedding patterns staining her skin, then across to the table littered with ornate jewellery. Gold, rubies and huge antique pearls caught the light. On the other side of the room hung her bridal gown, the sumptuous cloth of gold shimmering.

Jacqui followed her gaze. 'The trappings are there, but something is missing.' There was concern in her eyes. 'You don't look like a woman in love.'

Samira flinched, then made herself smile. She was making the best of her life, choosing hope over regret instead of locking herself away to fret over what she'd lost. She would build something positive and make a useful contribution, helping to raise a family.

She was being strong.

And, if the best she could hope to achieve didn't include romantic love, that suited her. She was far better without that.

'Not all brides are in love, Jacqui. Arranged marriages are common, especially between royals.'

'I know, I know. Asim said the same.'

Samira tensed. Jacqui had discussed this with Asim? She hated that she'd been the subject of such discussion, even though she knew it was because they cared for her. They'd been there when she'd needed them in her darkest hours. But she was fine now.

'It's just that I want you to have what I have, Samira.' Jacqui looked so earnest. 'I want you to be happy, to be loved and in love.'

'Thank you.' She reached out and touched Jacqui's arm. 'But I *am* happy. This is exactly what I want.'

Still her sister-in-law frowned.

'Not everyone wants to fall in love. Asim must have told you about our parents.'

Solemnly Jacqui nodded. 'They were unhappy.'

Samira's huff of laughter was bitter. 'They were miserable and they made life hell for us too. They were either so in love no one else mattered, or they were fighting like wild cats, doing anything to score a point over the other, even using us in their battles.' She looked down to find herself pleating the fine fabric of her skirt. Her chest tightened.

'Your parents were volatile and self-indulgent.' Jacqui's voice penetrated the memories. 'Love needn't be like that.'

'I know and I can't tell you how happy I am for you and Asim.' Samira paused. 'But I don't want love. I tried that and it was the biggest mistake of my life. I'm too much like my mother. I was swept off my feet by romantic dreams, blindly putting my trust in someone completely wrong for me.'

'Jackson Brent is a louse,' Jacqui growled. 'You can't blame yourself.'

Samira sat back in her chair, warmth filling her at her sister-in-law's instant support.

'I do blame myself. I wasn't a child. I made the decision to throw everything over, all I'd worked for and dreamed of, to be with him. I fooled myself into believing in him and I was utterly, devastatingly wrong.' Her palm crept across her belly as if to prevent the clenching pain, a phantom memory from four years ago.

'One mistake…'

'That was enough. What if I made the same mistake

again? I can't go through that again, Jacqui, I just can't.' Samira ducked her head, ashamed at the welling distress that filled her even after all this time. She drew a calming breath. 'I'm too like my mother. I let passion override judgement and I paid the price. But unlike her I won't make the mistake of staying on that merry-go-round.'

'And Tariq knows this?'

'Of course he knows.' Samira smiled, her confidence returning. 'Don't look so worried. This marriage is everything I want.'

'Samira.' Her name on Tariq's tongue made her blink. It sounded...different. The noise of the wedding banquet faded as she met his eyes.

Or was it she who was different? Hours spent at his side through the wedding ceremony and celebration had left her unaccountably on edge. She felt his presence with every cell of her body.

Applause filled the feasting hall as he took her hand and stood, drawing her up. He was resplendent in robes as white as the distant snow-capped peaks. His jaw was lean and hard, a study in power, his eyes a glint of cool green as he looked down at her and slowly smiled.

Instantly heat shimmered under her skin, a heat that intensified when his warm fingers slid against hers, enfolding them completely. Sensation trickled through her from her tight lungs, meandering all the way down through her belly to a single pulse point between her legs.

She inhaled sharply, eyes widening as he held her gaze. There *was* something different about Tariq. Something she couldn't identify.

'My queen,' he said in a voice barely above a whisper, yet it amplified in her ears, blotting out the sound of their guests. Or perhaps that was the thud of her pulse.

'Your Highness.' She dipped her gaze in acknowledgement. She owed him her loyalty as her new sovereign.

His fingers tightened around hers, making her look up.

'Your husband.' His nostrils flared as if drawing in her scent and shock buffeted her. Tariq looked so intent, so *close*, his tall frame blocking out everything else. Samira felt a heavy throb of anticipation deep inside as his head lowered purposefully towards hers.

Instantly, disconcertingly, anxiety shredded her composure. It was all she could do not to step back, but she was sure he felt the flinch of her hand in his.

His eyes narrowed, a twitch of a frown marking his brow. Then he lifted her hand. She watched him press a kiss to the delicate, hennaed pattern on her flesh and felt the warmth of those firm lips.

Her breath hitched, her breasts rising hard beneath the ponderous weight of ancient gold jewellery that suddenly seemed far too oppressive.

Tariq smiled. She felt the movement against her hand and wondered, dazed, what amused him. Finally, eyes still meshed with hers, he straightened to his full height.

The crowd stood, applauding so loud it was a wonder the crystal glassware on the tables didn't shatter.

A herald appeared before them, bearing a golden goblet studded with cabochon emeralds and amethysts. Tariq took it in one large hand.

'Long life to the happy couple,' roared the herald.

Tariq lifted the goblet and drank, then held it out to Samira, turning it so her lips touched the spot from which he'd drunk. Heat sizzled through her as he watched her over the rim and she swallowed the heady, sweet mixture that tasted of honey, cinnamon and unknown spices.

'May they be blessed with peace and happiness and honoured by all.'

Again Tariq drank. Samira watched, enthralled, as the muscles in his powerful neck moved.

He held the drink out to her, again presenting her with the same side of the goblet that he'd used. She told herself she imagined the taste of him there on the beaten gold. Yet it felt incredibly intimate, pressing her lips where his had been, even though she knew it was merely a symbolic gesture as old as the traditional marriage ceremony. She gulped a little too much, feeling the concoction catch the back of her throat.

Tariq's hand squeezed hers and Samira's tension eased a little. It would be all right. They were almost through the celebration that had somehow turned into an ordeal.

'And may they be blessed with strong, fine children.'

Samira was ready for it but still the words caught her a slashing blow to the midriff. She pasted on a bright smile and watched Tariq draw a deep draft from the golden chalice.

He lifted it to her mouth, tilting high so she had no choice but to swallow more than the tiny sip she'd planned.

The hall broke out into a pandemonium of applause and ululating cheers. But all she could see was Tariq's eyes. They'd darkened to gleaming tourmaline. Or were her senses blurring? She felt warm and somehow...undone.

Tariq lowered the goblet and Samira licked her bottom lip, catching a stray drop that lingered there. Tariq seemed fascinated with the movement and to her horror she felt tiny prickling darts of heat pepper her breasts and abdomen. Just as if he'd touched her.

Heat burned in her ears.

'What is that stuff?' she whispered.

He passed the goblet to the waiting herald, his eyes never leaving hers. 'It's harmless enough. A traditional mixture designed to promote virility.'

Samira snapped her mouth shut, her brain whirling as

Tariq turned to address the assembled throng. She told herself it was a necessary part of the ritual, no more. But the feel of Tariq's hand still gripping hers, the sensation of his long fingers threading through hers, his thumb stroking her palm, sent a warning buzzing through her.

Tariq watched from the doorway as his bride bent over the twin beds where his boys slept. A nightlight glowed at floor level and she looked like something from a fairy story, all shimmer and fragile, gossamer-fine fabrics.

But Samira wasn't an ethereal fairy. She was a warm, flesh-and-blood woman. He'd felt her pulse stir as he held her hand at the banquet, watched the rosy heat brighten her cheeks and plump up her lips as she drank their wedding toast.

His groin had tightened unbearably as he'd looked down into those wide, anxious eyes and he'd felt the double-edged sword of lust and caution at his throat. He wanted her so badly his skin grated with it.

It felt like he'd wanted Samira most of his life.

Now there was nothing, not even the guilt he carried over Jasmin, to stop him having her.

Yet seeing her bent over his sleeping sons, rearranging blankets and moving stuffed toys, he felt more than desire. Gratitude that she genuinely cared for them. How many other brides would have spent their wedding night checking on their stepchildren?

Yet wasn't that why she'd proposed marriage? For his children?

Tariq's jaw tightened. His pride shrieked outrage that she saw him as no more than a tool to get what she wanted.

He'd read her expression when she'd told him she couldn't have a baby. He'd seen her pain and it was part of the reason he'd consented to this marriage, despite his reservations. That and the curious certainty he couldn't simply turn his back on Samira as originally intended. She had something he needed.

It had given insight into her motivation for brazenly offering herself in marriage. And he'd been determined she'd make that offer to no other man but him!

Tariq spun away on his heel and stalked down the corridor. But Samira didn't offer herself, did she? She expected him to accept her with conditions. As if he wasn't a man with a man's needs and hungers. As if he didn't have a right to touch the woman who'd pledged herself to him, body and soul.

She'd thought she could dictate terms to him, the Sheikh of Al Sarath!

Perhaps she was more innocent than the world thought. He could have told her no marriage was as simple as it appeared on paper, not when it was lived by real people. Not even an arranged marriage executed for reasons of pragmatism and convenience.

A clammy hand wrapped around his chest, squeezing tight as shadows of the past rose.

When two people lived together as husband and wife the boundaries blurred. And in this marriage, despite Samira's fond imaginings, the boundaries were about to be ripped asunder.

Samira leaned back against the pillows, a paperback in her hand. A gentle breeze stirred the long, sheer curtains and soft lamplight made even the enormous, lavishly appointed room seem cosy. Yet she was too wired to relax.

Her mind buzzed with impressions. The noise and colour of the crowd at the wedding. The strange sense that, despite the throng, she and Tariq were isolated from the rest, each action, each word, weighted and momentous. The spicy smell of Tariq's skin as he'd held her hand and kissed it. The way his eyes had held hers as they'd shared that jewelled goblet.

That must be it, the reason her body was tight and achy. It was the potion they'd drunk. The alternative, that this was a reaction to Tariq, just wasn't acceptable.

Or perhaps it was the suspicion, fuelled by the gleam in Tariq's eyes today, that there might be complications in their marriage-on-paper-only arrangement. That look reminded her Tariq was a virile, red-blooded man used to taking what he wanted.

Samira rubbed at the goose bumps on her arms, telling herself she was being fanciful. Tariq had accepted her terms.

She turned to switch off the lamp and caught movement on the other side of the room.

'Tariq!' Her voice was a thready whisper.

He'd changed out of his wedding finery. Gone was the white robe and head scarf. Gone was the jewelled, ceremonial dagger. Gone was half his clothing!

This was Tariq as she'd never seen him. Her eyes rounded and her jaw sank open. The young man she'd once known had been long and lean but his body had changed in a decade, filling out the promise of those wide shoulders.

Her vision was filled with acres of bare, golden skin. She drank in the solidly muscled pectorals dusted with dark hair, the flex and bunch of more muscles at his taut abdomen as he prowled out of the shadows towards her. He walked proud, shoulders back, stride confident, reminding her that this man ruled all he surveyed.

Samira's throat dried as she took in the splendour of him. He was like a statue of a Greek god come to life—all warm flesh instead of cold marble. A long silver, slashing arc across his ribs and another smaller scar near his shoulder were the only things marring that perfection.

Yet they emphasised his earthy masculinity. She knew

he'd got the larger wound in his teens, practising the ancient art of swordsmanship. She'd heard him tell Asim that his uncle, who was his guardian, had given him no sympathy because he'd been foolish enough not to wear protective clothing, and worse, to let someone get the better of him. Tariq had grown up in a man's world where toughness was prized and no quarter was given for sentiment or weakness. Now he looked every inch the marauding male.

Not like a man committed to a platonic relationship.

A shiver ran through her, tightening her muscles and rippling across her skin. Her breath hissed between her teeth.

Her eyes dropped to the pale, loose trousers he wore, riding dangerously low.

Awareness slammed into her and she struggled back against the headboard, realising too late she was staring.

'What are you doing here?' Her voice was half-strangled in her throat.

'I came to wish my bride goodnight.' His mouth tipped up in a smile that was at once easy and far too disturbing, as it set her already racing pulse skittering out of control. 'It's customary between married couples.'

'But I... But we're not...'

'Not married? I think you'll find we are, Samira.'

His smile widened, grew sharp as his gaze dropped to her lips, then lower to her full breasts straining against the oyster satin nightgown. Instantly her nipples hardened, thrusting against the soft fabric. She crossed her arms, hiding them from view.

'I didn't expect to see you again tonight,' she said, mustering her control. Uneasily she watched him near the bed. He was so tall he loomed over it but she refused to shrink back. She had nothing to fear from Tariq. She'd known him, trusted him, as long as she could recall. Just because her traitorous body yearned for him, she was imagining he felt the same.

'You wanted a husband and family,' he said smoothly, as if he were right at home in her bedroom. She wished she had his sangfroid. She felt as out of her depth as a frightened virgin. 'Your life has changed, Samira. You need to accept that. You won't just see me at formal functions but at all hours, including the middle of the night if the boys are sick or need us. Even with the help of nannies you'll be on tap, not just when they're already bathed, fed and dressed.'

'Of course. I know that.' She nodded, breathing more easily. The reminder of the boys grounded her, easing her nerves at Tariq's presence. She leaned forward, relieved to be on solid ground. 'I went along to see them. They were sleeping soundly.'

'But you kissed them goodnight anyway.'

'How did you know?' Did he object? Did he think she was trying to take Jasmin's place? She was conscious that she'd stepped into the slippers of a dead woman.

'I saw you.'

Her head swung higher.

'You did? I didn't see you.'

He shrugged. 'I thought I'd give you time alone with them.'

Samira's lips curved in a smile. This was the Tariq she remembered: kind and thoughtful. Caring.

'Thank you,' she murmured. 'But you should have come in. I wouldn't want to keep you away from them.'

'I'm here now.' Suddenly he was sitting on the side of the bed, turned to face her, his hand planted beside her silk-clad hip, hemming her in. Shock ricocheted through her.

Furtively she moistened her bottom lip with her tongue. Whenever Tariq got this close her mouth parched.

'Is there anything you want?' Samira fought nervous tension and smiled at him. There were hundreds of reasons for him to stop by for a midnight chat. Arrangements to farewell the VIP guests tomorrow, her family included. Or perhaps some detail about the boys' routine.

'Yes.' The word was a low hum that stirred the butter-flies nesting in her belly. 'A goodnight kiss.'

'A—?' She goggled. She couldn't be hearing right. Samira shook her head, loose tresses sliding around her bare shoulders.

'Kiss.' He said it again, his face serious. His gaze dropped to her mouth and heat roared through her. Samira swallowed, her arms wrapping tighter across her torso. Her breasts felt too full and highly sensitised, the nipples blatantly puckering.

'But…why?'

She halted, her face flaming as realisation hit. She'd never felt so gauche. She wasn't some innocent. She un-derstood what it meant when a half-naked man entered his wife's bedroom at night and demanded a kiss. 'That's not what we agreed,' she said quickly. 'It's not part of our deal.'

'Your deal, Samira. Not mine.'

Her fingers gripped her upper arms like claws, digging into soft flesh. This couldn't be happening. 'But you heard me out. You understood.'

'I heard you explain you wanted a marriage that was no marriage.' He leaned infinitesimally closer and the air between them clogged. She couldn't seem to draw enough oxygen into her lungs. 'That doesn't mean I agreed. What I agreed was to make you my wife. That's exactly what I intend to do.'

Shock battered her as she read his intent. And a sense of betrayal so deep it sliced straight to her heart.

She'd *trusted* Tariq. That was why she'd approached him of all men. She knew his word was his bond and he'd implicitly accepted the conditions she'd put on their mar-riage. Yet now…

Bile rose in her throat. She could barely believe she'd been duped again by a man, and by *this* man.

He hadn't told her his intentions before the wedding. He'd waited till it was too late for her to withdraw.

He'd tricked her.

'Tariq!' Her voice was a hoarse scratch. 'As a man of honour—'

His finger on her lips silenced her. She gasped and tasted the salty, male tang of him. To her dismay she registered how good that tasted.

Samira became conscious of the way he caged her against the headboard. His other arm reached across her, his hand planted on the bed beside her hip, trapping her.

'No man of honour would accept what you proposed, Samira. Not if he had any self-respect.' He watched her closely, as if cataloguing her reaction. 'You came to the wrong man if you wanted some emasculated father figure.'

'Father figure?' Her eyes rounded. 'The last thing I want is to tie myself to a man like my father.' He'd been emotionally unstable, lacking in judgement and self-control. It was his example, and Brent's, that had driven her to seek marriage with someone dependable.

Tariq didn't look dependable right now. He looked unpredictable and dangerous, like a keen-eyed hunter sighting his prey.

Fear trickled down her spine.

'You're too young to be a father figure to me, Tariq.'

He shrugged and her mouth dried a little more. She stood no chance against his strength if he decided…

'You wouldn't force me!' The words shot out defiantly, yet she couldn't quite disguise the question in them.

Tariq reared back, his eyes flashing as if she'd insulted his manhood. 'Of course not. I'd never force a woman!' He lifted his hand from the bed as if to break that sense of entrapment. But it was too late. Samira was transfixed.

'Tell me what you want, then.' She swallowed hard but jutted her chin defiantly. She wouldn't give in without a fight.

'Just a kiss.' His eyes held hers. 'When I went to kiss you at the banquet in front of our guests, you turned as pale as milk.' He nodded as her mouth flattened. It was true. She hadn't been able to hide her reaction.

Relief flooded her, weakening her limbs. A kiss, that was all, not…

Her brain seized at the alternative.

'I refuse to have a wife who's afraid of me. Who can't bear to be close to me.' Something dark flashed in his narrowed eyes and her heart pounded faster. 'I need a wife who can take her place at my side without flinching.'

'I'm sorry,' she murmured stiffly. 'I don't know what happened.' Except she did. She'd seen Tariq the man, not the convenient spouse, and been terrified by her response. 'But we don't have to kiss.'

'Can you think of a better way to prove you won't cringe away next time I'm near you? The next time we're together in public? And there are the boys to consider. I don't want them thinking I intimidate you.' His deep voice held a hollow note she hadn't heard before.

Suddenly Samira saw herself as she must seem to him. Needy. Damaged. All the things she'd promised herself she'd never be again. Shame filled her.

She'd promised Tariq she'd be his partner, not an albatross around his neck. Despite his attempt to change the rules of their marriage, pride dictated she give him this much.

'That's all?' Her voice sounded scratchy and breathless. She couldn't dismiss his statement that he hadn't agreed to her marriage terms. But this wasn't the time or place to deal with that. She'd do it when they were fully clothed.

'That's all.'

'And then you'll leave?'

He nodded.

If she kissed him!

Her heart raced out of control at the thought.

Before Samira could have second thoughts she unwrapped her arms and braced her hands on the bed either side of her. A quick breath dragged in the disturbingly appealing scent of Tariq's warm skin, but she refused to think about it, or the way his eyes darkened as she closed the gap between them.

But there was no mistaking the imposing, masculine bulk of him, the bare-chested arrogance of him, or the skirling twist deep inside as she drew close. It made her lose her nerve.

At the last moment she turned her head, pressing her lips not to his mouth but to the firm, taut skin of his cheek. It was smooth, as if he'd just shaved, and it was surprisingly enticing. For an instant she hovered there, her mouth to his flesh, knowing an unheralded desire to explore, to lift her palms to his shoulders and angle her mouth over his.

With a gasp she pulled back, sliding her hands beneath her legs as if to stop them reaching for him again. Her sudden neediness scared her.

Eyes brilliant as gems held hers as blood pounded in her ears. He didn't say anything, though it was obvious she hadn't delivered a real kiss. It was a coward's kiss.

But it was the best Samira could do. Being close to Tariq made her pulse crazy and tied her in knots. Anxiety still feathered her backbone. Did he really intend to demand more?

Abruptly Tariq stood. Samira blinked, her gaze sliding over his amazing bronzed body.

Surely it wasn't regret she felt because he was leaving?

Recognising that she didn't want him to leave stole her voice.

'That's a start,' he murmured finally.

'A start?'

Tariq nodded. 'One day soon we'll be husband and wife in every sense of the word.'

Samira shook her head. He had it all wrong.

'Not because I demand it but because it's what we both want.' He leaned close, his eyes tourmaline shards that dared her to deny it. 'I promise you, Samira, you'll be with me every step of the way.' It was a threat but it sounded like a promise. A promise that sounded appallingly enticing.

She wanted to object, argue, say something to puncture his arrogant certainty. But instead her tongue cleaved to the roof of her mouth.

His gaze scorched and Samira felt the sizzle in every inch of her body. His slow smile hitched his mouth up at one side, creating a sexy groove down one cheek that made her insides clutch. He looked so utterly confident, as if he'd never had a doubt in his life.

'The next time you kiss me it won't be because I ask, Samira, but because you want me.'

CHAPTER FIVE

SHE WAS AT his side as they said farewell to their guests. Her dress, the colour of sun-ripened peaches, made her glow and brought out the brightness of her warm, sherry eyes. He'd guess that no one else noticed the smudges under her eyes. If they did they'd assume it was because he'd kept her from sleep with a night of unbridled passion. Even her blush looked like that of a new bride.

Tariq's belly clenched. Just thinking about Samira strung him tight as a bow. It was unnatural for a man and wife to live as celibate strangers, even for a night.

But Samira hadn't been ready. She'd been as uptight as a virgin, her nervousness palpable despite her bravado.

He wasn't a man to force any woman. That flash of fear in her eyes had stopped him in his tracks.

Yet he intended to have her as his wife in every sense. He only hoped he survived to enjoy her surrender. His hunger for her was stronger, richer, more compelling than it had been all those years ago. He ached with it.

Because she was the woman he'd desired and never had?

Because she'd been the object of his first real passion?

Stretching out his hand, he placed his palm on her back as she wished a visiting princess a safe trip. Samira stiffened but didn't move away. After a few moments, when his hand didn't shift, he felt her tension gradually ease.

Tariq suppressed a smile as he listened to a guest enthuse about yesterday's wedding celebration. It was like breaking in a filly, getting Samira used to his touch, persuading her to trust him. It would take patience but the prize would be worth it.

He glanced down, taking in her vibrant loveliness. Not just her exquisite features, but the warmth of her personality. Her hand fluttered as she emphasised a point and the delicate henna markings caught his eye. Markings that proclaimed her *his*.

Tariq stiffened as need cannoned into him.

He'd married Samira for all the sensible reasons she'd put forward, including his need to do the best for his boys. He'd responded to the desperation he'd read in Samira, the bone-deep instinct that told him she needed this, needed *him*, more than she was prepared to admit.

But there was one reason above all why he'd accepted her proposal.

He'd never wanted a woman as badly as he wanted Samira.

The truth buffeted him, dragging the air from his lungs. It was a truth he'd tried so hard to ignore.

At seventeen she'd been heartbreakingly lovely. Enough to send him rushing back to his homeland lest he do something unforgivable, like seduce his best friend's innocent sister. He'd felt guilty for years, knowing how dishonourable the carnal thoughts were that plagued him. He'd even, at one point, contemplated offering marriage, till he'd heard she had her sights set on a career in fashion. Tariq had needed a wife by his side, not living in the USA or Europe.

Yet, even in the years they'd been apart, just the sight of her photo in the press had the capacity to distract him. He'd never been able to forget her.

So when she'd come to him for help, offering herself in marriage…

He might be Sheikh, commander, ruler and protector of his people. But he was a man too.

'I wish you well, Tariq,' the visiting prince before him said. 'May your sons be many and strong, your daughters as beautiful as your lovely bride and your years long.'

Tariq clasped his outstretched hand, responding in kind.

It struck him how hard this must be for Samira, with everyone wishing them the blessing of children when she couldn't have any. Regret lanced him and he felt a sliver of hurt for her sake.

Yet she didn't flinch as one after another departing guest offered the same wishes. She was the ideal hostess, regal yet warm, charming and lovely, as if she hadn't a care in the world.

Tariq slid his hand in a comforting circle just above her waist. Would she realise he silently offered his support? He could do no more, not in public and not, he guessed, with a woman who guarded her emotions so closely.

Tariq's gentle caress at her back was strangely soothing. After last night she'd been on tenterhooks, anticipating the next time he'd reach for her, maybe demand another kiss. But this—she shifted her weight rather than press back against his warm hand—this felt like comfort.

At last the guests were gone and they were alone. Still his hand remained, his long fingers splaying heat across her upper back. She should move away.

'How are you holding up, Samira?'

She looked up and was surprised to read concern in Tariq's eyes.

'Okay, thanks.' Her brows twitched together. 'Why, don't I look it?' She'd done her best to disguise her sleepless night.

He shrugged and she felt the shift of his arm across her back. She'd forgotten how good it felt to be touched.

'You look gorgeous.' The gleam in his eyes did strange things to her insides. 'But with everyone harping on the prospect of children I wondered.'

Samira stiffened and stepped away, drawing in on herself. Instantly she missed his touch. She was torn between gratitude that he'd thought of her pain and fear she'd given herself away when she'd prided herself on being strong.

'It's nothing.' His steady scrutiny made her edgy. 'At least, I'm used to it.' She forced a smile to hide her discomfort. So many good wishes for something that could never be had reawakened that dull ache of pain at her core. She refused to give in to it. 'After the first hundred times, it's water off a duck's back.'

'It's over now,' he murmured, as if they didn't both know that for a lie. The speculation would start in a few months when people began looking for signs of pregnancy.

Samira's empty womb contracted hard but she ignored it. She couldn't have her own babies but she was now the mother of two sons. That would keep her too busy to worry about anything else. That and dealing with her new husband.

'As you say.' She nodded. 'It's all over.' His kind lie reassured her that she hadn't quite made the huge mistake she'd feared. Relief welled.

Last night Tariq had shattered her optimism with his declaration that he intended them to be lovers. She'd felt devastated and betrayed, haunted by the fear she'd once again chosen a man she couldn't trust. But now, reading the protectiveness in his body language and the concern in his eyes, she saw the man she'd once known and adored. The decent, caring man she'd thought she'd married.

'Finally we're alone,' he murmured. Samira stiffened, anxiety punching hard and low as he reached for her. His fingers wove through hers, big and strong, effective as any manacle as he turned towards the private royal entrance to the audience chamber. 'Come.'

'Where are we going?' Her breath hitched, distrust rising anew. It struck her that she no longer knew what to expect from the man she'd married.

He paused and looked down. She felt as if she was drowning in those clear, green depths. Had they always been so mesmerising?

'It's our honeymoon. We've got a week with not one official function. There are better places to spend it than the audience chamber.' His mouth tilted in a slow smile that sent fear scuddling through her.

It had to be fear. It couldn't be excitement.

'You told me last night you'd wait.' Her voice sounded stretched and she tried to conjure calm as panic rose.

Tariq's brows bunched. 'You think I'm about to ravish you?' He looked at their hands locked together, his so much larger and more powerful than hers. 'Is that really what you believe?'

Samira read the stern glint in his eyes and the clamped austerity of his jaw. She'd touched him on the raw.

'I don't know what to think,' she admitted. 'I thought I knew you but I was wrong. You made that clear last night.'

'You knew the boy, not the man.'

He stood proud, unashamed of the man he'd become, the man who'd duped her into believing she was safe with him when all the time he had his own plans. He'd tricked her into believing he'd married on her terms and yet remarkably at this moment she wanted to trust him.

Samira stared up at Tariq. Was he the man she'd known or a stranger? How much had he altered in the years since she'd felt she could trust him with her life?

There'd even been a time, in the distant past, when she'd thought she loved him. He'd been her first romantic crush, the one she'd spent hours daydreaming over with all the fervour of her teenage soul.

Long fingers smoothed her forehead and shivery heat tightened her skin. 'Don't fret about it, Samira.' He paused. 'I have a gift for you. That's all.'

'A gift?' Another one? He'd already presented her with a wealth of exquisite jewellery. Even for a princess born to the opulence of the Jazeeri royal court, her breath had been taken away by his gifts. 'You've given me enough.' She felt overwhelmed by his generosity. Her own gifts, though carefully chosen, weren't nearly as lavish.

'This is something from *me*, not an heirloom.'

There it was again, that glint in his eye that made her shiver. Mentally Samira shook herself. She refused to live her life walking on eggshells.

'That sounds intriguing.'

Tariq's swift, approving smile made her breath catch. He really was stunningly charismatic.

He led her deep into the heart of the palace's private apartments. Samira busied herself admiring the furnishings and the occasional glimpses across the city to the blue smudge of the mountains beyond. Anything to distract her from the intimacy of Tariq's hand enfolding hers, his tall frame imposing yet somehow reassuring as he shortened his stride to match her pace. Being close to him took some getting used to.

Finally they stopped before a wide door. 'After you.'

She pushed it open, only to freeze on the threshold. Slowly, disbelieving, she took in the large, airy space lit by extra-wide, full-length windows.

Samira swallowed, her throat tight, her eyes glazing at the unexpected perfection of it.

'It's wonderful,' she whispered.

'You can go in, you know.'

She hardly heard him. Already she was moving across

the hardwood floor to the massive table in the centre of the room set under powerful lamps. Her fingers trailed the edge of the work surface before moving across to the drawing board, tilted at an angle to catch the natural light. Then to the set of built-in cupboards. The custom-made drawers. The specially designed containers that held bolts of fabric: velvets, silks, lace, satin and chiffon. There was even a mannequin on a podium, again set under brilliant lighting.

Everywhere she looked, in every drawer and corner, was something that pleased her.

Slowly she turned, taking in the careful thought and attention to detail that had gone into making this the ideal work room.

She blinked hard as she recognised the ancient, slightly saggy lounge chair she'd used for the past four years when she'd wanted to curl up and sketch. Beside it was a small wooden table inlaid with mother-of-pearl. It held a sketch pad like the one she always used and a variety of crayons and pencils.

'Your sister-in-law helped me with the details. She sent through photos of your workshop in Jazeer.'

'But this is…' The words stuck in Samira's throat. 'This is far, far better. It's perfect.' She'd never had a custom-made studio. Despite her growing success she'd worked out of a large room she'd adapted in her brother's palace. But this—it was amazing. And it had been created especially for her.

A wave of excitement crashed over her, making her blood tingle. She itched to get to work here.

Samira pivoted to find Tariq just behind her. She grabbed his hand in both of hers, enthusiasm buoying her.

'I don't know how to thank you.' She shook her head, brim-full of emotion. He'd done this for *her*. No gift had ever been so special, so very *right*. 'Words don't seem enough.'

'Then don't use words.' His glinting eyes challenged her, as if he knew she felt over-full, needing an outlet for the surge of elation and wonder she felt.

Samira's breath hitched in automatic denial, the shutters she'd so carefully built instantly coming up to guard her from this over-emotional response.

She saw the moment he read the change in her. The moment his gaze altered from challenging to disappointed.

The moment he realised she didn't have the guts to follow through.

When he saw how scared she was.

In that instant the truth blasted her. She had all the emotions of other women. She felt pain and hope and delight but she'd spent years bottling them up, hiding them from the world and herself. Because she was scared they'd make her weak.

She'd let Jackson Brent do that to her.

No, she corrected. She'd done it to herself.

Her nostrils flared in disgust and inadvertently she drew in the heady spicy aroma of Tariq. It sent a trickle of feminine pleasure coursing through her.

She'd even learned to repress that in the last few years, hadn't she? She hadn't been interested in a man, much less turned on by one, in four years. She hadn't let herself.

Suddenly Samira saw herself as Tariq must—wary to the point of being pathetic.

Was she? Or was she merely cautious? Sensible to protect herself?

But there was a difference between being cautious and being a coward. Last night she'd been a coward and the knowledge was bitter on her tongue. All this time she'd told herself she was being strong. But in reality...

Samira let go of Tariq's hand, instead planting a steadying palm on his hard chest, the other on his shoulder as she rose on tiptoe.

Light flared in those cool eyes but he didn't move, merely stood stock-still, waiting.

She realised she'd stopped breathing and exhaled, then drew in a deep breath redolent of desert spice and hot man. Tariq. His scent enticed. Could he possibly taste as good? Suddenly she had to know.

Samira slipped her hand from his shoulder up to the back of his head, pulling till his mouth was a whisper from hers.

Atavistic warning clawed through her, screaming that she was about to cross a point of no return.

For once, need overrode caution. The need to trust herself, just a little. The need for a man's touch.

Her eyes closed as she pressed her mouth to his. His lips were warm and inviting. She angled her head a little, kissing him again, enjoying his hard body against her, the pleasure of his mouth touching hers.

Samira's other hand snaked up to wrap around his neck, holding him tight as she worked tiny kisses along the tantalising seam of his lips. She felt the exhale of his breath through his nostrils, harder than before, and licked where before she'd kissed. He felt so good. *This* felt so good. If only…

Delicious pleasure hit as he opened his mouth, sucking her tongue inside, drawing her into delight. It was so sudden, so powerfully erotic, that she crumpled at the knees, clinging to his tall frame as his arms wrapped her close.

His mouth worked hers, drawing her to him, delving her depths so she had no option but to surrender that last skerrick of caution.

Samira was captivated. Her whole body came alive in a way she'd never known. Surely no kiss had been like this—a slow kindling that burned bright and satisfying even as it demanded more and yet more?

She arched, moulding herself inch by inch to that strong body she hadn't been able to put from her mind. Still her lips clung to his, hungrier now as his grew more urgent, and a new fire ignited low in her body. Her hands tightened on him. Ripples of heat traced her skin, eddying at her breasts, her pelvis. At her back and hip where he held her so securely.

Her heart was hammering as she tore her lips away, gasping for air. Yet it wasn't lack of oxygen that made her withdraw, but shock at how a thank-you kiss had turned into something completely different. Gratitude and excitement had turned to curiosity, to pleasure and then, almost, to surrender.

She wanted nothing so much as to kiss him again, to lose herself in him.

Samira shivered, suddenly cold despite the hot pulse of blood under her skin. Fear warred with elation.

Tariq still held her, his gaze hooded, waiting, and her stomach churned.

She swallowed, trying to find her voice and not betray rising panic. 'That was…'

His mouth tilted a little at one corner. 'Delightful?' he mused in a low murmur that trawled through her insides, tying her in knots.

'Unexpected,' she gasped.

'A taste of things to come.' His smile deepened, his hold tightening just a fraction.

Instantly Samira stiffened, shaking her head.

She broke from his embrace, staggering back till she came up against the huge work table, her breath coming quick and shallow. Her hands splayed on its edge as she tried to lock her knees. She felt too wobbly to stand alone.

'No.' Her voice was hoarse but she didn't care. She had to make him understand.

She hated that he made her feel weak. She'd taught herself to be strong, hadn't she? She'd taken him by surprise when she'd proposed marriage. She'd been strong then. She refused to cower now.

'No.' Samira locked her hands before her, meeting his eyes directly. 'I told you I don't want love or sex.'

Tariq's teeth bared in a smile she could only describe as hungry. It made her wonder how the graze of his teeth on her skin would feel. 'You say that but your body tells a different story.'

He stepped forward but her outstretched hand stopped him. It took too long for her to realise her fingers had curled into his crisp cotton clothing. She tugged her hand back as if burned.

'Please, Tariq. Believe me when I tell you love is the last thing I want.' Except for the warm, sustaining love between a mother and her children. She'd imagined a special caring too, respect, trust and friendship between husband and wife, but shied from calling it love.

'You made that clear when you proposed. That was one of the reasons I agreed to marry you.'

'It was?' Her eyes widened.

'Definitely.' His gaze shifted, lifting to look past her towards the distant mountains. Instantly Samira felt some of her tension suck away, like a tide suddenly turning. 'The last thing I want is a wife who thinks she's in love with me.' His voice held a honed edge that made her shiver.

Because Tariq was thinking of Jasmin?

Obviously he was. Samira watched his dead gaze as he stared into the distance. She sensed he didn't see the view. It was his first wife he saw. Everyone spoke of how devoted they'd been, how her death had devastated him.

Samira's heart wrenched.

He looked as if a cold wall of steel had crashed down, cutting him off from her. Was his grief still so all-consuming?

Samira wanted to comfort him, except she guessed the last thing he wanted was a reminder that his beloved wife was gone, replaced by a woman he hadn't really wanted.

Suddenly she felt small and unreasonably...hurt.

That was ridiculous. She'd never expected more from him.

Of course Tariq didn't want love. He'd had that from Jasmin and now he couldn't love again. He was a one-woman man. Samira told herself she respected him for that.

He turned and eyes of crystalline green snared her. 'But there's no reason,' he murmured in a low voice of pure temptation, 'why we can't enjoy sex.'

Heat pounded into her. His stare didn't trail suggestively over her body. It didn't need to. It was potent, alight with a desire that made the blood sing in her veins. She struggled to cope with a barrage of sensations as her body responded to that sultry, knowing look. Her emotions jackknifed from distress to forbidden excitement.

'No. We agreed.'

'You agreed, Samira. I didn't.'

Panic rose anew as she tried and failed to ignore the heat in his eyes and, worse, the answering blaze of hunger in her belly.

It was an aberration.

She threaded her fingers together. 'I told you I don't trust myself with sex and love. I don't—'

'You think sex and love are the same?' His brows crunched together.

'I...' She tilted her chin up. She mightn't have Tariq's vast experience but she had enough. 'For me they are. I never slept with a man I didn't love.' Which meant she'd had one lover and he'd been the biggest mistake of her life. 'Sexual attraction makes you vulnerable. It blinds you to the truth, so you see only what you want to see.' It had been her mother's great weakness and her own. But she'd learned her lesson.

'Oh, Samira.' Tariq shook his head, his hand touching her chin in a fleeting caress that sent shock waves zinging through her. 'You're so inexperienced.'

She huffed out a gasp of mirthless laughter. 'You're the only one to think so.' There was an element of the press, and the public, that insisted on wondering whether she'd been to bed with every man ever photographed with her.

'Believe me, you don't need to be in love to enjoy sex.'

Samira supposed he was thinking of the many beauties who'd warmed his bed before his first marriage and, if rumour was right, in the period since his first wife's death. None had lasted long enough to make a claim on him.

'I know that.' She wasn't a complete innocent. 'But it was like that for me and I can't afford for it to happen again.' She couldn't survive such disillusionment a second time.

'You don't love me, do you?'

'No.' She clenched her jaw.

'Yet you feel this?' *This* was the graze of his knuckles across her breast, lingering at her nipple, making it harden. Her breasts seemed to swell and an arrow of fierce heat shot directly to her womb.

Samira jerked back against the table, shock skittering through her.

'Don't touch me like that!'

'Why not, when you enjoy it?'

She opened her mouth to deny it but he continued. 'I can see the flush of arousal at your throat so don't pretend I'm not right.' His gaze dipped from her neck. 'Your breasts are burning up, aren't they? Is there heat lower too? Deep inside, do you feel empty? Needy?'

Samira gasped as the muscles between her legs clenched

greedily, responding to Tariq's words. He knew her too well. Better than she knew herself.

'I can fill that emptiness, Samira. I can make it good for you. For both of us.'

He could too. Instinctively she knew it. Certainty gleamed in those penetrating eyes. Her body was inching forward, eager for his expert touch.

Samira grabbed hard at the table behind her. 'I don't want that.'

Slowly he shook his head. 'Of course you do. So do I.' His face was taut with a hunger that should have dismayed her, yet instead intrigued her. She imagined them together, here in this room, his big, capable hands gentle yet demanding on her flesh. She wanted...

No! She'd made that mistake once.

'I told you, Tariq, it's not for me. Intimacy and love are bound up together. I won't go there again.'

'You speak with such experience. How many lovers have you had?'

'One.' She jutted her chin. 'That was one too many.'

His gaze narrowed. His words, when they came, held a contained savagery she'd not heard from him before. 'You had your heart broken by a bastard who shouldn't have been allowed even to touch the hem of your dress.'

Samira blinked, taken aback by the depth of Tariq's anger.

'Take it from me, little one, sex can be quite, quite separate to love.' He paused and she sensed he chose his words carefully. 'That makes us an ideal match. I don't want love from you and you don't want it from me. We're on a level playing field. Neither of us will fall for some grand romantic illusion about this marriage.'

Was that bitterness in his voice?

Samira bit her lip. No doubt he was thinking of Jasmin and the fact no other woman could take her place in his heart.

'We have the marriage you wanted,' he continued. 'But we can have more. We can enjoy each other. It's only natural, you know.' This time his touch wasn't at all sexual, a mere brush of fingertips against her hair, yet she felt it all the way to her toes.

'Desire is a part of life. Why not enjoy it? After all, neither of us is in danger of falling in love.'

CHAPTER SIX

A SMILE CURVED Samira's mouth at the way Risay's small hand tucked confidingly into hers as they entered the stables. Shade engulfed them, with the scent of horses, hay and leather.

She paused, letting her eyes adjust, basking in the gentle pleasure of this outing with her new son.

Her son. The word shimmered like a vibration in the warm air, wrapping around her. How long before she grew accustomed to this wonderful new reality?

Her reverie was broken when Risay tugged her hand. Stiff-legged, he marched forward, gabbling in baby language to a man sitting amidst a selection of harnesses.

'Your Highness.' He rose and bowed, a bridle hanging from gnarled hands.

'Please, don't let me interrupt your work.'

With another bow he sat and picked up his polishing cloth. Light from a window caught the ornate silver decorations on the bridle. 'The little prince admires the harness,' he said as Risay strained forward, hand outstretched.

Samira smiled. Anything bright was sure to catch Risay's eye. 'We're looking for the Sheikh. I believe he's here somewhere.'

'Just in the training ring.' The stable hand gestured to the open space on the other side of the building.

The thud of hooves on dirt drew her attention and she

turned to look out of the wide doors. Movement caught her eye.

'I'll look after the young prince if you wish to talk with His Majesty,' the stable hand offered. 'We're old friends.'

Samira dragged her gaze away from the arena. Risay already half-sat on the man's lap, obviously at home, plucking at an intricately wrought harness.

'Thank you.' She nodded and moved towards the open doors.

In a sunlit arena a man and horse faced each other— the horse skittish, its gait high as it pranced, eyes rolling. Her heart jumped as Tariq, unperturbed, approached it. His lips moved and the horse's ears flicked.

Samira's skin drew tight as she caught the delicious, low cadence of Tariq's voice. That same voice had mesmerised her just yesterday.

Desire is a part of life.

Neither of us is in danger of falling in love.

The voice of temptation.

She'd told herself she was immune to such temptation. Yet her body betrayed her. Even here, now, when Tariq wasn't aware of her presence.

Fire trawled her veins, stirred the feminine pulse point between her legs, scorched her breasts. She just had to look at Tariq's powerful frame, hear his rich coffee voice, and she went weak at the knees.

Despair gripped her. Maybe her critics were right. Perhaps she was tainted for ever since she'd once given in to a man's blandishments. Perhaps desire had become an intrinsic weakness, no matter how hard she battled for a cool head.

Her eyes ate him up. He wore a collarless shirt that stuck to broad, muscled shoulders in the heat and pale trousers tucked into boots. Tall, confident and erect as a soldier, he was magnetic. His total lack of fear as the stallion side-stepped wickedly close made her gasp.

Heart in mouth, Samira moved nearer, watching the horse try to intimidate. A rider herself, she understood the stallion's magnificence and the danger. One strike of his powerful hoof could seriously wound.

Yet, as she watched, something changed. That sharply nodding head lowered. Wide nostrils flared as it scented the man who stood, murmuring, keeping eye contact with the big beast.

Seconds strung out to minutes and, apart from quick checks to see Risay was happy, Samira's gaze remained glued on the figure of her husband as he, by some magic, quieted the untamed horse. He didn't even lift his hand, just communed with it in a way she didn't understand.

Finally the horse stepped forward, its gait almost delicate, and blew gustily on his face.

A chuckle sounded in the still air, causing a ripple of sensation deep in Samira's belly. She pressed her hand to the spot, trying to prevent that warm, melting sensation from spreading.

Tariq lifted his hand and the stallion snuffled it. When Tariq turned and moved away, to Samira's amazement, the horse followed like a pet. It nudged his shoulder blade and he laughed, the sound carefree rather than triumphant.

Samira couldn't drag her eyes away. Something inside squeezed tight and hard at the power and pleasure radiating from him. It made her want to reach out and—

'Samira.' He'd seen her. Sensation jolted her as their eyes met.

In swift strides Tariq crossed the arena to stand before her, only a fence separating them.

Despite the breathless clutch of attraction, Samira found herself smiling. 'You have a shadow.'

He turned his head just as the stallion lipped at his shoulder. Tariq murmured something she couldn't hear to the big animal, then, swift as quicksilver, he was through the fence to stand before her, his eyes keen beneath lazy lids.

Samira breathed him in hungrily, clean sweat and warm spice. Moisture sheened his forehead and the burnished skin of his collarbone. Her eyelids flickered as the pulse between her legs quickened.

'How did you do that?' she asked, needing words to fill the expectant silence.

'Do what?' His eyes were on her mouth and her nipples pebbled in anticipation. She shuffled back a step.

'That.' She nodded to the stallion. 'The way you break in a horse.'

'Ah.' He drew the sound out as he followed her a pace. Heat beaded Samira's brow. He was too *close*. 'That's the secret.' He bent his head and his words feathered warm breath across her face. 'I don't break them. I gentle them.'

His eyes caressed her and she felt it like the graze of hard fingers along her throat and over her cheek.

She blinked. 'Gentle?' Was he some sort of horse whisperer?

'It's a matter of trust,' he murmured in that low voice with just a hint of gravel. It trawled through her insides, furrowing pleasure in its wake. 'Once they know I'm not going to hurt them, they learn to trust.'

The liquid heat in his eyes told her he was talking about more than horses.

She stiffened. 'You won't hurt them while they abide by your rules, you mean. You want to be master.' Just as he wanted to be hers. Disillusionment was still fresh in her memory. Of how he'd duped her into believing he was safe.

No man had ever looked less safe.

Or more appealing. That was the problem. Her heart hammered her ribcage as if yearning for her submission.

'You think it's about power?' Slowly he shook his head,

his gaze never leaving hers. 'You had the wrong teacher, Samira.' Heat scorched her skin at his words. They both knew he was referring to her ex-lover. 'It's all about partnership, mutual understanding and enjoyment.'

'Enjoyment?' Instead of disbelief, the single word sounded...needy. She swallowed hard, unable to break away from the enchantment Tariq wove around her with his rich voice and those slumberous eyes that yet danced with anticipation.

'Of course.' He smiled and something hitched in her chest. 'If we don't both enjoy the partnership it won't work.'

Tariq's words hung in the air like a promise. Partnership, enjoyment...was that what he offered where she saw only capitulation and danger?

Samira looked over his shoulder to the dark, glistening eye of the big stallion. Far from being cowed, mischief glinted there. And delight.

Or perhaps her imagination ran away with her. She shook her head, stepping back abruptly to break the spell Tariq wove around her.

Long fingers closed around her hand. His grip was firm but not unbreakable, yet she found herself stilling.

'We're not enemies, Samira.' His tone coaxed. 'We want the same thing.'

She swallowed the words all but bursting on her tongue. Emotionally charged accusations that stemmed from fear, not of Tariq as much as of herself, of this *weakness* she couldn't eradicate but dared not give in to again.

'Risay is here,' she said stiffly. 'Unlike his brother, he refused to settle for a nap without seeing you.'

Tariq's hand loosened around hers as she pulled away, yet even with four whole paces between them the imprint of heat still shackled her.

Then he moved past her in long, easy strides. He hunkered down to Risay's level and weathered his son's en-

ANNIE WEST

89

thusiastic embrace with a smile that confirmed what she already knew: that his boys were the light of his life.

He didn't look back over his shoulder at her. His whole attention was focused on his son.

To her dismay, Samira felt excluded. She wanted some of what he gave Risay: his attention, his loyalty. She wanted to bask in his smiles, share his laughter.

And more…so much more.

Laughter rang out, the sound curling around Samira's heart, making her smile. Adil shrieked with joy as his father threw him up and deftly caught him in strong arms. Water droplets caught the dying light as Tariq shook his head. Samira made herself look away. She'd spent too long furtively ogling his powerful body.

This time at the oasis had been far more confronting than the night of their wedding, when Tariq had come to her bedroom and insisted she kiss him. A week had passed and with each day the tension in her had twisted harder.

Her husband stood thigh-deep in the shallows, his swim shorts clinging to powerfully hewn thighs. The sight of him sent Samira's blood pressure hurtling into the danger zone.

She'd never been one to gawk at men. But she'd never spent time with a man like Tariq.

Her one and only lover had been handsome and oh-so-charming, wiry rather than muscular. He'd looked better modelling chic designer clothes than out of them. And she'd discovered that his charm was more often for the camera than for her. Yet here was Tariq, even more appealing in the role of doting father and considerate husband than he was in public.

His eye caught hers and a pulse of awareness passed between them, making her heart beat like a drum. One glance and instantly she reacted. It had been like that since the wedding, even though Tariq hadn't pressed her for more.

Each day, each hour, she waited for him to try persuading her into intimacy, only to be *disappointed* when he treated her with careful courtesy! After their conversation in the stables she'd expected him to make a move on her, confident of success. Yet he'd let her be. Only the warmth in his gaze and the way his hand lingered when they touched proved it hadn't all been a dream. She hadn't imagined his proposition.

Samira tore her gaze away, kneeling and opening her arms to Risay as he splashed through the shallows towards her.

The sight of the brilliant smile on his dear baby face tugged at her heart strings. He and his brother had welcomed her into their world with an uncomplicated enthusiasm that reinforced all her fond hopes.

Silently she vowed she'd repay their generosity with all the love and support they deserved.

Her arms closed around Risay and she snuggled him close. He was wet and cuddly and chuckled as inevitably he reached for her hair.

Samira let him play with the knot at the back of her head. Tiny fingers snagged and pulled. She sighed, acknowledging it was easier to do it herself. With a few swift movements she released her hair. It tumbled down and Risay clapped his hands, sitting with a splash in the shallow water, threading his fingers through her long tresses.

'What is it with you boys and my hair?'

'It's the novelty.' Tariq's voice seemed ridiculously deep after his son's high squeal of pleasure. And it held a husky note that brushed along her nerves like rich velvet. 'They've never seen anything like it.'

Samira looked up to meet his eyes. There it was again, that flash of brilliance that made her catch her breath. She was grateful her hair was loose. It hid the way her nipples swelled against her swimsuit, as if reaching out for his touch. The idea sent discomfort squirming through her.

Yet it was true. Every instinct she possessed urged her to forget her qualms and take what Tariq offered. This honeymoon with him and the twins at the 'small' summer palace on the edge of the desert and the mountains had worn down her doubts and her resistance.

They'd spent almost every waking hour together since he'd set aside royal responsibilities for a week and declared this family time.

It had become appallingly difficult, trying to remember exactly why intimacy with Tariq was such a bad idea when he was with her all the time.

'Sofia, their nanny, has short hair. So do the other staff.'

As he spoke his gaze followed the fall of Samira's hair. That took his stare down to her waist, then lower to the high-cut edge of her swimsuit and her bare thighs. Immediately fire zinged along her veins, concentrating at the sensitive spot between her legs. She shifted her weight and watched a tiny smile tug at his mouth. As if he knew exactly how she responded.

It wasn't the first time he'd seemed to know more about her desires than she did herself.

'Maybe I should get it cut.' Carefully she extricated Risay's fingers from her hair and distracted him with a brightly coloured bucket. 'I've been thinking about it for ages.'

'No!'

Her head swung up at his sharp tone. Tariq was frowning down at her, his game with Adil stopped. What was his problem?

'People cut their hair all the time, Tariq.' It was past time she updated her image. Jackson had suggested it more than once when they'd been together and Samira had worried that her reluctance proclaimed her old-fashioned or just plain cowardly. She'd had long hair all her life. But was that any reason to keep it?

'Please don't.'

Samira opened her mouth to say something offhand, until she read what was in Tariq's eyes and her mouth snapped shut. Heat seared her from top to toe and in every crevice and pulse point in between.

It struck her that this was the first time Tariq had asked her for anything.

She was so distracted she barely noticed Sofia bustling along to gather up the boys and take them back inside for dinner. Slowly Samira stood, stretching her toes to counteract the pins and needles in her feet from kneeling so long. Finding any excuse to look away from Tariq.

But he was still there, still watching, when she straightened. Surely he stood closer?

Her breath stalled. It wasn't just the magnificence of him. Or the fire in his eyes. This was Tariq, the man she'd known and trusted all her life. The man who'd made her dream of a family come true. The man who looked at her and made her feel utterly unlike the sensible, careful woman she'd striven to become.

'Promise me you won't cut it.' Before Samira could work out if that was a request or a command, Tariq reached for her.

He threaded his fingers in her hair, combing slowly from her ear, down past her jaw and throat, hovering for long moments near her breast, then down to where her stomach muscles automatically tensed as he ran out of hair. His hand came to a stop barely grazing the red Lycra at her hip bone.

The hiss of Samira's indrawn breath was loud in the silence. Her muscles clenched hard in response to his feather-light touch. She ordered herself to step back but her legs weren't listening.

'I like it the way it is.' He lifted a fistful of hair and held it to his face, burying his mouth in the dark locks, closing his eyes as he inhaled, his mighty chest rising as if sucking in her essence.

It was the most erotic thing she'd ever experienced. Every erogenous zone in her body slammed into awareness. Samira's mouth dried and her breasts tingled anew. Her knees wobbled alarmingly and she shot out a hand, grabbing his elbow. He felt hot and hard and flagrantly male.

Slowly he lifted his eyes and lightning jolted through her as their gazes met and held.

Could he feel how she shook? Did he hear the rasp of her uneven breathing?

She swallowed hard, telling herself she still had time to retreat. Nothing had happened.

Yet she knew that for a lie. This was… She shook her head. She had no words to describe this.

Tariq stood stock-still. Samira in a red one-piece swimsuit, her sable silk hair rippling in waves to her waist, equalled his most fervid imaginings. The perfume of her skin was in his nose and mouth, like the sweetest of all treats. His lips brushed the impossible softness of her hair and he wasn't sure he could let go.

Yet he'd promised not to rush her. He'd given his word.

This week of holding back from her had almost killed him. His breath sawed in his throat as he struggled to breathe.

He wanted so badly to reach for her. Holding back gouged a chasm through his midriff. But, despite the longing in her eyes, he saw the way her teeth sank into her bottom lip and the tight defensiveness of her shoulders.

Tariq looked into her beautiful face and suppressed a shudder of desire. His need for her was a ravening hunger that obliterated any satisfaction that she was obviously weakening. He'd assured himself it would be easy to enjoy the physical benefits marriage brought. Yet he felt himself hover on the edge of control.

It wasn't supposed to be like *this*. So all-consuming.

Guilt was a sudden sharp, twist of pain driving up from his gut to his heaving chest. How could he feel this rush of powerful desire when not much over a year ago his wife—

He slammed the door on that thought, but not before shame scored him.

Jasmin had asked him to do what was best for the boys, to find a woman who'd care for them as her own. Yet he'd been in no rush to fulfil his promise, appalled at the thought of marrying again. Nothing, he'd thought, would induce him to take another wife, to step into the quick-sand that was emotion.

Now, holding Samira's soft hair in his hand, feeling her touch on his arm, he wondered what the hell he'd done. How was he supposed to control *this*?

What he felt was too big, too deep, too raw and unfamiliar. He resented it, despised the weakness it revealed in him. His whole upbringing had been designed to eradicate weakness. His guardian's regimen of hard work, discipline and self-denial had honed Tariq into a man with the strength and single-mindedness to rule a nation, to lead in war if necessary, not to wallow in feelings or succumb to neediness.

Yet his fingers were stiffly reluctant as he released Samira and stepped back. Warm water eddied around his calves. He wished it was deep and icy so he could douse the heat in his blood and his phenomenal erection.

Abruptly he turned, wading out until the water reached his hips and then striking out for the other side of the oasis pool.

CHAPTER SEVEN

TARIQ STOOD, ARM braced high against the open window as he stared at the winking stars. The desert night sky glittered, diamond-bright. A soft breeze feathered across his chest and rippled his loose cotton trousers against his thighs. But it did nothing to cool him. Even the plunge in the oasis and a cold shower later hadn't brought relief from the heat simmering within.

What he needed was a distraction, but the children were in bed and paperwork couldn't hold his attention. Usually it was no effort to work through the evening. But he'd grown so used to Samira's presence, he missed it now. This last week he'd spent most of his time with her, getting reacquainted over a game of chess or backgammon, or discussing the boys. But he'd decided an evening apart was a wise precaution.

A mirthless laugh escaped. He'd planned to accustom her to his presence, use every moment of every day to remind her how good they'd be together and how foolish she was to try denying the inevitable.

How that had backfired!

He was the one so needy he all but climbed the walls with wanting. He was the one who couldn't settle.

He should have made her see reason that first night. Despite her haunted eyes it wouldn't have taken much to seduce her. She was such a sensual woman he could have overcome her doubts in no time.

Now he was paying the penalty for his scruples.

Tariq shoved aside the half-formed suspicion that mere lust shouldn't torture him so. After Jasmin, he knew he was incapable of feeling anything more profound for any woman.

He swung away from the window, intending to dress for a night ride across the desert, when a figure emerged from the shadows near the door.

'Samira!' Even in the gloom she took his breath away. Her long, pale nightdress shimmered with the lustre of a thousand pearls as it shaped her voluptuous form. Her hair lay loosely plaited over one shoulder, trailing down past her breast, lifting with every breath she took.

Tariq swallowed hard, his eyes travelling from her luscious breasts to her tiny waist and the smooth flare of her hips. She moved and a narrow slit revealed one leg all the way to her thigh. He breathed out gustily, trying to rein in his impulse to reach for her and slam her against his body.

'Hello, Tariq.'

'What are you doing here?' He flexed his fingers, then linked them behind his back, away from temptation.

'I want to talk with you.'

Tariq shut his eyes, trying to conjure the willpower he needed. She came to his room dressed like *that* and expected to chat? More and more he wondered just how experienced his bride was in matters of passion.

He'd reached the end of his tether.

'We can talk tomorrow, Samira. It's late.' He strode to the wide bed and dragged back the covers. If that didn't scare her away, nothing would.

Yet she stood her ground. In the dim light he saw her chin jut.

'This won't take long. I know how disrupting a visitor can be just as you're trying to get to sleep.'

Tariq repressed a grunt of laughter. So this was payback for him walking into her room the night of the wedding? If so she had no idea how *disruptive* that had been for him. If she knew she wouldn't have dared venture into the lion's den.

Deliberately he sat on the side of the bed and gestured for her to do the same, knowing she wouldn't.

'Thank you.' To his amazement, she sat down. Not at the far end of the bed, either, but a prim arm's length away.

Tariq took one look at the toned thigh peeping out from her satiny gown and dragged his gaze up to her face. She was tense but more than that he couldn't read in the gloom.

'I wanted to ask you…'

'Yes?' It came out as a growl because inevitably his gaze had dropped again to where she fidgeted with the slit now gaping wide on her thigh. There was only so much temptation a man could withstand.

When she didn't respond immediately he looked up to see her biting her lip.

'Yes?' He managed to sound a little more encouraging.

'How are you sure we can completely separate sex from…' she shrugged and spread one arm wide '…from anything else? How do you know we can keep sex and love separate?'

Tariq felt his pulse pound hard once, twice. He forced himself to sit back, planting his arms behind him on the bed. As if every cell of his being didn't clamour for him to reach for her now. If she'd come this far…

'Bitter experience.'

Her gaze had settled on his chest but now it swung up. 'Because of those other women? Because none of them have been able to fill the gap your wife left?'

'Partly.' The truth was far more difficult and painful. He had no intention of going there. 'I assure you, Samira, love isn't something you need fear from me.' Tariq's mouth twisted at the irony of his situation. If only she knew. 'And your experiences have cured you of that too.'

Slowly she nodded. 'Absolutely.'

'See? It's simple when you think it through. You've already taken a step to build a better life without it. To think with your *head* not your heart.' That was his strength, what he'd been trained to do from birth, eschewing anything that might cloud his judgement. He held out one hand, palm up, on the bed. 'I admire your courage in learning from your mistake and reaching out for what you really want.'

For long seconds she contemplated his outstretched hand. Then, just as his patience frayed, she laid her palm on his. It was delicate and soft, but not weak. He smiled as he folded his fingers around hers.

She was his. Just as he'd planned.

Victory tasted sweet in his mouth. But not as sweet as Samira would be. Already he was salivating, anticipating pleasures to come. He stroked his thumb from her palm up to the pulse point at her wrist and she shivered delicately, her nipples peaking against the clinging nightdress.

'You expect a woman to reach out and take what she wants?' There was a delightful breathless hitch to her voice that awoke a visceral possessiveness in Tariq.

He'd wanted Samira so long. Since the year she'd turned seventeen. Instead of abating, his hunger had intensified with each passing year, torturing him. At first Samira had been untouchable because of her youth and innocence, because of who she was, because their paths lay in different directions. Yet now, against the odds, here she was, his wife.

'Why not?' His voice emerged as a low rumble. 'It's what I'd do.'

His words hung in still air. Then a warm palm planted itself on his chest, fingers splaying as she leaned close. Tariq's breathing faltered. He felt the imprint of her hand right down into what passed for his soul. For a fleeting instant doubt hammered him, the remembrance of all he couldn't offer her.

Then her fingers moved, learning the shape of his body, and doubt fled.

This time it was simple attraction, he assured himself, heady with relief and anticipation. There would be no painful emotional complications.

This time it would be okay.

The knowledge reassured him and fed his arousal.

His eyelids lowered as he fought to rein in rampant hunger to a level that wouldn't panic her. His need was so profound.

'I want you, Tariq.' She whispered the words against his collarbone, pressing a kiss to his burning skin, then another and another, working her way in towards his throat, her mouth soft and hot.

Tariq arched back his head, exhaling with relief and shuddering anticipation. He grabbed her shoulders and with one surging movement hauled her onto his lap, groaning as her satin-clad bounty pressed against him. Her taut backside was on his thighs, his erection nudging her hip, the glorious weight of one full breast in his hand.

Was ever a woman created with the sole purpose of driving a man crazy?

He was near explosion point and they were still dressed. He hadn't felt such urgency since he'd fumbled with his first woman.

Tariq dragged in a breath that smelt of sugary cinnamon with a hint of musk. Sex and Samira, a heady combination.

His mouth found her shoulder and he bit down on the spot that curved up to her neck, knowing how sensitive it would be. The taste of her in his mouth was as heady as he remembered.

She gasped, twisting closer, her breasts thrusting, her

buttocks sliding across his legs. The friction of her hip against his shaft was excruciating pleasure. So was the knowledge that Samira was as aroused as he. She trembled all over as if sensitised to the very weight of the air against her body.

Tariq smiled and sucked gently at the spot he'd nipped. She grabbed his shoulders, fingers digging hard, her breath a low moan that was music in his ears.

'I told you I could make it good for you, Samira.'

But she was past answering. He wasn't even sure she'd heard. Her eyes were slits and her breath came in little pants as she shifted restlessly against him.

To hell with it. Foreplay could wait till the next time. This thing between them was too urgent, too elemental, for games.

He grabbed her waist, the silky material on her delicious body too flagrantly appealing. With a surge of energy he lifted her up to face him, the muscles in his arms locking hard to support her.

'Move your leg over mine,' he growled.

Her eyes opened, looking directly into his, and Tariq felt the impact of her stare thwack him in the chest. He read dazed confusion and a desperation that matched his own.

His arms shook as he lowered her gently onto his lap, pulling her close so her thighs wrapped around his hips. He struggled to breathe in, but the sensation of her heated core hard up against him was almost too much. He gritted his teeth, praying he had the stamina to last.

His hands slipped up her thighs and he found the lace-edged slit on one. Instantly his fingers were under the material, questing over skin every bit as enticing as the delicate, slippery fabric.

She shifted, rising clumsily on her knees, and somehow the silk ripped as his hand plunged higher.

'Sorry.'

For answer she shifted her weight onto one knee, then the other, dragging the material out from under her legs, clearing the way for him. By the time she'd done that he'd yanked open his trousers, freeing himself from the folds of fine cotton.

As she sat back down, Samira gasped and shuddered, her silk-clad breasts exquisitely arousing against his bare torso. Flesh on flesh, heat on heat…the sensations were exquisite torture. He wrapped his arms around her, holding her still against his recklessly pulsing heart.

Did he imagine a flicker of something like anxiety cross her taut features? It couldn't be. It was too late for second thoughts. Yet some part of his almost numbed brain still worked. To his amazement he found himself asking, 'You're sure?'

'Absolutely.' Her voice was that of a temptress, throaty and low. She speared her hands through his hair, clamping his head as she brought her lips to his. Sweet as wild honey, delicious as ambrosia. That was Samira. He plunged into her mouth, demanding complete submission. Elation filled him at her unstinting response. Yet even that wasn't enough.

He let one hand trawl high to the soft hair at the apex of her thighs. It was damp and she jerked at the fleeting brush of his hand. He circled back and she tilted her pelvis greedily, inviting.

An instant later, hands bracing her hips, he lifted her bodily, not breaking their kiss, and positioned her over his erection. She sighed against his lips as he drew her slowly down.

Tariq felt his brain fog, every part of him focused on the sensation of slick pressure as Samira bore slowly down on him. Had there ever been a moment like this? So tight, so perfect, so right?

The taste of her in his mouth, her scent filling his nostrils, the feel of her surrounding him… He shuddered, already too close to the brink.

He devoured her with a marauder's kiss, angling his body higher against hers till she took him all, and ecstasy hovered on the edge of his consciousness.

Samira moaned into his mouth and he swallowed her pleasure, the sound of it rushing through him in fiery trails.

Not yet. Not yet. He wasn't ready to relinquish this.

But there was no holding back. Already he was lifting her high, supporting her as she finally found the rhythm they both needed. Tariq tilted his hips and stroked deep as she returned to him then rose, riding him harder, drawing him in as far as she could.

Fire flashed and her hands grabbed tighter, her movements growing jerky. His blood sizzled, his skin tingling, every sinew and tendon straining as he felt the first ripple of her pleasure drawing him closer to the edge. The ripples became shudders; the synchronicity of their bodies grew staccato, almost out of rhythm. Samira tugged her mouth away, gasping his name as she shattered around him. He'd never heard anything so beautiful.

With a last, desperate surge Tariq powered up hard, touching heaven and spilling himself in spasms of bliss.

A lifetime later he came back to himself. He held Samira tight in his arms: warm and sumptuous. Her thighs locked around him, her body trembling, each movement teasing him with agonised delight.

Tariq breathed slowly, filling burning lungs. His brain still swam. He felt dazed, as if he'd passed through some mysterious rite of passage.

He frowned, unsettled at the way something at once familiar could feel so extraordinary.

Samira snuggled closer, her breathing muffled in his collarbone, wetness smearing his shoulder.

'Samira?' He wouldn't have known his own voice. It

was a hoarse, unfamiliar rasp. 'Are you crying?' Dismay rose at the suspicion that glorious, white-hot sex had turned to something else. Something fraught with female emotion.

She shook her head. The movement brushed her breasts against his chest and Tariq sucked in his breath as pleasure stirred anew.

'It's just a little overwhelming.'

'Good overwhelming?' He found himself soothing her back with gentle, circular strokes.

'Fantastic overwhelming.' She sniffed and blinked, her wet eyelashes spiky against him. 'I've never done it like that before.' Her head tipped up and huge, soft eyes met his. He knew an insane urge to fall into those glowing depths and lose himself for ever. 'Is that why it was so amazing?'

Tariq felt his eyes widen. She'd never had sex astride a man? It was hardly adventurous sex. Hastily he began revising his assumptions about her level of experience. It seemed that her famous ex-lover, despite his notoriety, had left Samira remarkably inexperienced.

Tariq couldn't stop his hands from skimming up her sides to brush the edges of her breasts. Her jump of pleasure and her startled stare, as if surprised at her body's response, told its own story.

'No, that's not why it was amazing. It's just us, Samira. The chemistry between us.'

And the fact that she'd been in his blood for over a decade. No wonder his orgasm had been so explosive.

He felt the sudden tension in her and knew at once she was second-guessing the implications.

'Good sex is like that, Samira. It's nothing to fret over.'

Finally Samira dropped her head onto his shoulder, slumping sated against him. He rested his chin on her head, feeling the tickle of her hair, the softness of her body against him, her tight, enticing heat.

And as easily as that he was ready again, heavy with arousal, deep inside her.

Samira's indrawn breath said it all.

Shock hammered him even as he moved tentatively, wresting a sigh and a little shiver of pleasure from her. Her lips pressed to his shoulder, her tongue swiping his damp flesh.

In all these years he'd never wanted any woman as much as he wanted Samira.

Nothing in his past compared with his passion for her.

Tariq swallowed an iron-hard knot of guilt but couldn't dispel the shame in his belly or the burn of desire.

He'd never wanted Jasmin like this.

That was significant enough.

But it was more than that. The truth stripped him of honour, eating into his corroded soul.

He felt more for Samira after a week than he'd felt for his first wife after four years of marriage.

What kind of man was he?

CHAPTER EIGHT

THE REMAINS OF the village were a pathetic mess, even after a team of engineers and builders had been hard at work. Samira struggled to keep her eyes on the faces before her, rather than stray past them to the pitiful rubble, the ruins of what had once been homes clinging to the edge of the narrow valley.

She swallowed hard. She'd never seen such devastation.

Yet the women around her in the new community centre were beaming, excited to welcome their queen. They'd turned the building, currently used for emergency accommodation, into an inviting space, like the interior of the vast nomad tents their forebears had used. Rugs lined the floor and walls and sweet treats were proffered on platters.

Tariq had been right. Her presence today, wearing sumptuous traditional dress rather than the more sombre outfit she'd planned, had been the distraction these women needed. And his insistence that they bring the boys had been a masterstroke.

Samira smiled and thanked the young girl with huge eyes who offered her tea in a tiny, filigree-edged glass. The girl ate up everything about her from her scarlet silk skirts to her old gold jewellery and henna-stained hands.

With their backs to the open doors, older women sat beaming, clucking over Adil and Risay as they played with a couple of local toddlers in the safety of the circle of adults. Some women wore traditional finery, silver coins

sewn into their scarves, their dresses trimmed with exquisite embroidery, bangles clinking on their arms. Others,
whom Samira guessed had been lucky to survive the flash
flood that had swept away half the village, wore plainer
garments. But even they were smiling.

Samira sipped the tea, declared it delicious and turned
to her nearest neighbour. Conversation was tentative at
first, but grew animated as the women lost some of their
shyness. Their talk centred on the recent devastation and
plans to rebuild.

Opinion was unanimous that the recovery effort had
been wonderful. Why, the royal Sheikh himself had been
here the day after it had happened! He'd taken a personal
interest in the rebuilding, insisting the plans be developed
in consultation with the community.

The Sheikh was so capable. So wise. So willing to listen.
So handsome.

A titter of laughter circled the room and all eyes focused on Samira.

To her amazement she felt heat wash her cheeks, just as
if she were a real bride besotted with her husband.

She wasn't besotted. But she *was* a bride. Ever since
the night she'd found the courage to face her fear and her
desire for Tariq and gone to him, she'd been swept up in a
world of sensual pleasure and breathless anticipation. Life
had never felt so…real, so vibrant and exciting.

Her gaze shifted outside to where Tariq, wearing jeans,
boots and a hard hat, clambered with a group of men over
rubble beside the scaffolding for a new building.

Predictably her mouth dried as she took in his towering
form. Broad-shouldered, slim-hipped, long-legged, he was
so masculine just the sight of him did funny things to her.

And the memory of the things he did with her in the
privacy of their rooms… Her blush intensified, to the delight of the women around her.

She smiled and shrugged, accepting their gentle ribbing with good grace. Why shouldn't she? She had it all. The children she'd craved, the husband who respected but didn't try to dominate her. And sex that could melt her bones, nights of glorious pleasure that left her feeling better than she ever had in her life.

What more could she want?

Tariq turned, following the gestures of the village elder and project manager as they discussed how the new site for the village was so much safer than the old one. They'd been over this before and his attention strayed to Samira sitting surrounded by women in the newly constructed community centre. Even from this distance he saw the stiff formality of the group had disappeared, replaced by what looked and sounded like a party.

A grin tugged his mouth as he heard laughter and saw an old woman pick up Adil and croon to him. It would do his sons no harm to get out of the palace and be with his people. Their people. Learning to mix with strangers would stand them in good stead for the future.

But it was his bride who drew his eyes.

From the moment she'd emerged in her finery this morning he'd wanted to bundle her back into her bedroom and strip away the gossamer silk that made her shimmer like some enticing gift waiting to be unwrapped. Or maybe it was the knowing glint in those warm, sherry eyes, reminding him of how they'd spent the better part of the night, naked and desperate for each other.

Even now, with the whole population of the village between them, he felt his blood rush south, his groin tighten as need stirred.

He found himself striding towards the village centre, the men following.

There was a stir among the women as they made ready

to serve refreshments to the men. He was given the place of honour, the headsman to his right, Samira to his left. He breathed in her sweetness and looked down, registering the slow-fading henna on her hands that marked her as his. Once more Tariq felt a surge of triumphant possessiveness.

As ever, it sideswiped him. Such intensity, such need, was unprecedented.

Black guilt hovered as it had after they'd had sex the first time. With it came a frisson of warning, as if someone stroked an icicle down his spine. A sense that with Samira he'd strayed into unknown, dangerous territory.

Tariq wrenched his mind free before the thought could take hold.

He had exactly what he wanted. Life was good. So good that for the first time since boyhood he toyed with the idea of cutting short his official duties to escape and enjoy himself.

Tariq exhaled slowly and forced himself to focus. He had responsibilities, duties. He was totally in control of the situation no matter how wayward his thoughts. He would keep everything in perspective, including his desire for his wife.

Tariq snared her wrist as they entered the royal apartments. 'Let Sofia put the boys down for their nap.'

'But it's no trouble. I like doing it.' Samira's confidence with them grew each day, and they had accepted her into their lives.

She'd done the right thing, proposing this marriage. The niggle of doubt that she'd tied herself to a man who'd tricked her, pretending to accept her terms, then breaking down her resistance to sex—well, it was only a niggle. After all, she enjoyed this marriage with benefits as much as he.

She'd been naive believing they could live together celibately. But in everything else, he'd been honest with her. Of course he had. This was Tariq. The man she'd known all her life.

'Leave them.' His voice was a low burr that burrowed to the core of her. 'You can do it tomorrow.'

She met his hooded stare and nodded, trying to dispel the heated blanket of awareness that engulfed her whenever he was near.

Sitting beside him at the village reception had been torture. The whole time she'd smiled and made polite conversation her skin had been drawn too tight, her blood pulsing too fast, her body crying out for his touch.

It had taken him no time at all to persuade her into intimacy. Persuade! She'd all but jumped him, once she'd accepted his assurance that intimacy and love could be separate.

And now... She gulped, watching his eyes darken. Now she struggled to pretend she didn't spend all her time thinking about him. She'd opened the Pandora's box of sexual closeness and was more in thrall to Tariq than she could ever have expected. Her breathing sharpened. With fear or excitement?

'We need to talk about today.' He turned abruptly towards their private corridor.

Talk? She stifled disappointment. 'Of course. I thought it went well. Did you?'

'Better than expected. Everyone sounded positive despite what they've been through.' Yet Tariq's words didn't ring with satisfaction. She caught an undercurrent of urgency in them and wondered what was wrong.

Samira hurried to keep up with his lengthening stride.

'They appreciate all you're doing. The women kept singing your praises.' A blush rose at the memory of their enthusiasm, the compliments for her fine husband who was not only strong but handsome and no doubt virile. 'You won their trust early, going there in person at the time of the emergency and helping with the rescue mission.'

Her pride in him swelled. Tariq was an outstanding leader, hands-on as well as strategic, not one who only sat back and supervised at a distance. His presence had brought real hope to the villagers.

'They're my people. Where else would I have been?'

He led the way into the first of their private sitting rooms but, instead of halting by the cluster of comfortable chairs, Tariq closed the door behind them, then strode on.

'Didn't you want to talk?' There was a breathless catch in her voice as she scurried to match his pace.

'Is that what I said?' The look he slanted her sizzled all the way to her toes.

Swiftly he turned. In her traditional flat slippers she felt tiny against his towering bulk. His shoulders blocked out the room and she had to tilt her neck to hold his gaze as a thrill of anticipation shot through her. She'd never felt so overwhelmingly feminine as with Tariq.

'What I *want*…' the rough texture of his voice weakened her knees '…is to be alone with you as soon as possible.'

His hands were on her, lifting her against a pillared archway. Shocked, she opened her mouth to speak but instead her breath came out in a gasp of satisfaction as he pressed close, his torso to her breasts, his powerful thighs hard and insistent, pushing hers apart.

Samira roped her arms around his neck, holding tight, reeling as a wave of desire crashed over her, threatening to drag her under. His solid heat inflamed her. An urgent throb of need pulsed at the spot where he wedged himself close, taking her from zero to boiling point in mere seconds. Even the tang of desert heat and male spice tickling her nose was arousing.

'The bedroom is just there,' she whispered, shimmying higher in his arms, pushing against his hard shaft, unmistakeable through the fine silk of her dress. Tariq's unashamed arousal and his urgent passion were a continual revelation.

As was her inevitable response.

It struck her anew how very controlled Jackson's lovemaking had been. Surely she shouldn't feel so *driven* by the need to have Tariq right here, right now, as if nothing mattered except having him inside her?

When had she become so wanton?

'You think I can last till the bedroom?' Tariq groaned and bent his head to bite her neck. Samira shuddered as pleasure ripped through her, turning her body molten.

Everything in her softened. Breasts, belly, womb all hummed with the need for more. Her hands tightened, grabbing handfuls of his thick hair, holding him hard as he kissed the sensitive skin of her throat.

'Hold on.' He moved, pressing her up against the wall. She heard the chink of his belt buckle, felt him fumble between them. Then he was fighting his way past her long skirts, shoving the silk up her legs till she felt a waft of air on her bare thighs.

She almost slipped but big hands hoisted her higher, guiding her legs till they encircled his waist. And all the time his eyes held hers. It was as if she hovered on the brink of diving into a fathomless mountain pool.

Except it was heat she felt as he ripped her panties away and she gasped with horrified delight. Pure fire she touched as with one sure thrust Tariq embedded himself deep within her.

She was so incredibly full, as if he stretched her to the limit. As if they'd become one, she thought hazily as he retreated, then thrust hard again, creating ripples of delight that took her straight to the edge. She grabbed tight, needing this oneness with him.

'Samira.' He ground the word, his jaw hard, his hands

heavy on her body. She revelled in his touch and moved eagerly with him. He paused, then surged again, taking her to new heights. 'You have no idea how I hunger for you.'

She tried to gulp in enough air to catch her breath. 'I do.' It made her desperate, this unquenchable need for her husband. But the more she gave, the more she trusted him, the stronger it grew. 'I want you all the time,' she gasped.

He stilled and she almost cried out in frustration. Till she registered his expression. She couldn't interpret it, but those eyes gleamed more brightly than ever. As if they could burn right through her.

When he stroked again, he took her to heaven's door. The world burst into fireworks. Through a haze of bliss she just caught his words.

'I've always wanted you, Samira. Always. And now you're mine.'

Samira lay sprawled across Tariq on the bed, her limbs dissolved, her head on his heaving chest. His heart hammered beneath her ear, rapid like hers. Her palm rested on his chest, fingers furrowed into the smattering of hair that she still found so intriguing.

'I don't think I can walk,' she whispered.

She felt more than heard his huff of laughter. 'Good. I don't want you going anywhere.' He pulled her closer, as if just the thought of her moving wasn't to be considered.

Samira smiled sleepily. She'd lost her shoes when he carried her here and her dress was twisted around her hips but she didn't have the strength to move. His breath was hot on her face and his hand played languidly with her hair, loose to her waist. She felt...replete. As if there was nowhere she'd rather be. Not in her work room. Not even with the twins.

'I like that you're so strong.' She rubbed her face against his skin, inhaling that delicious scent: essence of Tariq.

'The way you held me back there…' Just thinking about it made her inner muscles clench in remembered pleasure. Samira adored it when Tariq's loving was slow and thorough but hard and fast definitely had a lot to recommend it.

'I like that you're so eager for me.' She heard the smile in his voice and imagined his smug grin. No wonder. He'd overturned her 'no sex' rule in mere days and now she couldn't get enough of him.

It was just sex, of course. Sex and liking. A marriage with benefits.

Yet his earlier words lingered in her mind, teasing her.

'What did you mean—you've always wanted me? Since the day I came to you in Paris?'

Tariq said nothing. His fingers dragged through her hair, making her head tilt up. From here she saw his solidly hewn jaw and the strong column of his throat as he swallowed.

'Tariq?'

'Since then too. When you came to the hotel in that tight skirt and jacket I wanted to rip them right off you.' His fingers strayed across to her hip, distracting her as he traced delicate whorls of pleasure on her flesh.

Samira wriggled and clamped her hand on his, making him stop.

'Since then *too*? What does that mean?'

He sighed. 'You always were tenacious, weren't you?'

She'd had to be. If she'd waited for her parents to give her guidance she'd have waited all her life. She'd had to cling to her dreams, forging her career despite the roadblocks: disbelief that a princess actually wanted to learn to sew; prejudice from peers, teachers and the public who thought she wasn't serious or that she'd pulled strings to get her sought-after training place.

'It's not a trick question, Tariq. What did you mean?'

'What I said. I've always wanted you.'

The words shimmered in the air, simple yet devastating. Samira blinked, trying to get her head around them.

'Define "always".'

'You're not going to let it go, are you?' He lifted his head and fixed her with a stern eye. She stared back. He might be the Sheikh of Al Sarath but she was his wife. She had a right to know.

Tariq let his head drop back on the pillow. Beneath her hand his fingers resumed their leisurely exploration of her hip.

'I've wanted you for years. Since you were seventeen, to be precise,' he said at last, effectively stealing her voice. Samira's heart fluttered.

'I remember coming to Jazeer that winter as usual. My uncle encouraged me to learn as much as possible about our neighbouring states.' Silently Samira nodded. Tariq's stern uncle had been his guardian till Tariq had come of age. He'd raised his orphaned nephew along with his own much younger sons. She'd often thought that was why Tariq had been so patient with her. How many boys and young men put up with their best friend's kid sister following wherever they went?

But wanting her since she was seventeen? She felt like someone had upended her world, leaving it altered for ever.

At seventeen Samira had been increasingly aware of Tariq, not just as her brother's friend but as the sort of man a teenage girl could hang her dreams on: those dreamy eyes; the deep, smooth voice that did strange things to her insides and still did. That tough, lean body.

Her younger self had been embarrassed and excited by the new daydreams she'd begun to have about him. She'd even wondered if she'd given herself away and that was why he'd left so abruptly, never to return.

'I never suspected,' she said at last.

'Of course not. That would have been unforgivable. You were my best friend's sister. And you were far too young. You weren't meant to know.'

Samira frowned. 'Never?'

What if she'd known years ago that Tariq had been attracted to her? She'd spent long enough mulling over her mistakes to know her infatuation with Jackson Brent had stemmed as much from self-doubt and her need for love, as from his attractiveness and his efforts to charm her.

Despite her looks, perhaps because of them, Samira had always harboured a fear she was fatally flawed, all show and no substance. Maybe because her parents had never really cared for her, she'd always secretly believed she was unlovable. Hence her reckless leap into a relationship with the first man to sweep her off her feet.

Knowing that a man she respected, like Tariq, was attracted to her... Could that have changed her attitude and given her a little more confidence?

Or was that wishful thinking?

'You were untouchable, Samira. It wouldn't have been right. That's why I left.'

Had he really wanted so badly to touch her? There was something in his voice, an echo of regret that resonated deep.

Samira twisted, lifting her head to look at his face. His forehead was corrugated, his mouth set in a firm line.

'You left because of me?' A flurry of emotion hit her—regret, dismay and delight.

Tariq raised one arm, slipping his hand beneath his head. His biceps bulged, a reminder of his latent power. Heat streamed through her all over again. She blinked, distracted by the urgent flutter of response in her belly.

'What else could I do? I felt guilty, lusting after a kid who looked on me as a big brother.' His tone was hard.

'But you stayed away. You never came back.'

Tariq shrugged. 'It was better that way.'

What he left unsaid was that by the time she'd grown he'd lost interest, for he'd never returned. Instead she'd heard the rumours of his many lovers. Then he'd married Jasmin, whom everyone said was the love of his life. Of course he'd never have come back. Samira must have been a passing fancy. Given his distinction between sex and love, she could only guess he'd lost his heart to his first wife and knew no one could replace her.

He'd made no secret that first day in Paris that he hadn't wanted to marry. Because he still loved Jasmin? Samira had assumed so. But now, in Tariq's bed, the idea tore at something deep inside. Her chest squeezed as an ache filled her.

Had he married her out of pity?

Samira bit her lower lip and looked away, subsiding against his chest.

No. Not pity. The way Tariq touched her didn't feel at all like pity.

He wanted her physically. What they shared was simple and mutually satisfying. Now she had a family, a place to belong, real purpose. The boys were bonding with her and hopefully would come to love her. Tariq respected her. Plus there were the benefits of sex.

Why then did dissatisfaction grate at her? Why the bitterness on her tongue, the edge of disquiet?

Samira breathed deep, inhaling the musky man aroma she'd come to adore, and forced herself to relax. Automatically Tariq curled his arm around her, drawing her close, his breathing slowing beneath her ear.

She had everything she wanted, she reminded herself. More, given the glow of wellbeing in her sated body and heavy limbs.

Yet Tariq had unsettled her. His revelation made her realise she didn't know him as well as she'd thought. All these years she'd been certain of two people in her life: her brother, Asim, and his best friend, Tariq.

Now Tariq made her question what she thought she knew.

First had come the revelation he'd misled her, pretending to accept a paper marriage. Next the revelation she'd never known him as well as she'd thought. All those years ago he'd hidden how he felt from her.

Had she known him at all?

Surely the decent, caring man she'd known hadn't been a mirage? She saw him in the man Tariq had become.

But there was another side to her husband. He wasn't just a gentle giant. He was a virile, clever, powerful man who got exactly what he wanted.

What did he want from her?

She'd assumed he'd married her to acquire a mother for his children, a consort.

That and a sexual partner.

It couldn't be anything else. Despite their sizzling passion, Tariq always left her to sleep alone. He respected her privacy. He gave her the distance she wanted. He didn't demand an *emotional* bond.

Because she wasn't the wife he'd chosen for himself. Samira sighed, realising her thoughts had come full circle, back to Jasmin.

Tariq might share himself now with Samira, but he'd never love her because Jasmin held his heart.

Samira had understood that from the first. Why, then, did the knowledge dim her incandescent glow of pleasure?

Why did she feel so…lost?

CHAPTER NINE

'ALLOW ME TO congratulate you on your lovely bride. You've chosen well, my friend.'

Tariq followed the direction of the old Emir's gaze, though he knew what he'd see. Despite having been married for months now, his attention kept straying to the far side of the reception room, to his wife. As if he couldn't get enough of her. Samira glowed, her skin peach-perfect, her delicious body ripe and even more voluptuous than when they'd married. Those luscious breasts seemed fuller, more pert than ever.

He forced his attention elsewhere but his eyes snagged on the alluring curve of her smile, her graceful gestures.

Pride swelled. Samira was a superb hostess.

She chatted easily with guests: diplomats, VIPs and... Tariq noted a familiar handsome face and blond hair, the project manager overseeing the rebuilding project in the mountains. Nicolas Roussel hung on her every word. Samira took such an interest in the project that every time Tariq turned around Roussel was at her side.

Just as well Tariq knew she wasn't interested in any man but himself.

'Thank you.' He nodded, acknowledging the Emir's compliment. 'I count myself fortunate.'

For she didn't just excel at social events. Samira was also a caring queen. Her personal gift of sewing machines and bolts of fabric, sent to women in the flood-ravaged mountain villages, had been just right. It had lifted their spirits, as well as given them a potential source of income. She'd even commissioned fine embroidery from them for use in her designs and had laid the groundwork for a successful local enterprise.

'I admit I wondered about a queen who runs her own business.' The old man shook his head, raising his hand when Tariq would have spoken. 'But I stand corrected. It seems to me that your wife's experience as an entrepreneur gives her a broader view of the world. My wife and I have enjoyed her company during our visit. And,' he chuckled, 'my daughter is smitten with the gown your wife designed for her. She's a very talented woman.'

Tariq inclined his head. The Emir, ruler of a neighbouring state, was notoriously conservative and his good opinion hard-won. Samira had done well to impress him.

'I believe so.'

'It was sensible of you to lose no time providing a mother for those boys of yours. I hear she dotes on them. No doubt she's getting broody about having some of her own too, eh? It shouldn't be long.' He winked.

Tariq stiffened. The old man didn't say anything others weren't thinking. Yet Tariq remembered Samira's pale features as she'd told him she could never have children. Her pain had dragged at him like a plough scraping through rough soil.

'We're content as we are,' he said through tight lips.

'No need to poker up about it. I've seen the way you look at her. The pair of you can barely keep your eyes off each other. You're obviously both besotted.' He clapped an arm on Tariq's shoulder. 'You're a red-blooded man with a beautiful wife. Make the most of it.' He turned his head. 'Ah, I see I'm wanted. If you'll excuse me?'

Tariq had to work to keep his face bland as the older

man moved away. The Emir had rattled him more than he'd thought possible.

Besotted? Hardly. He was incapable of such unguarded emotion. That was a strength he'd accrued from his strict, unsentimental upbringing. There'd been no room for love in his formative years, no soft, feminine influence. It was only later he'd learned such invulnerability was also a flaw.

When he'd discovered Jasmin, carefully chosen for their arranged, dynastic marriage, loved him.

It had been unexpected, unwanted. Terrible.

For, no matter how much he respected and admired her, Tariq hadn't been able to return those feelings.

His mouth thinned. Samira had been adamant she didn't want romantic love. Perhaps he should have come straight out and told her he was incapable of it. If he'd been able to fall in love it would surely have been with Jasmin. She'd been gentle, loyal and hard-working, deserving of love. And he'd seen how she'd suffered when her feelings weren't returned.

He'd tried so hard and failed abysmally. She'd never won his heart, leaving him to conclude that, like his upright but emotionally isolated uncle, he didn't have a heart to win.

He'd done his best to make it up to her in attentiveness. But it hadn't been enough. He'd seen it in her eyes.

Tariq had failed her. The knowledge ate at him like a canker. Despite his wealth and power he hadn't been able to save Jasmin's life. Nor had he been able to give her the one thing she'd craved—love.

Abruptly Tariq turned his back on the group surrounding Samira, his heart pounding.

The Emir was mistaken. Samira didn't want love. She'd married him for his sons.

And he… He wanted her, craved her. He'd craved her even when she'd been with another man. Even when he'd been married to another woman.

So much for being a man of honour!

A chance sighting of a press photo of Jazeer's scandalous princess had been enough to send him into a lather of activity, extending his already full schedule in an attempt to work off desires he had no right feeling. Guilt had driven him to be the ideal husband to Jasmin in every way left open to him.

Tariq breathed deep. The past was past. He'd done the best he could for Jasmin. And as for wanting Samira—she was his wife now. Why shouldn't he desire her?

They had the perfect marriage. Respect. Affection. Phenomenal sex. But no illusions of love.

'Risay, you're becoming such a big boy.' Samira smiled encouragingly as he tackled the long noodles in his bowl, amazed at how he'd grown in the months since the wedding.

Beside him Adil was absorbed in pulling the pasta apart and dropping it from his high chair. He caught Samira's eyes, picked up another thread of pasta, then let it fall, crowing with delight as it hit the floor. Samira laughed. 'And you, Adil, are going to be a charmer with that cheeky smile and those big green eyes.'

Just like his father. No one would call Tariq cheeky, but his smile made her heart flip over. It transformed his face from austere to stunningly charismatic. Every time she saw it Samira's breath caught beneath her ribs.

She shifted in her seat. Strange that she had that slightly breathless feeling now, as if carrying the boys down the corridor and putting them in their high chairs was more effort than before.

'Is everything all right, madam?'

Samira smiled up at Sofia who'd just appeared with the boys' juice cups. 'Yes, thanks. Just getting a bit more comfortable.'

She tugged at the fabric of her skirt that had bunched high when she sat. How could the waistband need adjusting again?

She'd got in the habit of wearing loose dresses in private, but she'd been with a client today and had put on a narrow tailored skirt and jacket of peacock-blue in the retro fifties style Tariq appreciated so much. Probably because of the way it clung to her hips and thighs.

Samira frowned. Maybe she should give up wearing it until she slimmed down. She hadn't noticed herself eating more but clearly Tariq's excellent royal chefs were having an impact. If she didn't do something soon to get back in shape she'd be as fat as butter.

'Are you sure nothing's wrong, madam?'

'Nothing at all. Just a little too much good food.'

Sofia nodded and clucked her tongue as she removed Risay's empty bowl. 'Fitted clothes like that will get more difficult to wear. You'll be more comfortable in traditional dresses and loose trousers from now on.'

Samira sat straighter, surprised at the nanny's readiness to discuss her employer's weight. None of the servants at home in Jazeer would have dreamed of making it obvious they'd noticed.

'I didn't mean to offend, madam.' Sofia must have seen her surprise. 'It's only natural, though it does take some getting used to.' She patted her own narrow waist and Samira stared, perplexed.

'I'm sorry. You've lost me. What takes getting used to?' Samira stood up, ready to lift Risay from his chair.

'The way pregnancy changes your body. It can seem overwhelming the first time.'

For a heartbeat Samira stared, stunned, then her arms dropped to her sides, leaden weights. She'd expected this sort of speculation but still it was discomfiting.

'I'm afraid you're mistaken.' Deliberately she shaped

her lips into a casual smile. 'I'm not pregnant.' She would have to school herself to say it without sounding quite so hollow.

'You're not?' Sofia looked taken aback. 'I'm so sorry. I could have sworn… I've never been mistaken before. And you have the look.'

Despite herself Samira was curious. Her one experience of carrying a child had been over almost before she'd realised it. She'd never had regular periods and hadn't had any obvious symptoms so she'd been blithely unaware of the baby she carried. There had barely been enough time to adjust to the wondrous news before the trauma of losing it.

'There's a look?' She couldn't help asking, though she knew she shouldn't torment herself by prolonging this.

Sofia nodded emphatically. 'You've got it. There's a look in the eyes, and your skin glows, and…' She stopped, her gaze sliding away.

'And?'

Sofia shrugged. 'You've gained a little weight. Not only in the waist but here too.' Her hands plumped up her own breasts.

Suddenly Samira found herself sitting, her head spinning.

No. It was completely far-fetched. It was impossible.

And yet…

She bit her lip, admonishing herself for even that brief flight of fancy. There was a world of difference between wishful thinking and reality. She'd made it her business to live in the real world, not pine for what could never be.

She crossed her arms, then immediately dropped them at the graze of fabric over her nipples.

'Sensitivity there too.' Sofia added helpfully, as if reading her discomfort.

'I—' Samira shook her head. She would *not* go there. Her breasts had been sensitive for some time, but she couldn't tell the other woman it was because of the attention Tariq devoted to them. If he wasn't caressing her breasts with his hands, he had his mouth on them, knowing it drew exquisite pleasure from her. Her nipples tingled as she remembered the attention he'd lavished on them last night, and on every other part of her body.

Her breath sucked hard.

'Thank you for your concern, Sofia, but I'm afraid you're mistaken.' She stood briskly and began to help the nanny clear the boys' food away.

But, as she put the twins down for their nap, Samira couldn't shake the memory of Sofia's certainty. Samira's grandmother had prided herself on her uncanny ability to spot a pregnancy. She'd claimed it was a gift and that in all her decades she'd never been wrong.

Was Sofia also gifted with such insight?

If she was, she was badly mistaken this time.

Samira looked down at the boys, already drowsing after their busy day, and found her hand had crept unbidden to her stomach. It wasn't just her waist that thickened. Her belly curved out now too. Yet, though she'd always had a curvy figure, Samira had never had weight problems.

She bit her lip, trying to force down the tremulous hope that rose like a tiny green shoot in an arid desert.

The anguish of losing her tiny infant, and of hearing she'd never conceive again, was a raw wound in the darkness of her psyche. She couldn't afford to reawaken that pain with false hope.

Yet as she left the bedroom she found herself wondering.

Samira slumped down onto the side of the marble bath, staring at the test result. Her fingers shook so much she told herself she wasn't reading it right.

She pressed her palm against her abdomen as if she

could feel anything new there. Or as if the touch of her hand could protect the new life sheltering within.

Panic slammed into her. She hadn't been able to protect the baby she'd carried four years ago. How could she this time?

Nature hadn't wanted her to be a mother. Hadn't she been told she wouldn't conceive again?

Her skin tightened. Her forehead and the back of her neck prickled, turning clammy with the cold sweat of fear.

The test indicator clattered to the floor as Samira's vision hazed with nightmare memories. Blood and pain and the devastatingly gentle tone of a stranger telling her it was too late, she'd lost her child.

Instinctively Samira pressed her legs together so hard they grew numb. She blinked back the hot tears glazing her eyes and forced herself to think. She'd hunched over into a foetal position, body bowed and knees drawn up to protect the new life inside.

Her breath hissed, loud in the silence. She carried a new life!

She was pregnant. Against the odds she was pregnant.

And if one miracle could happen—her conceiving again—perhaps it was possible another miracle might happen and her child would be born alive and healthy.

Samira gulped over the burning ball of emotion in her throat.

If she'd learned one thing it was never to give up. She'd dragged herself from the darkest of places after the grief and scandal of her past. She refused to go back to living in the shadows.

Gingerly she straightened, taking stock of how she felt.

A smile hovered. She felt fine. More than fine, she felt fit as a fiddle, except for the way nerves made her stomach roil.

She breathed deep, then bent to pick up the test result, her fingers closing tight around it.

It could be a false positive. Gravely she nodded to herself as if she actually believed that. As if excitement wasn't skittering through her, as if her blood wasn't fizzing with elation and her toes curling.

What she needed was certainty, a doctor.

Again she nodded. Good, she was thinking clearly and logically.

Yet when Samira stood up she saw that the woman facing her in the mirror wore a smile so broad it could only be described as rapturous.

Tariq paused midstride and stared at the retreating back of the man following one of the maids at the far end of the corridor. An icy hand clamped his neck.

No, he was mistaken. It was a trick of the light. The obstetrician had no reason to visit the palace.

Yet Tariq was blindsided by memories of the last time he'd seen that doctor. Tariq had been hollow with shock, unable to believe the world had turned on its head. He'd been given his precious sons but at the cost of Jasmin's life. Joyful expectation had turned to disaster.

He'd grappled with the unnerving sense that he'd lost control. All his wealth and influence hadn't been able to save Jasmin. In fact, his need for an heir had caused her death.

Shaking off fraught memories, he continued on, opening the door to the royal suite and striding in. He wanted Samira. Just being with her made him feel good. How corny was that? Her warmth and understanding, her company, were as essential to him now as her physical generosity.

After that moment in the corridor, when dark tendrils from the past had wound around him, squeezing so he couldn't breathe, he needed Samira.

She wasn't in her room but he heard water running in her bathroom. His step quickened.

'Samira?' He rapped on the door.

Fragrant steam rose from the bath, hazing her skin, warming it to a delectable rose pink. His gaze dropped to the neckline of the unbuttoned shirt she clasped closed in one hand, then to her silky, loose trousers. She looked ripe and delicious. His hands twitched as he stepped into the bathroom.

'Tariq.'

The husky way she breathed his name recalled nights of carnal delight. He reached for her, the lingering tightness in his chest disintegrating as he wrapped his hand around her waist and felt her, warm and alluring, beneath his palm.

'I want you,' he growled, spreading his feet wide and hauling her in between his thighs. 'Now.'

Her lips tasted like heaven. Her body arched into his as he slid his hands down the sweep of her back and anchored them on her taut buttocks.

She sighed into his mouth and Tariq wanted nothing more than this, to be here with Samira.

'The bath!' She leaned back in his hold, twisting to look over her shoulder.

Tariq feasted on his view of bountiful breasts, plump above her creamy lace bra. He swallowed a groan.

Fortunately for his sanity Samira had yet to realise how utterly compelling he found her body. She didn't play coy games but always gave herself generously, participating equally in every erotic adventure.

He'd lifted his hand to caress her breast when she pulled away, bending to turn off the taps.

A tight smile curved Tariq's mouth as he appreciated the view. From her casually upswept hair, to the swell of her hips and neatly rounded bottom, Samira was all woman.

All his.

She turned, surveying him from under the long fringe of her lashes. He felt that look right to the soles of his feet.

In a more reflective moment he might worry about her ability to reduce him to molten hunger. Right now he was too busy enjoying himself.

He stepped forward, then halted, puzzled by her expression. She looked… He couldn't pin down her expression but sensed secret satisfaction. Her smile was pure Mona Lisa.

'Samira, what is it?'

She opened her eyes wide as if surprised he'd sensed the energy radiating from her. Tariq wondered that he hadn't noticed it sooner, but he'd been absorbed responding to other needs. Now he paused, surveying her face.

Her eyes glittered like faceted gems. He'd never seen them so bright. And there was something wistful about her smile that drew him on a level that had nothing to do with sex.

She was simply the most beautiful woman he'd ever seen.

His eyes traced the gentle curve of her mouth, the throb of her pulse at the base of her neck, and something punched hard and low in his belly. Something more than desire or possessiveness. Something he'd never known before.

'Samira, talk to me.'

'I have some news.' Her gaze cut from his and he noticed her hands twisting together.

Instantly Tariq tensed. He stepped forward and took her hands. They trembled in his and he frowned. 'Bad news?'

She shook her head, loose tendrils of ebony silk swirling around her throat. 'Good news. Unbelievable news.'

Her eyes met his again and heat scudded down his spine to flare out into his belly. Her radiant smile pulled his own lips wide. Anything that made her happy was worth celebrating.

'Don't keep me in suspense.'

Her hands turned in his, fingers clasping tight.

'The most wonderful news in the world. We're going to have a baby.'

CHAPTER TEN

THROUGH A HAZE of elation Samira watched Tariq's broad brow furrow in amazement. She nodded eagerly, urging him to accept it was true, though she found it hard to believe herself.

Time stood still on this moment of pure joy. The seconds slowed as he stared down at her, his features setting into lines of disbelief.

'It's true. Really.' She felt like a giddy kid, excitement fizzing in her veins.

'You told me you couldn't have children.' Tariq's eyebrows arrowed down in a black line and his tone sounded almost accusing.

'I did. That's what I thought, what I've believed for years.'

'You didn't think to check?'

Samira started at his harsh tone. This wasn't the reaction she'd expected. 'You don't sound happy.'

He shook his head as if to clear it, his expression surprisingly grim. 'I sound like a man whose wife assured him children were an impossibility.'

She frowned. Surely she imagined his disapproval? 'I was told by my specialist I couldn't have children.'

Even now those words rang like a death knell, making her shiver. For they *had* been a death knell. He'd broken the news after she'd lost her precious child. It had been a double blow, to miscarry then learn there could be no other babies in future.

'Here. You need to sit.' Tariq took her by the elbow and led her to the seat beside the bath.

Immediately she felt better. For an inexplicable moment she'd worried he wasn't pleased with her news. Samira sighed as she sat, her legs none too steady.

'Thank you. It's still a bit of a shock.'

'But you're absolutely sure?' His look was intent.

'The doctor just confirmed it.' Not just any doctor, but the best obstetrician in the capital. She slipped her hand across her abdomen, reassuring herself. 'He was just here. He assured me the earlier diagnosis was flawed. Obviously, since there's a baby.' She found her lips curving once more in a smile.

Tariq nodded. 'I thought I recognised him in the distance.'

For a moment Samira wondered how Tariq knew him, till she realised the same doctor might have attended Jasmin. She blinked and looked quickly away.

In her excitement Samira hadn't considered how her news would dredge up bittersweet memories for Tariq. No wonder he seemed a little...aloof. She'd been so wrapped up in excitement she hadn't thought of anything else.

'Doesn't he need to do further tests?'

Samira dragged her eyes back to Tariq, wary at his lack of animation. Surely, when he had time to acclimatise...?

'Yes, to make sure everything is normal. But the doctor was very reassuring and there's no question I'm pregnant.' She paused, savouring the words. They were an incantation of hope and joy. Her—a mother! 'The doctor thinks I'm already well along.'

'How is that possible?' Tariq's words sounded brusque. But then, he was still processing the news. No doubt he'd be beaming when it sank in.

'I didn't have any symptoms, except now I've started to

put on weight. Not even any morning sickness.' He didn't say anything and she felt heat climb her cheeks.

Still Tariq didn't say more, just stood watching her, his stance rigid. He was within touching distance but he hadn't reached for her since he'd helped her sit.

Suddenly that tiny distance between them seemed telling.

He'd had time now to absorb her news. Wasn't a father-to-be supposed to be pleased as well as surprised?

Tariq loved children. He was a family man through and through. Yet he watched her as if looking at a stranger.

Icy fingers played a fugue down Samira's spine. Her smile frayed around the edges.

'I realise it will mean some adjustments for Adil and Risay, to have a little brother or sister. But they're young enough to adapt.' Was that what bothered him? 'I already love them both and I promise they'll never be second best in my eyes.'

'The more the merrier?' Tariq's shoulders rose as he dredged up a deep breath. 'You were always up-front about your desire for children. Of course you're thrilled.'

'And you're not?' Looking up as he towered over her was giving her a crick in the neck. She stood up, hauling the edges of her shirt close together with stiff fingers.

'You have to admit it's…unexpected. You told me you couldn't have children.'

He'd said that before. She blinked as her skin crawled. Something wasn't right. Did he think she'd lied to him about being unable to conceive? Surely not.

Tariq looked down at those soft sherry eyes and saw hurt shimmer there. He hefted in another deep breath. He had to get hold of himself.

But from the moment Samira had said the word 'baby'

he'd frozen inside. The world had decelerated into slow motion, a sense of unreality filling him.

He'd believed he'd never have to face this again. He swallowed, a bitter taint on his tongue. For an instant he'd almost been tempted to think Samira had tricked him into fatherhood, pretending to be infertile. Till his brain had switched on. This was *Samira*. Honest, up-front Samira. She'd never behave so dishonestly.

Tariq reached out and stroked the hair off Samira's flushed cheek and she turned her head into his touch, sighing. With relief? He knew he hadn't responded as she'd hoped.

'It's very exciting news,' he managed at last. 'The twins will be delighted to have another playmate too, I'm sure.'

'You think so?' Samira smiled, her eyes sparkling. She was lit from within, almost incandescent. Tariq shied from the memory of Jasmin with that same expectant glow. And the unavoidable recollection of her months later, parchment-white and still, so very still, beneath the neatly folded hospital sheet.

'It's a miracle and a little scary.' Her hand reached out to grasp his. That was when he noticed she was trembling.

Instantly Tariq pulled her close, wrapping his arm around her slender shoulders. She leaned into him, hugging tight. How could he not have realised she'd be nervous as well as excited?

'Miracles can be a little frightening.' Tariq injected a smile into his voice. 'But you'll be in the best of hands, I promise.' Ruthlessly he thrust aside the knowledge that the best hands hadn't saved Jasmin. Samira didn't need to hear that.

'Thank you, Tariq. I know you'll look after me.' Her breath shuddered against his chest. She felt so fragile in his arms, so vulnerable. Reassuringly he tightened his hold, pretending to a certainty he was far from feeling. 'It's just...'

'Just what?'

It took her a long time to reply. When she finally did, the words came in a rush. 'I had a miscarriage four years ago.'

Her words stopped his voice. They all but stopped his heart.

He stepped back a fraction so he could look down into her face. The pain he saw there stabbed through him, slicing a furrow through his heart. She'd been pregnant?

His hands closed convulsively around her and he pulled her close, rocking her against him.

'That must have been devastating.'

'It *was*,' Samira whispered. 'It happened just after the news broke about Jackson's infidelities, when I returned to Jazeer to escape the paparazzi.'

Tariq felt her tremble and comforted her as best he could with long, slow sweeps of his hand at her back. All the time he felt a roiling burst of emotions deep in his gut. Frustration, anger and regret. Samira had gone through so much. Her lover's betrayal, public humiliation as the scandal hit the press and the paparazzi hounded her and, on top of that, such personal heartbreak.

'I had no idea. No wonder Asim kept you close in the palace.' If he'd known he'd have offered his help. But what could he have done?

'I sort of went into a meltdown.' Samira burrowed deeper into his chest. 'I didn't trust myself in the public eye and I hid out in the palace, not wanting to see anyone. I stayed there for months.'

'I'm not surprised.'

'Really?' Over-bright eyes lifted to meet his.

It felt as if he'd swallowed splinters of shattered glass when he saw the hurt in those huge eyes.

'Really.' Had she thought herself weak for taking time

to recover from such devastating blows? 'I can't imagine how you coped.' The idea of losing Risay or Adil made him break out in a cold sweat.

'I had no choice.'

Pain hammered him when he thought of her going through that alone. Tariq had known Samira for years and understood that, despite Asim's willingness to support her, Samira would have drawn in on herself, closing out the world and suffering in silence. He'd seen it when she was a kid. She didn't share her hurt. That was one of the reasons her proposal in Paris had blindsided him, because she'd opened up enough to let him glimpse her pain at not being able to conceive.

'You're not alone now,' he found himself saying. 'This is our baby and I'll be here to take care of you.'

He must have said the right thing because Samira's face lit up with a glow that rivalled the luminous desert sunset.

'Thank you, Tariq. I needed to hear that.'

He took her hand in his, so small yet so capable, and raised it to his lips. She tasted of sweet, heady woman and despite the gravity of the moment Tariq registered his body's eager response.

He'd never wanted a woman the way he wanted Samira. The thought of her, sexy and ripe with his child, sent his hormones into overdrive.

Until his brain engaged again.

She'd had a miscarriage. She'd been told she'd never be able to conceive again, yet against the odds she had. It didn't take a genius to realise the risks for Samira and the child had to be higher than average.

He mustn't do anything to endanger them. She might be in her second trimester, when the risk of miscarriage was supposed to lessen, but Tariq knew how unpredictable, how downright dangerous, pregnancy could be.

The image of Jasmin's still face rose again. She'd died

giving birth to the babies he'd planted within her, the babies he'd married her to acquire.

Tariq shuddered, fear icing his spine. He wouldn't let history repeat itself. He'd take every possible precaution.

And, he vowed, he'd do it without adding to Samira's natural anxiety. After one miscarriage she must be nervous about the outcome of this pregnancy. She didn't need his fears compounding her own.

'Come on,' he urged, gently brushing Samira's shirt from her shoulders, valiantly ignoring the delicious bounty of full breasts in that made-for-seduction lace bra. 'Let's get you into that bath while it's still warm.'

Samira complied with an alacrity that had him almost bursting out of his too-tight skin. She shimmied out of her trousers, wriggling her hips in a tantalising display that made him swallow hard. Tariq had to turn away, pretending to adjust the water temperature when she undid her bra and her ripe breasts swung free. His palms itched to reach for them and his groin tightened unbearably.

The final straw came as she shoved her panties off and swiped her hand over her waist and the slight swell of her belly. Her beatific smile stole his breath but the sight of her naked body, indescribably lush and feminine, almost broke him.

Quickly Tariq reached for her arm, ignoring the sultry invitation in her eyes.

'Hold onto me as you step in. Don't slip.'

'Of course I won't slip. You've got me.' Her words were a breathy laugh of joy that curled around his heart, making it beat fast and hard.

Stoically Tariq averted his eyes from the sight of her rose-tipped breasts bobbing in the water, the shadow between slender thighs that parted as he watched. Heat speared him.

'Join me?' Her voice was a throaty invitation, her fingers clinging to his. She knew as well as he did that he'd never once refused an invitation to get naked with her. On the contrary, he'd shocked her once or twice with the ways and places he'd chosen to sate the ever-present carnal desire they shared.

Tariq forced himself to stand tall, pulling his hand from hers. Samira's smile vanished, her brow wrinkling.

'Relax now.' He couldn't help himself and bent down to kiss her cheek, inhaling her sweetness. 'It's been a big day.'

Finally she nodded, disappointment tinging her expression. 'Yes. It's been a lot to take in.'

Tariq made himself step back. 'Your maid will be waiting in the bedroom when you're ready to get out. Just call and let her help you. Yes?' He waited till she agreed, then turned and made himself walk, stiff-legged, out of the bathroom.

He ached all over. He wasn't used to denying himself the pleasure of Samira's body. He'd never known such temptation as watching her strip before him, knowing she carried his child.

He'd found pleasure with Jasmin. He'd been thrilled by her pregnancy. But he'd never experienced anything like this.

Tariq wiped his hand across his face and discovered he was sweating.

Samira was pregnant with his child.

He would do whatever it took to keep the pair of them safe. He would take no chances. Tariq closed his eyes, feeling deep in his gut that churning fear of failure he'd known only once before.

His imagination failed him at the idea of losing her as he'd lost Jasmin.

No! He wouldn't let it happen again.

Not to Samira.

* * *

'Are you sure there's nothing bothering you, Samira?' Over the long-distance connection her sister-in-law, Jacqui, sounded concerned.

'No, no. I'm fine.'

'Except?'

Samira heard Jacqui's determination to get to the bottom of things. It was a trait that had made her a successful journalist before she'd taken to writing books.

'Come on, you can talk to me. Something's not right.'

Samira sighed and sat back in her favourite comfy chair, the one Tariq had transported all the way from Jazeer to her work room. Staring at the mountains bathed in shades of pink and gold by the dying sun, she reminded herself how lucky she was. The doctor had allayed the worst of her fears, assuring her there was no reason she shouldn't carry this baby to term.

'Everything is fine, truly. I don't have any complaints.' She paused, hearing Jacqui's waiting silence. 'It's just that Tariq is…' Again she hesitated. How could she admit her husband hadn't been in her bed in the weeks since she'd broken the news about the baby? Or that she missed him so badly his absence marred her joy at this miracle pregnancy?

How far she'd come from the woman who'd blithely assumed she could have a paper marriage with Tariq. Once she'd experienced his love-making she'd been hooked. Yet it wasn't just sex she missed, it was the intimacy. The pillow talk, the tenderness, the feeling of wellbeing and closeness that had no equal in her experience.

Was it anxiety about the pregnancy that made her so needy?

A huff of laughter came over the phone. 'If you ask me Tariq is just like Asim—proud, assertive and overprotective. It's a wonder to me that two such strong, opinionated men grew to be such good friends.'

'They bonded when they were very young. You know our home life wasn't easy.' Now, that was an understatement! 'And, from what Asim said, Tariq's upbringing was tough. His uncle expected him to be a man from an early age. I don't think there was time for fun, except when he visited us. He was too busy preparing for the demands of the sheikhdom.'

'From what Asim said? Hasn't Tariq told you about his past?'

Samira shrugged. 'I've known him all my life, so I know the important things.' Yet he'd surprised her. He was more complex, powerful and determined than she'd thought. 'Tariq isn't the sort of man to open up, seeking sympathy.'

'That makes two of you.' She paused. 'Maybe that's the problem. Perhaps you need to open up more to each other.'

Samira opened her mouth to protest, then stopped. 'Is that what you and Asim did?'

Again that gentle huff of laughter. 'Getting your brother to talk about feelings was almost impossible.'

'You managed it.' Asim and Jacqui were blissfully happy. They were one of the reasons she'd had the nerve to propose marriage. She'd wanted at least a modified version of their happy family, even if it was centred around respect and child-rearing rather than passionate devotion. She drew a fortifying breath. 'How did you do it?'

'What? Drag your brother, kicking and screaming, out of his comfort zone to confront his feelings?' Jacqui paused and Samira sat forward, eager for the answer. 'It wasn't easy.' There was no laugh in her voice now. 'I shared myself with him. I was totally honest.'

Samira cringed. Tariq already he knew her secrets: her desire for a family and her miscarriage, her hopes for this child. Surely that was enough? All she wanted was to resume the intimacy they'd shared until last month.

'Samira? Are you there?'

'Yes.'

'But you're not sure you wanted to hear that?'

Jacqui was too perceptive. 'You've given me a lot to think about.'

She just wasn't sure it was the answer for her.

Samira smoothed the rich cream satin over her thighs. It felt decadently luxurious. A baby bulge didn't stop a woman from appreciating beautiful lingerie.

She twisted in front of the workshop's full-length mirror. The neckline plunged deep, edged with the exquisite embroidery she'd commissioned in the mountains. She'd placed an order for more, knowing the delicate finery on the translucent fabric was just right for this design.

She had long-term plans to launch an exclusive range of lingerie. The project gave her a new creative outlet and would provide valuable income for the village women.

Her mouth twisted. Who'd have thought pregnancy would inspire her to design slinky nightgowns? She might be halfway through her pregnancy but hormones only made her more aware of her body's needs.

Or maybe that was Tariq.

Her hands bunched in the slithery fabric, her pulse tripping. Her husband made her hot and bothered with just a look or the casual brush of his hand.

Which was tragic when a casual brush of the hand was all she'd had from him since she'd told him about the baby. That and his solicitous grip at her elbow whenever she descended the long staircase to the royal reception rooms. He always managed to be at her side then, the epitome of protectiveness.

As if she were some feeble, ancient relative. The thought infuriated her. And hurt.

A commotion at the door had her spinning around just as a tiny body launched itself at her.

'Mama!' Small arms wrapped around her legs, hugging tight.

'Risay.' She bent to pick him up but wasn't fast enough.

'Let me.' Tariq was already there, disengaging hands that she saw now were sticky with honey, and lifting Risay high. 'I'm sorry about your...' He stopped as he took in her décolletage.

Instantly her nipples tightened, grazing the soft fabric. She drew in a sharp breath as heat shafted through her body at his look.

Naked but for a thin layer of satin, she felt too exposed. The speculative gleam in Tariq's eyes told her he hadn't missed her response. Worse, it created a needy, melting sensation between her legs.

'Mama!' Risay leaned towards her, arms outstretched, and she dragged her attention back to him, smiling at his cheeky grin.

'He's not supposed to bother you while you're working.' Tariq's voice was like the stroke of silken gauze across her bare arms and shoulders. She shivered and kept her eyes on Risay.

'I don't mind.' She took Risay's hand and leaned in, brushing his cheek with a gentle kiss. 'It's rare that they escape Sofia's eagle eye.' Footsteps made her turn. Sure enough, there was Sofia, tutting under her breath.

'My apologies, sir, ma'am.' She turned to the toddler who gave her a broad grin. 'And as for you, Master Trouble, you'll come back right now and finish your meal.'

'Mama,' he said defiantly.

Samira couldn't prevent a tiny smile of delight. Discipline was important, of course, and her hours in the work room were precious if she wanted to keep her business ticking over till she was ready to devote more time to it again. But she couldn't be angry that Risay wanted to be with her. Or that he called her Mama.

'I'll be along soon. After you've finished eating.'

Finally, with pouts that failed to hide his triumph, Risay let Sofia carry him out.

Tariq made to follow till Samira put out her hand. She'd avoided taking Jacqui's advice for too long. Now she was desperate enough to try even that.

'Don't go.' Slowly he turned and her breath stalled as she met his eyes. Her skin tightened, the hairs lifting on her arms at the intensity of that stare. Her hand dropped to her side as she battled that familiar upsurge of longing.

'Please?'

CHAPTER ELEVEN

TARIQ COULDN'T TAKE his eyes off Samira. The sheen of the clingy material she wore complemented the glow of her skin and the luminous brightness of her sherry-gold eyes. Stoically he tried not to stare at the swell of her breasts, tip-tilted with hard little nubs that thrust so invitingly towards him. The delicious sweep from waist to hip. The pronounced curve of her belly where she cradled his child.

He swallowed and ripped his gaze back up again.

His wife. His for the taking.

He read the invitation in her eyes and had to weld his feet to the floor rather than stalk back and haul her into his arms.

How he wanted her.

How he'd missed her.

All these weeks it had been hell holding back: being at her side in public or with the boys. Making sure she didn't work herself too hard. And all the time keeping his hands to himself.

When he did allow himself to touch her it was exquisite torture. He wanted so much more than her arm in his, the inadvertent brush of her hip or breast as they stood together, presiding at some function.

'Yes?' The word was harsh as gravel. He cleared his throat and tried for a softer tone. 'You wanted something?'

There was a flash in Samira's eyes that might have been anger but it was gone before he could be sure.

'Won't you stay for a while? I rarely see you.'

He saw her daily. Yet he knew what she meant. He'd been careful not to be alone with her.

'My schedule's very busy.' Nevertheless he moved back into the room and saw some of the tension ease from her slim shoulders.

'Surely you have some time for me?'

Some time! *All* his time was devoted to the complex issue of Samira and how she fitted in his life. How best to look after her and their child.

'Is there something wrong?' Tariq noticed the tiny smudges under her eyes. He frowned. He was used to her blooming with good health. Even now she looked radiant, but those shadows told a different story.

He crossed the room and took her arm, registering the softness of her inner arm and the swish of shimmery material against her naked skin as he led her to an armchair.

'Tell me about it.' He waited till she took a seat before retreating to lean against her work table. But her subtle cinnamon scent wafted across his senses. It was more intoxicating than any manufactured perfume.

'You've been avoiding me,' she said at last.

Tariq shrugged. 'My diary is full with the multilateral negotiations and the rebuilding project on top of all the usual commitments.'

Samira angled her head as if to view him better. He folded his arms.

'You know what I mean.' Her voice dropped to a low, sultry note. 'You don't come to my bed any more.'

Now she *had* surprised him. He hadn't expected a direct confrontation.

Why? Because she's so shy and docile? An inner voice sneered at his foolishness. Of course Samira would take the bull by the horns. For all her subtlety and grace in dealing with the public and fractious VIPs, she was no pushover.

She could be surprisingly forthright. The fact she'd had the nerve to propose marriage to him proved that.

And yet… Tariq sensed it took a lot for her to confront him. Her hands twisted in her lap while her neck and shoulders screamed tension.

'You want sex?' His mind raced, calculating how long it would take to get her out of that slinky bit of nothing and flat on her back beneath him.

It took far too much effort to crush the urge to act.

Tariq knew his duty. His uncle had drummed a sense of responsibility into him by the time he could walk, preparing for the day he'd be ruler.

Samira had a history of miscarriage. His duty was to keep her and their child safe. If that meant staying out of her bed for a few months, he'd do it. He'd do everything to protect her. Just as he had the country's top specialist on call and had cut back the hours of evening functions so Samira could rest.

He'd take no chances.

A shadow flickered in his soul and a chill crept up his backbone, lifting the hairs on his nape one by one. He drew a slow breath, not quite managing to dispel the fear he'd fail Samira as he'd failed Jasmin.

'Yes.' Samira shook her head, her brow furrowing. 'No. Not just sex.'

Tariq waited. Her shoulders lifted and dropped and he swallowed hard as those lush breasts jiggled temptingly.

'I want…' She shook her head and again he caught the perfume of her skin.

Everything about his wife—from her voice, the perfume of her skin, the taste of her on his tongue, to the lush perfection of her body—made him want more. Made him want in ways too numerous to calculate.

Tariq's hands clenched on the edge of the worktop. 'You want…?'

'I don't think I can put it into words.'

Despite his certainty that it would be better for them both if he found an excuse to leave, he didn't shift. How could he look after her if he didn't understand her?

'Try me.'

Samira looked up at him watching her, the intensity of his gaze wrapping around her, making warmth curl within. Yet he gave nothing away.

She'd come this far. All she had to do was be honest. *Share yourself*, Jacqui had said.

Unfortunately Samira had little experience of that. She'd learned to keep herself to herself in the ways that really mattered. But if it was worth having it was worth fighting for. Tariq, and the precious sense of wellbeing he'd given her before, were worth having.

'You know Asim and I weren't close to our parents?'

Tariq's eyebrows slanted in surprise at the change of subject. 'I knew.'

'You've heard their marriage wasn't easy?' Asim wouldn't have discussed it and Tariq wouldn't have asked, but he'd have to have been deaf not to hear the whispers.

'I don't listen to rumour. I prefer to deal in facts.'

Samira compressed her lips. Was he being deliberately unhelpful or just chivalrous?

'They lived in a world of their own. When all was well I never saw them because they were wrapped up in each other. But more often it was a war zone. Screaming rows and doors slamming, glass smashing and angry tirades.' She brushed her hands over the shivering skin of her arms. 'They were jealous and suspected other lovers. The best times were when they were away and we were alone with the staff.'

'I'm sorry. That must have been hard.'

Samira hesitated, groping for words. 'I'm not telling

you this to get sympathy, but so you understand what it was like.'

'I understand.'

But did he?

'The thing is…' She looked down to see she'd bunched the rich satin into a taut knot. Instantly she opened her hands and smoothed out the crushed fabric. 'The thing is, they didn't just play out their dramas between them. They used us.'

Samira kept her eyes down, not wanting to read Tariq's expression as acid memories made her flesh crawl.

'Each used to interrogate me, trying to use me as a spy against the other. I found out years later that a diplomat was dismissed because I told my father how he smiled and laughed when he was with my mother. I thought it nice *someone* laughed in the palace but my father was convinced they were having an affair. Possibly because he was having one with my nanny at the time.'

'You shouldn't have had to go through that.' The rumble of Tariq's voice drew her head up. His expression was sombre.

'It could have been worse.' She paused. 'It took me a long time to learn to be cautious but I learned my lesson when I was thirteen.' Samira stopped and focused on trying to slow her too-fast pulse.

'My mother invited me to tea with a friend and I was so excited to be included I didn't realise what was happening till too late. Her "friend" turned out to be a journalist, pumping me for information about my father. She took innocent anecdotes and twisted them into the worst kind of slimy innuendo about my father. The more I tried to set the story straight, the worse it got, with my mother putting words in my mouth and it all going down on record.'

Samira sank back in her seat, hating that it had been her mother of all people who'd made her feel unclean.

'My father managed to quash the story but my parents separated. Publicly the story was they were busy with regal responsibilities in different places.'

She met Tariq's grim stare and shrugged. 'I blamed myself but I finally learned to keep myself to myself.'

It was a lesson she'd stuck to until she'd met Jackson Brent and, in the throes of romantic excitement, thrown caution to the wind. His betrayal had cured her of romance and almost stolen her ability to trust.

Yet she trusted Tariq.

He'd moved away from the table to stand before her. The expression in his eyes made her heart somersault with hope.

Jacqui had been right. She just needed to open up to her husband. Explain and clear up whatever was holding him back. Then they could regain the easy, satisfying relationship she'd so enjoyed. Relief filled her. The unpalatable task of talking about the past would be worth it.

'You can't blame yourself for their marriage failing.'

'Eventually I worked that out. Plus I realised I didn't want a marriage like theirs.'

Her gaze lingered on the impressive breadth of Tariq's shoulders and chest and she congratulated herself on having made a far better marriage. She hadn't trusted so-called love. She'd married a man she respected, a man of integrity.

Yet being so close to him sent her wayward hormones into a chaos of yearning excitement.

'I told you this so you'd understand how much our marriage means to me.' She smiled up at him. 'After my parents' destructive marriage and my failed relationship, it took a lot even to consider marriage. I don't trust easily. But you've made this...' Samira waved her hand wide, suddenly on an emotional brink at the thought of all Tariq had done for her.

He'd given her so much. Not only had he shared his boys, he'd created a place for her in his world, accepting her and caring for her. She felt safe, content, part of the sort of family she'd never thought she'd have, yet with the freedom to pursue her dreams.

And then there was the child she carried.

She put her hands on the arms of her chair, ready to lever herself up.

'Don't! There's no need to get up.' Tariq dragged a straight-backed chair from the table and sat down, facing her, his long legs folded back beneath the seat. 'So, you're happy here. That's excellent.'

Samira blinked. 'More than that. What we've shared—it's more than I'd believed possible.' Despite her confident proposal, she'd wondered how well two virtual strangers could live and work together.

'You've been wonderful, Tariq. Thoughtful and generous, and reassuring when I need it.' It was as if he sensed and responded to her fears for the baby.

'It's my pleasure to look after you.' His words were crisply formal, as if she hadn't got through to him at all.

'I'm not talking about being looked after.' Her brow pleated as she sought the right words. 'What you've given me is precious and I want you to know I appreciate it.' She smiled, rubbing at her baby bulge as she felt the fluttery movements of their child.

Tariq followed her gesture and stiffened. Samira was thrilled he'd given her a child. No surprises there. That was why she'd married him, to become a mother.

He exhaled slowly. No man liked to feel used but Samira came perilously close to making him feel that now.

He hadn't been consulted about this child. If he had, he'd have admitted the twins were enough for him. After losing Jasmin in labour, another child was the last thing on his mind.

His blood chilled thinking about that time.

What did Samira want from him? Why tell him now about her miserable childhood? He felt frustrated and appalled by it but could do nothing to alter the past.

Despite his considerable experience, women could still be a mystery.

He watched Samira closely, noting her over-bright eyes and flushed cheeks. She was emotional, he'd almost say overwrought, except there was no question that she was happy.

'Thank you,' he murmured. 'I'm pleased you're content.' Samira had been fulsome in her thanks and, despite the demons that rode him, he understood how precious this baby was to her. 'I want you to be happy.'

She nodded, her eyes glowing, and Tariq stood abruptly. He needed to leave before he did something unforgivable, like maul the woman he'd pledged not to touch.

He'd done his research. He knew sex with Samira wasn't likely to endanger her or the baby. But how likely had it been that Jasmin, after a completely normal, healthy pregnancy, should die? He couldn't take the risk. Not again. Not Samira.

'I need to leave, but I'll see you later with the boys.'

'Wait!' Samira stood too, her hand smoothing the nightgown over her bump. 'You're going? But you haven't answered me.'

'There was no question.' Heat seared him with each passing second. He had to get out of here before his resolve cracked.

She drew herself up. Yet even when she looked downright regal all he could think of was how good she'd feel in his arms, melting against him. How good she'd taste.

'I want to sleep with you.' Her words were pure, husky

temptation to a man on the edge of control. 'But I want
more too. More of *us*. The way we were before I told you
about the baby.' Her eyes held a dewy sheen of happiness
he'd thought reserved for their child. But now Samira was
looking at him in a way that did strange things to his in-
ternal organs. He couldn't identify the sensation and that
disturbed him.

'Being with you...' Her shoulders lifted as she spread
her arms palm upwards. 'I can't tell you how much our
marriage means. It's changed me. I never expected I'd feel
anything like this.'

Tariq stiffened.

She hadn't expected to feel anything like this?

Like what?

He remembered Jasmin's soft, hopeful gaze whenever
he'd entered a room, whenever they were together. They'd
contracted to marry but somewhere during their dynastic
marriage she'd fallen in love.

And he'd been unable to return that love. He'd felt her
disappointment in every searching, loving look.

Tariq swallowed hard, tasting the rusty metal tang of
horror as he registered the softening in Samira's expression.

'I want to be a wife to you in every way, Tariq.' Her
smile could light up a city. But it could devastate too. His
chest cracked wide as he saw what was in her eyes.

Love.

Love for him.

A love he was congenitally incapable of returning.

His breath caught, snared by his galloping heartbeat.
Sweat broke out across his forehead and there was a drum-
ming in his ears as past and present merged. Pressure built
in his chest as if from welling emotions. Except he didn't
do emotion, not of that sort.

This couldn't be happening again. A wife who looked

to him for love. A wife carrying his child. A wife who yearned for something that wasn't in him to give. A wife he feared he couldn't keep safe from hurt.

The day Jasmin had died the doctor had looked at him with sympathy, believing he dealt with a heartbroken husband. Tariq had felt like a sham, utterly unworthy.

Tariq had assured himself theirs was a decent marriage, a practical one, that he'd been a thoughtful and loyal husband even as he'd regretted Jasmin's unfortunate *tendre*. But it was only when she'd died that the enormity of what he'd done had smashed into him, blasting away cosy excuses. Jasmin had lost her life because of him and his need for heirs.

Now the past reinvented itself. He saw it in Samira's hopeful expression. In her outstretched hand.

Tariq's heart slammed against his ribs, his skin breaking into a clammy sweat as the walls pushed in on him, the weight of them crushing the air from his lungs.

He stepped back and watched her arm fall. His gut went into freefall as he saw surprise morph into hurt. But he couldn't lie. Not even for her. 'I'm sorry, Samira, but you're asking too much.'

Tariq spun on his heel and strode from the room.

CHAPTER TWELVE

YOU'RE ASKING TOO MUCH.

The words had hung in the air between them too long. It had been weeks since Tariq had burst out with them and still they bit deep, hurting just as keenly as the day he'd said them.

Samira looked down the long table lit by antique candelabras. Beyond the twenty guests invited to this intimate royal dinner sat Tariq, resplendent in white robes and a head scarf edged with gold.

He faced her down the table but his attention was on his guests. He conversed with the American ambassador and some leading entrepreneurs while at the same time making a couple of visiting provincial leaders feel welcome.

Tariq handled his responsibilities easily. He was an expert negotiator. According to his staff he was a born administrator. His people loved him because he was a man of action who ruled fairly and provided well for them.

The twins adored him. He made time for them in ways her father never had. And, if Tariq was a fraction too strict on discipline, she and Sofia moderated his demands.

Few men could handle so many responsibilities. Yet Tariq did. Nothing was too much effort.

Except being with his wife.

That was *asking too much.*

Bile filled Samira's mouth and she choked it back, her

knife and fork clattering to her plate. The delicious meal turned to ashes in her mouth.

Tariq made time for everyone but her.

As if sensing her regard, he looked up.

Even from this distance his laser-bright stare captured her, pinning her to the seat. Samira's heartbeat fluttered, her breath quickening. Despite the heavy weight of pregnancy she felt that telltale softening at her core in preparation for his touch.

A touch that would never come.

Samira bit her lower lip before it could tremble.

She despised her weakness for a man who patently didn't want her.

Oh, he'd been happy enough to take her when they were first married. He'd *insisted* on it, as if a platonic marriage was an affront to his manhood.

But once her waistline had thickened, and she'd become more apple than hourglass, Tariq had lost interest. Her appeal had clearly been skin-deep.

She'd known her looks would fade with age but hadn't expected to lose her allure so soon, or realised how devastating that would be.

Samira choked down aching self-pity and forced her gaze to the blur of faces around the table.

Tariq had made it abundantly clear she was in the same category as the multitude of women who'd kept him company before and after his first marriage. They'd been gorgeous and expendable. Once he'd had his fill, they'd been history.

Was there even now some beauty waiting for this dinner to end so he'd come to her? Pain knifed Samira's ribs, slashing at her, tearing her breath.

After all, she'd given him permission to take lovers. She didn't want to believe it, not after what they'd shared, but, having experienced Tariq's phenomenal sex drive, she doubted he'd stay celibate long.

Nothing could have reinforced the fact she was a poor second to his beloved first wife more than the way he avoided her. He treated her charmingly, always concerned for her wellbeing, but in an avuncular way, as if she was a charge to be cared for, not a wife to be cherished.

How dared he?

Fury was a pummelling beat high in her chest.

He'd seduced her for his pleasure, then left her high and dry when his interest waned. As if she could be dismissed once he'd had his fill!

How was she supposed to continue in this marriage? Better never to have given in to his seduction and lived as strangers than succumb to his charisma, fall for the man, then have him reject her.

Pain jabbed deep as realisation struck.

Fall for the man...

Samira sucked in a panicked breath. No, it wasn't that. It couldn't be. She'd never be foolish enough to risk her heart again by falling in love with any man. Not even Mr Almost Perfect Tariq.

Yet her anguished heart somersaulted at the very thought of the word.

Love.

Love for Tariq.

Had she fooled herself all this time, telling herself she could have everything she wanted with him but not risk her heart?

'Your Highness, are you all right?' The words reached her through a thick fog. 'Your Highness?'

Slowly she dragged her head around to find Nicolas Roussel leaning close, his hair gleaming gold in the wavering darkness that edged her vision.

'Do you need a doctor?' The Frenchman's voice was

low and urgent. He reached as if to touch her arm, then hesitated, as if remembering her royal status. His blue eyes were concerned.

At least there was one man here who cared about her!

Even as the thought lodged, Samira knew she was being melodramatic. Tariq cared. Just not enough.

The thought brought a sob to her lips and she clapped a hand over her mouth, horrified that her emotions had her teetering on the brink.

Tariq had enjoyed her as a lover till her sexual allure faded, and he cared about her as the stand-in mother for the twins, as his consort and hostess. He just didn't care about her the way she did him.

Love.

Samira's heart pounded so hard it felt like it might jump out of her chest.

How long had she been pretending to herself?

How long since she'd fallen for her husband?

'I'm calling a doctor.' A chair scraped as Nicolas made to stand.

'No!' Her hand shot out and grabbed his wrist. As if from a distance she saw her fingers wrap, white-knuckled, around his arm. She couldn't seem to let go. 'I'm all right, truly.'

Samira tried for a smile and knew she'd failed when he looked at her doubtfully.

'Truly.' She tried again, her tense facial muscles stretching. 'It's just…' she leaned towards him and he bent close '…sometimes I get a little uncomfortable.'

His gaze skated across her belly, then up again.

Samira nodded, prising her fingers loose from his arm and sitting back in her seat, willing herself to look calm despite her too-rapid pulse and the sick lurching of her stomach. It was a half-truth, after all, since she'd suffered from indigestion recently. Better to let her guest think it was that bothering her than the discovery she was in love with her husband. A husband who had rejected her.

Pain wrapped gnarled hands around her heart, squeezing tight.

'I understand.' Nicholas's smile was warm. 'My sister recently had a baby. She said sitting for too long was difficult.'

'Ah, you *do* understand.' Samira prided herself on her light tone, as if she had nothing on her mind but a little heartburn. She'd spent years learning to project grace and charm even when her private world had been a disaster. Desperately she dredged up every lesson she'd learned and gave him a dazzling smile. 'Tell me…' She leaned closer. 'Did your sister have a boy or a girl?'

The next course was being served when Samira looked up to discover Tariq staring down the table. His jaw was tight, his mouth a grim line. And the look he sent Nicolas Roussel should have incinerated the charming Frenchman where he sat.

Samira's breath stalled as hope fluttered high in her chest. Surely that incendiary stare signalled possessiveness? She'd never seen Tariq jealous, but that fixed glare held an unmistakeable threat.

Her heart took up a quick, excited rhythm.

Until Tariq's gaze shifted to her and his face went completely blank. One minute she could have sworn she saw bloodlust in his eyes, the next she was left wondering if it had been a trick of the light.

Tariq inclined his head infinitesimally, favouring her with the small, polite smile which was the most animation she ever saw in him now.

How she hated that smile. It reminded her of all they'd once shared and all she still craved.

Then he turned to the ambassador and didn't look her way again, clearly dismissing her from his thoughts.

Samira was surprised no one at her end of the table noticed the sound of her heart cracking wide open.

Tariq looked up from the draft treaty document as the door to his private study slammed open. One look at his wife's taut features and he surged to his feet. She was in the final stages of pregnancy and he was constantly on tenterhooks, wary of a crisis.

'That will be all for now,' he told his secretary, his eyes fixed on Samira.

Never had she come to his office without invitation. Their lives proceeded in neat, contained patterns, intersecting only at official functions and when they spent time with the boys.

She looked tense. Was it the baby? Tension knotted his gut. He started towards her, then stopped at the look she sent him. Not pain or distress, but anger.

Tariq frowned. In all the time they'd been married he'd never seen Samira furious. In fact he hadn't seen anger on her features since she'd been a kid. He hadn't realised it before but even in her teens Samira had been self-contained, as if she controlled her natural volatility.

Finally they were alone, his secretary closing the door behind him.

'Won't you sit down?'

She lifted her chin and regarded him along her pert nose. His breath snagged. She'd never looked more beautiful, more alluring, her eyes glittering bright as gems, her lush body vibrating with passion. He wanted to reach out and stroke away the tension in her shoulders, kiss her into compliance, mould his hands to her deliciously rounded belly and...

'You cancelled my meeting.'

Tariq blinked, trying to get his mind back into gear.

'You're not denying it?' Her hands went to her hips,

pulling the red silk of her loose dress tight, accentuating her heavily pregnant form. Could she feel his baby moving inside?

He cleared his throat and forced his gaze up, stoically ignoring the inevitable tension in his groin. Every time he looked at her he felt it. Every time he thought of her. Keeping his distance was killing him.

'You're concerned about a missed meeting?'

'I'm concerned...' she paused, dragged in a breath '...that you believe you have the right to interfere with my schedule.'

'Ah. The meeting in the mountain villages.'

She nodded. 'We were going to discuss the opportunities for local women. Yet I find it's been removed from my diary with no explanation.'

'It was to take place at the same time as the redevelopment meeting but as I'm no longer available it will be rescheduled. Besides, it's a long way to the mountains now you're so far through your pregnancy. You need to be careful of yourself.'

Given her militant look he refused to admit he'd cancelled the meeting solely to prevent her travelling late in pregnancy. He wanted Samira here, where the best medical care was available.

He thrust from his mind the fact that hadn't saved Jasmin.

Samira's delicate eyebrows arched high. 'I'm careful. Besides, I have people fussing around me if I so much as lift a finger.'

Tariq nodded. He was taking no chances with her well-being.

'Do you have any idea when it will be rescheduled?' Her narrowed eyes told him she wasn't convinced.

Tariq spread his hands. 'I leave those details to my staff but I doubt it will be soon.'

For a full minute Samira didn't say anything and it

struck him how much he missed the easy camaraderie they'd once shared. Being with her had been pure pleasure, not just in bed, but out of it too. Until she'd announced her pregnancy. Until he'd seen love shining in her eyes and known he couldn't give her what she wanted.

Tariq looked again. It wasn't love he read in her face.

'Very well.' She drew a slow breath. 'I'll have my secretary organise a separate meeting with the women's representatives. I have some business proposals that won't wait.' Before he could voice an objection she added, 'I'll invite them here to the capital.'

'An excellent idea.' He'd prefer it if Samira reduced the hours she spent working, but at least she'd given up her plan to travel. His breathing eased.

'I'll ask Nicolas to attend. His expertise is invaluable.'

Tariq stiffened. Was that provocation in her bright eyes as she turned and left the room? Had she guessed how he hated the sight of her with Roussel?

It didn't matter how often he reminded himself the man was capable, trustworthy and honest. The sight of Samira smiling with the Frenchman, so obviously attuned to him, set Tariq's teeth on edge.

Roussel had his wife's ear and her smiles while Tariq was forced to kick his heels at a distance. It didn't matter that he was the one who'd rebuffed Samira. Or that caution decreed he keep his distance. The strain of holding back from her drove him close to breaking point.

Roussel, of all people! Tariq hadn't missed the fact that the Frenchman had the blond hair, slim build and charming smile of Samira's first lover, Jackson Brent. Clearly she was drawn to the type.

A type that was altogether different from Tariq's towering bulk. Of course it was. She'd made no bones about the fact she'd married him for his children, not himself.

And if she'd enjoyed sex with him… Well, hadn't he made sure she did? That meant nothing.

A crash reverberated as his fist slammed into the wall. Tariq looked down, vaguely surprised at the blood scoring his knuckles. Pain wrapped round his hand and flashed up his arm.

Could he have got it wrong?

Was it possible his wife wasn't in love with him after all?

Samira gasped as pain wrapped around her and she clung to the shower screen. All day she'd felt out of sorts, unable to settle and her back aching. Now she knew why. Her baby was coming early. What had begun as ripples of discomfort had grown into full-blown contractions so fierce she had trouble remembering to breathe.

Was it supposed to be like this so quickly? She hadn't had time even to get out of the bathroom after trying to ease her discomfort with a warm shower.

Panic rose. If she slipped she doubted she could get up. She'd imagined a slow onset of labour, nothing so intense and overwhelming. What if something was wrong? What if her baby was in danger?

Suddenly the distance to the door seemed never ending.

Belatedly she remembered to slow her breathing, concentrate on exhaling. When at last the pain abated, her gaze snagged on the phone by the bath. Slowly, her hand groping for support, she made her way to it.

'Yes?' The deep voice burred in her ear as another contraction began.

Samira opened her mouth but only managed a gasp.

'Who is this?'

She clung to the receiver, her hand shaking. 'Tariq,' she finally managed. It was a hoarse whisper, the best she could manage, but he didn't answer. Her phone clattered to the floor.

Fear notched high and she blinked back tears of frustration. She needed Tariq. Here. Now. To tell her everything was okay and that the baby would be fine.

Samira rode out another contraction, bracing herself against the cool tiled wall, trying to force down fear that, despite her uneventful pregnancy, she might lose this baby too.

The door crashed open.

'Ah, *habibti*.' The deep voice curled reassuringly around her. 'It's all right. I'm here. I'll look after you.'

She closed her eyes as strong arms wrapped around her naked body and lifted her high against a solid chest.

'Tariq.' She breathed deep, inhaling that unique tang that was his, her body melting into the comfort of his embrace. 'I thought you hadn't heard me. I thought—'

'Shh. It's all right. I've got you. I won't leave your side.'

Hours later Samira looked up into eyes that had darkened to moss green. That wide, proud forehead was wrinkled with concern but his smile was brilliant.

'She looks like you,' he murmured in a voice that brushed like velvet over her skin.

'Right now I'm not sure that's a good thing.' Euphoric and still stunned at the abrupt but safe delivery of their wonderful, tiny daughter, Samira had no illusions about her appearance. She'd be exhausted if she weren't floating in seventh heaven.

'It's an excellent thing.' Tariq stepped closer, holding their child in the crook of his arm. Samira's heart rolled over at the sight of him holding that tiny, precious life so gently. 'You're the most beautiful woman I've ever known. No one can hold a candle to you.'

Samira told herself he was being kind but the way his eyes gleamed as he looked between her and the baby stopped the words in her mouth. He looked...smitten.

She blinked, fighting back what she told herself were tears of exhaustion.

'Samira? What is it?' Instantly Tariq was at her side. 'Are you in pain?' Already he was reaching for the call button to summon medical staff.

She shook her head. 'I'm just a little overcome.'

Not just by the birth, which had been unusually short for a first delivery. But by Tariq. He'd been with her the whole time, a rock to cling to, his words of encouragement just what she needed, his strength giving her strength.

Through it all she'd seen in his eyes something far more profound than concern for her physical wellbeing. No husband could have been more tender, more supportive or proud.

No matter what he'd said before, Tariq *cared*. She knew it as surely as she knew she'd just been through a life-changing experience.

Carefully he sat on the edge of the hospital bed. 'Everything will be all right.'

Looking into his glowing eyes Samira could believe it. Surely the miracle she'd hoped for had happened? He wasn't distancing himself now, erecting barriers between them.

He reached out to brush the hair back from her face, his touch a gentle caress of her flushed cheek.

Slowly, infinitely slowly, he leaned forward to press his lips to hers in the sweetest of kisses. Her lips parted and she tasted the intriguing salty, male tang of him. His tongue slicked hers, drawing her essence into his mouth, and she sighed at the rightness of it.

'Sleep now, Samira.' The words washed over her as her eyelids fluttered shut.

She smiled. Beyond all expectation everything was going to be all right.

CHAPTER THIRTEEN

SAMIRA WATCHED SILENTLY from the doorway as Tariq paced the nursery with little Layla in his arms. As ever, her heart somersaulted in her chest as she saw him with their daughter. There was no doubt she was the apple of his eye, as precious to him as the twins.

He'd always been good with children, hadn't he? It was one of the reasons Samira had married him.

Pain scored deep. *Pity he wasn't as good with wives.*

Correction: *with her.* He'd been an adoring, devoted husband to his first wife. But then he'd doted on Jasmin, everyone said so.

Samira's hand curled around the door jamb as anguish sucked the air from her lungs and swiped the strength from her knees.

Weeks ago in hospital, she'd mistaken Tariq's delight in their baby for something else. She'd believed he cared for *her* in the way she craved. But she'd been horribly mistaken.

It was as if those moments of intimacy had never been.

She pressed the heel of her hand to the tearing ache in her chest. Yet nothing could stop the grief ripping her apart.

Terrible as it had been before Layla's birth to know Tariq didn't love her, she'd found the strength to bear it. But now, after her luminous joy in the hospital when she'd been so *sure* he cared, the awful, polite emptiness of their marriage was destroying her.

Samira couldn't take much more. Even her bones felt brittle with the effort of holding herself together on the outside when on the inside she was a shattered, bleeding mess.

She'd given her heart to Tariq but he wasn't interested. What she'd thought was genuine tenderness in the hospital had been a mirage, an illusion brought on by exhaustion and wishful thinking.

All her life she'd known the dreadful danger of 'love'. She thought she'd plumbed the depths when Jackson had betrayed her and that, as a result, she'd immunised herself against its power. Only now she realised what she'd felt for her faithless lover was nothing in comparison to this soul-wrenching love for her husband.

She must have made some sound of distress for Tariq swung around.

Her heart dipped as she read the familiar signs when he saw her—the instant stiffening of his shoulders, the guarded expression, the distance he somehow put between them even without physically moving.

Samira grabbed harder at the door jamb.

'Hello, Tariq.' Her voice was husky but firm and she jutted her chin higher.

'Samira, shouldn't you be resting?'

Her mouth twisted mirthlessly. She was always being told to rest when she wanted to be with him.

'I want to see my baby. Between you and the staff I barely get any time with her.' Bitterness made her exaggerate. She wanted to lash out at Tariq, sick of this distant politeness that was all they shared now.

She breathed deep, seeking calm.

For so long she'd craved a child, believing it would fill the stark emptiness within. And it was true; Layla was the light of her life. The tenderness she felt whenever she looked at her daughter had no comparison.

But too late Samira had realised a baby couldn't make

her whole. Only she could do that, except she'd made the mistake of giving away a vital part of herself to Tariq. The man who'd never be the husband she wanted because he was still in love with his dead wife. The man who viewed her not with love but as a responsibility.

Shoring up her strength, she walked into the room, not even flinching at the careful way Tariq passed their baby over so as not to touch Samira.

She compressed her lips, biting down the reproach that hovered on her tongue.

What was the point in berating him? He couldn't help what he felt. In other circumstances she'd be full of admiration for a man so loyal to his one true love.

Something wrenched deep inside and she turned away, blinking back hot tears as Layla nuzzled at her breast. Love for her little girl filled her, yet even that couldn't bring peace.

She was trapped in a web of her own devising.

'Goodnight, Tariq.' She didn't look at him. Slowly, her body cramped with a soul-deep ache, she settled in the low chair by the crib and undid the belt of her robe.

Tariq's hands clenched as he watched Layla suckle at her mother's breast. He never tired of the sight, despite the raw discomfort it brought him. Who'd have believed watching a woman feed a baby would be so arousing?

Not just any woman but Samira.

Even with dark circles under her eyes and her skin pale with tiredness, his wife made him hard with wanting. More, she twisted his gut in knots.

He tried to do the right thing, to keep some physical distance while she recuperated from childbirth. Just remembering that labour made his belly churn.

It had been excruciating torture, watching Samira suffer, and pretending to a confidence that all would be well when at the forefront of his mind was the memory of Jasmin's lifeless face after her emergency delivery.

Even now, weeks after Layla's birth, he woke in a sweat most nights from nightmares where Samira didn't survive. Where nothing the doctors did could save her, because Tariq hadn't got her to the hospital soon enough.

The image of her when he'd burst into the bathroom and found her in labour still haunted him. She'd looked so *vulnerable*. If he'd needed anything to shore up his resolve to keep his distance until the doctor said intimacy was safe, it was that.

'You're still here?' Samira looked up, a frown on her delicate features.

He stiffened. 'It's late. There's nowhere else I need to be.'

She opened her mouth as if to speak, then turned instead to watch Layla.

As if he wasn't there.

Tariq scowled. He wasn't used to being dismissed. Even if his self-imposed rule was to avoid being alone with her so as not to be tempted into doing something he shouldn't.

This was different. This was Samira withdrawing from *him*. Not physically, but mentally. She'd been like this since the hospital.

Tariq hated it. Every instinct clamoured that this wasn't right.

He'd told himself after the baby was born they'd resume the relationship they'd had before. Surely he'd imagined the love he'd seen in her face months earlier? For she'd shown no evidence of it since. If anything, her partiality for Roussel's company, never enough to provoke gossip, but still marked, seemed to indicate he'd been mistaken about that.

Yet, right from that first day home from the hospital, things had gone wrong. Tariq had excused himself to let Samira rest, finding one reason after another to keep away. When he'd finally returned, timing his appearance with

that of the twins and their nanny, there'd been no welcome
in Samira's eyes. She'd looked bruised with fatigue and
there was an unfamiliar blankness in her expression as
she'd listened to his excuses about catching up with work.
As if she just didn't care.

That had shocked him. Though they'd grown apart before the birth, he'd always felt Samira *cared* for him. Her
indifference was a blow he couldn't shrug off. It bothered
him more than he'd thought possible.

He'd refrained from pressing her, understanding she
needed time to recuperate; making excuses, knowing she
must be exhausted from labour. He'd found more and more
work to occupy him, giving her the space she needed.

But it wasn't working. Something was horribly wrong.

The spark had gone out of her, the vibrant energy that
was an essential part of Samira. Her eyes no longer tracked
him across the room and he hadn't seen her smile in weeks.

His belly hollowed. He missed that. Missed the way
her eyes used to light up when she saw him; how she'd
lower those long, lustrous eyelashes to screen her expression when she realised he'd noticed her hungry stare. How
her pulse had fluttered faster when he took her hand, even
when they were in a receiving line at a royal function.

Nor had he missed the way she called Layla *her* baby,
not *theirs*.

Cold crept along his spine. The gap between them
yawned wider each passing day. It was no longer something he could control.

She'd always wanted a child. Now she had one of her
own. Was that why she shut him out?

Were he and the twins superfluous?

Tariq's heart hammered against his ribs. The chill along
his backbone turned to a glacial freeze, stiffening every
muscle and seizing his lungs.

It couldn't be. It was just weariness from the birth. The

doctor had advised time and patience. Maybe a change of scenery to lift her spirits. Tariq had planned a visit to the small palace where they'd honeymooned, as soon as he could get away.

'I've been thinking.' He stepped closer and Samira half-turned her head but didn't meet his eyes.

That epitomised all that was wrong between them. Tariq couldn't seem to reach her any more. It wasn't anger that ate at him but concern that maybe this was something he couldn't put right.

Blanking out the idea, he stepped in front of Samira, willing her to look up.

'Yes?' Once more her gaze skated towards his face but never settled.

With infinite effort he managed not to sound gruff. 'A change of scenery might be welcome. A little break away.'

Instantly Samira's gaze meshed with his and he felt the impact of that stare right to the soles of his feet. At last! It was the closest they'd come to connecting since the night the baby had been born. Then she'd looked at him with such softness in her eyes, he'd felt like a god among men.

Yet now for the first time he had no inkling what she felt. The realisation pulled his flesh tight as the hairs at his nape stood on end. Never, in all the years he'd known her, had Samira been so unreadable, so blank. It was as if a light had been switched off inside her.

Fear clutched greedily at his innards. He felt like something precious had slipped away from him.

'You must be a mind reader.' Her voice was low and husky, as if from a tight throat. 'I was thinking the same thing.'

'Excellent.'

But before he could explain his plans she spoke again. 'I need to go to Paris.'

'Paris?' He stiffened.

She nodded and once more her gaze slid away. He wanted to grab her by the chin and force her to look him in the eye. Then he glanced down at Layla, still feeding at her breast, and pulled himself up.

'Yes. Next week.'

'You want to go to Paris?' Why there?

'Yes.' Her voice had that husky quality that always ignited his libido.

Perhaps he'd panicked needlessly. If Samira fancied a trip to the city women equated with romance, how could he object?

Relief fizzed in his blood. The doctor had been right. She was just tired. Tariq would see to it her stay in the French capital was memorable. His mind raced with possibilities.

'That's an excellent idea. Not next week, though. I'll still be tied up in negotiations. But in another week or two I can manage it.'

Satisfaction filled him. Everything was going to be okay. His mouth hitched in an approving smile.

'No. I'll go next week.' There was no answering smile. If anything, her expression was sombre.

'I'm sorry, Samira. That's not possible. You know how important this treaty is. I'm doing the best I can to speed things up but I'm needed here.'

She shrugged. 'Layla and I can go without you.'

For the first time in his life Tariq experienced the sensation that the floor had dropped away beneath him. He almost stumbled where he stood.

'You can't be serious!'

'Of course I'm serious.' She tilted her head, as if curious at his reaction.

What did she see on his face? Outrage? Anger? Fear? For fear was what billowed up in waves from the pit of his stomach. Fear as strong as he'd felt when he'd thought he might lose her in childbirth.

He was losing Samira. She'd drifted away from him and he had no idea how to grab her back.

His palms itched with the need to haul her close, imprison her against him and not release her. But that wouldn't work. She was with him now physically, but mentally, emotionally, she was in some other place. Some place he couldn't reach.

Never had the emotional minefield of the female psyche been so unfathomable.

What did she want from him?

How could he get back what they'd lost?

The metallic tang of alarm filled his mouth. Samira in Paris without him? In the city where Nicolas Roussel lived since his contract had finished?

Tariq tried to banish jealousy, telling himself Samira had more class than to betray him.

Yet the idea of Samira and Layla alone, apart from him and the twins, filled him with cold, draining dread.

He shook his head, biting down a terse refusal. It was on the tip of his tongue to forbid her but he knew, whatever his rights as Samira's husband, that wasn't the way to win her over. Brute force wouldn't work, no matter how tempting.

He'd never felt at such a loss.

'It makes more sense to wait.' He dredged up a shadow of a smile that threatened to crack the taut flesh of his face. 'In two weeks I'll have this wrapped up, I promise.' He'd do whatever it took to conclude the treaty in record time. 'Then we can all go together.'

But she was already shaking her head. 'There's no need. I know you're tied up here.'

Something flickered in her expression and Tariq's eyes narrowed. Had she deliberately proposed the visit at a time she knew he couldn't get away?

'Besides, I've already promised—'

'Promised whom?' Nothing could disguise the raw edge of anger in his words. Who was she meeting? If it was…

'That French cabinet minister.' Samira stared up at him with rounded eyes. 'She contacted me months ago about a designing a dress for her wedding.'

'You don't do wedding dresses.'

She shrugged. 'It's not a conventional bridal dress. It's her second marriage and she wants something different. I promised when she was here and I'm running out of time.'

Tariq wanted to bellow that he didn't give a damn about what sort of dress a foreign politician wanted. He didn't give a damn about anything but having Samira look at him the way she used to. To feel the sunshine of her smile as she laughed with him and the boys or lay in his arms, sated and content.

Samira disengaged the now drowsy Layla, revealing one lush breast, its raspberry nipple glistening, and a jolt of need jabbed direct to Tariq's belly. His hunger for her was so predictable, so strong, he'd given up trying to fight it. But it was nothing compared with his need for that intangible connection between them that had disappeared like rainwater on desert sand.

Swiftly Samira covered herself and lifted Layla to her shoulder.

The sight of them together, mother and child, smashed open something hard and tight in his chest. He could almost feel the blood cascade from the unseen wound as he faced the possibility Samira had given up on their marriage.

'Don't worry, Tariq. We'll be fine in Paris.' Samira's smile was perfunctory. 'Layla's nanny will take care of her while I'm busy.'

'How long will it take?'

She shrugged and looked down at their baby. 'A few days, a week. But you're right. A change of scenery will be good. I think I'll stay on for a while. There's no rush for me to return, is there?'

Every sinew and muscle strained as Tariq held himself back, forcing himself not to shout that there was every reason for her to return. That she wouldn't be permitted to leave the country. Her place was here with him and their boys. He had no intention of letting either her or their daughter leave.

Pain radiated along his jaw from his gritted teeth. But it was nothing to the tearing stab of frustration and fury he felt as he fought for control.

He told himself he was a civilised man, a husband who understood a wife might need space and understanding after childbirth.

He would find a way to keep her. He had to. In the meantime…

'Very well. Since you've promised the woman, you'd better see her. I'll have my staff organise your visit.'

Yet, even though he knew he was doing the sensible thing, the civilised thing, though he knew she'd have the best care from hand-picked staff, his gut knotted.

He turned and strode from the room before he could give in to the impulse to snatch his wife up, sling her over his shoulder and secrete her in the ancient harem where stout doors and old-fashioned padlocks would keep her just where he needed her.

Walking away, giving her the breathing space she needed, was the hardest thing he'd ever done.

CHAPTER FOURTEEN

SAMIRA PUSHED THE pram along the bank of the Seine, watching the golden lights come on as the sky darkened. A cruise boat went by filled with tourists. Laughter floated across the water and her steps faltered as she remembered Tariq's deep, inviting chuckle as he relaxed with her and the boys.

She dragged in an uneven breath. She missed the boys, even after just a day away.

And she missed Tariq.

How stupid was that when she saw him so rarely? When they led separate lives?

Yet there was no escaping the truth, even here in Paris. She was in love with her husband. As for clearing her head and finding a solution by getting away from him, that had been an abysmal failure.

All her trip to France had achieved was to make her homesick. She wanted to be back in Al Sarath.

How telling that her adopted country felt like home now. Because the people she loved most were there.

But what would she return to? A rapturous welcome from the twins and polite indifference from Tariq.

She had two options. Go back to the palace and live a life devoted to her children and her work. She'd pretend her heart wasn't broken but it would be torture being so close to the man she could never have. Or take Layla and leave Tariq and the boys. It would be the scandal of the century. Worse, she'd never be allowed to see Adil and Risay again. Or Tariq.

Both options were untenable.

Yet what other choice did she have?

She looked up to see a couple entwined together in the shadows of the embankment. Abruptly she stopped, her heart slamming against her ribs. Her breath snatched as heat pricked her eyes. Searing emotion blocked her throat as she remembered Tariq holding her like that. As if he'd never let her go.

How much she wanted from him!

Too much. She hunched over the pram, pain stabbing low and fierce.

Out of her peripheral vision she caught a shadow of movement, one of her discreet security detail making sure she was all right. Yet another reminder of Tariq.

As if she didn't already have that. Slowly she straightened and glanced down at her daughter's sleeping face. Layla's dainty rosebud lips were such a contrast to the determined little chin she'd got from her father. A tremor racked Samira, starting high in her chest and radiating out to weaken her limbs.

It didn't matter what she did or where she went, she couldn't escape her feelings for Tariq. She'd been appallingly naive, proposing marriage to a man whom, she realised too late, she'd been half in love with all her life. She'd been worse than naive in falling for his 'sex without emotion' idea. With her past she should have protected herself better. Now it was too late.

The breeze along the river picked up and she shivered. It was time she got Layla back to the hotel. Past time she came to some conclusion about the future.

Shoulders slumped, she forced herself to walk on.

Samira had just passed Layla to her nanny for a bath and turned towards her own room when a door on the far side of the suite's opulent sitting room opened.

'Tariq?'

Samira's hand went to her throat as a familiar form filled the doorway. Her chest squeezed around a heart that thumped an arrhythmic beat.

She blinked, unable to believe her eyes. But there was no mistaking that broad-shouldered frame, or that proud visage. Elation filled her. Until she remembered this couldn't be the reunion she craved.

Yet, despite the stern voice telling her to be calm, she couldn't repress the sheer joy of seeing Tariq again.

His face was taut and unrevealing but his eyes glittered like gemstones and his thick hair stood up as if he'd run his fingers through it.

She frowned. 'What's wrong? Is it the boys?' She was halfway across the room in an instant.

'The boys are with Sofia, settling down for a story. I promised you'd see them before they slept.'

Samira lurched to a halt, relief slamming into her, stopping her headlong progress.

'They're here?' Automatically she looked past him. 'You've brought the boys?'

He nodded, his expression terse.

'What about the treaty? You shouldn't be here.' Tariq was a vital part of the negotiations that everyone hoped would bring stability to their region.

'Tariq? What's happened?' The talks had been going well. Surely they hadn't fallen in a heap after all the hard work he'd put into them?

'Nothing's happened.' He stepped away from the door, snicking it shut behind him. His presence filled the room, making her ridiculously light-headed.

'But you had back-to-back meetings all week.' Confusion filled her, made worse by the unfamiliar look on Tariq's face. He looked sombre, grim even, but with an edge of something else, something stark that made her skin prickle. Now he was closer, she saw the bleak look in his eyes.

'Nothing's happened to Asim or Jacqui, has it?'

Instantly he shook his head, closing the gap between them with his long stride. 'They're fine. They send their love.' His hands engulfed hers and to her amazement Samira felt the tiniest hint of a tremor in them.

'Tariq, you're frightening me.'

'Frightening *you*?' He shook his head, the action so minute she wondered if she'd really seen it. 'I didn't mean to.' He drew a slow breath and his massive chest rose. 'There's been no accident, no tragedy. Everything's fine.'

Except it wasn't. Everything in Samira warned that things were far from right when Tariq, the strongest, most self-assured man she knew, looked as if he'd been knocked off-centre. It wasn't just the rumpled hair and raw emotion in his eyes. It was his quickened breathing, the grooves of pain around his mouth, the tension in his broad neck and over-tight grip.

'I think I'd like to sit.' She didn't really want to. She wanted him to pull her into his arms and never let her go. But she couldn't admit to that.

'Come.' He drew her over to a wide sofa with a magnificent view over Parisian rooftops to the glittering Eiffel Tower.

Samira didn't spare the view a glance, too intent on the feel of her husband's hard, powerful hands holding hers as if they were fragile flowers. How long since he'd touched her?

She knew the answer instantly. In the hospital, when he'd kissed her. It seemed a lifetime ago. A lifetime since she'd known hope.

Now she read unease in the lowering angle of his brows and the way his gaze didn't settle but kept moving, flicking across her features and back again. It scared her.

'You've met with your client?' he asked before she could question him.

'This morning. It went well.' For the first time in her life Samira felt no upsurge of creative energy at the prospect of designing something beautiful. Not even a thrill at extending her talents with the challenge of designing a wedding dress. For years her work had been a refuge and a solace. Today, though, it had been hard to summon the enthusiasm she needed to satisfy her client.

'Good.' His nod was abrupt. 'That's good.'

He fell into silence and Samira watched him swallow, the movement jerky, as if something blocked his throat. Suddenly realisation hit.

'It's you, isn't it? Something's happened to you.' Her fingers curled hard around his, trying to draw strength from his familiar heat. 'What is it, Tariq?' Her mind flew from one awful prognosis to another. Was he suffering some dire illness? Her heart plunged. She tasted the rust tang of blood as she bit down hard on her lip.

'You can't leave.'

'Sorry?' Samira gaped up into blazing eyes that captured hers with their searing intensity.

'You have to stay.'

'I don't understand. What are you talking about?'

'This.' With a lift of the chin he indicated the presidential suite and the city of Paris beyond. 'I can't let you go. I need you with me.'

Samira watched his eyes darken to a shadowed moss green, felt the sizzle of response deep inside as he claimed her for himself and couldn't repress a spark of triumph.

How masochistic could she get? It wasn't her he wanted, just what she represented—a hostess, a consort, a mother for his children. A chattel.

'Tariq?' Her voice was a thin stretch of sound as she struggled to contain her emotions. Suddenly she was shaking all over, her hands palsied in his hold, her chin wobbling.

Appalled, Tariq saw the change in Samira. He'd wanted for so long to smash through her barriers, to see again some life and emotion in her. Now he did, but she looked like she was breaking under the strain.

Yet he hung on tight. He wasn't releasing her again.

It was selfish of him.

It was needy.

And he wasn't budging.

'You're mine, Samira. You belong with me.' Her hands lay limp in his. 'Samira! Say something.'

'What do you want me to say?' She sounded impossibly weary. 'You don't deserve the scandal that would come if I walked out on you.' His heart all but stopped at her admission she'd thought of deserting him permanently. 'But I can't live under the same roof with you again.'

There. She'd said it. His worst nightmare had come to pass.

Terror grabbed greedily at him, digging its talons right down to the bone. Pain eviscerated him.

He opened his mouth to speak but no sound came. After what seemed a lifetime he found his voice. It was brittle with self-mockery. 'And I once believed you loved me.'

Samira's indrawn breath hissed in the silence. 'Neither of us wanted love, remember?'

Tariq nodded, the irony of his situation hitting full-force. 'We don't always get what we want, though, do we?'

'Tariq?' She leaned forward. 'What are you saying?'

He could have drowned in those serious, honey-brown eyes. He owed her the truth, the whole truth.

'I married you believing I could have everything and give little in return. I could have the sexiest, most beautiful woman as my wife, in my bed. I could have your smiles and gentle charm and your passion. All I had to do was sit back and take advantage of my good fortune, no emotional strings attached.'

He drew a shaky breath. 'Until I realised I had it all completely wrong.' He grimaced at his blind stupidity. 'Thinking you'd fallen in love scared the life out of me.' His blood had run cold at the idea of another one-sided love affair. 'I told myself I did the right thing, withdrawing from you.'

Her eyes were huge. 'That's why you gave me the cold shoulder? Because you thought I was in love with you? That's why you didn't come to my bed?' Samira's voice sounded unfamiliar, sharp with pain. Shame filled him.

Tariq looked down at their linked hands, hers so small in his, yet he was under no illusion that he was the stronger of the pair. He was a hollow sham of the man he'd thought himself.

He forced himself to meet her frowning stare. 'At first it was to protect you and the baby. I couldn't let anything happen to you. I needed to keep you safe and sex...' He shrugged. 'You'd already had one miscarriage and I knew how suddenly things could go wrong.'

To Tariq's surprise, Samira's hands tightened on his. 'You were thinking of Jasmin?'

'How could I not? She was fine through her pregnancy, but at the end...' He shook his head. 'I couldn't take any chances. And then, when you told me you wanted more, you wanted *us* together, I panicked.'

'Because you didn't want me falling in love.' Her voice was flat and barren. He hated the way it sounded and that he was the reason for that.

'Because I didn't know any better.' He lifted her hands and pressed his lips to first one, then the other, drawing in the sweet taste of her, sucking her delicious cinnamon scent deep into his lungs.

He had to find a way to keep her. Even if it meant baring his imperfect soul.

'I didn't know any better *then*. I thought love was a curse. Until it hit me.'

Samira stared up into a face hollowed by pain. For a heady second, she'd hoped he meant he felt love too. But that couldn't be. The desolation in his eyes was too profound.

'Tariq? I think you'd better explain.'

'You married a man who didn't believe he could love.'

Familiar pain smote her. 'I know. Jasmin.'

'Yes.' His lips firmed. 'But not the way you think.' His sigh seemed dredged from the depths of his being.

'You don't have to tell me.' Samira didn't think she could bear hearing Tariq rhapsodise about his one true love. Not now when her heart lay cracked and bleeding.

But he wouldn't let her hands go. And the tortured look in his eyes... How could she walk away from him?

'That's one thing I must do, *habibti*—tell you. If nothing else.' Even that casual endearment tugged at her emotions.

He shifted on the sofa, his knees hard against her legs, and Samira forced herself to stay where she was because, whatever ailed Tariq, he needed her for this moment at least.

'I did Jasmin a terrible disservice.' His voice was rough gravel.

'Because you couldn't save her?' Samira had heard enough, now and in Al Sarath, to realise Tariq blamed himself for his first wife's death. 'You did all you could. Everyone says so, even at the hospital. But some things are beyond our power. The medical team did all they could and they're trained for such things.'

Yet there was no lightening of the shadows in his eyes.

'She died because of me. Because I wanted heirs.'

Samira squeezed his hands, unable to bear his anguish.

'She wouldn't have blamed you, Tariq. She loved you.' Samira spoke from the heart, knowing a kindred connection with Jasmin. If the other woman had felt even half of what she, Samira, did, she'd have absolved him.

'She did love me.' His voice was hollow. 'But I didn't love her.'

Samira started. He hadn't loved Jasmin? She felt as if the world revolved too fast, tilting crazily around her.

'Sorry?'

Tariq turned away, but whether he saw the view of Paris out of the window or something else she didn't know.

'I didn't love her. I didn't know how.' He paused. 'I wasn't brought up to love anyone except, of course, my country. My uncle put all his energies into raising me and my cousins to be capable, strong and honest, men who would never shirk from duty or hardship in the right cause.'

'So I gathered.' Samira remembered the stern older man she'd met during one of Tariq's visits to Jazeer. His smile hadn't reached his eyes and, though he'd been polite to the little princess, it was clear he'd been far more interested in the display matches of fencing, wrestling and riding in which his nephew competed.

Tariq's eyes met hers. 'It was an all-male household. Love wasn't a factor in our lives. We were trained in toughness and above all self-sufficiency. So when it came time to marry—'

'You decided on an arranged marriage.' She'd imagined Tariq swept off his feet by love for Jasmin when instead he'd done as generations of sheikhs before him had done and made a dynastic marriage.

'Not quite immediately.' Something flickered in his eyes, something bright and hot. Then he blinked and it was gone. 'But you're right. Jasmin was suitable in every way: charming, well-born, beautiful and...' He paused. 'A genuinely nice woman.'

Samira blinked. *A genuinely nice woman.* That, finally, convinced her Tariq hadn't been in love with his first wife.

Did he think of Samira as a *genuinely nice woman* too? She didn't think she could bear it.

'And she loved you.' Samira's stomach plummeted in a sickening rush as she realised how much she had in common with Jasmin. Both of them had been in love with a man who didn't return their feelings. How had Jasmin borne it?

'Not initially, at least I believed not. I was absolutely honest about my reasons for marriage. I didn't pretend to romance. But as time went by...' He shook his head. 'Jasmin loved me. She didn't hide it, and she never reproached me for not returning her feelings, but I saw the hurt in her eyes.'

His hands tightened on Samira's and she felt the tension in him.

'She was a caring wife, a good queen. I tried to give her what she most wanted. I tried so hard but I just didn't have it in me. I failed her.'

Samira wanted to tell him that falling in love wasn't something you tried to do. It just happened. But that would bring no comfort. Not to him or to her.

They were in the same place now, weren't they? One loved and one didn't. She compressed her lips, holding back the flood of useless words that hovered on her tongue, choking back distress.

Finally she spoke. 'No one can switch love on just because they want to. You did your best. Everyone says you were devoted to her.'

'I tried. But it wasn't anything like what she felt for me.' His eyes snared hers and Samira's heart gave a mighty thump. 'I realised that when I met you again in Paris.'

'When you met *me*?' Confusion filled her. She knew she shouldn't prolong the agony of this conversation but she couldn't wrench herself away.

He loosened his grip on her hands and looked down, watching his long fingers stroke hers, tracing the exquisite solitaire ruby ring that had been his betrothal gift. What was he thinking?

'When I saw you again I felt things I hadn't felt in years. Emotions I'd pushed aside. New feelings too, things that were unfamiliar.'

Samira stared.

He sat up, his gaze mesmerising. 'I'd wanted you years ago, when you were on the verge of womanhood. I wanted you even more when I saw you in Paris. So desperately I couldn't bear the thought of you walking out and proposing to some other man who'd agree to marry you in an instant.'

'You didn't show it.' If anything he'd been cold—disapproving and haughty.

'Didn't I? I hardly knew what I was doing.'

Samira tugged her hands free and surged to her feet, stepping away from him. 'So, you *wanted* me.' She swallowed hard. Nothing had changed. Tariq was a virile man and he wasn't used to being denied. 'But why did you have to *marry* me?'

She choked back a sob of despair. If they hadn't married she wouldn't have fallen in love with him. She wouldn't feel this awful desolation.

Large hands settled on her upper arms. His warmth branded her and she shut her eyes, telling herself she'd pull away in a moment.

'Because I felt more for you, Samira, than I ever have in my life. Because I felt things I couldn't put a name to. Things that made me feel...different.'

His breath feathered her hair, his chest pressing against her shoulders. 'I needed you in my world as I've never needed anyone. I couldn't imagine life without you in it. I didn't just want you in my bed or at my side at banquets and receptions. You were a part of me and I couldn't bear to release you again.'

'Tariq?'

She made to turn but he stopped her, his body close as a shadow, warming her back. His words, his presence, were almost too much to cope with, but nothing in this world would tear her away.

'I wanted you in every way a man can conceivably want a woman, Samira. I'll always want you like that.' His words were pure magic, hypnotising her and evoking tentative joy. 'I love you. I just didn't recognise what it was.'

'You love me?' Her heart seized, then catapulted into life again.

He pressed his lips to her hair in the gentlest caress and her eyelids fluttered as emotion filled her. She had to be dreaming. Yet with his words in her ears, his touch on her body, it felt so *real*.

'I think I came close to loving you all those years ago, though I couldn't put a name to it then. Certainly I planned to marry you, until I heard you were going to study overseas.'

'And that stopped you?' Still she couldn't believe it.

'I felt guilty lusting after a teenager. What right had I to come between you and your dreams? Besides, I needed a wife in Al Sarath, not in Paris or New York.'

'I don't… I can't believe it.' It was too far-fetched. 'You said you couldn't love.'

'All my life I thought so.' His mouth moved against her scalp. 'I didn't realise, you see. I spent so long telling myself that because I couldn't give Jasmin what she wanted. Yet the moment you walked back into my life there was no escaping. It was a *coup de foudre*—a flash of lightning hitting me out of the blue.'

'You never said anything.' Samira struggled to be sensible, not let herself be swept away by the wave of elation rising inside.

Tariq loved her?

'I didn't know what it was.' His lips caressed the side of her neck and she shivered, her resistance cracking. 'I just knew I needed you. When I thought you might love me I was terrified, fearing I'd let you down too. Until you withdrew and it hit me what I'd lost.'

'*You* withdrew from *me*!'

'I was a coward. I'd never felt anything like this. It scared me witless. All these months I've wanted to hold you close and never let you go, but I but didn't dare. I was frantic I might lose you.'

As he'd lost Jasmin. Suddenly she registered that Tariq's big body was shaking.

She spun around. Blazing eyes of darkest tourmaline captured her gaze and his raw emotion blasted her. She felt she looked straight into his soul.

'I love you, Samira. I know I haven't made you happy but give me a second chance. I can't lose you.' His voice was uneven and Samira stared, stunned by such vulnerability in this man who was always calm and in control.

'I don't want to lose you either, Tariq.' It was hard to swallow over the knot in her throat.

'But you left.'

'I couldn't bear the rejection any longer. You'd grown so cold. You never wanted to be with me.'

In a single, swooping movement Tariq wrapped his arms around her and tugged her tight against him. His body was furnace-hot, burning right through the chill that had clamped her. She had to arch her neck to meet his gaze and what she saw there was the most wondrous sight in the world.

Samira never wanted to move. Her hands splayed across

his chest where his heart hammered, its racing beat a match for hers.

'My little love.' His smile was crooked. 'I was trying to give you space because I thought I was making you unhappy. You needed to recover from the birth and—'

'What I needed was you to hold me and never let me go.'

'Really?' Doubt showed in his expression.

'Absolutely.'

'I've still got a lot to learn about...' His shoulders rose expressively.

'About love?' He nodded and Samira breathed deep. 'You think I don't? Love was the one thing I've tried to avoid as long as I can remember. Especially after Jackson.'

Tariq's embrace firmed, pulling her against hard muscle and bone. 'Don't talk about him.'

'It doesn't hurt now.'

'I don't care. I don't want his name on your lips.' In a flash the autocrat was back. She looked up at Tariq's strong face and elation rose.

'Because you're jealous?' It didn't seem possible that a man like Tariq—proud, powerful and so very dear— could be jealous.

'Of course I am.' He paused, watching her intently. 'You haven't told me how you feel, Samira.'

Wasn't it already crystal clear?

'I love you, Tariq.' It felt so good to say it aloud for the first time.

The look on his face made her gulp and something in her chest rose and swelled. Joy overwhelmed her and her eyes glazed.

'You don't look happy about it.' His voice was gruff.

She blinked. 'Don't you know women cry when they're happy?'

'You're happy?' He traced one finger over her cheek

and she sighed at the overwhelming sense of rightness at his touch. 'You really love me?'

'I really, truly love you.'

'And I wuv you.' A tiny arm wrapped around her legs and Samira looked down to see Risay, his hair tumbling over his forehead, his pyjamas askew, with his arms around the pair of them. 'I stay wiv Mummy.'

No little boy had ever looked more adorable with his big brown eyes and wide smile.

'Bringing in the reinforcements to argue your case, Tariq?' she said shakily as he bent to lift their son high off the ground.

Her husband's answering grin ignited that inevitable spark deep inside. 'A good general marshals all his forces to win victory.'

'Is that how you feel—victorious?' She kissed Risay on the cheek and slanted a sideways look at her husband.

He shook his head. 'Not victorious. I don't think I could ever take this for granted.'

He bent and kissed her full on the mouth, ignoring Risay's giggles, and Samira clutched him close, her heart welling with tenderness and awe.

'But I'm the happiest man alive. And I intend to make you the happiest woman.'

EPILOGUE

'SHE'S A DARLING, isn't she?' Samira looked at the delicate features of their little daughter as Tariq placed her in the cot and drew up the sheet. The sight of him, such a big, brawny hunk of a man, so infinitely gentle with the tiny, trusting child made her heart turn over.

He was everything she could ever want in a man and more. Far more.

He turned, pausing when he saw her expression. Then he reached out, drawing her close. Her breath sighed out as he pressed her head to his shoulder and she felt the strong, steady beat of his heart. She slid her arms around him, squeezing tight.

'She *is* a darling.' His voice rumbled up against her ear. 'Just like her mother.'

Samira smiled. After two years of marriage, she was complacent, knowing Tariq always spoke the truth to her now. There was nothing but honesty between them and a deep, abiding love that filled her world to the brim.

Callused fingers tilted her chin up. 'Thank you, *habibti*.'

Her brow knitted as she met his eyes and felt the inevitable snap and sizzle between them.

'What for? I was the one who wanted another baby.'

'And it was a pleasure to let you persuade me.' Heat gleamed in those mesmerising eyes and Samira's breath caught.

'You didn't take much persuading.'

'What can I say?' Tariq smoothed his palms down her back and she arched into him. 'I enjoy your persuasion so much.'

Her heart skipped a beat at the look he gave her. Sometimes she couldn't believe how lucky she was.

'Not every man would agree to adopt.' But she'd had to ask. The little orphaned girl, born in one of the mountain villages and destined for an orphanage, had stolen her heart.

'Then I'm happy not to be every man.' Tariq's words dragged her back to the present. 'Not every man is fortunate enough to marry his soul mate.'

He bent and pressed a gentle kiss to her brow, the tender salute melting her insides, making her cling tight.

'Thank you, my sweet, for your generosity in naming her Jasmin. Not many women would do that.'

Samira shook her head, smiling. Secure in Tariq's love, she no longer felt jealous of his first wife. 'She was a special person. Look at the sons she produced.'

It had been a chance symbolically to lay the ghost of Tariq's guilt to rest. The shadows had gone from his eyes now that he'd stopped looking back to the past, too focused on the present and his growing family.

'You're a woman in a million, Samira.' He cupped her face and brushed his firm lips across hers, stealing her breath.

'I'm glad you think so.'

'Oh, I know so.' Something glittered in his eyes and Samira had no trouble identifying it now.

Love. Love that he didn't bother to mask.

As ever, her pulse pounded in response, joy making her mouth curve in a smile that came straight from her soul.

An instant later he'd scooped her up in his arms, holding her high against his chest as he strode out the door and back through their suite.

He didn't stop in the sitting room where his official files and her latest sketches awaited them. Instead he kept going into the bedroom.

'Tariq! You told me you had work you wanted to finish tonight.'

He stopped at the foot of the wide bed, slanting a knowing look her way. Instantly heat eddied deep inside.

'It can wait,' he growled, his gaze tracking over her body. 'Besides, I'm being a supportive husband, showing an interest in my wife's career.' His mouth kicked up at one side in a hungry smile that made her breath hitch. 'Take off that wrap and show me the new nightgown you've designed.'

Samira leaned in and pressed a kiss to the bare skin at his collarbone, tasting the salt tang of his warm flesh, feeling her pulse riot inevitably in response.

'Of course, Your Highness.' She sent him a sultry look that made him groan. 'Your wish is my command.'

* * * * *

THE DOCTOR
TAKES A PRINCESS

LEANNE BANKS

This book is dedicated to all those
underestimated women with tender hearts
and big fears who hide it all with a big smile.
Thank you for being so much more
than we give you credit for.

Prologue

Ryder McCall raced the double baby stroller into the elevator just as the doors started to close. The twin boys cackled with glee at the wild ride as he pressed the button for the eighth floor. He'd already rescheduled the appointment with his attorney three times and he would have done it again if he'd known the nanny was going to bail on him. Again.

In the back of his mind, he counted his pulse. His heart rate was higher now than when he'd run a half marathon last year. His life was far different now, he thought as he glanced at the boys and caught a swishing movement behind him. Stepping to the side, he saw a woman dressed in a pink cocktail gown that skimmed over her creamy shoulders and her curvy body. The dress ended just above her knees, revealing a tempting glimpse of her legs and high-heeled sandals. The medical expert in him knew the negative impact of high heels on the human body, but the man in him was trying to remember the last time he'd been out with a woman. He was having a tough time remembering.

The woman smiled at him and gestured toward the twins. "They're adorable. I bet they keep you busy."

He nodded. "More than you could—"

The elevator suddenly jolted and dropped several feet, then stopped.

Ryder glanced at the boys at the same time he heard the woman's intake of breath. "Everyone okay?"

The twins just looked at them with wide eyes.

"Are we stuck?" the woman asked, her brow furrowed with worry.

"Let me see," he said and pushed the button for another floor. The elevator didn't move. He pushed the button to open the doors and nothing happened. He pushed the alarm button and a piercing sound filled the elevator.

The woman covered her ears. "Oh, my—"

A voice came on an intercom. "This is building security. Do you have a problem?"

"We're stuck," Ryder yelled over the terrible pulsating alarm. He heard a sob from one of the boys. A half beat later, the other started, louder.

"So sorry, sir. We'll come and fix it soon."

"Soon," he echoed as the twins began to cry in earnest. "When is soon?"

"As soon as possible," the woman on the intercom said and there was a clicking noise. The alarm shut off, but the boys were in high gear.

"Oh, the poor things. They must be frightened," the woman in the elevator said. She paused a moment, then shrugged. "Here, I'll hold one of them."

Ryder shot a skeptical glance at her. "They haven't had their baths and they're very messy eaters." Tyler was wearing a gross combination of yellow and orange on his blue shirt while Travis clearly had not enjoyed his strained peas. Green smudges decorated the light blue shirt that matched his brother's.

The woman made a tsking sound. "Well, we have to do something. We can't let them keep screaming." She set her purse on the floor and held out her hands. "Go ahead, give one of them to me," she insisted in a voice that sounded as if she were accustomed to having her orders followed.

As a medical doctor and acting chief adviser for the residents at Texas Medical Center, he, too, was accustomed to having his orders followed. This time, though, he decided to allow the woman to take Tyler because the baby was clearly beyond upset. As soon as he set the boy in her arms, she bobbed as if she'd handled a crying baby before. Ryder hauled Travis out of his stroller seat and also bobbed.

The woman made soothing sounds and Tyler gradually quieted between hiccups. As usual, Travis took a little longer. He was the louder boy of the two.

"That's better," she said. "Who am I holding?"

"Tyler," Ryder said. "This is Travis. I'm Ryder McCall. Thank you for your help."

"You're quite welcome," she said in a voice that seemed to combine several accents, none of which originated from Texas. "I'm Bridget," she said and fanned herself with the shawl draped over her arm. "Whew, it's getting warm already."

"And it's only going to get hotter until they fix the elevator. Are you feeling faint?" he asked, aware that plenty of people would grow light-headed in this situation.

She shook her head. "No."

"I'd offer you some water, but I was in a hurry when I left the house, so all I've got are bottles for the boys."

"Well, at least you have that," she said and glanced at her watch. "I hope we're not stuck for long. Perhaps I should call my friends." She bent toward the floor and shook her head. "I'm sorry, Tyler. I'm going to have to put you down for a moment," she murmured and carefully placed the tot in his stroller seat. She picked up her phone and punched some numbers, then frowned.

"Let me guess," Ryder said. "No service."

She nodded.

"Figures. The steel doors can sustain most catastrophes known to man, so they're bound to make it difficult to get a cell connection."

She bit her lip and winced. "Oh, I wonder if someone will call my security."

"They're on their way," he said, wondering if she hadn't understood the conversation he'd had with the woman earlier. Maybe she hadn't heard correctly, he thought, between the alarm bleeping and the boys screaming. "At least, they better be on their way. I hope the boys don't—"

"Need a diaper change?" she asked, nodding in understanding. "Time for the—"

"Nanny," he said in complete agreement. "I just wish I could find one who would stay around longer than two weeks."

"That sounds difficult. Are you working with an agency?"

He nodded. "Part of the problem is I work long hours."

"Hmm, and your wife?"

"I don't have a wife," he said.

Her eyes widened. "Oh, that must make it very difficult."

Ryder sighed. "I'm actually the boys' godfather. My brother and his wife were killed in an automobile accident one month ago."

Bridget gasped. "That's terrible. Those poor boys, and you, oh my goodness. Do you have any help at all?"

"Not unless I hire them," he muttered. "Do you have any children?"

She shook her head quickly, the same way he would have before he'd learned he would be raising the boys. "Two baby nieces," she said.

"That's how you knew to bob up and down with Tyler," he said.

"Yes," Bridget said and glanced at her watch again, growing uneasy. She'd agreed to the charity appearance she would be attending as a favor to her sister's long-time friend, and her security was only a three-button code away if she should need them. If her sister's friend became uneasy, however, she might call Valentina.

Valentina might call security to check on her and…
She shuddered at the public scene that would cause.
Bridget was here in Dallas to do the job her brother had
asked of her and as soon as she was done, she was off
to Italy.

It was so warm that she was getting past the glow
stage. Right now, she probably looked like she'd just finished a spinning class, although she did those as rarely
as possible. Getting sweaty wouldn't matter that much
to her if she weren't being photographed. During the last
year and a half, however, it had been drilled into her that
her appearance in front of the camera was a reflection
of her country. It was her duty to look immaculate and
to avoid scandal at all cost.

Bridget had slipped a few times on both counts. She
might be a princess, but she wasn't perfect. Nor was
she particularly patient. She could tell that Ryder, the
other adult in the elevator, wasn't patient either. He was
glancing upward as if he were assessing the structure
of the lift.

"You're not thinking of climbing out, are you?" she
couldn't resist asking.

"If no one shows up, I may have to," he said.

"And what were you planning to do with the babies?"
she demanded, panicked at the prospect of being left
alone with the twins. Now that she thought of it, Ryder's
presence had made her feel much more reassured.

He shot her a level look. "The purpose of getting out
would be to ensure safety for all of us."

He looked like a no-nonsense kind of man, strong,
perhaps intolerant of anyone weaker than himself.

Which would include her. Okay, she was making assumptions. But what else could she bloody do? She was stuck in an elevator with the man. She couldn't deny the appeal of his strong jaw and lean but muscular body. She also couldn't deny her admiration that he had taken on his brother's orphaned twins.

An instant parent of twin boys? The mere thought made her sweat even more. Bridget would have forced herself to accept her responsibility in such a situation, but hopefully with sufficient support. Multiple children, multiple nannies.

She sighed, glancing at the emergency button. "We've heard nothing. Do you think we should call again?"

"It will make the boys cry again," he said, clearly torn.

"I'll take Tyler," she said and picked up the baby. He flashed her a smile that gave her a burst of pleasure despite their situation. "You're a little flirt, aren't you?" she said and tickled his chin.

Ryder stabbed the button and the shrieking alarm started. Tyler's smile immediately fell and his eyes filled with fear. He began to scream. His brother began to wail.

Seconds later, the alarm stopped and a voice came on the intercom, but Bridget couldn't make out the conversation with Ryder as she tried to comfort Tyler. The only thing she knew was that Ryder had spoken in a firm, commanding voice that rivaled that of her brother's, and anyone in their right mind had better obey.

The intercom voice went away, but the babies still cried. Bridget and Tyler bobbed. "What did they say?"

"They said they would take care of us in five minutes," he yelled over the cries of the boys.

"How did you do that?"

"I told them I was climbing out in three," he said.

"Effective. I wonder if I should try that sometime," she mused. "Is there anything else we can do to settle them down?" she asked loudly, still shielding Tyler's closest ear with her hand.

A long-suffering expression crossed his face. "Just one thing," he said. "Row, row, row your boat, gently down the stream."

Bridget stared in amazement at this man who reminded her of a modern-day warrior singing a children's song and something inside her shifted. The sensation made her feel light-headed. Alarm shot through her. Or perhaps, it was the heat. Pushing the odd feeling and any self-consciousness aside, she sang along.

Six minutes later, the elevator doors opened with a swarm of firemen, paramedics and Bridget's security guard standing outside.

"Your Highness," her security guard said, extending his hand to her.

"Just a second," she said, putting Tyler into his stroller seat.

"Your Highness?" Ryder echoed, studying her with a curious gaze. "Why didn't you—"

"It—it causes a fuss," she said. "Will you be okay? Will the children be okay?"

"We're fine," he said, and she felt foolish for questioning such a capable man.

"Well, thank you," she said and extended her hand

to his, noting that his hands were smooth, but large and strong. She felt an odd little spark and immediately pulled back. "And good luck."

"Your Highness, a medical professional is waiting to examine you," her security said as she stepped off the lift.

"I don't need a medical professional," she murmured. "I need a cosmetic miracle."

Chapter One

Sitting at the kitchen table of her brother-in-law's ranch, Bridget watched Zach Logan hug her sister Valentina as if he were leaving for a yearlong journey. Instead, she knew he would be gone for only a couple of nights. Bridget resisted the urge to roll her eyes. Zach and Valentina just seemed so gooey in love.

"Call me if you need anything," he told her, then swung his young daughter, Katiana, up into his arms. "Are you going to be good for your mommy?"

Katiana solemnly nodded.

"Give me a kiss," he said.

The toddler kissed his cheek and wrapped her little arms around his neck.

Despite her earlier reaction, the scene tugged at Bridget's heart. She knew Zach and Tina had gone through some tough times before they'd gotten married.

Zach shot Bridget a firm glance that instinctively

made her sit up straighter. He was that kind of man, confident with a strong will. Although she was happy Tina had found happiness with him, Bridget knew she would want a totally different kind of man. Charming, average intelligence, playful and most likely Italian.

"You," he said, pointing his finger at Bridget. "Stay out of elevators."

She laughed. "I can only promise that for a few days. When I go back to Dallas, I'm sure I'll have to face more elevators if I'm going to complete Stefan's latest job for me. If I have anything to do with it, I'm going to take care of it as quickly as possible."

Tina shot her a sideways glance. "Are you saying you're already tired of us?"

Bridget shook her head and walked to give her sister a hug. "Of course I'm not tired of you. But you know I've had a dream of having a long-delayed gap year in Italy and studying art for years now. I want to make that dream come true while I'm still young."

Tina made a scoffing sound, but still returned the hug. "You're far from losing your youth, but I agree you deserve a break. You've taken on the bulk of public appearances since I left Chantaine and moved here. I don't understand why you didn't take a break before coming here. I'm sure Stefan would have let you."

Stefan, their brother, the crown prince, could be the most demanding person on the planet, but what Tina said was true. He not only would have allowed Bridget a break, he had also encouraged it. "I want a year. A whole year. And he believes Chantaine needs more doctors. I agree. Especially after what happened to Eve—"

Her voice broke, taking her by surprise. She'd thought she'd gotten her feelings under control.

Tina patted her back with sympathy. "You still feel guilty about that. I know Eve wishes you didn't."

Bridget took a careful breath, reining in her emotions. "She saved my life when the crowd was going to stampede me. Pushed me aside and threw herself in front of me. I'm just so glad she survived it and recovered. I don't know what I would do if she hadn't…" Her throat closed up again.

"Well, she survived and you did, too. That's what's important," Zach said and pulled Bridget into a brotherly hug. "And now that you're in my territory, I want you to think twice before getting on elevators."

Tina laughed. "So protective," she said. "It's a wonder he doesn't find some kind of testing device for you to use so you won't get stuck again."

Zach rubbed his chin thoughtfully. "Not a bad idea. Maybe—"

"Forget it," Bridget said, the knot in her chest easing at the love she felt from both her sister and her brother-in-law. "I'll be fine. Think about it. How many people do you know who have gotten stuck in elevators? Especially more than once?"

"You were a good soldier," Tina said in approval. "And you still showed up for your appearance at Keely's charity event."

"She probably wasn't expecting me in my sad state with droopy hair and a dress with baby-food stain on it."

"Oh, she said they loved you. Found you charming.

Were delighted by your story about the elevator. Most important, the donations increased after your arrival."

"Well, I guess baby-food stains are good for something, then. I'll leave you two lovebirds to finish your goodbyes in private. Safe travels, Zach."

"You bet," he said.

Bridget scooped up her cup of hot tea and walked upstairs to the guest room where she was staying. Her sister had redecorated the room in soothing shades of green and blue. The ranch should have given Bridget a sense of serenity. After all, she was miles from Stefan and his to-do list for her. She was away from Chantaine where she was recognized and haunted by the paparazzi whenever she left the palace. But Bridget never seemed to be able to escape the restlessness inside her. That was why she'd decided to skip a short vacation and take care of this significant task Stefan had asked of her. After that, she could take her trip to Italy and find her peace again.

No one had ever accused Bridget of being deep. She voiced her distress and upset to her family at will, but presented the rest of the world with a cheery effervescent face. It was her job.

Some of the conditions she'd witnessed during the past year and a half, the sights and sounds of children sick in the hospital, Chantaine's citizens struggling with poverty, cut her to the quick and it had been difficult to keep her winsome attitude intact. It irritated her how much she now had to struggle to maintain a superficial air. Life had been so much easier when she hadn't faced others in need. Life had been easier when someone hadn't been willing to sacrifice her life for the sake of Bridget's safety.

Even though Eve had indeed survived and thrived since the accident, something inside Bridget had changed. And she wasn't sure she liked it. Eve and Stefan had fallen in love and married. Eve cared for Stefan's out-of-wedlock daughter as if she were her own. On the face of it, everything was wonderful.

Deep down, though, Bridget wondered if her life was really worth saving. What had she done that made her worthy of such an act?

She squeezed her eyes shut and swore under her breath. "Stop asking that question," she whispered harshly to herself.

Steeling herself against the ugly swarm of emotions, Bridget set her cup of tea on the table. She would complete the task Stefan asked of her. Then maybe she would have settled the score inside her, the score she couldn't quite explain even to herself. Afterward she would go to Italy and hopefully she would find the joy and lightness she'd lost.

After three days of being unable to meet with the head of residents at Texas Medical Center of Dallas, Bridget seethed with impatience. Dr. Gordon Walters was never available, and all her calls to his office went unanswered. Thank goodness for connections. Apparently Tina's friend Keely knew a doctor at University Hospital and there just happened to be a meet and greet for interns, doctors and important donors at a hotel near the hospital on Tuesday night.

Bridget checked into the hotel and her security took the room next to hers. One advantage of being at Zach's ranch meant security was superfluous. Not so in Dallas. She dressed carefully because she needed to impress and to be taken seriously. A black dress with heels. She resisted the urge to paint her lips red. The old Bridget wouldn't have batted an eye.

Frowning into the bathroom mirror in her suite, she wondered what that meant. Well, hell, if Madonna could wear red lipstick and be taken seriously, why couldn't she? She smoothed her fingers over her head and tucked one side of her hair behind her left ear. She'd colored her hair darker lately. It fit her mood.

She frowned again into the mirror. Maybe she would dye it blond when she moved to Italy.

She punched the code for her security on her cell phone. Raoul picked up immediately. "Yes, Your Highness."

"I'm ready. Please stay in the background," she said.

"Yes, ma'am. But I shall join you on the elevator."

A couple moments later, she rode said elevator to the floor which held the meeting rooms and ballrooms. A host stood outside the ballroom which housed the cocktail party she would attend. "Name?" he asked as she approached him.

She blinked, unaccustomed to being screened. Doors opened at the mention of her title. Not in Texas, she supposed. "Bridget Devereaux and escort," she said, because Raoul was beside her.

The man flipped through several pages and checked off her name. "Welcome," he said. "Please go in."

"The nerve of the man," Raoul said as they entered the ballroom full of people. "To question a member of the royal family," he fumed as he surveyed the room.

Bridget smiled. "Novel experience," she said. "I'm looking for Dr. Gordon Walters. If you see him, by all means, please do tell me."

Thirty minutes later, Bridget was ready to pull out her hair. Every time she mentioned Dr. Walters's name, people clammed up. She couldn't squeeze even a bit of information about the man from anyone.

Frustrated, she accepted a glass of wine and decided to take another tack.

Dr. Ryder McCall checked his watch for the hundredth time in ten minutes. How much longer did he need to stay? The latest nanny he'd hired had seemed okay when he'd left tonight, but after his previous experiences, he couldn't be sure. He caught a glimpse of the back of a woman with dark brown wavy hair and paused. Something about her looked familiar.

The dress was classic and on a woman with a different body, it would have evoked images of that actress. What was her name? Audrey something. But this woman had curves which evoked entirely different thoughts. The sight of the woman's round derriere reminded Ryder of the fact that he hadn't been with a woman in a while. Too long, he thought and adjusted his tie.

Curious, he moved so that he could catch a side view of her. Oh yeah, he thought, his gaze sliding over her feminine form from her calves to her thighs to the thrust of her breasts. He could easily imagine her minus the dress. His body responded. Then he glanced upward to her face and recognition slammed into him.

The woman speaking so animatedly to one of his

top residents, Timothy Bing, was the same woman he'd met in the elevator the other night. Princess whatever. Bridget, he recalled. And of course, his top resident was utterly enthralled. Why wouldn't he be? The poor resident was sleep-deprived, food-deprived and sex-deprived.

Ryder was suffering from the same deprivation albeit for different reasons. He wondered why she was here tonight. Might as well cure his curiosity, he thought, if he couldn't cure his other deprivations. He walked toward the two of them.

Timothy only had eyes for Her Highness. Ryder cleared his throat. Both Timothy and the woman turned to look at him.

Timothy stiffened as if he were a marine and he'd just glimpsed a superior. Ryder almost wondered if he would salute. "Dr. McCall," he said.

Bridget looked at him curiously. "Doctor?" she echoed. "I didn't know you were a doctor."

"We didn't have much time to discuss our occupations. Your Highness," he added.

Out of the corner of his vision, he saw Timothy's eyes bulge in surprise. "Highness," he said. "Are you a queen or something? I thought you said you were a representative of Chantaine."

Bridget shot Ryder a glare, then smiled sweetly at Timothy. "I am a representative of Chantaine. A royal representative, and I hope you'll consider the proposal I gave you about serving in Chantaine for a couple of years in exchange for a scholarship and all your living expenses."

Ryder stared at the woman in horrified silence. She

was trying to seduce away one of his prized residents. Timothy was brilliant. His next step should be to one of the top neurological hospitals in the States.

Ryder laughed. "Not in a million years," he said.

Bridget furrowed her brow. "Why not? It's a generous offer. Dr. Bing would benefit, as would Chantaine."

"Because Dr. Bing is not going to make a gigantic misstep in his career by taking off for an island retreat when he could be one of the top neurological surgeons in America."

Bridget's furrow turned to a frown. "I find it insulting that you consider a temporary move to Chantaine a misstep. Our citizens suffer from neurological illnesses, too. Is it not the goal of a doctor to heal? Why should there be a prejudice against us just because we reside in a beautiful place? Does that mean we shouldn't have treatment?"

"I wasn't suggesting that your country doesn't deserve medical care. It's my job, however, to advise Dr. Bing to make the best decisions in advancing his career and knowledge."

Princess Bridget crossed her arms over her chest and looked down her nose at him. "I thought that was Dr. Gordon Walters's job, although the man is nowhere to be found."

Timothy made a choking sound. "Excuse me," he said. "I need to…" He walked quickly away without finishing his sentence.

"Well, now you've done it," she said. "I was having a perfectly lovely conversation with Dr. Bing and you ruined it."

"Me?"

"Yes, you. The whole tenor of our conversation changed when you appeared. Dr. Bing was actually open to considering my offer to come to Chantaine."

"Dr. Bing wanted to get into your pants," Ryder said and immediately regretted his blunt statement.

Bridget shot him a shocked glance. "You're the most insulting man I've ever met."

"You clearly haven't met many residents," he said wearily. "I apologize if I offended you, but Timothy Bing doesn't belong in Chantley or wherever you said you're from."

"Chantaine," she said between gritted teeth. "I will accept your apology if you can direct me to Dr. Gordon Walters. He is the man I must meet."

Ryder sighed. "I'm afraid I'm going to have to disappoint you. Dr. Gordon Walters is not here tonight. He hasn't been working in the position as chief resident adviser for some time. It's not likely he'll return."

She cocked her head to one side and frowned further. "Then who will take his place?"

"No one will take his place. Dr. Walters is rightfully loved and respected. I am serving as his temporary successor."

Realization crossed her face. "How wonderful," she said, when she clearly found the news anything but.

Bloody hell, Bridget thought, clenching her fingers together. Now she'd put herself in a mess. She took a deep breath and tried to calm herself. Yes, she and Dr. McCall had engaged in a spirited discussion, but surely he would come around once he heard more about Chantaine and the program she was offering.

"Well, I'm glad I've finally found the person who is currently in charge. Our first meeting in the elevator showed that you and I are both responsible, reasonable adults. I'm sure we'll be able to come to an understanding on this matter," she said, imbuing her words with every bit of positive energy she could muster.

Dr. McCall shot her a skeptical glance. "I'll agree with your first point, but I can't promise anything on the second. It's good to see you again, Your Highness." His gaze gave her a quick sweep from head to toe and back again. "Nice dress. Good evening," he said and turned to leave.

It took Bridget an extra second to recover from the understated compliment that inexplicably flustered before she went after him. "Wait, please," she said.

Dr. McCall stopped and turned, looking at her with a raised eyebrow. "Yes?"

"I really do need to discuss Chantaine's medical needs with you. I'm hoping we can come to some sort of agreement."

"I already told you I couldn't recommend that Timothy Bing spend two years in your country," he said.

"But you have other students," she said. "I'm sure you have students interested in many different areas of medical care. Coming to Chantaine would enable the physicians to get hands-on experience. Plus there's the matter of the financial assistance we would offer."

"I'm sorry, Your High—"

"Oh, please," she said, unable to contain her impatience. "Call me Bridget. We've sung together in an elevator, for bloody sake."

His lips twitched slightly. "True. Bridget, I'm not

sure I can help you. Again, my number-one priority is guiding my students to make the best career decisions."

Her heart sank. "Well, the least you can do is give me an opportunity to discuss Chantaine's needs and what we have to offer."

He sighed and shrugged his shoulders in a discouraging way, then pulled a card from his pocket. "Okay. Here's my card. My schedule is very busy, but call my assistant and she'll work you in."

Work her in. Bridget clenched her teeth slightly at the words, but forced a smile. "Thank you. You won't regret it."

"Hmm," he said in a noncommittal tone and walked away.

She barely resisted the urge to stick out her tongue at him.

Raoul appeared by her side. "Are you all right, Your Highness? You look upset."

"I do?" she asked, composing herself into what she hoped look like a serene expression. She was finding it more and more difficult to pull off instant serenity these days. "I'm fine," she said. "I've just encountered a slight obstacle to completing my assignment for Chantaine."

She watched Ryder McCall's broad shoulders and tall form as he wove through the crowd. Slight obstacle was putting it mildly, but she'd learned that a positive attitude could get a woman through a lot of tricky spots. "I need to know everything about Dr. Ryder McCall by morning, if not before," she muttered and glanced around the room. It was amazing what one could learn about a person in a social situation such as this. She might as well make the best of it.

* * *

Ryder walked into his house braced for chaos. His home life had become one big state of chaos bigger than the state of Texas since he'd inherited his brother's boys. Instead of pandemonium, his home was dark and quiet, except for the sound of a baseball game. Ryder spotted his longtime pal Marshall lounging on the leather couch with a box of half-eaten pizza on the coffee table and a beer in his hand.

"Your sitter called me," Marshall said, not rising. "As your official backup. She said one of her kids got sick, so she couldn't stay. Just curious, where am I on that backup list?"

Pretty far down, Ryder thought, but didn't admit it. There were two middle-aged neighbors, an aunt on the other side of town and his admin assistant before Marshall. Ryder suspected he'd called in favors too often if everyone had refused but Marshall. "Thanks for coming. How are the boys?"

Marshall cracked a wily grin. "Great. Gave them a few Cheerios, wore them out and tossed them into bed."

"Bath?" he asked.

"The sitter took care of that before I got here. That Travis is a pistol. Didn't want to go to sleep, so I gave him my best Garth Brooks."

Ryder gave a tired smile. "Must have worked. I'll give a quick check and be right back."

"Cold one's waiting," Marshall said.

Ryder trusted Marshall to a degree, but he didn't think leaving the kids with his buddy from high school on a regular basis was a good idea. He wouldn't put it past Marshall to slip the boys a sip from his beer if he was desperate enough. When pressured, Marshall could get a little too creative, like the time he hot-wired the car of one of the school's top wrestlers because his own car had died.

Marshall owned a chain of auto-mechanic shops across Texas. He wore his hair in a ponytail and tattoos were stamped over his arms and back. He hadn't attended college, but he'd made a success of himself. Most people couldn't understand their friendship because they appeared to be total opposites, but a mutual appreciation for baseball, some shared holiday dinners which had always included hotdogs and hamburgers and the fact that they both tried to show up during the hard times had made them like family.

With his brother Cory gone, Marshall was the closest thing to family Ryder had. His gut twisted at the thought, but he shoved the feeling aside and gently opened the door to the nursery. He'd learned to walk with stealthlike quiet during the last month. The possibility of waking the boys made him break into a cold sweat.

Moving toward the closest crib, he glanced inside and even in the dark, he knew that this was Tyler, and he was in Travis's bed. Travis was in Tyler's bed. He wasn't going to complain. They were both lying on their backs in la-la land. Which was exactly where he would like to be.

Instead, he walked on quiet footsteps out of the room and gently closed the door behind him. Returning to the den, he saw Marshall still sprawled on his sofa with the same beer in his hand.

"They're asleep," Ryder said and sank into a leather chair next to the sofa. He raked his hand through his hair.

"I coulda told you that," Marshall said. "I made sure they would sleep well tonight."

He shot a quick glance at Marshall. "You didn't give them any booze, did you?"

Marshall looked offended. "Booze to babies? What kind of nut job do you think I am?"

"Well, you aren't around kids very much," Ryder said.

"Maybe not now, but I was an in-demand babysitter in junior high school. Some things you don't forget. And just in case you're worried, this is my second beer. I wouldn't go on a bender when I was taking care of your kids."

Chagrined, Ryder rubbed his chin. "You got me. Sorry, bud. Being in charge of two kids is making me a little crazy."

"A little?" Marshall said and shook his head. "You've turned into the nut job. You know what your problem is, you're no fun anymore. Those babies sense it and it gets them all uptight, too. It's like a virus. You spread it to the babysitters and it makes them crazy, so they quit. You need to get laid and go to a ball game."

"Thanks for the advice," Ryder said. "I'll take your advice in a decade or so."

"Lord help us if you wait that long," Marshall said. "Maybe I could set you up with somebody. Take the edge off."

Ryder slid him a sideways glance. "I'll pass. You and

I may root for the Texas Rangers, but we don't share the same taste in women."

"Your loss," Marshall said, sitting upright. "I know some women who could wear you out and make you sleep like a baby."

"I've learned babies don't always sleep that well."

"It's your aura," Marshall said. "That's what Jenny, my ex, would say. Your aura is poisoning your environment."

"A dependable nanny is what I need," Ryder said.

"Well, if you can get a sitter, I've got tickets to the Rangers game on Thursday. Take care, buddy," he said, rising from the couch and patting Ryder on the shoulder. "Keep the faith, bud. And move me up on that backup list. I'm more dependable than your Aunt Joanie. I bet she's always busy."

Ryder smiled despite himself. "You got it. Thanks. If I can find a sitter, I'll go to that game with you."

"I'll believe it when I see it. 'Night," Marshall said and loped out of the house.

Ryder sank farther into his chair, kicked off his shoes and propped his shoes onto the coffee table. He considered reaching for that beer, but drinking anything would require too much energy. Hearing the roar of the crowd and the occasional crack of the bat hitting the ball from the game on his flat-screen TV with surround system, he closed his eyes.

Making sure the twins were safe, taking care of his patients and covering for Dr. Walters were the most important things in his life, but he knew he needed help, especially with the twins. He'd never dreamed how difficult it would be to find dependable caretakers for the boys. His head began to pound. He could feel his blood pressure rising. Pinching the bridge of his nose, for one moment, he deliberately chose *not* to think about the next nanny he would need to hire and the deteriorating mental health of his mentor, Dr. Walters.

Ryder thought back to his high school days when he'd been catcher and Marshall had pitched. They'd won the state championship senior year. That weekend had been full of celebration. He remembered a cheerleader who had paid attention to him for the first time. She'd given him a night full of memories. Blonde, curvy and wiggly, she'd kept him busy. He hadn't lasted long the first time, but he'd done better the second and the third.

His lips tilted upward at the memory. He remembered the thrill of winning. There had never been a happier moment in his life. He sighed, and the visual of a different woman filled his mind. She had dark shoulder-length hair with a wicked red mouth and cool blue eyes. She wore a black dress that handled her curves the same way a man would. She would be a seductive combination of soft and firm with full breasts and inviting hips. She would kiss him into insanity and make him want more. He would slide his hands into her feminine wetness and make her gasp, then make her gasp again when he thrust inside her….

Ryder blinked. He was brick-hard and his heart was racing as if he were having sex. He swore out loud.

He couldn't believe himself. Maybe Marshall was right. Maybe he just really needed to get laid. His only problem was that the woman in his daydream had been

Problem Princess Bridget Devereaux. Yep, Marshall was right. Ryder was a nut job.

Bridget read Dr. Ryder McCall's dossier for the hundredth time in three days. He hadn't had the easiest upbringing in the world. His father had died when he was eight years old. His mother had died two years ago.

Ryder had played baseball in high school and won an academic scholarship. He'd graduated first in his college class, then first in his medical-school class.

His older brother, Cory, had played football and earned a college scholarship. Unfortunately, he was injured, so he dropped out, took a job as a department-store manager and married his high-school sweetheart. They'd waited to have children. Six months after the birth of twin boys, they'd attended an anniversary dinner but never made it home. A tractor trailer jackknifed in front of them on the freeway. They both died before they arrived at the emergency room.

An unbelievable tragedy. Even though Bridget had lost both her parents within years of each other, she had never been close to them. Ryder had clearly been close to his brother. Now, a man who had previously been unswervingly focused on his studies and career, was alone with those precious motherless babies.

Her heart broke every time she read his story. This was one of those times she wished she had a magic wand that would solve all of Ryder's problems and heal his pain. But she didn't. As much as she wished it were true, Bridget was all too certain of her humanity.

In the midst of all of this, she still had a job to do. She needed to bring doctors to Chantaine, and Dr. McCall's assistant hedged every time Bridget attempted to make an appointment. She would give the assistant two more tries, then Bridget would face Ryder in his own territory. If he thought an assistant would keep her at bay, he had no concept of her will. Surprise, surprise, especially to herself. She may have portrayed an airy, charming personality, but underneath it all, she was growing a backbone.

Chapter Two

Ryder left the hospital and picked up the boys after the latest sitter unexpectedly informed him that her child had a medical appointment she could not skip. He had an important meeting with several members of the hospital board this afternoon which *he* could not skip. He hated to press his admin assistant into baby service again, but it couldn't be helped.

After wrestling the boys in and out of car seats and the twin stroller, he felt like he'd run a 10K race as he pushed the stroller into his office suite. Instantly noting that his admin assistant was absent from her desk, he felt his stomach twist with dread. She'd left her desk tidy and organized as usual. She'd also left a note on his desk. He snatched it up and read it.

Miss Bridget Devereaux called 3x this a.m. I can't put her off forever. Gone to my anniversary celebration as discussed. Thank you for letting me off.

—Maryann

Ryder swore out loud then remembered the boys were in the room with him. "Don't ever say that word," he told them. "Bad word."

He recalled Maryann asking for the afternoon off—it had to have been a week or so ago. He'd been busy when she asked and hadn't given it a second thought. Now, he had to juggle his boys and an important meeting. He shook his head. Women managed children and careers all the time. Why was it so difficult for him? He was a healthy, intelligent man. He'd run marathons, worked more than twenty-four hours straight, brought a man back to life in the E.R., but taking care of these boys made him feel like a train wreck.

Ryder sat down at his desk and flipped through his contact list on his computer for someone he could call to watch the boys during his meeting. He sent a few emails and made three calls. All he got were voice mails.

"Well, hello, Phantom Man," a feminine voice called from the doorway.

Ryder swallowed an oath. Just what he needed right now. He didn't even need to look to know it was *Princess Persistent*. But he did and couldn't deny that she was a sight for sore eyes. Wearing another black dress, although this one looked a slight bit more like business wear, she smiled at him with that wicked red mouth that reminded him of what he hadn't had in a long time.

Dismissing the thought, he lifted his hand. "I have no time to talk. Important meeting in less than—" He glanced at the clock. "Thirty minutes. Got to find someone one to watch the boys."

"Not having any luck?" she asked.

"No."

"You sound desperate," she said, sympathy lacking in her tone.

"Not desperate," he said. "Pressed."

"Oh, well as soon as you give me a time for our meeting, I'll get out of your way."

"I already told you I don't have time," he said in a voice that no one in their right mind would question.

She shrugged. "All I want is for you to pull up your calendar and ink me in," she said. "You already agreed."

"Not—"

She crossed her arms over her chest. "You have your job. I have mine."

Travis arched against the stroller restraints as if he wanted out. The baby wore an expression of displeasure, which would soon turn to defiance and fury, which would also include unpleasant sound effects. Ryder loosened the strap and pulled him into his arms.

Tyler looked up expectantly and began the same arching action against the stroller. Ryder withheld an oath.

"Want some help?" Bridget asked.

"Yes," he said. "If you could hold Tyler, I have one more person I can—" He stopped as he watched her settle the baby on her hip. An idea sprang to mind. "Can you keep them for an hour or so?"

Her eyes widened in alarm. "An hour?" she echoed. "Or so?"

"Just for this meeting," he said. "I'll leave as soon as possible."

She shot him a considering look. "In exchange for an opportunity to discuss Chantaine's medical proposition with you, and you having an *open mind.*"

"I agree to the first half. The second is going to be tough."

"How tough would it be to take your twins to your important meeting?" she challenged.

The woman was playing dirty. "Okay," he said. "As long as you understand, my first priority is my residents' professional success."

"Done," she said. "Did you bring a blanket and some food?"

"Whatever the sitter keeps in the diaper bag," he said, relief flowing through him like a cool stream of water. "Thank you," he said, setting Travis in the stroller seat. "I'll see you after the meeting," he said and closed the office door behind him.

Bridget stared at the babies and they stared at her. Travis began to wiggle and make a frown face.

"Now, don't you start," she said, pointing her finger at him. "You haven't even given me a chance." She set Tyler in the other stroller seat and dove into the diaper bag and struck gold. "A blanket," she said. "You're going to love this," she said and spread it on the floor. Afterward, she set Travis on the blanket, followed by Tyler.

The boys looked at her expectantly.

"What?" she asked. "You're free from the bondage of the stroller. Enjoy yourselves." She narrowed her eyes. "Just don't start crawling or anything. Okay? Let's see what else is in the bag."

Unfortunately, not much. She used up the small

container of Cheerios within the first fifteen minutes and fifteen minutes after that, both boys had lost interest in the small set of blocks. She pulled out a musical toy and helped them work that over for several minutes.

Peekaboo killed a few more minutes, but then Bridget started to feel a little panicky. She needed more snacks and toys if she was going to keep the little darlings entertained. Grabbing some blank paper from Ryder's desk, she gave each boy a sheet.

Travis immediately put it in his mouth.

"Let's try something else," she said and crumpled the paper.

He smiled as if he liked the idea. Great, she thought. More paper. She crumpled a few sheets into a ball and tossed it at them. They loved that. They threw paper all over the room.

After a few more minutes, Travis began to fuss, stuffing his fist in his mouth.

"Hungry?" It would help so much if they could tell her what they needed. Luckily two bottles were also stuffed in the bag. She pulled out one and began to feed Travis. Tyler's face crumpled and he began to cry.

"Great, great," she muttered and awkwardly situated both boys on her lap as she fed them both their bottles.

They drained them in no time. Travis burped on her dress.

Bridget grimaced. A second later, Tyler gave her the same favor.

At least they weren't crying, she thought, but then she sniffed, noticing an unpleasant odor. A quick check revealed Travis had left a deposit in his diaper.

* * *

Ryder opened the door to his office prepared for screaming, crying, accusations from Bridget. Instead the boys were sprawled across her lap while she sang a medical magazine to the tune of *Frère Jacques*. He had to admit it was pretty inventive. His office looked like a disaster zone with papers strewn everywhere and he smelled the familiar, distinct scent of dirty diapers. He must have wrinkled his nose.

She did the same. "I didn't think it would be considerate to toss the diapers into the hallway, so they're in the trash can. I bundled them up as best as I could."

The boys looked safe and content. That was what was important. "It looks like you had a good time."

"Not bad," she said with a smile. "Considering my resources. You're really not set up for babies here."

"I can't agree more," he said and snatched up a few wads of paper. "What were you doing?"

"Playing ball with paper. It worked until Travis was determined to eat it." She gingerly lifted one of the boys in Ryder's direction. "So, when do we have our discussion?"

He tucked Tyler into the stroller and followed with Travis. Ryder was tempted to name a time next year but knew that wouldn't be fair. Better to get it over with. "Tonight, at my house," he said. "Do you like Chinese?"

"I prefer Italian or Mediterranean," she said, frowning as she rose to her feet. "At your house?"

"It's the one and only time I can guarantee for the foreseeable future."

She sighed. "It's not what I hoped for. How am I going to have your undivided attention?"

"Maybe we'll get lucky and they'll go to sleep," he said.

Four hours later, Bridget could barely remember what she'd said or eaten for dinner. The boys had taken a nap in the car on the way home and woken up cranky. She suspected they hadn't gotten enough of an afternoon nap. Although she resented the fact that she wasn't getting Ryder's undivided attention during their discussion, she couldn't really blame him. In fact, despite the fact that he was clearly a strong man, she could tell that caring for the twins was wearing on him. He loved them and would protect them with his life, but the man needed consistent help.

It was close to eleven before the twins truly settled down.

"I'd offer you a ride to wherever you're staying, but I can't pull the boys out of bed again," he said, after he had made the trip up and down the stairs five times.

His eyes filled with weariness, he raked a hand through his hair. Her heart tugged at his quandary. The urge to help, to fix, was overwhelming. "My security is always close by. He can collect me. It's no problem."

"I keep forgetting you're a princess," he said.

"Maybe it's the baby formula on my dress," she said drily.

"Maybe," he said, meeting her gaze. The moment swelled between them.

Bridget felt her chest grow tight and took a breath to alleviate the sensation.

"I'm sure you're tired. You could stay here if you want," he offered. "I have a guest room and bath."

Bridget blinked. She *was* tired, but staying here? "I don't have a change of clothes."

He shrugged. "I can give you a shirt to sleep in."

The prospect of sleeping in Ryder's shirt was wickedly seductive. Plus, she *was* tired. "I'd like to get your nanny situation in order for you."

"That would be a dream come true," he said. "Everything I've done so far hasn't worked."

"There may be a fee for an agency," she said. "I'm not sure how it works here. I'll have to ask my sister."

"I took the first and second suggestions that were given to me and they didn't pan out. It's imperative that I have excellent care for the boys. "

"I can see that," she said. "But do you also realize that you will have to make some adjustments as time goes on? Later, there will be sports and school activities where parents are expected to attend." Bridget remembered that neither of her parents had attended her school activities. Occasionally a nanny had shown up, but never her parents. "Have you figured out how you'll address that?"

He frowned thoughtfully. "I haven't figured out much. I haven't had custody very long. It's still a shock to all of us. I know the boys miss their mother and father, but they can't express it. I hate the loss for them. And I'm not sure I'm such a great choice as a parent. I've been totally dedicated to my career since I entered med school. Add to that how I've been filling in for Dr. Walters and it's tough. I don't want to let down my residents or the twins."

Bridget studied Ryder for a long moment. "Are you

sure you want to step in as their father? There are other options. There are people who would love to welcome the boys into their—"

"The boys are mine," he said, his jaw locking in resolution. "It may take me some time, but I'll figure it out. The boys are important to me. I held them minutes after they were born. I would do anything for them. We've just all been thrown a loop. We're all dealing with the loss of my brother and sister-in-law. I will be there for them. I will be."

She nodded slowly. "Okay. I'll try to help you with your nanny situation."

He paused and the electricity and emotion that flowed between them snapped and crackled. "Thank you."

She nodded. "It's late. I may need to borrow one of your shirts and I should talk to my security."

"No problem," he said, but the way he looked at her made her feel as if he'd much prefer she share his bed instead of taking the guest bed alone.

Bridget took a quick shower and brushed her teeth with the toothbrush Ryder supplied. Pushing her hands through the sleeves of the shirt he left in the guest bedroom for her, she drank in the fresh scent of the shirt. She climbed into bed, wondering what had possessed her to get involved in Ryder's situation and she remembered all the things she couldn't control or influence. Maybe, just maybe she could wave a magic wand in this one and help just a little.

It seemed only seconds after she fell asleep that she heard a knock at the door. She awakened, confused and disoriented. "Hello?"

"Bridget," a male voice said from the other side of the door. "It's me, Ryder."

The door opened a crack. "I just wanted you to know I'm leaving."

Her brain moved slowly. She was not at the hotel. She was at Ryder's townhome. "Um."

"The boys are still asleep."

She paused. "The boys?" She blinked. "Oh, the boys."

He came to the side of her bed. "Are you okay?"

"What time is it?"

"Five a.m."

"Is this when you usually leave for work?"

"Pretty much," he said.

"Okay," she said and tried to make her brain work. "What time do they usually get up?"

"Six or seven," he said. "I can try and call someone if—"

"No, I can do it," she said. "Just leave my door open so I can hear them."

"Are you sure?"

"Yes. Check in at lunchtime," she said.

"I can do that," he said and paused. "Did anyone ever tell you how beautiful you are when you're half-asleep?"

Unconsciously, her mouth lifted in a half smile. "I can't recall such a compliment."

"Nice to know I'm the first," he said, bending toward her and pressing his mouth against hers. Before she could say a word, he left.

Bridget wondered if she'd dreamed the kiss.

She fell back asleep for what must have been 30 seconds and she heard the sound of a baby's cry. It awakened her like cold water on her face. She sat upright, climbed out of bed and walked to the boys' room. She swung open the door to find Travis and Tyler sitting in their cribs and wailing.

"Hi, darlings," she said and went to Travis. "Good morning. It's a wonderful day to be a baby, isn't it?" She saw a twisty thing on the side of the crib and cranked it around. The mobile turned and music played. "Well, look at that," she said and touched the mobile.

Travis gave a few more sobs, but as soon as he looked upward, he quieted as the mobile turned.

Bridget felt a sliver of relief. "Good boy," she said and went to Tyler's bed and cranked up the mobile. Tyler looked upward and gave up his halfhearted cry, staring at the mobile.

Diaper change, she thought and took care of Travis. Then she took care of Tyler and hoisted both boys on her hips and went downstairs. She fed them, changed them again and propped them on a blanket in the den while she called her sister's friend for a reference for the best nanny agency in Dallas. Three hours later, she interviewed four nannies in between feeding the twins and changing more diapers and putting them down for a nap. When they fussed at nap time, she played a CD more repetitious than her brother's top-adviser's speech on a royal's duty. She'd heard that lecture too many times to count. The huge advantage to the babies' CD was that it included singing. Bridget wondered if she might have been more receptive to the lecture if the adviser had sung it.

The second prospective nanny was her favorite. She received letters of reference on her cell phone within an hour and sent a generous offer that was immediately accepted. After she checked on the boys, she ordered a nanny/babycam. Next in line, she would hire a relief nanny, but right now she needed a little relief of her own.

Bridget sank onto the couch and wondered when her day had felt so full. Even at this moment, she needed to use the bathroom, but she didn't have the energy to go. She glanced at herself, in her crumpled dress from yesterday with baby formula, baby food and liquid baby burp. That didn't include the drool.

Crazy, but the drool was sweet to her. How sick was that? But she knew the twins had drooled when they'd relaxed and trusted her.

She laughed quietly, a little hysterically. Anyone in their right mind would ask why she was working so hard to find a nanny for a doctor with two baby boys. Maybe a shrink could explain it, but these days, Bridget had a hard time turning down a cause of the heart. And Ryder and the boys had struck her straight in the heart with a deadly aim. She hoped, now, that she would feel some sort of relief.

Leaning back against the sofa with her bladder a little too full, she closed her eyes. Heaven help her, this baby stuff was exhausting.

Ryder left the office early, determined not to leave Bridget totally in the lurch with the boys. Stepping inside the front door, he found Bridget, mussed in the most alluring way, asleep on his couch.

She blinked, then her eyes widened. "Oh, excuse me. Just a second," she said, then raced down the hallway.

He listened carefully, automatically these days. A CD played over the baby monitor, but there were no other sounds. A double check never hurt, he thought, and strode upstairs to listen outside the nursery door.

Nothing. He opened the doorknob in slow motion and pushed the door open. Carefully stepping inside, he peeked into the cribs. Both boys were totally zoned out. He almost wondered if they were snoring but refused to check.

Backing out of the room, he returned downstairs to the den. Bridget was sipping from a glass of water.

"Are they still asleep?" she asked.

He nodded.

She grimaced. "I hate to say this. You have no idea how much I hate to say this, but we need to wake them or they'll be up all night. And I'm not staying tonight."

"Yeah," he said, but he was in no rush.

"I hired a nanny. She can start Monday. I've also ordered a baby/nannycam for your peace of mind. The next step is hiring a relief nanny because the twins are especially demanding at this age. Well, maybe they will be demanding at every age, but we have to deal with the present and the immediate future."

Ryder stared at her in disbelief. "How did you do that?"

She smiled. "I'm a fairy princess. I waved my magic wand," she said. "Actually I got into the best nanny agency in Dallas, used my title, interviewed four highly qualified women in between changing diapers, selected one applicant, received references, blah, blah, blah and it's done." She lifted her shoulders. "And now I'm done."

"I'm sure you are. In any other circumstance, I would invite you out to dinner for the evening."

"Lovely thought," she said. "But I feel extremely grungy. The opposite of glamorous. I'm going to my sister's ranch for the weekend. You can call me next week about all the doctors you want to send to Chantaine."

His lips twitched. "You don't really think I'm going to sell out one of my residents for this, do you?"

"Sell out is such a harsh term," she said with a scowl. "I believe it's more accurate that you're giving them an opportunity for hands-on experience in a beautiful environment with a compensation that allows them to concentrate on treatment rather than their debt."

He lifted an eyebrow. "Pretty good."

She shrugged. "It's the truth. My security is waiting to drive me to my sister's house. Can you take it from here?"

"Yes, I can. Do I have your number?" he asked. "For that dinner I promised."

She looked at him for a long, sexy moment that made him want to find a way to make her stay. "Some would say I'm more trouble than I'm worth," she said.

"They haven't seen you with twins," he said.

She smiled slightly and went to the kitchen. Out of curiosity, he followed and watched her scratch a number across the calendar tacked on the fridge. "Good enough?" she asked.

"Good enough," he said.

"Don't wait too long to call me, cowboy doctor," she said and walked toward the front door.

"I won't," he said, his gaze fixed on the sight of her amazing backside. "G'night, gorgeous."

She tossed a smile over her shoulder. "Same to you."

Bridget felt Valentina search her face. "Twin boys? Dr. Ryder? What does any of this have to do with you?"

It was Saturday morning. Noon, actually, as she sipped her tea and entered the world of the waking. "I didn't mean to get involved, but I didn't have a choice. I mean, the boys were orphaned. Ryder is grieving at the same time he's trying to take care of the babies. Trying to take on someone else's job because he's medically unable."

Tina stared at her in disbelief. "Are you sure you're okay? Maybe you need more rest."

Bridget laughed. "I'm sure I'll take another nap, but the story won't change tomorrow. It was something I had to do." She paused. "You understand that, don't you? When you have to fix it if you can?"

Tina's face softened and she covered Bridget's hand with hers. "Oh, sweetie, I'm so sorry," she said, shaking her head.

"For what?"

"The Devereaux fixing gene has kicked in," she said. "It's a gift and a plague."

"What do you mean?"

"I mean, you finally understand what it means to be a Devereaux Royal," she said, her expression solemn. "If you see a need, you try to fill it. If you see a pain, you try to heal it. It's your purpose. It's our purpose."

"So, I'm going to be doing stuff like this the rest of my life?" Bridget asked, appalled.

Tina nodded and Katiana banged on the tray of her high chair, clearly wanting more food.

"Oh, I hope not." Bridget didn't want to feel that much. She didn't want to get that emotionally involved. Surely, she could get this out of her system once and for all with Ryder and the babies and then get back to her true self in Italy.

Bridget sighed. "What I really want to do is wrap up

this doctor thing as soon as possible. I'm concerned it may not happen as quickly as I like."

"Why not?" Tina asked as she gave Katiana slices of peaches.

"I don't understand it all, but the way Ryder talks about it, going to Chantaine would be death for a physician's career. Sounds a bit overdramatic to me, but I need to get further information. In the meantime, Stefan has asked me to make some more official appearances, so I'll be traveling and spending more time in Dallas."

Tina frowned. "I don't like that," she said. "I thought you were going to spend most of your time here with me."

"I'll still be coming to the ranch as often as possible, but you know how Stefan is. He likes to maximize our efforts."

"How well I remember," Tina said with a groan. She dampened a clean cloth and wiped off Katiana's face and hands.

Katiana shook her adorable head and lifted her hands. "Up," she said.

"Of course, Your Highness," Tina said and gave her daughter a kiss as she lifted her from the chair.

Katiana immediately pointed at the floor. "Down."

"Please," Tina said.

Katiana paused.

"Please," Tina repeated. "Can you say that?"

"Psss," the toddler said.

"Close enough," Tina said with a laugh.

Bridget stared at her sister in jeans and a T-shirt and sometimes had to shake her head at the sight of her. "I'm just not used to seeing you quite so domesticated."

"I've been living here for more than two years now."

"Do you mind it? The work?" she asked. "At the palace, you could have had several nannies at your beck and call."

"I have Hildie the housekeeper, who may as well be Katiana's grandmother, and Zach. I like the simplicity of this life. Before I met Zach, I always felt like I was juggling a dozen priorities. Now between him and Katiana, the choice is easy."

"Must be nice," Bridget muttered as Hildie, Zach's longtime housekeeper, strode through the door carrying a bag of groceries.

"Well, hello, all Your Highlinesses. We've got a roomful of royalty today. Miss Tina, did you offer your sister some of that strawberry bread? Looks like you're having a late breakfast. Although that should come as no surprise considering when she got here last night," Hildie said, lifting her eyebrow.

Bridget wasn't quite certain how to take the stern-looking gray-haired woman. Tina insisted the woman had a heart of gold, but she seemed to rule the house with an iron hand. "Good morning, Miss—"

"Call me Hildie, and it's afternoon. Do you feel like some pancakes or a turkey sandwich? You looked pretty rough when you got in last night," Hildie said as she began to put away groceries.

"She was taking care of twin babies," Tina said, clearly still amazed.

Hildie's jaw dropped. "Twin babies," she said. "You?"

Bridget grimaced. "I know it's totally improbable. Hopefully I won't be put in that type of situation again."

"She was helping a doctor who had become a

guardian to his brother's two babies because the brother and sister-in-law were killed in an accident."

Hildie shook her head, her brow furrowing in deep sympathy. "That's terrible, just terrible. You did the right thing," she said to Bridget. "Let me fix you a pie. I'll fix you any kind you want."

Surprised, Bridget felt a rush of discomfort mixed with pleasure. "Oh, I don't need a pie. You're delightful to suggest it, but—"

"I insist," Hildie said.

Tina lifted her shoulders helplessly. "You're going to get a pie whether you like it or not. You may as well pick what you like, and I guarantee it will be the best pie you've eaten."

"Well, if you must, I would like the most decadent chocolate pie you can bake."

Hildie cackled with laughter. "Chocolate. You can tell the two of you are sisters. And you may try to hide it, but you have that fix-it compulsion just like your sister."

"I don't have that compulsion," Bridget insisted. "It's temporary. Like a virus. As soon as I take my long break in Italy, I'll be cured."

Hildie laughed again and shot her a look of sympathy. "Don't worry, Your Highliness. It may take a while, but you'll figure it out."

Bridget frowned because it seemed that Hildie knew something she didn't. Hmm. The prospect didn't please her, but the chocolate would help.

Chapter Three

Three nights later, Ryder met Bridget at an exclusive Mediterranean restaurant in Dallas. He remembered she'd said she preferred Mediterranean and Italian food. With the Dallas skyline outside the window beside them, he couldn't look anywhere but at her. Her blue eyes sparkled with a combination of sensuality and warmth. Her black dress—yet another one—dipped into a V that cupped her beautiful breasts and her lips were, again, red.

"Thank you for joining me," he said after they'd placed their order.

"Thank you for inviting me. Who's watching the twins?" she asked.

"A neighbor and her daughter. I'm paying double. Amazing how easy it was for them to commit when I said that," he said.

She laughed. "They're adorable but exhausting. How was the new nanny?"

"Scary efficient. This was her first day and she's already whipping all of us into shape," he said, amazed at how good he felt just to be with Bridget.

"Good. Next step is to get a backup," she said and took a sip of wine. "In the meantime, about Chantaine's medical program…"

He stifled a groan. "Do we have to discuss business?"

"Briefly," she said and lifted an eyebrow. "Remember that we held our discussion while the twins were screaming *after* I had cared for them during your meeting and—"

"Okay, okay," he said. "Do you want me to be blunt?"

"I would love it," she said, leaning forward and propping her chin on her hands.

"The truth is, there's no true professional advantage for the residents to go to Chantaine after they graduate. There's no extra education, association with an expert, or certification."

"So money is not enough," she said.

"No," he said.

"Hmm." She tilted her head. "So the whole game would change if Chantaine could offer exposure to a noted expert in a particular field?"

He nodded.

She took another sip of her wine. "Thank you."

He could tell her brain was already racing. "You're plotting and planning," he said.

She smiled, her sexy red lips lifting upward, sending a sensual heat through his veins. "Yes, I am. I'll figure something out. It's the Devereaux way."

"I did an internet search on you," he admitted. "You've *mostly* stayed out of trouble. How did you manage that?"

"I'm flattered. Of course, I did research on you right after the cocktail party. How did I stay out of trouble?" she asked. "It's all relative. My sisters did me a huge favor. I wouldn't wish it on her, but Ericka went to rehab, and then after that, Tina got pregnant. What a scandal. So my little tumbles—"

"Like the time you got smashed at the nightclub in Chantaine and made a scene—"

"That was Stefan's fault. Eve was with me and he couldn't stand the fact that she wasn't with him." She waved her hand. "But I won't fault him too much. He'd just discovered he had a baby from an earlier affair and was trying to work out his relationship with Eve."

"I remember reading an article about some sort of incident. A gang. She was hurt."

He stopped when he saw her gaze darken with emotion.

"She saved my life and nearly lost her own," Bridget said quietly as she ran her finger around the top of her glass. "It all happened so fast. I wish I had responded differently. She was hurt. She almost died." She lifted her glass and took a quick sip. "It was wrong. Her life shouldn't have been put in jeopardy for my sake."

He was shocked at the stark guilt he saw on her face. "These things happen. Decisions are made in microseconds. She's a Texas girl. She acted on instinct."

She bit her lip. "Maybe I need to learn some of those Texas-girl instincts," she muttered.

"Your instincts are pretty damn good. You took care of the twins when we were in a jam," he said.

"That's different," she said.

"Not as far as I can see. I won't lie to you. I can't make any promises about sending doctors to Chantaine. On the other hand, I've thought about having you in my bed way too much. I wish I could say it's just because you've got a killer body and I've done without, but the truth is, there's something else about you that gets me going."

Her lips parted in startled disbelief. "I—" She broke off and shook her head. "I don't know what to say."

"You don't have to say anything. I just wanted you to know," he said.

She met his gaze and he could tell she was undecided. He saw want and hesitation, and he understood it, but he was driven to find a way to get her to meet him halfway.

After a delicious dinner, Ryder drove Bridget to her hotel and insisted on walking her to her room. "You know security is watching me," she said as they stood outside her door.

"Do you want to step inside your room?"

An illicit thrill raced through her. Her guard would report to Stefan and he would fuss. She would dodge his calls the same way she had after spending the night at Ryder's house. What a hassle. "For just a moment," she said and slid her key card into the lock.

Ryder pushed open the door. Seconds later, she felt her back against the door and his mouth on hers.

"Do you know what your red mouth does to me?"

he muttered and plundered her lips. He slid his tongue into her mouth, tasting her, taking her.

Her heart slammed against her ribs. She couldn't resist the urge to lift her fingers to his hair and scalp.

He groaned in approval and rocked his hips against hers.

Bridget gasped, her breath locking somewhere between her lungs and throat. Somehow, someway, she craved his warmth and strength. His passion and need struck her at her core.

"I want you," he said. "You want me. Let me stay for a while."

A terrible wicked temptation rolled through her. If he stayed, he would fill her and take her away from her uncertainty and emptiness. She knew he could take care of her, if only for a little while.

He French-kissed her, sending her around the world at least a couple of times.

"You want me to stay?" he asked, sliding his mouth down over her ear.

She inhaled, grasping for sanity. Closing her eyes, she tried to concentrate. "Yesandno," she said, running the words together. She dipped her head so that her forehead rested against his chin. "This is a little fast."

He gave a heavy, unsatisfied sigh. "Yeah, it is. But it's strong."

She nodded. "Sorry," she whispered.

"It's okay," he said cradling the back of her head. "It wouldn't work out anyway."

"Why is that?" she asked, leaning back to look at him.

"I'm a doctor. You're a princess," he said.

"So?" she asked.

"The two don't mix," he said. "And never will. Sweet dreams, Your Highness."

He left and Bridget stared at the door, frowning. *Why couldn't they mix?* Not that she *wanted* them to mix. And the *sweet dreams* thing really grated on her. That was what Eve had often said. It had seemed so sweet when she'd said it. Not so with Ryder. Bridget snarled. He was gone. Good riddance.

Ryder heard a knocking sound and shook his head as he glanced up during the meeting he was in to discuss the performance of the residents.

Dr. Wayne Hutt, Ryder's nemesis, knocked on the table again. "Dr. McCall?" he said. "Anyone home?"

"Pardon me," Ryder said in a crisp voice. "I was studying my notes."

"Apology accepted," Hutt said. "Drs. Robinson and Graham are having attendance issues."

"Dr. Robinson is concerned about the welfare of his family in rural Virginia and Dr. Graham's wife has just gotten pregnant," Ryder said. "They just need a little time to refocus. It won't be a problem."

"How can you be sure?" Hutt challenged.

Ryder fought his antipathy for his associate. "I'm sure," he said. "Just as Dr. Gordon Walters would be sure," he said, pulling rank because everyone knew Dr. Walters trusted Ryder over anyone else.

Hutt gave an odd combination of a frown and grimace.

Dr. James Williams, chief of everything, nodded.

"We'll give these two interns two weeks to make adjust-ments. Dr. McCall, you'll speak to them?"

"Yes, sir."

Seven minutes later, the meeting ended, thank God. He returned to his office and sent emails to Drs. Rob-inson and Graham to set up appointments. He answered another fifty emails and stood to make late rounds with his patients.

A knock sounded outside his door and Dr. Hutt walked inside. "Hey, Ryder. Late night. I'm surprised you can do this with the twins."

Ryder resisted the urge to grind his teeth. "I've hired a new nanny and am getting new backup. Thanks for your concern. I need to do late rounds."

"Just a minute," Hutt said. "How's Dr. Walters doing? No one's talking."

"He's working through his recovery. These things take time," Ryder hedged.

"That's pretty vague," Hutt said.

"You know I can't discuss the confidential status of patients," he said.

"But Walters isn't really your patient," Hutt continued.

"He's my mentor and friend, the closest thing I've had to a father since my own father died when I was a kid. I'm not discussing his condition," Ryder said.

"It must not be good," Hutt said. "You know if the twins are too much for you, I'll be glad to step in and help."

Ryder just bet Hutt would like to step in and *help*. What Hutt really wanted was a promotion. What Hutt really wanted was to snatch Walters's position away from Ryder. Although Ryder hated that Walters couldn't fulfill his duties any longer.

"Thanks for the offer," he said.

"Seriously, Ryder. I have a wife and a child. The wife is the critical element. She makes it easy for me to do my job. When you don't have a wife…"

"I have a good new nanny," he said.

"It's not the same as a wife," Hutt counseled.

"Hmm. See you. Good night," he said and headed out the door. What Hutt didn't understand was that Ryder had never had any intention of getting married and having children. He'd observed his parents' disastrous marriage, his father's death and his mother's subsequent descent into alcoholism and death.

After that, Ryder had resolved that he wanted to heal people. Bag the personal relationships, with the exception of his brother and his family. His family became his patients, and after he completed his residency, his family included the new residents. And always Dr. Walters. He would never take a wife. His mind wandered to a visual of Bridget the last time he'd seen her, her eyes catlike with sensuality, her mouth soft and sensual, taking him into her. His mouth into her. When he really wanted to give her a lot more.

Ryder swore under his breath. This was all libido. He'd taken care of this issue before with other women doctors as career-driven as he was. No-ties sex provided a release that allowed him to do his job. Maintaining his focus on his profession and the twins was the most important thing. Bridget was just a distraction.

Bridget wandered around the medical association meeting and was bummed that Ryder wasn't there. He was probably taking care of the twins. She felt a deep tug of sympathy and quickly tried to brush it aside. Ryder didn't want her sympathy. They would never work. Remember? She covered her irritation with a smile as she nodded at someone else she didn't know.

Halfway through the evening, the shrimp bowl was refilled and Bridget put a few on her plate.

"I always wait for the refill at these things," a distinguished older man said to her.

She nodded in agreement. "I agree. Fresh is better. Bridget Devereaux," she said, extending her free hand.

"Dr. James Williams, University Hospital," he said shaking her hand. "Are you a pharmaceutical sales rep?"

She opened her mouth and it took a moment to speak. She smiled. "Not exactly. I'm representing the country of Chantaine. Very small country in the Mediterranean. We're trying to recruit more doctors. We're offering complimentary living expenses and paying special scholarships in addition to salary for a two-year stay."

Dr. Williams lifted his white eyebrows. "Really? I'll have to speak to my physician in charge of residents about that. Perhaps a couple of them could benefit from that."

"I would appreciate that very much. I'm sure you're a very busy man. Would you mind if I touch base with you in a week or so?"

"Not at all," he said. "Some of our residents have money challenges. Don't we all in this economy?"

"So true," she said. "Are you the speaker tonight?"

He shook his head. "No, I'm lucky. Eat and leave."

She laughed. "Don't rub it in," she said.

He laughed in return. "Tell me your name again. I don't want to forget."

"Bridget Devereaux," she said, deliberately leaving out her title. "I represent Chantaine. I'm honored to meet you."

"My pleasure to meet you, Miss Devereaux," he said, and ate his shrimp cocktail.

Bridget worked the room the rest of the night and arranged a visit to the pediatric wing at Texas Medical Center to make a public service announcement for public health. She also met several doctors who wanted to pursue a more personal relationship, but she demurred at the same time that she gave them her card which contained a number for her assistant.

By the time the evening was done, her feet were also done. Her mind wandered to Ryder and the babies, but she tried to push her thoughts aside. With a glass of white wine in her hand, she kicked off her high heels and watched television in her suite at the hotel.

She closed her eyes. Soon enough she would be in Italy with a gorgeous Italian man keeping her company. She smiled at the image, but soon another image flashed in its place. Ryder, sans shirt, stood before her and dragged her into his arms and began to make love to her. He was so hot that smoke rose between them, but the sensation of his skin against hers made her dizzy. His kiss made her knees weak. He made her want in a way she never had....

She felt herself sinking into the couch, her body warm and pliable. And alone.

Bridget blinked and sat up against the couch. This was just wrong. He'd already said they wouldn't work because of who he was, because of who she was. A part of her rebelled against the notion one moment. The next, she didn't. She didn't have room for this drama in her life. She had goals. She had Italy in her future.

Bridget washed her face and brushed her teeth, determined to put Ryder from her mind. As she fell asleep, though, she dreamed of Ryder and the boys.

A few days later, Ryder followed up on a surgery patient midday. The young man had been admitted to the E.R. with appendicitis. Ryder had operated and needed to give his stamp of approval for the teen to be discharged. He was stopped because there was filming in the pediatric unit.

Slightly irritated, he checked his text messages on his cell and answered a few.

"She's a princess making a video," one nurse said to another.

He snapped his head up at the comment. "Princess?" he repeated.

"Yes," the nurse said. "But she's very nice. Not at all snooty. I got her coffee and she was very grateful. More than a lot of doctors."

"She wasn't trying to save lives," Ryder said.

The nurse shrugged. "Anyone can say please and thank you, and she did."

Minutes later, Bridget appeared, lighting up the room with her smile. The chief of Pediatrics accompanied her, clearly dazzled.

"Thank you," she said. "Thank you so much from Chantaine and me. You have been wonderful."

"Isn't she wonderful? Now *that* is a princess," the nurse said.

Ryder wanted to make a wry, cynical response, but he was too busy staring at Bridget. And the damned pediatric chief. She seemed to glow. He remembered how she'd felt in his arms, how that wicked red mouth had felt against his. He remembered how she'd made him smile. Not many people had managed to do that during the last few months.

She squeezed the pediatrics chief's arm, then glanced around the room and waved. Her gaze locked with his and he felt a surge of need all the way down to his feet. It was sexual, but more, and confused the hell out of him. She gave a quick little wave and returned her attention to the pediatric chief.

Ryder felt an inexplicable surge of jealousy. *Where the hell had that come from?* Pushing it aside, he continued to his patient's room for the final exam. Less than five minutes later, he headed down the hallway toward his office. Rounding a corner, he nearly plowed into Bridget and Dr. Ware, the pediatrics chief, who was chatting her up. His body language said he wanted to eat her with a spoon. His hand placed on the wall above her head, he leaned toward her. Ryder fought the crazy urge to push him away, but turned his head instead.

"Ryder. Dr. McCall," Bridget said.

He slowed his steps and turned around and nodded in her direction.

"How are you? The twins? The new nanny?" she asked, her gaze searching his.

Ware stepped beside her. "Whoa, she knows a lot about you, McCall. How did that happen?"

Ryder shrugged. "Just lucky, I guess. I'm good. The twins are good and the new nanny is fantastic. I could say I owe you my life, but I'd be afraid you'd take it."

She shot him a look of mock offense. "You know better than that. Besides, it's not your life that I want," she said with a laugh.

Ware looked from one of them to the other, clearly curious. "What *does* she want? And why in the world wouldn't you give it to her?"

"She wants my residents," he said, meeting her gaze.

"After they've completed your program," she insisted. "Plus, I only want to *borrow* them for a couple of years, and they'll be well compensated."

"You could throw her one or—" Dr. Ware's pager sounded. "Please excuse me. I need to go. You have my card, Your Highness. Give me a call. Anytime," he said with a hopeful smile and rushed away.

Bridget sighed and turned to Ryder. "Are you going to do the civilized thing and ask me to join you for lunch?"

"If I haven't been civilized before, why should I start now?" Ryder retorted because Bridget made him feel anything but civilized.

"I suppose because you owe me your life," she said with a glint in her eyes.

He gave a muffled chuckle. "Okay, come along. I better warn you that lunch won't last longer than fifteen minutes."

"Ah, so you're into quickies. What a shame," she said and began to walk.

"I didn't say that," he said, but resisted the urge to pull at his collar which suddenly felt too tight.

"I can't say I'm surprised. All evidence points in that direction."

"How did we get on this subject?" he asked.

"You said you wouldn't last more than fifteen minutes," she said, meeting his gaze with eyes so wide and guileless that he wondered how she did it.

"I said *lunch* won't last—" He broke when he saw her smile. "Okay, you got me on that one. I hope you don't mind cafeteria food."

"Not at all," she said as they walked into the cafeteria.

He noticed several people stared in their direction, but she seemed to ignore it. They each chose a couple dishes and he paid for both, then guided her to a less-occupied table at the back of the room. "How did your video go today?"

"Hopefully, well. I interviewed Dr. Ware about preventative health for children. I also need to do one for adults. But enough about that. How are the twins?" she asked, clearly eager for information.

"I think the new nanny is making a big difference for them. This is the most calm I've seen them since I took custody of them," he said. "The nanny also suggested that I do some extra activities with them, but I haven't worked that into the schedule yet."

"What kind of activities?" she asked, and took a bite of her chicken.

"Swimming," he said then lowered his voice. *"Baby yoga."*

"Oh. Do you take yoga?" she asked and sipped her hot tea.

"Never in my life," he said. "The nanny seems to

think this would increase bonding between the three of us."

"That makes you uncomfortable," she said.

He shrugged. "I hadn't planned on having kids. I guess I'm still adjusting, too."

"You've been through a lot. Perhaps you should see a therapist," she said.

"We're doing okay now," he said defensively.

"I don't suggest it as an insult. The palace is always giving us head checks especially since my sister Ericka had her substance-abuse problem. I'm surprised it's not required in this situation."

"A social worker has visited a few times to check on things. She actually suggested the same thing," he said reluctantly. "She said I need to make sure I'm having fun with the boys instead of it being all work."

"There you go," she said. "I think it's a splendid idea. You just seem incredibly overburdened and miserable."

"Thank you for that diagnosis, Your Highness," he said drily and dug into his dry salmon filet. "Funny, a friend of mine said something similar recently."

"We all have to protect against burnout. I would say you're more in danger of it than most."

"Is there such a thing as princess burnout?" he asked.

"Definitely. That's what happened to my sister Valentina. She carried the load too long."

"And what are you doing to prevent burnout?"

"I have an extended break planned in my future. In the meantime, I try to make sure I get enough rest and solitude whenever possible. As soon as I wrap up the doctor assignment, I'll get a break. I'm hoping you'll toss me one or two of your residents as Dr. Ware suggested to get the ball rolling."

"It's going to be more difficult than that," he said.

"I don't see why it needs to be. It's not as if I'm seriously asking for your top neurosurgeons. We would love a general practitioner or family doctor. In fact, we would prefer it."

"You and the rest of the world. We actually have a shortage of family physicians, too."

"Again, I'm only asking to *borrow* them."

"What do you think of Dr. Ware?" he asked, changing the subject again.

"He's lovely. Unlike you, he's totally enchanted with my position and title."

"Part of my charm. Part of the reason you find me irresistible."

"You flatter yourself," she said.

"Do I?" he challenged. "You've missed me."

"Of course I haven't. You already said nothing would work between us. Of course, that was after you tried to shag me against the hotel door. I mean, you obviously have the attention span of a fruit fly when it comes to women and—"

He closed his hand over hers. "Will you shut up for a minute?"

Surprisingly, she did.

"I dream about you whenever I get the rare opportunity to sleep. I've dialed your number and hung up too many times to count. You can't want to get involved with me right now."

"It's not for you to tell me what I can and can't want. Lord knows, everyone else does that. Don't you start."

"Okay," he said wearily.

"So what are you going to do about it?" she challenged.

If he said what he *wanted* to do, he could be arrested. "I think I'll show instead of tell," he said and watched with satisfaction as her throat and face bloomed with color. He wondered if her blush extended to the rest of her body. It would be fun to find out.

Chapter Four

Two days later, Bridget's cell phone rang and her heart went pitter-patter at the number on the caller ID. "Hello," she said in a cool voice.

"Hello to you, Your Highness. How are you?" Ryder asked.

"I'm actually getting ready to make an appearance for a children's art program in Dallas," she said, smiling at the people who were waiting for her.

"Okay, I'll make this quick. Are you free tonight?"

She rolled her eyes. The man clearly had no idea how many demands were placed on her once people got word she was in the area. "I'm not often free but can sometimes make adjustments. What did you have in mind?"

"Swimming," he said.

"Excuse me?" she said.

"Swimming with the twins and pizza," he said.

"The pizza had better be fabulous. Ciao," she said and disconnected the call, but she felt a crazy surge of happiness zing through her as she followed the museum representatives inside the room where the children and press awaited.

Bridget gave a brief speech about the importance of art at all levels of society and dipped her hands and feet in purple paint. She stepped on a white sheet of paper, then pressed her handprints above and finished with her autograph.

The crowd applauded and she was technically done, but she stayed longer to talk to the children as they painted and worked on various projects. Their warmth and responsiveness made her feel less jaded, somehow less weary. Who would have thought it possible?

After extensive rearrangements of her schedule, Bridget put on her swimsuit and had second thoughts. What had possessed her to agree to join Ryder for a swim class when she was in a nearly naked state? She didn't have a perfectly slim body. In fact, if honest, she was curvy with pouches. Her bum was definitely larger than her top.

Her stomach clenched. Oh, bloody hell, she might as well be thirteen years old again. Forget it, she told herself. It wasn't as if anything could happen. She and Ryder would have two six-month-old chaperones.

Within forty-five minutes, she and Ryder stood in a pool with Tyler and Travis. Tyler stuck to her like glue, his eyes wide and fearful. "It's okay," she coaxed, bobbing gently in the water.

Ryder held Travis, who was screaming bloody murder.

"Are we having fun yet?" he asked, holding his godson securely.

"Should we sing?" she asked, trying not to be distracted by Ryder's broad shoulders and well-muscled arms and chest. For bloody's sake, when did the man have time to work out?

"They would throw us out," he said. "You look good in water."

She felt a rush of pleasure. "Thank you. Is Travis turning purple?"

"I think it's called rage," he said.

"Would you like to switch off for a moment?"

"Are you sure?" he asked doubtfully.

She nodded. "Let me give him a go," she said.

Tyler protested briefly at the exchange, then attached himself to Ryder. Travis continued to scream, so she lowered her mouth to his ear and began to quietly sing a lullaby from her childhood. Travis cried, but the sound grew less intense. She kept singing and he made sad little yelps, then finally quieted.

"Aren't you the magic one?" Ryder said.

"Luck," she said and cooed at the baby, swirling him around in the water. "Doesn't this feel good?" she murmured.

By the end of class, they'd switched off again and Travis was cackling and shrieking with joy as he splashed and kicked and Ryder whirled him around in the water.

As soon as they stepped from the pool, they wrapped the boys in snuggly towels. Ryder rubbed Travis's arms. She did the same with Tyler and he smiled at her. Her heart swelled at his sweetness. "You are such a good boy. Isn't he?" she said to Ryder.

"You bet," Ryder said and pressed his mouth against Tyler's chubby cheek, making a buzzing sound. Tyler chortled with joy.

"That sound is magic," she said.

Ryder nodded as he continued to rub Travis. "Yeah, it is." His glance raked her from head to toe and he shook his head. "You look pretty damn good."

Bridget felt a warmth spread from her belly to her chest and face, down her legs, all the way to her toes. "It's just been a long time for you," she said and turned away to put some clothes on Tyler.

A second later, she felt Ryder's bare chest against her back. An immediate visceral response rocked through her and she was torn between jumping out of her skin and melting. "Yeah, it has," he said. "But that shouldn't make you so damn different from every other woman I've met."

Her stomach dipped. "Stop flattering me," she said. "Get your baby dressed. You don't want him chilled."

After pizza and a raucous bath time, Ryder and Bridget rocked the babies and put them to bed. Ryder would have preferred to usher Bridget into his bed and reacquaint himself with the curves he'd glimpsed in the pool, but he would have to bide his time. Hopefully not too long, he told himself as his gaze strayed to the way her hips moved in her cotton skirt. He'd thought he was so smart getting her out of most of her clothes by inviting her to the baby swimming class. Now he would live with those images all night long.

"Wine?" he asked, lifting a bottle from the kitchen before he joined her in the den.

She had sunk onto the sofa and leaned her head back against it, unintentionally giving him yet another seductive photo for his mental collection. One silky leg crossed over the other while the skirt hugged her hips. The V-neck of her black shirt gave him just a glimpse of creamy cleavage. For once, her lips were bare, but that didn't stop him from wanting to kiss her.

Her eyes opened to slight slits shrouded with the dark fan of her eyelashes. "One glass," she said. "I think everyone will sleep well tonight."

Speak for yourself, he thought wryly and poured her wine. He allowed himself one glass because he wasn't on call.

"It's amazing how much they can scream, isn't it?" she said as he sat beside her.

"They save up energy lying around all the time. It's not like they can play football or baseball yet."

"Have you thought about which sport you'll want them to pursue?" she asked.

"Whatever keeps them busy and tired. If they're busy and tired, they won't be as likely to get into trouble," he said.

"So that's the secret," she said with a slow smile. "Did that work for you?"

"Most of the time. I learned at a young age that I wanted a different life than the life my parents had."

"Hmm, at least you knew your parents," she said.

"Can't say knowing my father was one of my strong points."

"Well, you know what they say, if you can't be a good example, be a terrible warning."

He chuckled slightly and relaxed next to her. "I don't want to be the same kind of father he was. Drunk. Neglectful. Bordering on abusive."

"You couldn't be those things," she said.

"Why not? You've heard the saying, an apple doesn't fall too far from the tree."

"You've already fallen a long way from that so-called tree," she said. "Plus, you may be fighting some of your feelings, but you love those boys." She lifted her hand to his jaw. "You have a good heart. I liked that about you from the first time I met you."

"And I thought it was my singing voice," he said and lowered his mouth to hers, reveling in the anticipation he felt inside and saw in her eyes.

She tasted like a delicious combination of red wine, tiramisu and something forbidden that he wasn't going to resist. Ryder was certain he could resist her if he wanted. If there was one thing Ryder possessed, it was self-discipline. The quality had been necessary to get him through med school, residency and even more so now in his position at the hospital and with the twins.

For now, though, Ryder had decided he didn't want to resist Bridget. With her lush breasts pressing against his chest, discipline was the last thing on his mind. She was so voluptuously female from her deceptively airy attitude to her curvy body. He slid one of his hands through her hair as she wiggled against him.

A groan of pleasure and want rose from his throat as she deepened the kiss, drawing his tongue into her mouth. The move echoed what he wanted to be doing with the rest of his body and hers. He wrapped his hands around her waist. He slid one down to her hips and the other upward to just under her breast.

He was so hard that he almost couldn't breathe. She was so soft, so feminine, so hot. With every beat of his heart, he craved her. He wanted to consume her, to slide inside her....

Ryder slid his hand to her breast, cupping its fullness. Her nipple peaked against his palm. The fire inside him rising, he tugged a few buttons of her blouse loose and slipped his hand under her bra, touching her bare skin, which made him want to touch every inch of her. He couldn't remember wanting to inhale a woman before.

The next natural step would be to remove her clothes and his and after that, caress her with his hands and mouth. After that, he wanted to slide inside her.... She would be so hot, so wet....

All he wanted was to be as close to her as humanly possible.

From some peripheral area of his brain, he heard a knock and then another. Her body and soul called to him. He took her mouth in another deep kiss.

Another knock sounded, this time louder, but Ryder was determined to ignore it.

Suddenly his front door opened and Marshall burst into the room.

"Whoa," Marshall said. "Sorry to interrupt."

Ryder felt Bridget pull back and hastily arrange her shirt. "Who—" she said in a breathless voice.

"My best friend from high school, Marshall," Ryder said. "He has a key," he continued in a dark voice.

Marshall lifted his hands. "Hey, I called and you

didn't answer. I started getting worried. You almost always answer at night. We've had a beer three times during the last week." His friend stared at Bridget and gave a low whistle. "And who do we have here?"

Irritated, Ryder scowled. "Show a little respect. Prin—" He stopped when Bridget pinched his arm. Staring at her in disbelief, he could see that she didn't want him to reveal her title. "Bridget Devereaux, this is Marshall Bailey."

His friend moved forward and extended his hand. Bridget stood and accepted the courtesy.

"Nice to meet you, Bridget," Marshall said. "It's a relief to see Ryder with a woman."

Embarrassment slammed through Ryder and he also stood. "Marshall," he said in a warning tone.

"I didn't mean that the way it sounded. The poor guy hasn't had much company except me and the twins." Marshall cleared his throat. "How did you two meet anyway?"

"Okay, enough, Mr. Busybody. As you can see, I'm fine, so you can leave."

"Oh no, that's not necessary," Bridget said and glanced at her watch. "I really should be leaving. I have an early flight tomorrow."

"Where?" Ryder asked.

"Chicago. They have a teaching hospital. I'll be meeting with the hospital chief to present the proposal for Chantaine's medical exchange."

"Oh," he said, surprised at the gut punch of disappointment he felt when he should feel relieved. "I guess this means you've given up on our residents."

"No, but you haven't been at all receptive. My brother

Stefan has instructed me to explore other possibilities. Your program was our first choice due to the quality of your residents and also the fact that you have so many family doctors and prevention specialists. But because you're unwilling to help…"

"For Pete's sake, Ryder, help the woman out," Marshall said and moved forward. "Is there anything I can do?"

Marshall was really getting on Ryder's nerves. "Not unless you have a medical degree and are licensed to practice," Ryder said.

"I believe my driver is here. Thank you for an action-packed evening," she said with a smile full of sexy amusement.

Ryder would have preferred a different kind of action. "I'll walk you to the car," he said, then shot a quick glance at Marshall. "I'll be back in a minute."

Ryder escorted Bridget to the limo waiting at the curb. A man stood ready to open the door for her. Ryder was disappointed as hell that she was headed out of town. Stupid. "So how long will you be gone?" he asked.

She lifted a dark eyebrow and her lips tilted in a teasing grin. "Are you going to miss me, Dr. McCall?"

His gut twisted. "That would be crazy. The only thing I've been missing for the last month is sleep," he lied.

"Oh, well, maybe you'll get lucky and get some extra sleep while I'm gone. Ta-ta," she said and turned toward the limo.

He caught her wrist and drew her back against him. The man at the car door took a step toward them, but she waved her hand. "Not necessary, Raoul."

"You must enjoy tormenting me," he said.

"Me?" she said, her blue eyes wide with innocence. "How could I possibly have the ability to torment you?"

"I don't know, but you sure as hell do," he muttered and kissed her, which only served to make him hotter. He turned her own words on her. "So, Your Highness, what are you going to do about it?"

She gave a sharp intake of breath and her eyes darkened as if her mind were working the same way as his. She bit her lip. "I can call you when I return from Chicago."

"Do that," he said.

Ryder returned to his house to find Marshall lounging on the sofa and drinking a glass of red wine. "This isn't bad," he said.

"Glad you like it. In the future, give me a call before you drop in. Okay?"

Marshall looked injured. "I did call you. You just didn't answer." He shook his head and gave a low whistle. "And now I understand why. That's one hot babe, and she reeks money. A limo came to pick her up? You sure know how to pick 'em. How did you meet her?"

"In an elevator," Ryder said, not wanting to give away too many details. As much as he liked his old friend, Ryder knew Marshall could gossip worse than an old lady.

"Really?" Marshall said, dumbfounded. "An elevator. Was it just you and her? Did you do anything— adventurous?"

"Not the way you're thinking," Ryder said in a dry tone, although if it had been just him and Bridget in that elevator without the twins, his mind would have gone in the same direction.

"Well, I'm glad you're finally getting some action," Marshall said.

Ryder swore. "I'd say you pretty much nixed that tonight. Between you and the twins, who needs birth control?"

Marshall chuckled. "Sorry, bud, better luck next time. I thought I'd see if Suzanne was hanging around tonight. She stays late for you sometimes."

Realization struck Ryder. "You didn't come by to see me. You came to see my nanny. I'm telling you now. Keep your hands off my nanny. She's not your type."

"Who says?"

"I say."

"Why isn't she my type? She's pretty. She's nice," he said.

"She's six years older than you are," Ryder said.

"So? She doesn't look it. She's got a fresh look about her and she's sweet. Got a real nice laugh," Marshall said.

"I'm not liking what I'm hearing," Ryder said, stepping between Marshall and the television. "So far, Suzanne is the perfect nanny. I don't want you messing with her. The boys and I need her."

"She's an adult. She can decide if she wants me to mess with her," he said with a shrug.

"Marshall," he said in a dead-serious voice. "She's not like your dime-a-dozen girls running fast and loose. She's not used to a guy like you who'll get her in the sack and leave her like yesterday's garbage."

Marshall winced. "No need to insult me. I've had a few long-term relationships."

"Name them," Ryder challenged.

"Well, there was that redhead, Wendy. She and I saw each other for at least a couple of years."

"She lived out of town, didn't she?" Ryder asked. "How many other women were you seeing at the same time?"

Marshall scowled. "Okay, what about Sharona? We lived together."

"For how long?"

"Seven weeks, but—"

"Enough said. Keep your paws off Suzanne."

Marshall slugged down the rest of the wine and stood. "You know, I'm not a rotten guy."

"Never said you were."

"I just haven't ever found the right girl," Marshall said.

"As long as you and I understand that Suzanne is not the right girl for you, everything will be fine."

Three days later, Bridget returned from her trip to Chicago. She hadn't snagged any doctors, but she'd persuaded one of the specialists she'd met to visit Chantaine and offer lectures and demonstrations. She was getting closer to her goal. She could feel it. Even though what she really wanted to do tonight was soak in a tub and watch television, she was committed to attend a charity event for Alzheimer's with the governor's son, who was actually quite a bit older than she was. Part of the job, she told herself as she got ready. She thought about calling Ryder, but every time she thought about him, she felt a jumpiness in her stomach. Bridget wasn't sure how far she wanted to go with him because she knew she would be leaving Dallas as soon as she accomplished her mission.

There was something about the combination of his strength and passion that did things to her. It was exciting. And perplexing.

Preferring to have her own chauffeur, Bridget met Robert Goodwin, the governor's son, in the lobby of her hotel. He was a distinguished-looking man in his mid-forties who reminded her of one of her uncles. She decided that was how she would treat him.

Her bodyguard Raoul, who occasionally played double duty in making introductions, stepped forward. "Your Highness, Robert Goodwin."

She nodded and extended her hand. "Lovely to meet you, Mr. Goodwin. Thank you for escorting me to an event that will raise awareness for such an important cause."

"My pleasure, Your Highness," he said, surprising her when he brought her hand to his mouth. "Please call me Robert. May I say that you look breathtaking?"

"Thank you very much, Robert. Shall we go?"

By the time they arrived at the historical hall, Bridget concluded that Mr. Goodwin's intentions were not at all uncle-like and she prepared herself for a sticky evening. Cameras flashed as they exited the limo and Mr. Goodwin appeared to want to linger for every possible photo as he bragged about her title to the reporters.

"Everyone is excited to have a real princess at the event tonight. People paid big bucks to sit at our table."

"I'm delighted I could help the cause." Sometimes it amazed her that a single spermatozoa had determined her status. And that spermatozoa had originated from a cheating jerk of a man who had never gotten her first name right. Her father.

"Would you join me in a dance?" Robert said, his gaze dipping to her cleavage.

"Thank you, but I need to powder my nose," she said. "Can you tell me where the ladies' room is?"

Robert blinked. "I believe it's down the hall to the left."

"Excuse me," she said and headed for the restroom, fully aware that Raoul was watching. She wondered if she could plead illness. After stalling for several moments, she left and slowly walked toward her table. Halfway there, Ryder stepped in front of her.

"Busy as ever," he said.

Her heart raced at the sight of him. "So true. I arrived back in town this afternoon and had to turn right around to get ready for this event."

"With the governor's son," Ryder said, clearly displeased.

"He could be my uncle," she said.

"Bet that's not what he's thinking," Ryder countered.

She grimaced and shrugged. "It's not the first time I've had to manage unwelcome interest, and if my appearance generates additional income for this good cause..."

"True," he said, his eyes holding a misery that grabbed at her.

"What brings you here?"

"Dr. Walters. He has had an impact on hundreds of doctors, but now he can't recognize himself in the mirror."

"I'm so sorry," she said, her heart hurting at the

expression on his face. "Seeing you, hearing you, makes me glad I came. I'm ashamed to confess that I was tempted to cancel because I was so tired after returning from Chicago."

His gaze held hers for a long emotional moment. "I'm glad you didn't give in to your weariness this time."

"Even though I have to face Mr. Anything-but-Good Robert Goodwin," she said.

"Give me a sign and I'll have your back," he said.

She took a deep breath. "That's good to know. I can usually handle things. This isn't the first time."

His gaze swept over her from head to toe and back again. "That's no surprise."

Her stomach dipped and she cleared her throat. "I should get back to my table. I'm told people paid to sit with me. I'm sure it has nothing to do with my title."

His lips twitched. "Not if they really knew you," he said.

"You flatter me," she said.

"Not because you're a princess," he said.

"Call me tomorrow."

"I will," he said.

Bridget returned to her table and tried to be her most charming self and at the same time not encouraging Robert Goodwin. It was challenging, but she was determined.

After the meal had been served, he turned to her. "I'm determined to dance with you."

"I'm not that good of a dancer," she assured him.

He laughed, his gaze dipping over her cleavage again. "I'm a good leader," he said and rose, extending his hand to her. "Let me surprise you."

Or not, she thought wishing with all her heart that he wouldn't surprise her. She didn't want to embarrass the man. She lifted her lips in a careful smile. "One dance," she said and stood.

They danced to a waltz, but he somehow managed to rub against her. She tried to back away, but he wrapped his hands around her waist like a vise, drawing him against her. Suddenly, she saw Ryder behind Robert Goodwin, his hand on his shoulder. Robert appeared surprised.

"Can I cut in?" Ryder asked.

Robert frowned. "I'm not—"

"Yes," Bridget said. "It's only proper."

Robert reluctantly released her and Ryder swept her into his arms.

"Thank goodness," she murmured.

He wrapped his arms around her and it felt entirely different than it had with Robert. She stared into his eyes and felt a shockwave roll through her. "When did you learn to dance?"

"A generous woman taught me during medical school," he said, drawing her closer, yet not too close.

Bridget felt a spike of envy but forced it aside. "She did an excellent job."

He chuckled. "It was all preparation," he said. "Everything we do is preparation for what waits for us in the future."

"I would have to be quite arrogant to think your preparation was for me," she said, feeling light-headed.

"You look beautiful tonight," he said, clearly changing the subject. "I hate having to share you with anyone else."

Her stomach dipped. "It's part of who I was born to be. Duty calls," she said.

"But what does Bridget want?" he challenged. "Meet me in the foyer in fifteen minutes."

"How?" she asked.

"You'll figure it out," he said.

Chapter Five

She would figure it out, Bridget thought as she sur-reptitiously glanced at the diamond-encrusted watch that had belonged to her grandmother. Two minutes to go and she was supposed to be introduced to the crowd within the next moment.

"As we continue to introduce our honored guests, we'd like to present Her Highness, Princess Bridget Devereaux of the country of Chantaine."

Bridget stood and smiled and waved to the applaud-ing crowd. She hadn't known she was a table head, but it wasn't unusual for event organizers to put her in the spotlight given the chance. Because of her title, she was a source of curiosity and interest.

Spotting Ryder leaning against the back wall as he pointed to his watch, she quickly squeezed her hand together and flashed her five fingers, indicating she needed more time. Then she sank into her seat.

Robert leaned toward her. "I was cheated out of my dance. We need to hit the floor again."

"I wish I could, but my ankle is hurting," she said.

Robert scowled. "Maybe because of the man who cut in on our dance."

She lifted her shoulders. "Perhaps it's the long day catching up with me."

"You're too generous. We could try a slow dance," he said in a low voice.

"Oh no, I couldn't hurt your feet that way," she said. "But I would like to freshen up. Please excuse me," she said and rose, wondering why she was going to such extremes to meet Ryder when she was supposed to be concentrating on making an appearance.

Her heart was slamming against her rib cage as she tried to take a sideways route through the tables along the perimeter of the room. With every step, part of her chanted *This is crazy—this is crazy.* But she kept on walking, so she must indeed be crazy. She stepped into the foyer and glanced around the area.

Something snagged her hand. She glanced over her shoulder and spotted Ryder as he pulled her with him down a hallway. "Where are we—"

"Trust me," he said and pulled her toward the first door they came upon. It was an empty dark room with a stack of chairs pushed against a wall.

"What are we doing?" she asked, breathlessly clinging to him.

"Hell if I know," he said, sliding his hands through her hair and tilting her head toward his. "I feel like a car with no brakes headed straight for you."

"So, we're both crazy," she said.

"Looks that way," he said and lowered his mouth to hers.

Her knees turned to water and she clung to him. His strength made her feel alive despite how tired she felt from her long day of travel. Shocked at his effect on her, she loved the sensation of his hard chest against her breasts. She wanted to feel his naked skin against hers. She growled, unable to get close enough.

He swore under his breath as his hands roamed over her waist and up to the sides of her breasts. "I can't get enough of you," he muttered and took her mouth in a deep kiss again.

She felt dizzy with a want and need she denied on a regular basis. It was as if she was suffering from a more delicious version of altitude sickness. His mouth against hers made her hotter with every stroke of his tongue. More than anything, she wanted to feel him against her.

"Ryder," she whispered, tugging at his tie and dropping her mouth to his neck.

He gave a groan of arousal. "Come home with me. Now," he said, squeezing her derriere with one hand and clasping her breast with the other.

Too tempted for words, she felt the tug and pull of duty and courtesy over her own needs. Bloody hell, why couldn't she just this once be selfish, irresponsible and rude? A sound of complete frustration bubbled from her throat. Because she just couldn't. She was in the States on official business from Chantaine and she'd been assigned to represent a cause important to her and her people.

"I can't," she finally managed. "It would just be

wrong and rude and it's not just about me. I'm sorry," she whispered.

"I don't know what it is about you, but you make me want to be more reckless than I've ever been in my life. More reckless than flying down Deadman's Hill on my bicycle with no hands when I was ten."

Bridget felt the same way, but she was holding on by the barest thread of self-restraint. Suddenly the door whooshed open and closed, sending her heart into her throat. Her head cleared enough to realize this situation could provide the press with an opportunity to paint her family in a bad light.

She held her breath, waiting for a voice, but none sounded.

"It's okay," he said as if he understood without her saying a word. "Whoever opened the door must have glanced inside and not spotted us. I'll leave first, then you wait a minute or two before you leave. I'll warn you if it looks like there's a crowd waiting for you."

She paused, then nodded slowly.

Ryder gave her shoulders a reassuring squeeze and kissed her quickly, then walked toward the door. Bridget stood frozen to the floor for several breaths and gave herself a quick shake. She moved to the door and listened, but the door was too thick. She couldn't hear anything. Counting to a hundred, she cracked open the door and peeked outside. No crowd. No photogs. Relief coursed through her and she stepped outside.

"Your Highness, I was worried about you," Robert said from behind her.

Her stomach muscles tightened and she quickly turned. "Robert, how kind of you."

"What were you doing in there?" he asked.

"My sense of direction is dismal," she said. "I went right when I should have turned left. Thank you for coming to my rescue. Now I can return to our table."

He slid his hand behind her waist and she automatically stiffened, but he seemed to ignore her response. "We can leave, if you like. I could take you to my condo...."

"Again, you're being kind, but we're here for an important cause."

"Afterward—"

"It's been a full day for me flying from Chicago. I appreciate your understanding that I'll be desperate to finally retire," she said. One of her advisers had instructed her that one should speak to another person as if they possessed good qualities...even if they didn't.

"Another time, then," Robert said, clearly disappointed.

Bridget gave a noncommittal smile, careful not to offer any false hope.

When Bridget didn't hear from Ryder for three days, she began to get peeved. Actually, she was peeved after day one. He'd behaved like he was starving for her and couldn't wait another moment, then didn't call. She considered calling him at least a dozen times, but her busy schedule aided her in her restraint.

On Tuesday, however, she was scheduled to meet with a preventative adult health specialist in preparation for a video she would be filming with the doctor as a public service announcement for Chantaine.

Afterward, she meandered down the hall past his

office. She noticed Ryder wasn't there, but his assistant was. Bridget gave in to temptation and stepped into the office. "Hello. I was wondering if Dr. McCall is in today."

The assistant sighed. "Dr. McCall is making rounds and seeing interns, but he may need to leave early for family reasons. May I take a message?"

"Not necessary," she demurred, but wondered what those family reasons were. "Are the twins okay?" she couldn't help asking.

The assistant nodded. "I think so. It's the nanny—" The phone rang. "Excuse me."

The nanny! The nanny she'd selected for Ryder and the boys had been as perfect as humanly possible. Perhaps more perfect. What could have possibly happened? Resisting the urge to grill the assistant about her, she forced herself to walk away. Her fingers itched to call him, but she didn't. It would be rude to interrupt his appointments with patients or the residents.

Bothered, bothered, bothered, she stalked through the hallway. The pediatric department head saw her and stopped in front of her, smiling. "Your Highness, what a pleasure to see you."

"Thank you, Doctor. How are you?" she said more than asked.

"Great. Would you like to get together for dinner?" he asked.

"I would, but I must confess my immediate schedule is quite demanding. Perhaps some other time," she said.

"I'll keep asking," he said and gave her a charming smile that didn't move her one iota.

Brooding, she walked down the hall and out of the hospital to the limo that awaited her. A text would be less intrusive, she decided, and sent a message. Two minutes later, she received a response. *Nanny had emergency appendectomy. Juggling with backup.*

WHY DIDN'T YOU CALL ME? she texted in return.

Her phone rang one moment later and she answered. "Hello."

"It's been crazy. I've even had to ask Marshall for help."

"Why didn't you ask me?" she demanded.

"You told me your schedule was picking up. I figured you wouldn't have time," he said.

True, she thought, but she was still bothered. "You still should have called me."

"You're a busy princess. What could you have done?" he asked.

Good question. She closed her eyes. "I could have rearranged my schedule so I could help you."

Silence followed. "You would do that?"

She bit her lip. "Yes."

"I didn't think of that."

"Clearly," she said.

He chuckled. "In that case, can you come over tomorrow afternoon? My part-time nanny needs a break."

"I'll confirm by five o'clock tonight," she said. "I have to make a few calls."

"Impressive," he said. "I bet your reschedules are going to be disappointed. Too bad," he said without a trace of sympathy.

She laughed. "I'll call you later," she said and they hung up and her heart felt ten times lighter.

The following afternoon, Bridget relieved the backup nanny while the twins were sleeping. From previous experience, she knew her moments of silence were numbered. She used the time to prepare bottles and snacks for the boys.

Sure enough, the first cry sounded. She raced upstairs and opened the door. Travis was sitting up in his crib wearing a frowny face.

"Hello, sweet boy," she whispered.

He paused mid-wail and stared at her wide-eyed.

"Hi," she whispered and smiled.

Travis smiled and lifted his fingers to his mouth.

Bridget changed his diaper. Seconds later, Tyler awakened and began to babble. Tyler was the happier baby. He was a bit more fearful, but when he woke up, he didn't start crying immediately.

Bridget wound Travis's mobile and turned her attention to Tyler. She took each baby downstairs ready to put them in their high chairs. Snacks, bottles, books, Baby Einstein and finally Ryder arrived carrying a bottle of wine.

"How's everybody?" he asked, his gaze skimming over her and the boys, then back to her. "Did they wear you out?"

"Not too much yet," she said. "It helps to have a plan."

He nodded. "With alternatives. I ordered Italian, not pizza. It should be delivered soon."

"Thank you," she said.

"I'm hoping to lure you into staying the night," he said.

"Ha, ha," she said. "The trouble with luring me after an afternoon with the twins is that I'll be comatose by nine o'clock at the latest. I talked to your part-time sitter and she told me Suzanne will be out for a few more days. Is that true?"

He nodded. "She had laparoscopic surgery, so her recovery should be much easier than if she'd had an open appendectomy."

"Then I think the next step is to get a list of your backup sitters and inform them of the situation and make a schedule for the children's care. So if you don't mind giving me your names and contact information, I can try to get it straight tomorrow."

He blinked at her in amazement. "You're deceptively incredible," he said. "You give this impression of being lighthearted and maybe a little superficial. Then you turn around and volunteer to take care of my boys, recruit doctors for your country and make countless appearances."

"Oooh, I like that. Deceptively incredible," she said, a bit embarrassed by his flattery. "Many of us are underestimated. It can be a hindrance and a benefit. I try to find the benefit."

Ryder leaned toward her, studying her face. "Have you always been underestimated?"

She considered his question for a moment, then nodded. "I think so. I'm number four out of six and female, so I think I got lost in the mix. I'm not sure my father ever really knew my name, and my mother was beginning to realize that her marriage to my father was not going to be a fairy tale."

"Why not?"

"You must swear to never repeat this," she said.

"I swear, although I'm not sure anyone I know would be interested," he said.

"True enough," she said. "My father was a total philanderer. Heaven knows, my mother tried. I mean, six children? She was a true soldier, though, and gave him two sons. Bless her."

"So what do you want for yourself?" he asked. "You don't want the kind of marriage your parents had."

"Who would?" she said and took a deep breath. "I haven't thought a lot about it. Whenever Stefan has brought up the idea of my marrying someone, I just start laughing and don't stop. Infuriates the blazes out of him," she said, and smiled.

"You didn't answer my question," he said.

His eyes felt as if they bored a hole through her brain, and Bridget realized one of the reasons she was drawn to Ryder was because she couldn't fool him. It was both a source of frustration and relief.

"I'm still figuring it out. For a long time, I've enjoyed the notion of being the eccentric princess who lives in Italy most of the year and always has an Italian boyfriend as her escort."

"Italian boyfriend," he echoed, clearly not pleased.

"You have to agree, it's the antithesis of my current life."

"And I suspect this life wouldn't include children," he continued with a frown.

Feeling defensive, she bit her lip. "Admit it. The life

you'd planned didn't include children...at least for a long while, did it?"

He hesitated.

"Be honest. I was," she said.

"No," he finally admitted. "But not because I was in Italy with an Italian girlfriend."

"No, you were planning to do something more important. A career in medicine. Perfectly noble and worthy, but it would be hard to make a child a priority when you have the kind of passion you do for your career. A child would be...inconvenient."

He took a deep breath. "We choose our careers for many reasons. I wanted to feel like I had the power to help, to cure, to make a difference. It was more important for me to feel as if I were accomplishing those goals than building a family life." He shrugged. "My family life sucked."

"There you go," she said in complete agreement. "My family life sucked, too. In fact, I wanted to get so far away from it that I wanted to move to a different country."

He chuckled. "So how is it that Princess Bridget is changing diapers and taking care of my twins?"

Bridget resisted the urge to squirm. "I won't lie. I once thought children were a lot of trouble and not for me, but then I got a couple of adorable nieces. I still thought I wouldn't want to deal with them for more than a couple hours at most with the nanny at hand to change diapers, of course." She bit her lip. "But it's just so different when they're looking at you with those big eyes, helpless and needing you.... And it would just feel so terribly wrong not to take care of them."

"And how do I fit into it?" he asked, dipping his head toward her.

"You are just an annoying distraction," she said in a mockingly dismissive whisper.

"Well, at least I'm distracting," he said and lowered his mouth to hers.

Bridget felt herself melt into the leather upholstery. She inhaled his masculine scent and went dizzy with want. He was the one thing she'd never had but always wanted and couldn't get enough of. How could that be? She'd been exposed to everything and every kind of person, hadn't she?

But Ryder was different.

She drew his tongue deeper into her mouth and slid her arms around his neck. Unable to stop herself, she wiggled against him and moaned. He groaned in approval, which jacked her up even more.

From some corner of her mind, she heard a sound.

"Eh."

Pushing it aside, she continued to kiss Ryder.

"Eh."

Bridget frowned, wondering....

"Wahhhhhhh."

She reluctantly tore her mouth from Ryder's. "The babies," she murmured breathlessly, glancing down at Travis as he tuned up. The baby had fallen on his side and he couldn't get back up.

"Yeah, I know," Ryder said. "I'm starting to understand the concept of unrequited l—"

"Longing," she finished for him because she couldn't deal with Ryder saying the four-letter L word. It wasn't possible.

"Bet there's a dirty diaper involved," Ryder muttered as he tilted Travis upright.

"Could be," she said and couldn't bring herself to offer to change it. She covered her laugh by clearing her throat. "I wouldn't want to deprive you of your fatherly duty."

He gave her a slow, sexy grin. "I'll just bet you wouldn't."

"It's an important bonding activity," she said, trying to remain serious, but a giggle escaped.

"Can't hold it against you too much," he said. "You've been here all afternoon."

Bridget rose to try to collect herself. Her emotions were all over the place. Walking to the downstairs powder room, she closed the door behind her and splashed water against her cheeks and throat. Sanity, she desperately needed sanity.

The doorbell rang and she returned as Ryder tossed the diaper into the trash before he answered the door. He paid the delivery man and turned around, and Bridget felt her heart dip once, twice, three times…. Adrenaline rushed through her, and she tried to remember a charming, gorgeous Italian man who had affected her this way. When had any man affected her this way?

Oh, heavens, she needed to get away from him. She felt like that superhero. What was his name? Superman. And Ryder was that substance guaranteed to weaken him. What was it? Started with a K…

"Smells good. Hope you like lasagna," Ryder said.

"I can't stay," she said.

"What?" he asked, his brow furrowing.

"I can't stay. I have work to do," she said.

"What work?" he asked.

"Rescheduling my meetings and appearances. I also need to take care of the childcare arrangements for the twins."

He walked slowly toward her, his gaze holding hers. She felt her stomach tumble with each of his steps. "You're not leaving because you have work to do, are you?"

She lifted her chin. "I'm a royal. I always have work to do."

He cupped her chin with his hand. "But the reason you're leaving is not because of work, is it?"

Her breath hitched in her throat.

"You're a chicken, aren't you?" he said. "Princess Cluck Cluck."

"That was rude," she said.

"Cluck, cluck," he said and pressed his mouth against hers.

After making the schedule for the twins' care, Bridget paid her sister an overdue visit. Valentina had threatened to personally drag her away from Dallas if Bridget didn't come to the ranch. Her sister burst down the steps to the porch as Bridget's limo pulled into the drive.

"Thank goodness you're finally here," Tina said.

Bridget laughed as she embraced her sister. "You act like I've been gone for years."

"I thought you would be spending far more time here, but you've been appearing at events, traveling to Chicago. And what's this about you helping that physician with his twin babies? Haven't you helped him enough?"

"It's complicated," Bridget said. "He's had some childcare issues. I think they're mostly resolved now."

"Well, good. I think you've helped him quite enough. Now you can spend some time with me," Tina said as she led Bridget into the house. "I have wonderful plans for us. Two aestheticians are coming to the ranch tomorrow to give massages and facials then we spend the afternoon at the lake."

"Lake?" Bridget echoed. All she'd seen was dry land.

"It's wonderful," Tina reassured her. "The summer heat and humidity can get unbearable here. We have a pond with a swing, but we're going to the lake because Zach got a new boat. Zach and one of his friends will be joining us tomorrow afternoon. Then we'll have baby back ribs for dinner."

Bridget's antennae went up at the mention of Zach's friend. "You're not trying to set me up, are you?"

"Of course not. I just thought you'd enjoy some no-pressure male companionship. Troy is just a nice guy. He also happens to be good-looking and eligible. And if you two should hit it off, then you could live close to me and—" Tina paused and a guilty expression crossed her face. "Okay, it's a little bit of a setup. But not too much," she said quickly. "Troy and Zach are business associates, so we'll have to drag them away from talk about the economy."

Bridget's mind automatically turned to Ryder. There was no reason for her to feel even vaguely committed to him. Her stomach tightened. What did that mean? she wondered. "I'm not really looking right now," Bridget said.

"I know," Tina said. "As soon as you take care of the

doctor project, you're off to Italy and part of that will include flirtations with any Italian man who grabs your fancy. But if someone here grabs your fancy…"

"Tina," Bridget said in a warning voice.

"I hear you," Tina said. "Let's focus on your amazing niece."

"Sounds good to me. I've missed the little sweetheart," Bridget said as they walked into the kitchen.

"Missed her, but not me!" Tina said.

Bridget laughed. "I adore you. Why are you giving me such a hard time?"

Tina lifted her hand to Bridget's face and looked deep into her gaze. "I don't know. I worry about you. I wonder what's going on inside you. You smile, you laugh, but there's a darkness in your eyes."

Bridget's heart dipped at her sister's sensitivity, then she deadpanned. "Maybe it's my new eyeliner."

Tina rolled her eyes. "You're insufferable. I always said that about Stefan, but you're the same, just in a different way."

"I believe I've just been insulted," Bridget said.

"You'll get over it. Hildie made margaritas for us and she always makes doubles."

Chapter Six

Bridget's morning massage coupled with one of Hildie's margaritas had turned her bones to butter. By the time she joined Tina, Zach and Troy on the boat, she was so relaxed that she could have gone to sleep for a good two hours. For politeness' sake, she tried to stay awake, although she kept her dark sunglasses firmly in place to hide her drooping eyelids.

Troy Palmer was a lovely Texas gentleman, a bit bulkier than Ryder. Of course Ryder was so busy he rarely took time to eat. A server offered shrimp and lobster while they lounged on the boat.

"Nice ride," Troy said to Zach.

Zach smiled as Tina leaned against his chest. "My wife thought I was crazy. She said I would be too busy."

"Time will tell," Tina said. "But if this makes you take a few more breaks, then I'm happy."

"You're not neglecting my sister, are you?" Bridget asked as she sipped a bottle of icy cold water.

Zach lifted a dark eyebrow. "There's a fine line between being the companion and keeper of a princess."

"I believe that's what you Americans call baloney. You work because you must. It's the kind of man you are. I love you for it," Tina said. "But I also love the time we have together."

Zach's face softened. "I love you, too, sweetheart."

Bridget cleared her throat. "We're delighted that you love each other," Bridget said. "But I'm going to have to dive overboard if we don't change the subject."

Tina giggled. "As you wish. Troy, tell us about your latest trip to Italy."

"Italy?" Bridget echoed.

"I thought that might perk you up," Tina said.

Troy shrugged his shoulders. "I go three or four times a year. Business, but I usually try to work in a trip to Florence."

"Oh, Florence," Bridget said longingly. "One of my favorite places in the world."

Troy nodded. "Yeah, I also like to slip down to Capri every now and then…"

Bridget's cell phone vibrated in the pocket of her cover-up draped over the side of her chair. She tried to ignore it, but wondered if Ryder was calling her. Dividing her attention between Troy's discussion about Italy and thoughts of Ryder, she nodded even though she wasn't hanging onto his every word. Her phone vibrated again and she was finding it difficult to concentrate.

She grabbed her cover-up and stood. "Please excuse me. I need to powder my nose."

"To the right and downstairs," Zach said. "And it's small," he warned.

"No problem," she said cheerfully and walked around the corner. She lifted her phone to listen to her messages. As she listened, her heart sank. Tomorrow's sitter was canceling. She was calling Bridget because Ryder was in surgery and unreachable.

Pacing at the other end of the boat, she tried the other backup sitters and came up empty. Reluctantly, she called Marshall who answered immediately.

"Marshall," he said. "'Sup?"

"Hello, Marshall," she said. "This is Bridget Devereaux."

"The princess," he said. Ryder had told her that Marshall had performed a web search and learned who she was. "Princess calling me. That's cool."

"Yes," she said, moving toward the other end of the boat. "There's some difficulty with sitting arrangements for Ryder's boys tomorrow morning. I was hoping you could help me with a solution."

"Tomorrow morning," he said. "Whoa, that's a busy day for me."

"Yes, I'm so sorry. I would normally try to fill in, but I'm out of town at the moment," she said.

"I might have a friend—"

"No," she said. "As you know, Ryder is very particular about his backup sitters. He won't leave the twins with just anyone."

"True," Marshall said. "Although I'm last on the list." Silence followed.

"I'm last on the list, aren't I?" Marshall asked.

"Well, you're an entrepreneur," she managed. "Ryder

knows you're a busy man with many demands on your time."

"Yeah," Marshall said. "How much time does he need?"

"Five hours," she said, wincing as she said it.

Marshall whistled. "That's gonna be tough."

"Let me see what I can do," she said. "I'll make some more calls."

"If you can have someone cover things in the early morning, I could probably come in around ten."

"Thank you so much. I'll do my very best," she said.

"Bridget," Tina said from behind her.

"Bloody hell," she muttered.

Marshall chuckled.

"To whom are you speaking?" Tina demanded.

"A friend," Bridget said. "Forgive me, Marshall. My sister is after me."

"Good luck. Keep me posted," he said.

"Yes, I will," she said and clicked off the phone. She turned to face her sister with a smile. "I'm just working out the timing of an appearance."

"Which appearance is that?" Tina asked.

"In Dallas," Bridget said. "I must say I do love Zach's new toy. I think it will be a fabulous way for the two of you to relax."

"Exactly which appearance in Dallas?" Tina said, studying her with narrowed eyes.

"Stop being so nosy," Bridget said.

Tina narrowed her eyes further. "This is about that doctor with the twins, isn't it?"

"His sitter for tomorrow has cancelled so we have to find another."

"We?"

Bridget sighed. "If you met him, you'd understand. He performs surgery, advises residents and he's an instant father."

"Perhaps he should take some time off to be with his new children," Tina muttered.

"It's not that easy. His mentor has Alzheimer's and he's trying to fill his position unofficially."

Tina studied her. "You're not falling for him, are you?"

Bridget gave a hearty laugh at the same time she fought the terror in her soul. "Of course not. You know I prefer Italian men."

Tina paused, then nodded. "True, and although you love your nieces, you've always said you couldn't imagine having children before you were thirty."

"Exactly," she said, though she felt a strange twinge.

"Hmm," Tina said, still studying her. "Is this doctor good-looking?"

Bridget shrugged. Yes, Ryder was very good-looking, but that wasn't why she found him so compelling. Giving herself a mental eye roll, she knew Tina wouldn't understand. "He's fine," she said. "But he's not Italian."

Tina giggled and put her arm around Bridget. "Now that's our Bridget. That's the kind of answer I would expect from you. Come back and relax with us."

Bridget smiled, but part of her felt uncomfortable. She knew what Tina was saying, that Bridget wasn't a particularly deep person. The truth was she'd never wanted to be deep. If she thought too deeply, she suspected she could become depressed. After all, she'd been a fairly average child, not at all spectacular. She hadn't flunked out in school, but she hadn't excelled at anything either. Except at being cheerful. Or pretending to be cheerful.

"I'll be there in just a moment. I need to make a few calls first."

"Very well, but don't take too long. Troy may not be Italian, but he's very good-looking and spends a fair amount of time in Italy."

"Excellent point," Bridget said, although she felt not the faintest flicker of interest in the man. "I'll be there shortly."

Several moments later, Bridget used all her charm to get the part-time sitter to fill in for the morning. Relieved, she called Marshall to inform him of the change.

"Hey, did you hear from Ryder?" he asked before she could get a word in edgewise.

"No. Should I have?" she asked, confused. "I thought he was in surgery."

"He's apparently out. He just called to tell me Dr. Walters passed away this morning," Marshall said.

Bridget's heart sank. "Oh no."

"Yeah. He's taking it hard. He hadn't seen Dr. Walters in a while and he'd been planning to try to visit him later this week." Marshall sighed. "Dr. Walters was the closest thing to a father Ryder had."

Bridget felt so helpless. "Is there something I can do?"

"Not really," Marshall said. "The twins will keep him busy tonight and that's for the best. The next few days are gonna be tough, though."

She saw her sister walking toward her and felt conflicted. "Thank you for telling me."

"No problem. Thanks for taking care of the childcare for tomorrow morning. Bye for now."

"Goodbye," she said, but he had already disconnected.

"You look upset," Tina said.

"I am."

After 9:30 p.m., Ryder prowled his den with a heavy heart. His mentor was gone. Although Dr. Walters had been mentally gone for a while now, the finality of the man's physical death hit Ryder harder than he'd expected. Maybe it was because he'd lost his brother so recently, too.

Ryder felt completely and totally alone. Sure, he had the twins and his profession, but two of the most important people in the world to him were gone and never coming back. He wondered what it meant that aside from his longtime friend Marshall, he had no other meaningful relationships. Was he such a workaholic that he'd totally isolated himself?

A knock sounded on his door, surprising him. Probably Marshall, he thought and opened the door. To Bridget. His heart turned over.

"Hi," she said, her gaze searching his. She bit her lip. "I know it's late and I don't want to impose—"

He snagged her arm and pulled her inside. "How did you know?"

"Marshall," she said, then shot him a chiding glance. "I would have preferred to hear it from you."

"I thought about it," he said, raking his hand through his hair. "But you've done enough helping with the babies."

"I thought perhaps that you and I were about more

than the babies, but maybe I was wrong," she said, looking away.

His heart slamming against his rib cage, he cupped her chin and swiveled it toward him. "You were right. You know you were."

"Is it just sex? Are you just totally deprived?" she asked in an earnest voice.

He swallowed a chuckle. "I wish."

Her eyes darkened with emotion and she stepped closer. She moved against him and slid her arms upward around the back of his neck. She pulled his face toward hers and he couldn't remember feeling this alive. Ever.

His lips brushed hers and he tried to hold on to his self-control, but it was tough. She slid her moist lips from side to side and he couldn't stand it any longer. He devoured her with his mouth, tasting her, taking her. Seconds later, he realized he might not ever get enough, but damn, he would give it his best shot.

He slid his fingers through her hair and slid his tongue deeper into her mouth. She suckled it and wriggled against him. Her response made him so hard that he wasn't sure he could stand it. His body was on full tilt in the arousal zone.

He took a quick breath and forced himself to draw back. "I'm not sure I can pull back after this," he said, sliding his hands down over her waist and hips. "If you're going to say no, do it now."

Silence hung between them for heart-stopping seconds.

He sucked in another breath. "Bridget—"

"Yes," she whispered. "Yes."

Everything in front of him turned black and white

at the same time. He drew her against him and ran his hands up to her breasts and her hair, then back down again. He wanted to touch every inch of her.

She felt like oxygen to him, like life after he'd been in a tomb. He couldn't get enough of her. He savored the taste and feel of her. Tugging at her blouse, he pushed it aside and slid his hands over her shoulders and lower to the tops of her breasts.

She gave a soft gasp that twisted his gut.

"Okay?" he asked, dipping his thumbs over her nipples.

She gasped again. "Yesssss."

He unfastened her bra and filled his hands with her breasts.

Ryder groaned. Bridget moaned.

"So sexy," he muttered.

She pulled at his shirt and seconds later, her breasts brushed his chest. Ryder groaned again.

The fire inside him exploded and he pushed aside the rest of her clothes and his. He tasted her breasts and slid his mouth lower to her belly and lower still, drawing more gasps and moans from her delicious mouth. Then he thought about contraception. Swearing under his breath, he pulled back for a second. "Give me a few seconds," he said. "You'll thank me later."

He raced upstairs to grab condoms and returned downstairs.

"What?" she asked.

"Trust me," he said and took her mouth again. He slid his hand between her legs and found her wet and wanting.

Unable to hold back one moment longer, he pushed

her legs apart and sank inside her. Bridget clung to him as he pumped inside her. She arched against him, drawing him deep.

He tried to hold out, but she felt so good. Plunging inside her one last time, he felt his climax roar through him. Alive, he felt more alive than he'd felt for as long as he could remember.... "Bridget," he muttered.

Her breath mingled with his and he could sense that she hadn't gone over the top. He was determined to take her there. Sliding his hand between them, he found her sweet spot and began to stroke.

Her breath hitched. The sound was gratifying and arousing. A couple moments later, she stiffened beneath him. He began to thrust again and she came in fits and starts, sending him over the edge.

He couldn't believe his response to her. Twice in such a short time? He wasn't an eighteen-year-old. "Come to bed with me."

"Yes," she said. "If I can make my legs move enough to walk upstairs."

He chuckled and knew the sound was rough. Everything about him felt sated, yet aroused and rough. "I'll help."

"Thank goodness," she said.

He helped her to her feet, but when they arrived at the bottom of the steps, he swept her into his arms and carried her up the stairs.

"Oh, help," she said. "I hope I don't give you a hernia."

"If you do, it'll be worth it," he said.

She swatted at him. "You're supposed to say I'm as light as a feather even though I may weigh half a ton."

"You took the words out of my mouth. You're light as a feather," he said.

She met his gaze and her eyes lit with a glow that both warmed and frightened him. "Excellent response," she said and took his mouth in a sensual kiss that made him dizzy.

"Whoa," he said and stumbled the rest of the way to his room. He set her on the mattress and followed her down. "You smell amazing," he said inhaling her scent. "You taste incredible," he said and dragged his tongue over her throat. "I want to be inside you all night long."

Her breath hitched again and she swung her legs around his hips. Sliding her fingers into his hair, she pulled his mouth to hers. "Do your best," she whispered and he thrust inside her.

Later that night, Bridget awakened, finding herself curled around Ryder. She was clinging to him. Her body said she wanted all of him, as much as he could give, as much as she could receive. But it wasn't just her body that craved him; some part deep inside her felt as if she belonged exactly where she was.

Her breath abandoned her. How was she supposed to manage this, this physical, yet highly emotional relationship with a man like Ryder? It wasn't even a man like Ryder. It was Ryder himself.

Ryder slid his thigh between hers, sending her sensual awareness of him into high mode. "You're awake," he said, sliding his arms around her. "You weren't planning on going anywhere, were you?"

"No. Just thinking."

"I'll put a stop to that," he said and distracted her again with his lovemaking. Afterward, she fell asleep.

The sound of a baby crying awakened her minutes later…. *Had it really been hours?* she wondered as she glanced at the alarm clock. Looking beside her, she saw that Ryder had already left the bed. The second baby started crying and she rose from the bed and pulled on one of Ryder's shirts. Thank goodness it covered her nearly to her knees because she'd left her own clothes downstairs.

She met Ryder in the hallway as he carried a baby in each arm. "Sorry our good-morning song woke you," he said with a wry, sleepy grin. His hair was sleep-mussed and a whisker shadow darkened his chin. Shirtless, he wore a pair of pajama pants that dipped below his belly button. She couldn't remember when he'd looked more sexy.

Reining in her thoughts, she extended her hands to take one of the twins. "I can help."

Tyler immediately fell toward her and she caught him in her arms.

"He made that decision pretty quickly. Can't fault his judgment," he said with a chuckle. "I already changed their diapers."

"Really?" she said, astonished.

"Don't look so surprised," he said as he led the way down the stairs. "My baby-care skills are improving."

"Congratulations," she said and put Tyler into one of the high chairs while Ryder slid Travis into the other high chair. She immediately put a few Cheerios on the trays while she prepared the bottles.

Ryder prepared the oatmeal. "You're getting faster at this baby stuff, too."

"I watched Suzanne one morning and took notes. She's so efficient."

"I'll be glad when she can come back," he said.

"Oh, speaking of that," she said. "The part-time sitter should be here any—"

A knock sounded at the door and Bridget felt a sliver of panic as she glanced at her bare legs and thought of her clothing strewn across the den. "Oh, bloody—Stefan will have my head. I'll be back in a couple moments," she said and grabbed her clothes and scrambled upstairs to get dressed. She glanced in the mirror and tried to tame her hair before she returned to the stairs.

Ryder met her halfway with an inscrutable expression in his eyes. "Embarrassed to be caught with an American doctor?"

"Not embarrassed so much as I wouldn't want my brother Stefan to find out. He really prefers we maintain a squeaky-clean image. And unfortunately we never know when someone may leak something to the press. That can turn into a huge mess."

"So you keep all your lovers hidden?" he asked.

"There haven't been that many," she said. "Do you really want paparazzi standing outside your door assaulting you with questions about me?"

"Good point," he said. "I'm going up to my study for a while. Dr. Walters's wife has asked me to write a eulogy for his memorial service."

Bridget's heart twisted at the grief Ryder was clearly trying to conceal. "I'm so sorry. Are you sure I can't do anything for you?"

His lips twitched. "You did a damn good job distracting me last night."

She felt her cheeks heat. "I was thinking of a cup of tea."

He shook his head. "I drink coffee. Breakfast would be nice, though."

She blinked. "Food. You want me to prepare food?" she echoed, at a loss. She'd taken one cooking class in her younger years and couldn't remember anything from it except how to put out a fire on a stove top.

He chuckled. "Sorry. I forgot your position, Your Highness."

She immediately felt challenged by his tone. "Well, it's not as if I can't prepare a meal. I just don't do it on a regular basis."

"When was the last time?" he asked.

She lifted her chin. "I prepared lunch for the twins just last week."

He laughed again, this time louder. "Bottles and jars of fruits and vegetables."

"They seemed to like it," she said. "Okay, what would you like for breakfast?"

"I'm guessing eggs Benedict would be too much to ask," he said.

She glowered at him.

"Okay. I'll go easy. Scrambled eggs, toast and coffee."

"I'll be right back with it," she said, muttering to herself as she continued down the rest of the stairs. This was ridiculous. Why should she care if Ryder considered her unskilled in the kitchen? He obviously respected her other talents such as organizing his childcare.

After a brief consultation with the sitter, however,

Bridget burned everything, even the coffee. She cleaned up her mess and started over, this time cooking everything on low. It seemed to take forever, but she finally got the job done and took the tray to Ryder's upstairs study.

He opened the door, wearing a distracted expression. "Thanks," he said, took the tray and closed the door.

She frowned, but took a breath. He was performing a difficult task. He needed understanding and patience.

Bridget went to his bedroom and arranged for a cleaning service. In her opinion, the house needed regular servicing. The sitters shouldn't be expected to clean in addition to keeping the twins. The twins were already a handful. An hour later, the cleaners arrived and she decided to take more coffee to Ryder.

She knocked on his door with the cup outstretched.

"Thanks," he said, still distracted as he accepted the cup. He closed the door again. She hesitated to interrupt, but thought it best to remove the dirty dishes, so she knocked again.

He opened the door, his eyebrows furrowed. "What?" he asked, almost in a curt voice.

"I thought I would take your dishes from breakfast," she said.

"Breakfast?" he said, his brow furrowing more.

"Yes, the eggs and toast you requested," she said.

"Oh," he said and went into his office. Seconds later, he returned with his uneaten eggs and toast.

"You didn't touch them," she said.

"Yeah, sorry. I'm really hung up over this eulogy."

Her frustration spiked. "I fixed these eggs and you didn't take a bite."

"I apologize. Really," he said, his face grief-stricken. In another instance, she would have screamed. But she knew Ryder was suffering.

"Fine," she managed in a tight voice. "What would you like for lunch?"

"Oh, anything. A ham sandwich. Thanks, *B,*" he said and closed his door again. *B?* She'd never been called *B* in her life.

She helped the sitter with the boys, then took another trip to Ryder's study with a ham sandwich.

"Thanks," he said and accepted the sandwich.

"Are you okay?" she asked before he could close the door in her face.

He shook his head. "I'm not there yet." He leaned forward and pressed a quick kiss against her mouth.

After that brief meeting, Bridget left because she sensed Ryder needed his space and she was determined to respect it.

Ryder finally finished writing the eulogy. He had no idea what time it was until he glanced at the clock. 4:30 p.m. Whoa. Later than he intended. Good thing he'd cancelled all his appointments and that this wasn't a surgery day. Stretching his neck, he glanced around the room and noticed the sad-looking ham sandwich on the table on the other side of the room.

His heart swelled at the thought of Bridget bringing him food, reaching out to him. Taking the plate, he walked downstairs expecting to see the fresh, sexy face of Bridget Devereaux.

Instead he was greeted by Marshall.

"Hey, dude," he said. "How's it going?"

"Okay," he said. "The twins?"

"Down for a nap," Marshall said.

"Bridget?"

Marshall lifted a brow and smoothed back his hair with his hand. "She was here?"

"Yeah. She fixed me breakfast and a sandwich for lunch," Ryder said, frowning.

"Breakfast," Marshall repeated.

Reluctant to reveal details about his relationship with Bridget, he shrugged. "She showed up early. You should know. You told her about Dr. Walters. I was working on his eulogy."

Marshall winced. "Sorry, bro. I'm guessing she left a while ago. The sitter didn't say anything about her."

Ryder's gut tightened. "Okay, I guess she had other things to do."

"Well, she *is* a princess," Marshall said.

"Yeah," Ryder said.

"You're starting to fall for her, aren't you?" Marshall asked.

"Hell no."

Chapter Seven

"Dr. Walters was more than a brilliant doctor. He was a father figure to many of us who'd never known a father. He was an advocate at the same time that he demanded the best of every resident who crossed his path. He was the best man I've ever known," Ryder said and glanced at the large group who had gathered to remember Dr. Walters.

His gaze skimmed the crowd and stumbled over a classy young woman wearing a black hat and black dress. *Bridget.* Her presence gave him a potent shot of strength.

He continued with the rest of his eulogy, then made his way toward Bridget. The seat beside her was empty. Her eyes widened as he stepped in from the aisle.

"Thanks," he whispered, sitting down and clasping her hand between them.

"There was no other choice than to be here for you," she whispered.

His heart swelled at her words and he squeezed her hand, trying to remember the last time someone had been there for him like this. No expectation, just support and some kind of emotion close to love. Yet it couldn't be love, he told himself.

Her hand, however, sure felt great inside his.

A couple hours later, Ryder and Bridget joined Mrs. Walters for an afternoon meal. Dr. Walters's widow seemed to have aged a decade within the last year.

"You were his favorite," she said to Ryder, her eyes full of pain as she smiled. "He wasn't supposed to have a favorite, but he did."

Ryder's heart squeezed tight. "He was the father I never had. He challenged me and empathized with me. He made me want to be my best."

Mrs. Walters nodded. "He was an inspiring man."

"I'm lucky that he was my mentor," Ryder said.

Mrs. Walters nodded and frowned. "He was a wonderful, wonderful man. But we never had children. Our family life was always dependent on his schedule." She paused. "If there was one thing he might have changed before he…went away…" She swallowed over her grief. "I think he may have spent more time with his family. Me. His brothers and sister. Until he began to fade, he didn't realize how important relationships were." She closed her eyes for a moment, then shrugged. "I'm rambling." She patted Ryder's hand. "Never forget that you are more than that hospital. Never," she said.

Shaken by her fervent expression, he took a quick breath. "I won't," he said.

Within a half hour, he escorted Bridget to his car. "Come back to my house," he said.

She paused a half beat, then nodded. "Yes."

Moments later, they walked into his house. The sitter sat on the couch reading a book. "Hi," she said. "Everything go okay? The twins are sleeping and they've been no trouble."

"Good to hear it," he said. "I'm gonna change my clothes. Will you be here for a while?"

The sitter nodded. "I'm scheduled to be here till six. Then I have a class."

"Thanks," he said and turned to Bridget. "There's a place I want to take you."

"If it involves hiking or swimming, I'll need to change clothes," she warned him.

"You'll be okay."

Seven minutes later, he pulled in front of a waterfall fountain. Man-made but spectacular.

"It's beautiful," she said as they walked close to the fall and lifted her face to the spray. "Have you been here often?"

"Yes," he said, squeezing her hand.

"I can see why," she concluded and closed her eyes. "Whenever I have a few minutes near water, it reminds me of Chantaine. For all my complaining about being chained there the last year, I can't deny the effect water has on me. Makes me wonder if I have a gill somewhere. What about you?" she asked. "You've been landlocked most of your life, haven't you?"

"Yes, but I find that spending some time near water,

and I mean more than a shower or swimming pool, balances me out. Especially if something is bothering me."

"It's natural that Dr. Walters's passing would upset you," she said.

"It's more than that," he said. "Now that he is really gone, his position with the residents will need to be filled."

"You want it very much, don't you?" she asked.

Ryder felt torn in two completely opposing directions. "I feel a huge responsibility. The other doctor who would want the job comes off as callous. He doesn't care about helping residents with problems. His first instinct would be to cut them from the program. Dr. Walters probed deeper before making that kind of decision and he made himself available to residents for conference. The goal at our hospital is to approach the physician as a complete person so that he or she, in turn, treats the patient as a complete person."

"The doctors in your program are very fortunate to receive that kind of benefit, but based on what Dr. Walters's wife said, it must be difficult for the adviser to strike the balance as a complete person." She sighed. "In a different way, serving our country as royals can be an all-consuming proposition. Makes you wonder if there's such a thing as balance outside of a yoga class."

Her yoga reference made him smile. "How is it you can make me feel better on such a dark day?"

"One of my many delightful skills." She glanced again at the fountain. "Have you ever wanted to jump in one of these and get completely wet?"

"Yes," he said. "Where I was raised we had a small

fountain in the town in front of a bank. When I was a little boy, I jumped in it and stomped around. Got a paddling that kept me from sitting down for a week."

"Was it worth it?" she asked.

"Before and during, yes. Afterward no."

"I almost took the plunge once in Italy, but I knew I would be arrested and there would be a big fuss."

"So you restrained yourself," he said.

She frowned. "Yes, but one day. Maybe soon after I'm able to bring back some doctors to Chantaine and I take my long vacation in Italy..."

"Is that why you're in such a rush to import doctors?"

"Trust me, I've earned this break. Even Stefan agrees, but he and I both know Chantaine needs doctors. After my sister-in-law was injured so horribly while saving my life, it became even more clear. I still—"

The darkness in his eyes surprised him. "You don't still hold yourself responsible, do you?"

She paused a half beat too long. "Of course not. The gang stampeded her. Even security was taken by surprise," she said as if by rote.

"But you still feel responsible," he said.

"She wouldn't have been there if I hadn't begged her to join me," she said. "For someone to put her life on the line for me, and it wasn't as if she had taken an oath to protect me. She just did it because of who she is."

"And because of who you are," he said.

"Now that's a stretch," she said. "I spend a lot of time at charity events and school and business openings. It's not as if I'm in a research laboratory finding cures for dreadful diseases."

"No, but you're helping raise money for those

research scientists, and someone needs to do it. Don't underestimate your importance. You inspire people to give more than they usually would."

"Perhaps," she said, but clearly wasn't convinced. "Now I just need to find a way to inspire doctors to come to Chantaine. At least I've already got one specialist willing to hold seminars," she said, then shook her head. "But today isn't about me or Chantaine. It's about you, Ryder. How else can I help you with your grief?" she asked in a solemn tone.

His mind raced in a totally different direction down a path filled with hot kisses and hot bodies pressed against each other. He couldn't help but remember the sight of her naked body in his bed. He couldn't help but want her again.

Her eyes widened as if she could read his mind. "You're not serious," she said. "Men. Sex is the solution for everything."

"There are worse ways to deal with grief," he said.

"True, but with the sitter at your house, it would be difficult to indulge that particular solution," she said.

"You're right," he said. "I should get back to the hospital. I canceled my schedule for the rest of the day, but making up for a lost day is hell."

"Absolutely not," she said, then bit her lip. "I suppose we could go to my suite."

His gut twisted at the prospect of holding her again. He didn't understand his draw to Bridget. All he knew was that his life had seemed full of darkness and when he was with her, he felt lighter. With his demanding schedule, he felt as if he needed to snatch whatever stolen moments he could with her. "That's an invitation I can't imagine turning down," he said, sliding his fingers over a silky strand of her hair.

Her breath hitched and he found the response gratifying and reassuring. He was damn glad to know he wasn't the only one feeling this crazy attraction.

After an afternoon spent drowning his devils in Bridget's bed, a cell-phone alarm sounded.

"Time to go," Bridget said, then rubbed her mouth against his cheek and pulled away.

He caught her just before she rose from the bed. "What's the rush?"

"It's five-thirty. The sitter will be leaving at six," she said with a soft smile and pulled on a robe.

"Damn, it's that late?" He glanced at the alarm clock beside the bed to confirm her announcement and shook his head. He raked his hand through his hair. "Hey, come back to the house with me. We can get something delivered."

"I'm sorry, I can't. I have a previous commitment this evening. I'm attending a forum to promote the prevention of gang violence. As I'm sure you can imagine, this is a cause near and dear to my heart. The Dallas district attorney will escort me," she said.

Ryder's gut gave a vicious twist. He'd heard the current D.A. was quite the lady's man. "I'm guessing Corbin made those arrangements," he said, unable to keep his disapproval from his tone.

"I believe he did. I'm only using a part-time assistant while I'm in Texas, but the arrangements went through her. She left me a dossier on him, but I've been too busy to scan it."

"I can tell you what you need to know," he said rising from the bed. "Aiden Corbin was elected two years ago and is a hound dog when it comes to women."

"What exactly is a hound dog?" she asked.

Ryder scowled. "It's a man who will do just about anything to get women into his bed."

"Is that so?" she said and shot a sideways glance at him. "It seems to me I've met several *hound dogs* here in Dallas."

"Hey, I'm no hound dog. I'm a hardworking doctor trying to take care of my brother's twin babies."

"It's really hard for me to buy your defense with you standing naked in front of me," she said, her glance falling over him in a hot wave that made it hard for him to resist pulling her right back into bed.

"I'm not used to being with a woman who has to fight off my competitors with a stick," he said.

She blinked. "Competitors," she echoed. "That would suggest I view these men on the same level as you, which I don't."

"What level is that?"

She paused then frowned. "Different. Besides, I don't have to beat the men off with a stick. And you must remember their primary attraction to me is due to my title and perhaps the erroneous view that I'm loaded."

"You underestimate your appeal."

"Hmm," she said. "Minus my title, I'm extremely average."

"You're wrong," he retorted. "You're beautiful and talented. You're…magic," he said, surprising himself with his words. Even though they were all true, they weren't the kinds of things he would usually say.

Bridget paused. Her eyes shimmering with emotion, she threw herself against him and wrapped her arms around him. "That's the nicest thing anyone has ever said to me. I'm not sure I agree, but it's quite wonderful that you would actually think those things about me. Thank you, Ryder. I will cherish your words forever," she said, then pulled away.

Something about her thank-you reminded him that his relationship with Bridget was temporary. That was fine with him. Lord knew, with everything on his plate, he didn't have time for a real relationship with a woman. For that matter, he'd never taken time to have a *real* relationship with a woman. He'd always been too busy with his career. So this relationship was no different, he told himself, but something about that didn't settle right with him.

That night, after he'd tucked the twins into their cribs and watched the rest of the ball game, he half glanced at the local news. Just as he was about to switch the channel, a video of Bridget and the D.A. appeared.

"Her Royal Highness, Bridget Devereaux of Chantaine, accompanied Dallas's district attorney, Aiden Corbin, to a special discussion at the Dallas Forum tonight. Reporter Charles Pine reports."

"Your Highness, welcome to Dallas. I'm curious, how can a small, idyllic island like Chantaine have a gang problem?"

"My country is quite idyllic, and we're quite fortunate that we have only occasionally had problems with gangs. Still, there have been incidents, and we are always exploring ways to prevent such problems in the future. Mr. Corbin has generously offered to present his experiences and knowledge by visiting our country in the future."

"Sounds like a rough gig, Mr. Corbin," the reporter joked.

Corbin gave a wide smile that looked lecherous to Ryder. "The princess is being very generous with her public and charitable appearances while she visits our city. The least I can do is to share my expertise in return."

Ryder bet the D.A. wanted to share more than his expertise. His stomach burned from the pizza he'd eaten earlier. His cell phone rang and he saw the caller ID belonged to Marshall.

Ryder answered the call, but Marshall started talking before he could open his mouth.

"Hey, what's your babe doing with our slimeball D.A.?"

"It's just business," he said, grinding his teeth at the same time.

"Business with the horn dog of the century?" Marshall asked. "If she was my woman, I wouldn't let her anywhere near Corbin."

Ryder bit his tongue. He'd had the same strange primitive reaction, but he had to contain himself.

"Whoa," Marshall said after the short silence. "You didn't say anything. Does that mean she's fair game? Because I gotta tell you that's one sweet piece of—"

"Don't even think about it," Ryder said. "With a sharp knife, I could disembowel you in less than sixty seconds."

Marshall gave a dirty chuckle. "Gotcha. I was just

kidding. I'm focused on someone else. I could tell something was cooking between the two of you. The way you act about her. The way she acts about you."

"What do you mean the way she acts about me?"

"Well, she's busted her royal ass trying to make sure your boys have got good care," Marshall said. "Speaking of good care, I took a bucket of chicken to your nanny the other day. Seemed the charitable thing to do."

"You took food to Suzanne?" Ryder said. "I told you to leave her alone."

"It was just chicken. She's been recovering, for God's sake. Give the poor girl a break," Marshall said.

Ryder narrowed his eyes. "You don't deliver chicken unless you're hoping for something for yourself."

"I'm insulted," Marshall said. "I can be a nice guy. Listen, I don't have time for this. I'll just tell you that you might want to keep an eye on your little princess because Aiden Corbin is known for poaching. G'night, Mr. M.D."

Ryder opened his mouth to reply, but he knew Marshall had clicked off the call. Marshall had always called him Mr. M.D. when he thought Ryder was getting too big for his britches. Trouble was, what Marshall had said about Corbin was right. The other trouble was Ryder had no real claim on Bridget, so the only thing left for him to do was stew. No way, he told himself. There was no good reason to stew over a temporary woman. He'd never done it before, and he wasn't going to start now.

Bridget left two messages on Ryder's cell during the next two days, but he hadn't answered. She worried that something may have happened. What if there'd been a problem with the nanny? Had his workload tripled as a result of Dr. Walters's death? She already knew he'd been reluctant to touch base with her when things weren't going well, so she decided to make a quick trip to his office at the hospital.

He was in a meeting with a resident, but just as she started to leave a message with his assistant, the resident exited his office.

"I'll let him know you're here," his assistant said.

Another moment later, Ryder opened his door. "Come in," he said.

Wondering at his abrupt tone, she entered his office and watched as he closed the door behind her. "I was concerned when I didn't hear back from you. Is everything okay with you and the twins?"

"No problem," he said. "Suzanne returned to work and the boys seem to be fine."

She frowned at how remote he seemed. "Are you sure you're okay? You seem—"

"Busy," he said in a firm voice.

"Well, I didn't mean to bother you," she said.

"I have another two or three minutes," he said.

Her jaw dropped of its own volition. "Excuse me?"

"I said I have another two or three minutes. Then I need to go to a meeting."

"Why are you acting this way?" she demanded.

"What way?"

"As if we're strangers," she said. "As if we've never shared a bed."

His eyes suddenly darkened with turmoil. "We don't have a committed relationship."

Bridget's heart twisted. She felt as if he'd slapped her. "Does that mean you have to act rude and uncaring?"

He paused. "No, but we both know this isn't a long-term relationship. You have your reasons. I have mine. There's no need to pretend anything different."

If she felt he'd slapped her before, she now felt he'd stabbed her. "I wasn't pretending. I was just caring," she said. "Clearly a mistake," she said and turned toward the door.

He grabbed her arm just before she reached the doorknob.

She turned, feeling more confused than she could remember in her life. "Why are you acting this way?"

"Our relationship isn't normal," he said.

"Well, you're not normal and neither am I, so why should it be?"

"I have no right to comment on what men you spend time with," he said

Realization swept over her. "Oh, for bloody sakes, is this about the D.A.?"

"Saw you on the news," he said. "He was trying hard."

"And got nowhere," she said. "Do you really think I would hop into bed with him after I'd just been with you? Do you really think I would hop into bed with anyone? You must think I'm the most promiscuous woman ever born."

"You get a lot of offers," he said and she could see he was torn. He was accustomed to being in control and now he wasn't.

"I get offers because I'm a princess, not because I'm me," she said.

"Not—"

She shook her head. "Okay, we'll have to agree to disagree. Again. The point is I haven't engaged in a meaningless affair, well, ever," she said. "It's just not my nature. And my affair, I'm not sure I like that word. My relationship with you isn't meaningless. I don't exactly know what it means because you and I seem to be headed in different directions. But I'm incredibly drawn to you. I can't explain it and I don't particularly like it. It's bloody well inconvenient, but damn it, you're important to me."

He stared at her for a long moment, then gave a short, humorless laugh. "Ditto."

"What does that mean?"

"Exactly what you said. I'm willing to ride this horse to the end of this race if you are."

Bridget had to digest his words. She wasn't accustomed to such references.

"I mean we'll take it till the end and then kiss each other good-bye," he said.

The word good-bye bothered her, but she didn't feel as if she had any other choice.

"Deal?" he asked, extending his hand.

She slowly placed her hand in his. "Deal."

He pulled her against him. "Come over tonight," he said.

Her heart slammed against her rib cage. "I'd like to, but I have a previous engagement."

"Damn," he said. "Just tell me it's not with Aiden Corbin."

She shook her head. "It's with the head of Pediatrics."

Ryder swore. "That's better?"

"You told me if I bring medical experts to Chantaine to do temporary training, then I'll have a better chance of attracting doctors."

"Why can't you choose old, married experts?" he grumbled.

She smiled. "Introduce me."

He lowered his head and gave her a long kiss that made her head spin.

When he pulled back, they were both breathing hard. "What about tomorrow night?"

"I have an engagement," she said. "But I'll rearrange it."

"Okay. Tomorrow night is another water class for the twins. I'll order takeout for us." He gave her a quick firm kiss. "You'd have more fun with me than the Pediatrics department head tonight."

Ryder arrived home a few minutes late that night to find Marshall's truck parked in front of his house. He opened his front door to find Marshall bouncing Tyler on his knee while Suzanne was changing Travis's diaper.

Tyler squealed. Marshall grinned. "Looks like somebody's glad to see you," he said and immediately handed the baby to Ryder.

Ryder's heart lifted at the baby's obvious joy and he kissed him on his soft cheek. Travis also gave an ear-splitting shriek.

Suzanne glanced up at him. "I've already fed them, but they're a little worked up. That may be due to Marshall," she said with a faintly accusing expression.

"Hey, I was just entertaining them until you got

home," Marshall said and picked up Travis. "I thought I'd try to give Suzanne a break from the heavy lifting."

Uh-huh, Ryder thought. "It's okay. I'm glad they're in a good mood. Can you give me a quick minute to talk to Marshall?"

"Of course," Suzanne said. "There's no rush. And if you want to change clothes, I can wait for that, too."

"Thanks," he said and gave a sharp jerk of his head to go outside to Marshall.

Ryder carried Tyler in his arms and Marshall carried Travis. "What the hell do you think you're doing?" Ryder demanded.

"Hey, I'm just helping out your nanny. You don't want another one to quit because of these wild boys, do you?"

"Suzanne had no intention of quitting. She's just recovering from her appendectomy," Ryder said.

"All the more reason for me to stop by and help her. These boys are getting bigger every day."

"She doesn't need your help."

"Says who?" Marshall challenged.

"Says me," Ryder retorted. "You just want to get into her pants."

Marshall shot him a quelling glare that would have worked with any other man.

Not Ryder. "Stay away from my nanny."

"You're just edgy because you're not getting any," Marshall said.

"That's none of your damn business," Ryder said.

"It is if it makes you act like a jerk," Marshall said, then sucked in a quick breath. "Listen, I like Suzanne. I think she likes me. I wanna give this a try."

"She's not your kind of woman," Ryder said.

"Well, maybe I've been going after the wrong kind of woman."

Ryder groaned. "If you wreck my nanny, I'll kill you."

"Give me a chance," Marshall said. "She is."

Ryder swore under his breath. "Okay, but if you mess up her mind…"

"Yeah, yeah, yeah," Marshall said. "When are you supposed to see your princess again? For the sake of all of us, I hope it's soon."

Filled with misgivings, Ryder watched his nanny drive off in Marshall's wake to a restaurant. Maybe he was just jealous, a voice inside him said, and he brushed it aside. The boys were rowdy and demanding and absorbed every ounce of his energy by the time they fell asleep.

When he awakened the following morning to the sound of Travis screaming at the top of his lungs, he could have sworn it was the middle of the night. Instead, it was 6:30 a.m.

Stumbling into the twins' bedroom, he picked up the baby and held him against him. "Hey, bud, what's up? You're okay."

Travis's cry melted to a whimper, and Ryder sensed the baby was missing his real father and mother. The thought twisted his gut. Poor kid would never know his real dad and mom. He was stuck with Ryder, and Ryder knew he would never be the father his brother would have been.

Chapter Eight

Later that morning, Ryder joined the chief of staff with Dr. Hutt in a meeting to discuss the future of the adviser program.

"There's been some debate over how we should continue this program in the future now that Dr. Walters is no longer with us," the chief of staff said.

"It's one of the things about our program that makes it distinctive and appealing to residents," Ryder said. "I can't imagine changing it."

"I agree that the program should continue," the chief said. "But Dr. Walters was one of a kind and we may need to make changes."

"Not if those changes will negatively impact the residents," Ryder countered.

"The residents needed to be toughened," Hutt said. "They've chosen the medical profession. It's a demanding field, so they need to be ready to take on their jobs.

Long hours and dedication to excelling in their fields are critical."

"They also need to deal with their patients as individuals. We enforce that teaching by treating them as individuals," Ryder said, feeling his back get up, ready for a fight.

"You're too soft on them," Hutt said.

"You treat them like a machine because that's how you treat your patients," Ryder said.

"Gentlemen," the chief of staff intervened. "There's no need for insults."

Ryder resisted the urge to glare at him and took a quick breath. "Forgive me," he said. "But Dr. Walters was very important to me. It would be an insult to him if I didn't present his point of view in this discussion."

"And you think I'm not," Hutt said. "Dr. Walters was my adviser, too. I worshipped the ground he walked on. What he taught me was the importance of discipline."

Ryder couldn't disagree. Discipline was critical to a doctor's success. "I've never disagreed with the importance of discipline, but Dr. Walters also emphasized to me to remember the human element."

"You're both right," the chief said. "And you've both clearly demonstrated your superior ability as medical doctors. The difficulty is that Dr. Walters spent an unbelievable amount of time counseling residents at the same time he managed his patient load. There was rarely a time he wasn't here at the hospital. Neither of you can make that kind of time commitment."

"I have a very understanding wife."

"I have a perfect nanny."

"Therefore," the chief of staff said. "I am going to assign both of you as intern advisers."

That sounded like a horrible idea to Ryder. "I can't imagine that Dr. Walters would approve."

"Unfortunately, Dr. Walters isn't here to give his advice. I agree that the advisership is one of the unique features of our program, but I can't in good conscience assign the total advisership to you, Dr. McCall, given your new family obligations."

"The two of you will have to work together or I will find new advisers," the chief continued. "The three of us will meet in two weeks."

Ryder led the way out the door, barely resisting the urge to slam it shut behind him. "This is a joke," he muttered.

"Hey, I don't want to work with you either. Just because you were Gordon's favorite doesn't mean the rest of us didn't see how great he was. And don't try to deny it. How did you get the financial relief you needed when your mother was dying?" he challenged.

Ryder's fingers itched to punch Hutt in his face. "He pointed me in the direction of several teaching opportunities. One of them worked out. It was that or wait tables. How did *you* get through med school?"

"You know how I got through. My parents paid for me. I started partying a little too much once I graduated and he told me I had to toe the line or go somewhere else. Rode my butt every time I walked into the hospital. I learned the hard way the importance of discipline."

"I did, too. I just learned it about ten years earlier than you did because I had to," he said and turned away.

Hutt caught his arm. "Just curious, what would it

take for you to give up the advisership and let me take it over?"

"A miracle," Ryder said.

"Too vague. I can't shoot for that," he said.

His colleague's response took him by surprise. "You gotta understand the guys who don't have parents who can pay their way. You gotta understand the guys who don't get into school because their daddy knows somebody. I'm not sure you can get there. Ever."

"You're an ass," Hutt said.

"So are you," Ryder said.

"Maybe that's why the chief is making us work together."

"Unless he's hoping we'll kill each other," Ryder muttered and went to his office.

That night, although Ryder physically did everything the teachers instructed them to do with the babies, Bridget could tell his mind was somewhere else. She tried not to focus on it as she watched Tyler put his face in the water and blow bubbles.

"Good boy," she said, praising the baby. "Good for you. Such a brave, brilliant boy."

Travis must have taken a competitive cue because he plunged his face in the water and lifted it, choking. Frightened, he began to cry.

"Oh no, that water went down the wrong way," she said, passing Tyler to Ryder and holding out her hands for Travis. "Poor thing. No need to go diving," she gently chastised him. "Watch," she said and lowered her mouth to the water and blew bubbles.

Ryder followed her lead and blew bubbles, making a sound with his deeper voice.

Travis quickly dried up and stared.

"Do it again," she said.

Ryder repeated and Travis let out a belly laugh.

Bridget couldn't resist laughing, too. "What a brilliant sound," she said. "Do it again."

Ryder dipped his head and shot her a dark, mocking look. "Yes, Your Majesty." He blew bubbles and this time, both Travis and Tyler laughed.

"Well done," she said. "Just a couple more times."

"Want to give it another go?" she asked Travis. "We can do it together." She lowered her mouth to the water to blow bubbles. "Come on."

Holding him securely, she dipped his chin in the water. He made a motorboat sound with his lips. Slowly, she lowered his mouth and he made the same sound. Just before he breathed in water, she pulled up his chin, and again he let out a belly laugh.

"Good boy," she said. "Brilliant."

"You never say that to me," Ryder muttered.

"Perhaps you need to try harder," she retorted.

He groaned and she felt his gaze sweep over her body with a flash of instant need before he hid it. 'You could drive a man insane, Your Majesty," he said.

"Your Majesty is incorrect. If you're going to address me correctly, you should say Your Highness. Or if you want to irritate me, you could use the term my brother-in-law's housekeeper uses. Your Highliness."

"I like that," he said. "Has a nice ring to it. Your Highliness."

She scowled. "So what put you in a bad mood at

work? Did one of your patients develop a secondary infection?"

"Hell no," he said frowning. "How did you know something happened at work?"

She rolled her eyes. "Because you're here and not here at the same time. You do everything the teachers say, but you're not really here. Some women would be insulted."

"It's probably best if I'm not completely here because looking at you in that bathing suit could make things embarrassing for me when I step out of the pool. But because you asked, there are some complications with the resident advisory position. I have to deal with the equivalent of the M.D. devil."

She winced. "That can't be enjoyable. Then again, would he be easier to deal with than you?"

He shot her a deadly look. "If you don't mind dealing with someone who will lie to your face."

She frowned. "Bloody hell for both of us," she muttered under her breath.

The teacher ended the class and Bridget and Ryder climbed out of the pool with the boys. Bridget changed Travis's drenched diaper while Ryder changed Tyler's. "You and your brother are the most brilliant, fabulous boys in the world. Never doubt it," she said and rubbed her nose against Travis's.

The baby laughed and grabbed at her. Her heart twisted in her chest. "So sweet."

"You're good with them," Ryder said.

"Shocking, isn't it?" she said.

"I think both of them have a crush on you," he said, leaning toward her. "Or maybe all three of us."

She smiled, feeling a surprising flood of warmth flow inside her. "You think they really like me? I've never thought of myself as good with babies."

Travis pressed a wet, open-mouth kiss against her cheek.

"Yeah, they clearly hate you," Ryder said.

She sighed. "I never thought I could adore babies this much."

"Me either," he said, drawing Tyler against him. The baby snuggled against him. "Not sure about this father-hood thing. I didn't have the best example."

"Neither did I," she said. "He couldn't ever remember my name."

"You're joking," he said, disturbed by the complacent expression on her face.

She shrugged. "My mother's job was to reproduce. There were a bonus of girls. She stopped after the second son which was after Phillipa and me."

"You weren't close to your mom either, were you?" he guessed.

"Hers wasn't a happy marriage. My mother had high hopes when she married my father, but she ended up terribly disappointed. So yes, I'm ill-prepared to be a loving mother. The only part of my background that gives me hope is my siblings. Stefan and Tina were more like parents to me."

"I guess that's another thing we have in common. We didn't have the best parents in the world. We were just on opposite ends of the spectrum. Yours were royal. Mine were dirt-poor," he said. "How did I get lucky enough to have a princess half-naked in a pool with me?"

"And your twin boys," she added, laughing. "I'm glad they like me. It's amazing how they get under your skin."

"Yeah," he said, looking down at Tyler. "I just hope I can figure out how to keep them safe, happy and feeling like they can conquer the world."

"I think you will," she said. "If anyone can, you can."

"The great thing about the swimming class is that it totally wears out the boys and they sleep like babies should," Ryder said, sitting on the couch beside Bridget with his hand wrapped around hers. "The bad thing is that it wears me out, too."

She gave a low, throaty chuckle that grabbed at his gut. "Times ten," she said.

"If you're as tired as I am, then you better stay the night," he said.

She slid him a sideways glance. "My driver could take me home. It would be no problem."

"Maybe not for him, but it would be for me," he said, drawing her head toward his and taking her mouth in a long kiss.

When he pulled away, Bridget sighed. The sound was magic to him. He couldn't get enough of her and he hated himself for it, yet he couldn't avoid it.

"Does that mean you'll stay the night?" he asked. "I can promise I'll wake you up in the middle of the night."

She lifted her hand to the back of his head and drew his lips to hers. "Just do your best," she said and he vowed he would.

The next morning, Bridget awakened to the sound of babies crying and the sight of an empty bed. She'd stayed the night with Ryder, and he had apparently left early this morning. Pulling one of his shirts around her and buttoning it, she walked toward the nursery.

Walking inside, she nearly bumped into Suzanne.

"Oh, please excuse me," Bridget said, covering a yawn.

Suzanne yawned in response. "No problem," she said. "I arrived a little late and Dr. McCall left right out the door."

"He has a lot on his mind," Bridget said.

Suzanne nodded. "I can tell. You can go back to bed. I can handle the boys."

"No, I'll carry him downstairs," Bridget said, changing Travis, then picking him up and holding him against her. "No need to cry. You're probably still tired from all that swimming."

"They can steal your heart pretty quickly, can't they?" Suzanne asked, smiling at Bridget as she cuddled the baby.

"Yes, I never dreamed I could feel this much affection for two little semi-humans who spit peas at you, scream bloody murder and can get downright stinky. Whenever anyone asked me how I felt about babies, I always thought they were fine if they belonged to someone else."

"I was just the opposite," Suzanne said. "I wanted to have children, but I couldn't. My husband felt the same way. That's a big part of the reason he left."

Saddened by Suzanne's confession, Bridget frowned as she followed the nanny downstairs. "But there are other ways, adoption, surrogacy...."

"He wanted children the natural way," Suzanne said.

"I'm sorry. It was clearly his loss. I have to believe there's a better man in your future," Bridget said.

Suzanne's cheeks turned pink. "Maybe, but I'll never marry again. The ending was just too painful. What about you? Is marriage in your future?" she asked as if she wanted the attention diverted away from her.

Bridget blinked, uncomfortable with the question, so she gave her automatic response as she put Travis into a high chair. "No time soon. Italy is calling me first, and then we'll see."

"What about Dr. McCall?"

"Oh, he's not interested in marriage. He has his hands full with the boys and his practice and the residents at the hospital. I'm certain it's not in his plans to marry anytime soon."

"Plans can change in an instant," Suzanne said. "I bet he didn't plan to be a daddy to twins either."

"So true," Bridget agreed, growing more uncomfortable with the conversation with each passing second. "It's definitely been a shock. That's enough of an adjustment without adding a wife into the mix."

"Hmm," Suzanne said as if she didn't quite agree but wouldn't say more.

Bridget felt a rush of relief. "Can you handle the feeding? I'd like to take a shower."

"No problem. Take your time," Suzanne said.

As Bridget stepped under the warm spray of water in Ryder's shower, she smelled the scent of his soap and felt surrounded by him again. She wondered if she and Ryder were making a mistake by becoming involved. She preferred the notion that her attraction to him was strong but temporary; however, between her surprising, growing feelings for the babies and her assignment to set up a program for doctors to Chantaine, their relationship was complicated at best.

Bridget dressed and allowed her hair to air-dry with the plan to perform her daily makeover at her hotel suite. She lingered at Ryder's house, playing with the twins until her phone rang and it was Stefan.

Her stomach sank with dread at the prospect of talking to her brother. So far, she'd successfully avoided speaking to him directly by keeping him apprised via email. Stefan was a wonderful, good-intentioned but interfering brother, and because he was crown prince, he could get more than a bit bossy. His new wife, Eve, had helped to rein him in, but the man had been born to rule. Some traits could never be eradicated.

"Hello, Stefan. My, you're up late. How are you?" she asked, moving away from the twins so he wouldn't hear them in the background.

"I'm fine. I need to discuss the progress with the doctor program—"

Tyler let out a loud scream as Bridget left his sight. Bridget winced, walking quickly toward one of the downstairs bathrooms and closing the door.

"What was that? It sounded like a wild animal," he said.

Close enough, she thought ruefully. "It was a baby. I guess it's naptime. Now, regarding the doctor program, I've hit a snag with—"

"Baby," he echoed. "What are you doing with a baby? You don't like children."

"I don't dislike children," she said. "I've just never spent much time with them. That was a twin infant I met by chance. I've gotten to know the family because they've had a bit of a crisis. Everything is headed in the right direction now, though. About the doctors for Chantaine—"

"This wouldn't be one of Dr. Ryder McCall's twin nephews, would it? Valentina told me you've been spending quite a bit of time with Dr. McCall and his children."

Valentina had snitched on her. She would have to be more careful what she said to her sister. "It turns out Dr. McCall is the resident adviser for the Texas Medical Center. I've been trying to persuade him to participate in our program, but he says that working on Chantaine isn't prestigious enough because we don't already have any specialized programs or research in place."

"Chantaine, not prestigious enough," he said, his tone dripping with fury.

Bridget had indicated that she'd not made as much progress as she wanted because the head adviser was ill and the hospital was undergoing transition, which was partly true. She'd hoped she wouldn't have to tell Stefan the full truth because she'd known he would be offended. "I reacted the same way. Told him he was the most insulting man I'd ever met. Now to accomplish my task, I'm stuck trying to get him to compromise," she said with sigh.

Silence followed. "Bridget, you're not trying to use seduction as a way of convincing the man, are you?"

Bridget laughed, partly from hilarity, partly from hysteria. If Stefan only knew. Heaven help her if he did. Then again, Raoul would talk if pressed. "If only it were that easy," she said. "The man is almost as stubborn as you are," she said.

Another silence passed, and Bridget could feel her brother's tension through the phone line. "That doesn't bode well for our plan. You've begun to approach other hospitals."

"Yes, I have, but I'm getting similar, though more politely worded, responses. Because of that, I've begun to invite various high-level doctors to Chantaine to conduct training and seminars. So far, three doctors have committed."

"Excellent," he said. "We may need to expand our search."

"I know. I'm hopeful that if I can recruit some additional specialists that we'll be able to overcome the objections of our top choices for hospitals," she said.

"Bridget," he said. "I know that part of the reason you feel strongly about this is because of what happened to Eve," he said.

"Of course I do. Thank goodness she received the care she needed in time."

"I feel the same way. Just keep your meetings businesslike," he said.

Bridget frowned. "What do you mean?"

"I mean, you can be charming and you're young and attractive. These men could become enamored with the idea of seducing a princess. I wouldn't want your reputation to suffer as a result of any misplaced determination."

"Now, I believe I'm insulted. Do you really believe I'm so easily swayed? And do you think this is the first time I haven't had to put up with unwanted advances?"

"There's no reason for you to be insulted. I'm just looking out for you. What do you mean, unwanted advances?" he demanded. "Raoul is supposed to stay on top of that."

"Unless you have something further to say that could be construed as helpful, I believe we've spoken long enough. I have things to do as I'm sure you do, too."

"Bridget, do not hang up on me. I'm not finished," her brother commanded.

She was tempted to push the button to disconnect. So tempted that her finger itched. "I'm waiting," she finally said.

"Phillipa is coming to Texas for a visit," he announced. "She's been acting depressed for the last few weeks and she's had a terrible time working on her dissertation. Eve thinks getting away from Chantaine and taking a break from her studies will help her."

Her stomach twisted in concern. "You don't think she's ill, do you?"

"No, she's been checked out by the royal doctors, but after Ericka's drug problems, I can't take any chances."

Alarm shot through Bridget. Her sister Ericka had become dependent on drugs and spent more than one stint in rehab. Thank goodness, she'd left her problems behind and she was now happily married to her French film-director husband. "I can't believe our Pippa would get involved with drugs. Not after how much all of us suffered when Ericka was having her problems."

"I don't think she is, but she's lost weight and seems miserable and distracted. A change of pace will refresh her."

"Between Valentina and me, we'll do our best," she promised.

"The initial plan is for her to spend most of her time at the ranch, but I'm sure she'll come into Dallas for a visit," he said.

"Yes," she said. "Thank you for letting me know. And how are Eve and Stephenia?"

"Eve is wonderful. Stephenia is a terror, but I swear I think she's already learning to read. Still quite demanding that I read to her every night if at all possible," he said, his tone a mixture of exasperation and tenderness.

"You're a lucky man, Stefan, to have a wife and daughter who love you," she said, then couldn't resist adding, "along with your loyal, subservient siblings."

He gave a short laugh. "Yes to both, although my siblings will never be subservient."

"It's not in our genes," she said. "Give my love to Eve and Stephenia."

"I will. And Bridget," he said, "if you can't work things out with this Dr. McCall soon, we'll move past him and onto someone more cooperative."

Bridget's stomach twisted at the thought. "I hear what you're saying."

"Good," he said. "All for now. We'll talk soon."

Bridget took a deep breath as the call was disconnected. Her mind raced with thoughts about Phillipa, Ryder and the twins, and her assignment to recruit new doctors to Chantaine. She grew dizzy under the opposing priorities and returned to the den with the idea of heading outside to clear her head.

On her way, however, Travis screeched at her.

"His version of hello?" she said to Suzanne.

"I think so," Suzanne said. "It's time for their morning nap and Tyler is almost there. Travis is next."

"I'll take him," Bridget said and went to the blanket on the floor to pick up the baby. "How are you doing, mister?"

He made an unintelligible sound and plastered his open mouth against her in a wet baby kiss.

Her heart turned over. "You're such a flirt," she accused in a voice she knew was far too affectionate.

He put an open-mouth kiss against her cheek again.

"Too much," she said and cuddled him.

Travis snuggled against her and sank his head against her throat. He sighed and seconds later, his breathing became more regular. Another half minute and she felt drool sliding down her neck.

It was the sweetest moment of her week. Or month. Or longer.

"You have a calming effect on him," Suzanne whispered. "He looks like he could sleep right there against you forever."

Travis sighed against her skin and she felt the terrible urge to tear up. Heaven help her, she needed to get her emotions under control.

Travis wiggled again and clung to her as if she were the most important person in the world. Her heart dipped at the way the baby made her feel. He was so vulnerable. She wanted to take care of him, make him feel safe…. Yet, he wasn't her baby.

Bridget savored his baby scent and the sensation of his healthy, chubby baby body in her arms. What an addictive combination. She wanted to hold him until nighttime…or later… Is this what happened to parents?

Perhaps this is why babies survived. They made you want to take care of them. Forever.

It took another few moments in the rocking chair, but Bridget finally decided Travis could hit the sack. She carried him upstairs to the nursery and gently placed him in his crib. Tyler was already asleep. Travis was the fussier baby. That should have made him less desirable, but Bridget considered it a challenge to comfort him and help him fall asleep.

"Very good for a princess," Suzanne said from the doorway. "Are you sure you don't have some magic you're hiding in your back pocket?"

Flattered, Bridget quietly stepped from the room and pulled the door shut behind her. "You should know better. The only magic with babies is if they feel safe."

"They both feel safe with you," Suzanne said.

Bridget's heart twisted. What did all of this mean? "I should go. I have appointments and phone conferences."

"Princess things to do," Suzanne said with a gentle smile.

Bridget nodded. "But if you have a problem with the twins, call me."

Suzanne sighed. "You hired me to take care of the twins. Yet you feel you need to help. Why is that?"

Bridget's stomach clenched again. "I'm not any kind of expert. It's like you said earlier. They sneak up on you and grab your heart."

Chapter Nine

After Bridget finally tore herself away from the babies, she threw herself into her task of soliciting visiting medical experts for Chantaine. It irritated her when the experts laughed off her proposal, but she persevered and won two maybes and one new definite yes for her efforts.

Between her schedule and Ryder's, they only managed text messages and a few phone calls. Although she was tired by bedtime, she was surprised at how much she missed Ryder and the boys. Just as she fell asleep, her cell phone rang. Her heart skipped at the caller ID.

"Hello," she said.

Before she could say another word, he said. "Dinner. Tomorrow night. 7:00 p.m. No excuses. It's been too long."

She laughed, crazy thrilled to hear his voice. "Oh my. Is it a doctor thing that you give orders like a royal?"

"Maybe," he said. "I can't talk. I've got to check on a patient," he said.

"This late?" she asked and heard the sound of voices in the background.

"He's diabetic and he's experiencing some complications from surgery. I'll stay another hour to make sure he's stable. Tomorrow night, I'm taking you out."

The next morning, soon after Bridget awakened, she received a call from her sister Tina. "We're coming to town for dinner tonight. You must join us."

"Oh no. I'm sorry, but I already have a commitment," Bridget said, immediately feeling edgy because she knew Tina had talked to Stefan.

"Is it business or pleasure? Because if it's pleasure, we can all go out together," Tina offered.

Bridget paused. Her dinner with Ryder promised pure pleasure, but if she discussed Chantaine's medical program, it could be construed as business.

"I can tell by your hesitation that it's pleasure," Tina said before Bridget could pull an excuse together. "We'll pick you up for a six-thirty dinner at the Longhorn Club."

"It'll have to be a 7:00 p.m. dinner," she automatically corrected. "Ryder has already set the time and I'm sure he'll be busy going from the hospital, home and back out again. In fact, this may not be such a good idea after all. He's extremely busy lately. I haven't seen him myself in three days."

"Three days," Tina repeated. "If that's such a long gap of time between your dates, then I would say the two of you are getting quite cozy. All the more reason for me to meet him."

Resenting her sister's interference, Bridget frowned. "And which member of the royal family gave your husband Zachary the stamp of approval while the two of you were seeing each other?"

"None, but my pregnancy put a different spin on the situation—" Tina gasped. "You're not pregnant, are you?"

"Of course not," Bridget said.

"But the two of you must be serious for you to get all snippy with me," Tina continued. "The only way you can disprove it is if you and your doctor meet Zach and me for dinner tonight. Ciao, darling," she said and hung up.

Bridget swore at the phone and tossed it on her bed. She didn't want to share Ryder with her sister or anyone else at the moment. She was appalled to admit, only to herself, that she'd missed Ryder and the twins terribly during the last few days. It had taken every bit of her self-control not to dash over to his house to hold the babies or to visit Ryder at the hospital. She knew, however, that she was growing entirely too attached to all three males. And now Ryder would have to face an inquisition from both her sister and her brother-in-law. She wouldn't blame Ryder if he ran screaming.

Deciding to give him the easy way out, she sent him a text message. *Change of plans. My sister and her husband insist we join them for dinner. I'll understand if you can't join us.*

When he didn't immediately answer, she suspected he was trying to word his response and took a shower, feeling glum, bordering pouty. Amazing how one phone call from her nosy sister could send her mood into the pits. When she got out of the shower, her cell phone dinged to indicate a message.

I'm in. Where?

Her heart turned cartwheels and she gave him the name of the restaurant along with a warning that her sister's interrogation could rival the American's CIA. Although she much preferred sharing an evening with Ryder without the company of her sister, she couldn't deny she was excited to get to see him, period.

That night, Bridget fought a surprising spate of nerves on the way to the restaurant. "Tell us more about your doctor," Tina said.

"You'll meet him soon enough," she said. "He's very work-oriented, but he's making adjustments now that he's the guardian for his twin infant nephews." She deliberately changed the subject. "Stefan told me Phillipa will be coming for a visit soon. He sounded worried. Have you had a chance to talk with her?"

"I've called, but she hasn't returned my call, which has me concerned. What about you?"

"I just left a message telling her I was looking forward to seeing her. She may need to relax a little before she's ready to talk. I didn't want to put any more pressure on her. I wondered if it was related to her studies, but Phillipa has always thrived under academic pressure."

"I think a little quiet time at our ranch will help her and we can come into town for a little fun. Of course, you could spend more time at the ranch, too," Tina said in a pointed voice.

"I have a task to complete and I can't do it from the

ranch," Bridget said, refusing to give in to her sister's dig. "Now I'm in the process of trying to lure medical specialists to come to Chantaine so we can attract more medical doctors to our program."

"And what about your Dr. McCall? How would he feel about visiting Chantaine?"

Bridget laughed at the thought, yet felt a twinge of sadness at the same time. "He's far too busy with his work at the hospital and with the twins. I can't imagine his even considering it."

"Oh, I don't know," Tina said. "Maybe because the two of you are so close—"

"Not that close," Bridget said flatly.

"If you're looking for doctors who would like to combine a vacation with teaching in Chantaine, I might know a few," Zachary offered.

"Oh, that would be fabulous. Please do let me know of any of your connections," Bridget said.

"Zachary recruited an obstetrician to the small town close to the ranch, so he might be able to give you some tips," Tina said.

"Part of it is finding the right person. Not every doctor wants to practice in a big city hospital. You may have your heart set on Texas Medical Center, but the truth is some highly qualified doctor in a backwater town might like the idea of spending some time on an exotic island with easy access to Europe."

"Thank you," she said, her mind already exploring possibilities. "I hadn't thought of that."

Tina squeezed her husband's arm. "What an intelligent, resourceful man."

"Well, I got you, didn't I?" he said and Bridget felt a

twinge of longing. How would it feel if Ryder acted the same way toward her? Biting her lip, she gave herself a hard mental shake. She had other plans. Italy beckoned.

She arrived at the exclusive restaurant and was seated with Tina and Zach. Ryder arrived fifteen minutes later, appearing distracted as he strode to the table. "Sorry," he said and leaned down to kiss her full on the mouth. "I've missed the hell out of you," he whispered.

He turned to Tina and Zach. "Your Highness," he said. "Your Highness's husband."

Both Tina and Zach chuckled. "Please call me Tina," she said.

"And I'm Zach," he said, rising to offer his hand.

"Excuse me if I'm checking my cell phone messages. I have a patient teetering on the edge tonight. He's diabetic and I would have preferred not to operate, but this wasn't an optional procedure."

"Is this the same patient you were watching last night?" Bridget asked.

"Yes," Ryder said. "He improved, but I'm concerned about circulation to his extremities."

Bridget automatically extended her hand toward his beneath the table. Ryder responding by clasping it against his knee. "If you need to leave," she began.

"I can stay for now. I just need to check my messages," he said.

"We're glad you could join us," Tina said. "You've certainly captured Bridget's attention and that's not easy to do."

Bridget fought a rise of heat to her cheeks. "Tina," she said.

"Really?" Ryder said. "That's encouraging news

because wherever she goes the men are chasing after her."

"I told you that's just because of my title," Bridget said.

"Not true," he said.

"Exactly," Tina said, and Bridget felt her sister study her intently.

Bridget picked up the menu. "I wonder what the specials are tonight."

The waiter took their orders, Ryder frequently checked his phone messages and even excused himself once to make a call.

"Is this what you want for your future?" Tina asked. "He's been half-focused on his phone throughout the entire meal."

"He could have cancelled, but he came. If someone important to you was in the hospital, wouldn't you want to know his doctor was this conscientious?"

Tina frowned. "I suppose. I just can't see you being happy with someone so intent on his career."

Bridget leaned forward. "Ryder and I haven't made any mention of commitment," she whispered. "We're just enjoying each other's company."

"As long as he's not enjoying the company too much," Zach said.

"I'm not pregnant, if that's what you're asking," she said.

"Low blow," Tina said.

"You deserve it," Bridget said, feeling pushed to the edge. "Stefan told me you tattled about me seeing Ryder. I would have expected better from you."

"It's my duty to look after you," Tina said.

"Isn't that the same thing Stefan said to you?" Bridget challenged.

Tina gasped in offense. "Well—"

Ryder reappeared at the table, relief written on his face. "Good news. My patient's condition is improving."

"Excellent news," Bridget said as the waiter cleared the plates from the table.

"Excellent," Tina agreed, though she shot Bridget a sharp look. "Bridget tells me you've recently taken over the guardianship of twin baby boys. That must have been traumatic for all of you. My sympathies on the loss of your brother and sister-in-law."

"Thanks," Ryder said. "Bridget has actually helped smooth the waters with the twins. She found a nanny who has been a perfect fit. Until she stepped in, I was scrambling. I had several quit on me. With my profession, I need dependable childcare."

"Well done, Bridget," Tina said, appearing impressed and vaguely surprised.

"Your friend Keely helped. She gave me the name of the top nanny agency in Dallas," Bridget said.

"But Bridget interviewed the candidates and selected the final choice," he said.

"Bridget isn't known for her affinity for babies," Tina said.

Thanks for nothing, Bridget thought.

"Neither am I," Ryder said bluntly. "But she stepped right in. She's been a lifesaver. The boys adore her."

"And what about you?" Tina asked. "What are your intentions?"

"Tina," Bridget scolded.

"It's a good question," Zach said, backing up his wife.

Bridget balled her fists in her lap. "You do not have to answer that question, Ryder."

Ryder placed his hand over hers underneath the table. "I don't mind answering. Bridget and I have just met. Neither of us know what the future holds. Based on the demands our lives place on us, I know our relationship is temporary."

Bridget's heart fell to her feet. Even though she agreed with Ryder's assessment, hearing the words wounded her to the quick. *She was temporary.*

The interminable meal finally ended fifteen minutes later. Ryder shook hands with her sister and brother-in-law, then brushed a kiss against the corner of her mouth. "Miss you," he murmured just for her ears. "Call me."

A few moments later, she sat in the back of her brother-in-law's SUV, still feeling shell-shocked.

"I can see why you like him," Tina said. "He's his own man and clearly isn't after you because you're royalty. Plus, it doesn't appear that he intends to keep you from going to Italy," she added with a low laugh.

Bridget couldn't muster the careless response she should have been able to toss back to her sister. Silence stretched inside the car.

"Bridget, are you okay? Why are you so quiet?" Tina asked, turning around to look at her.

Bridget thanked heaven for the darkness. "I'm just tired," she said.

"Are you sure? You were always such a night owl."

"I'm sure," she said, trying not to resent her sister for pressing Ryder. It had been so much easier for her when her relationship with Ryder had remained undefined. Some part of her must have craved the sense of possibility with him. He was so different from any man she'd ever known. Ryder and the babies almost made her rethink Italy.

Blessedly, Zach pulled in front of her hotel. Relief rushed through her. If she could just get upstairs without another inquisition. "It was so wonderful seeing both of you. Thank you for dinner," she said and stepped outside the car when the valet opened her door.

Tina rushed outside her door. "Bridget," she said, studying her face. "I know something is wrong."

"Nothing is wrong," Bridget said, pushing a strand of her hair behind her ear. "I told you I'm just tired."

"I don't believe you," Tina said. "I can sense you're upset."

Bridget lost her patience. "Why should I be upset? You just grilled my boyfriend and me. I had a perfectly wonderful evening planned with him, but instead we went to dinner with you and might as well have been sent to walk across coals."

She watched her sister's face fall in desolation. "I'm so sorry," Tina said. "Zach and I just wanted to make sure this man wasn't going to take advantage of you."

"Would you have wanted Zach to receive the same kind of grilling you gave me?"

"I didn't know you felt the same way about Ryder that I felt about Zach," Tina said.

"It doesn't matter how you judge my feelings. It matters how I judge my feelings. I'm an adult. I don't need my sister, brother, brother-in-law and everyone else legislating or judging who I see." She lifted her chin. "Have a little faith in me for a change."

Tina's eyes turned shiny with tears. "Oh, I'm so

sorry. I did the same thing to you that I didn't want done to me."

Bridget took a quick sharp breath. She hated to hurt her sister, but Bridget needed Tina to believe in her. Just a little. "Yes, you did. Do you really believe I'm so stupid that any man can get my attention?" she asked, then continued before her sister could continue. "I know I acted like a spoiled brat when I had to come back from Italy after two weeks to cover for you, but I still came back and I still covered. I'm not a total ditz."

"Oh, Bridget," Tina said, shaking her head and clasping Bridget's hands. "I never thought you were a ditz. I always knew you were underestimated. I owe you a huge debt for stepping in for me and also dealing with Stefan. I just don't want you to be hurt."

Bridget bit the inside of her lip. Too late for that, she thought. "I won't be," she reassured her sister and gave her a hug.

"Don't be mad at me," Tina whispered.

"I'm not," Bridget said.

"Promise?" Tina asked.

"Promise," Bridget said.

"You'll never bring another man around me, will you?" Tina asked.

"It'll be a while," Bridget said with a rough laugh. "I need to hit the sack. Long day tomorrow. I love you." She waved to Zach and gave her sister one more hug, then walked inside the hotel toward her suite. When she got inside, she collapsed on her bed and gave in to her tears.

Bridget soldiered through her appointments the next day. Just after four-thirty as she was headed back to her hotel to change for a dinner appearance, she received a call from Suzanne.

"Your Highness, I probably shouldn't call you, but I thought you should know," the nanny said in a tear-filled voice.

"What is it? What's wrong?" Bridget asked.

"It's Travis. His fever shot up to 105 degrees," she said. "We had to take him to the hospital because it was too late for the pediatrician."

Bridget's heart sank to her feet. "Where is Ryder?"

"He's at the hospital," she said. "In the emergency room with a pediatric specialist." She gave a muffled sob. "I'm at Ryder's with Tyler."

She fought the urge to hyperventilate. Nothing could happen to that baby. Nothing. "I'm going to the hospital."

"Ryder didn't tell me to call you," Suzanne said.

"Well, he bloody well should have," Bridget said and told her driver to head for the hospital.

Ryder had never felt so helpless in his life as he watched his nephew, now his son, suffer the tests necessary to make him well. Travis screamed at the top of his lungs. "I'm sorry, Dr. McCall, but I think we're going to need to do a spinal tap."

Sweating everything but blood, Ryder nodded. "Do what you have to do to make him well." Ryder was well aware that Travis's condition was deteriorating. He couldn't remember feeling this kind of terror ever before.

After the spinal, Ryder heard a ruckus outside the examination room. A nurse entered. "I'm sorry, but there's a woman outside. She says she's a princess. She insists to be allowed inside with you and your son."

The nurse may as well have hit him with both fists. *She's a princess.* It was Bridget. A crazy sliver of relief slid through him. *Your son.* The words echoed inside his brain over and over. "Let her in," he said.

Seconds later, Bridget burst into the room wearing a hospital gown. She glanced from him to Travis, who was curled up exhausted on the table. Ryder would have preferred his cranky cries to his silence. He touched the baby's arm.

Bridget touched Ryder's.

Struggling with a terrible sense of desperation, he covered her hand with his.

"Can I hold him?" she asked.

"Not yet." They'd been instructed to wait to hold Travis, who was hooked up to an IV.

"He's going to be all right," she said softly as she held Ryder's hand. "He's a strong baby."

"He's always the one to cry the loudest and the longest," Ryder said, surprised at the strength of the fear he was fighting. Medically, he understood everything that was being done, but some part of him felt it wasn't enough. There had to be more. There had to be a way.

A few more moments passed. Bridget squeezed his hand and took a deep breath. "Can we hold him now?" she asked the nurse when she entered the room.

"For just a few moments," she said. "Take care for his IV."

Bridget sat and held Travis. His vital signs showed less stress within a moment of her cuddling him. Ryder took his turn holding the baby a while later and he was surprised to see he had the same effect on him.

Sometime later, the pediatrician strode into the room. "Lab results are back. Strep," he said. "With antibiotics, he'll be better in no time."

"Are you sure?" Bridget asked. "He seems so listless."

The pediatrician smiled gently. "With the right treatment, these little guys recover so quickly they make me look like a miracle worker. You just need to make sure everyone who's been exposed to him receives preventative treatment, too."

"Tyler," Bridget said to Ryder.

"And Suzanne and the other sitters. Thanks, Carl," he said to the pediatrician. "I know you stayed late for this. I owe you."

"I'm glad it was so easy," he said and glanced at Bridget. "And I don't believe I've met your wife."

Ryder felt a twist of awkwardness, but rushed to correct his colleague for Bridget's sake. "She's not my wife, but we've been damn lucky to have her around. This is Bridget Devereaux."

Carl nodded. "You clearly have a calming effect on the baby. You must be a natural."

Bridget laughed wryly. "I'm not sure I'd call myself a natural, but I'm relieved Travis will be okay. Thank you so very much."

"No problem. We'll have him stay the rest of the night. I wouldn't be surprised if he'll be ready to be released by midday. I'll talk to you later," he said and headed out the door.

Ryder stared at Bridget tenderly holding his nephew, his child, as if Travis were her own child. Something inside him shifted. Stone walls he'd long considered closed cracked open and he felt a burst of sweet oxygen in places that had felt dead. The expansion inside him was almost painful. For a second, he looked away to gather his defenses, to put himself back together the way he needed to be.

When he looked at her again, he saw a tear drop from her eye to Travis's gown. She gave a quick sound of distress and swiped at her cheek.

The sight of her tears shocked him. Bridget was no crybaby. "Are you okay?"

"I apologize," she said, not lifting her head. "I was just so frightened for him. And I felt so helpless."

He couldn't not reach out to her. Pushing her hair from her cheek, he felt the dampness of her tears against the back of his fingers. "Yeah," he said. "Me, too."

She finally met his gaze. "They're so fragile. One minute, he was screaming bloody murder and trying to scoot to get a ball, and the next...this," she said, looking down at Travis as he slept, his energy clearly spent fighting his infection.

Moved more than he'd thought possible, Ryder kissed her cheek. "Thank you for coming."

"There was no other place more important for me to be," she said and met his gaze again.

The powerful emotion he saw in her gaze resonated inside him so strongly that it took his breath. What the hell was going on? Later, he told himself. He would figure it out later. For the moment, his priorities were perfectly clear. Travis and Bridget.

Just as Carl predicted, within hours, Travis began to make a miraculous recovery. He downed a bottle and afterward seemed to be looking for the rest of the meal. "They told us to go slow on the solids," Bridget said as she fed the baby some applesauce.

"But he looks like he's wanting a steak dinner," Ryder said, pleased with Travis's improvement.

Bridget laughed. "I agree, but he won't be getting that from me."

"He won't be getting that from anyone, no matter how cranky he gets," Ryder said protectively.

Moments later, Carl dropped by, examined the baby and released him. Bridget wanted to ride home with him and the baby. As they walked out of the hospital in the hot summer sun, two men with cameras and microphones suddenly swarmed them.

"Princess Bridget, you've been spending a lot of time with Dr. Ryder McCall and his nephews. Are the two of you serious or is this just a fling?" the reporter asked.

Anger rushed through Ryder, and he stepped in front of her before she could respond. "It's none of your business. Leave her alone. Can't you see we're bringing a recovering baby home from the hospital?"

"But the people want to know," the reporter continued.

"The people don't need to know. It's none of their business," Ryder said.

"You obviously don't understand that royals belong to their people," the man said and tried to shove Ryder aside to get to Bridget.

"Leave her alone," Ryder said and knocked the man to the ground.

A half second later, Bridget's security guard swept her and the baby into a limo.

"But, Ryder," Bridget protested as her guard closed the door of the limo.

The reporter on the ground winced in pain at the same time he shouted to the cameraman, "Did you catch all that? It'll be worth a fortune."

Chapter Ten

"You must leave Dr. McCall's house this instant," Stefan said to Bridget over the phone.

Bridget rolled her eyes. "I'm not going to do that. We just brought Travis home. He still needs comfort and Ryder can't do it all."

"Bridget, you're not the mother of these children. You have other duties, and now that the paparazzi has found you, Dr. McCall's house will be stalked day and night. For your safety, let alone your reputation, you can't stay there."

"Oh, to hell with my reputation. If I'm going to be crucified by the press, I can't think of a better reason."

"You're not thinking rationally," Stefan said. "Perhaps I should pull you from this assignment for your own good."

Bridget's heart froze. "You wouldn't dare," she said.

"Of course I would dare," he said. "I must make the calls for everyone's best interest."

"Give me two weeks," she said, determined to keep the desperation out of her voice. "You owe me that."

Silence followed. "It's true that Phillipa will be coming soon, but your doctor friend will need to be prepared for extra security at his house," Stefan said. "I get the impression he doesn't like a lot of intrusion in his private life. He may not like being told what to do."

"Of course he won't," she said. "Would you?"

"That's different," Stefan said.

"He won't what?" Ryder asked from the doorway, his shirt clinging to him in perspiration.

Her heart jumped and she covered the receiver. "It's my brother. He's being impossible."

"I'm not being impossible," Stefan said. "Let me talk to the doctor."

"Let me talk to your brother," Ryder said.

Bridget cringed. "I'd really rather the two of you meet in different circumstances."

"Sorry, sweetheart," Ryder said.

"Now is the time," Stefan said.

Bridget reluctantly handed the phone to Ryder. "Just start out with Your Highness," she whispered.

Ryder took the phone. "Good to meet you, Your Highness," Ryder said. "Your sister has been a godsend to my family."

Silence followed and Ryder tilted his head to one side.

"My position as adviser to the residents at my hospital can't be influenced by my feelings for your sister,"

Ryder said. "I can't send doctors to Chantaine if it's not in their best interest."

Bridget heard Stefan's raised voice and turned her head, wincing.

"I'm sure you understand my responsibility," Ryder said. "Just as you must make the best decisions for your country, I must make the best decisions in advising my residents."

Another quick silence followed, and Ryder met her gaze. "I have no objection to having additional security so that Bridget can come and go here as she pleases. I don't want what happened today to happen again."

A moment later, he said, "We agree on more than you think. Maybe we'll meet in person sometime. Bye for now, Your Highness."

He turned off the phone and handed it to her. "Your brother is a tough negotiator. Not as charming as you," he added with a low laugh. "And I'm sure he's not as hot."

She bit her lip, but couldn't keep from smiling. She closed her eyes for a second, then opened them. "I can be a lot of trouble. My family can be a lot of trouble."

He shrugged. "Everything can be trouble. Depends on whether it's worth it. Come back in the den. Travis is calling for you."

Bridget stayed the day and the day turned to evening. Ryder gave the okay for additional security around the house. He asked Raoul to keep it as invisible as possible. Raoul agreed. Ryder found he couldn't dislike Bridget's guard because he felt the same need to protect her. He was still trying to remember the time he'd punched someone in defense of a woman....

And he would damn well do it again and again for Bridget....

When those reporters had rushed him and Bridget, he'd acted instinctively, with a primitive response. They'd gotten way too close for comfort to Bridget and his baby. His head was still swimming with the reality.

Ryder hadn't realized how important Bridget and the babies had become to him. It was turning him inside out.

That night, against Raoul's advice, she stayed the night. Ryder took her to his bed and stripped off her clothes. He kissed every inch of her, then took her with every beat of his heart and every beat of hers.

His gaze wrapped around hers. At the same time that he took her, Ryder felt taken. In a way he'd never felt before.

Bridget clung to Ryder as he tried to rise from the bed in the morning. He gave a low chuckle that rippled through her.

"Don't want me to leave?"

"I don't," she said, sliding her hands over his muscular chest. "Pippa is coming to Dallas."

"Pippa?" he echoed, scouring her gaze.

"My sister Phillipa," she said. "She's having some problems. I'll have to entertain her a bit. You and I may not have as much time to be together."

"What kind of problems?" he asked, leaning down on his left forearm.

"I'm not sure, but she's stressed enough that my brother sent her here to visit Valentina and me."

He gave a slow nod. "You have a complicated family."

Her heart twisted. "I warned you."

He nodded. "So you did. When do I see you again?"

"I'll have to call you. I'm not sure when she arrives in the States."

"Call me today. I have surgery, but I'll check my messages in between."

Bridget scrambled to make her appointments for the day, then met Ryder at home that night. In between cuddling the twins, they ate sandwiches prepared by Suzanne and Ryder's friend Marshall.

"They seem to be growing very cozy," she said to Ryder as they leaned back against the sofa with the TV playing a ball game about which neither cared.

"Who?" Ryder asked, sliding his hand around hers.

"Suzanne and Marshall," she said.

Ryder groaned. "Don't tell me that. Marshall doesn't have a good history with women. His maximum time is weeks, not months. Days are more likely."

She shrugged. "You never know. Maybe she's the one. Maybe he's ready for the real thing and he's decided she's the real thing."

She felt him study her. "What do you think about the real thing?"

"I think the real thing starts on its own and then you have to keep it going," she said, but when she looked at him, she felt herself spin with emotion. "What about you?"

"I don't know. I always thought it was a figment of everyone's imagination," he said.

"And now?"

He shrugged his muscular shoulders. "Now, I'm not so sure."

Bridget hit the campaign trail for doctors for Chantaine hard. As one of her last resorts, she even met with the administrator of another medical hospital in Dallas. They were more open to her proposal of sending doctors to her country.

Bridget felt torn at the prospect. She wanted only the best for her country, but she couldn't automatically turn down the hospital's interest. It was more than Ryder could offer. The knowledge stabbed at her. She hated that he couldn't feel her passion for her country the same way she did.

In the meantime, she took deep breaths and decided not to make any impulsive decisions. That night, after rocking the babies, she joined Ryder in his bed. He made love to her with a passion that took her breath away.

Ryder drew her into his arms, flush against his body. She felt his heart beat against her chest. She had never felt closer to another human being in her life.

Travis recovered quickly. It seemed that one moment the baby had been listless and the next he was raring to go, trying to pull up and almost scooting, heaven help them all.

Phillipa arrived at DFW and Bridget greeted her sister with open arms. Bridget was concerned to see that Phillipa had indeed lost weight and there were circles beneath her eyes. "Hello, my darling," Bridget said. "I'm so glad to see you."

Phillipa slumped against her for a moment. "It's so good to see you, too," she murmured, squeezing Bridget tightly.

Bridget's concern deepened, but her instincts told her to mask it. At least for now. "I must prepare you for the Texas humidity," she said. "You can cut the air with a knife. We're headed to Tina's ranch. I'm sure she'll be calling any minute. She's dying to see you." Seconds later, her cell phone rang. "Just as I said." She picked up. "Yes, Tina, she's here and as soon as we get her luggage, we're headed straight for your house."

Bridget nodded and smiled. "Soon, soon. Ciao for now."

She hustled Pippa into the limo, plied her with a couple margaritas, and chattered during the drive to Tina's about Texas and the twins and Ryder. "Of course, Stefan is complaining," she said. "I swear he'd like to put us all in convents."

"So true," Phillipa said. "How did you deal with him?"

Bridget made a mental note of Phillipa's comment. Was Phillipa's problem romance? "Avoidance is the best policy," she said. "Emails. Text messages. Direct conversation is the worst because Stefan is disgustingly intuitive. If he would only get Eve pregnant, maybe he would be a bit distracted."

Phillipa chuckled. "Eve doesn't want to rush another child. She wants to give Stephenia plenty of time to adjust."

"Blast her practicality," Bridget said and took her second sip of her first margarita. "Well, you should know that Tina will arrange for massages and spa treatments.

Zach may take us out on his fabulous boat. We also have a social ball to attend in four days."

"Social ball," Phillipa echoed, clearly concerned.

"Oh, it's nothing to worry about," Bridget soothed. "It's a charity gala in Dallas. Tina and Zach will attend. If you like, we can make an appearance and bug out. You know I'm quick like that when it suits me. Stefan has fussed about it enough. Plus we can go shopping before and you can get a great dress out of it."

Pippa gave a mild smile. "So we don't have to stay all night?"

"Of course not," Bridget said, patting her sister on her knee. "Have the doctoral studies become a pain in the butt? You know, you work entirely too hard."

"My studies are fine, but Stefan insisted I take a break," she said.

"He means well," Bridget said. "But he still needs some work. I'm hopeful Eve can continue his needed transformation."

Phillipa sighed and took another sip of her margarita. "Bridget, you have no idea how much I've needed to see you."

Still concerned, Bridget managed a laugh. "Well, prepare yourself for an overdose."

Pippa smiled and Bridget felt as if she'd scored a small victory. Later, as they arrived at the ranch, Tina rushed down the steps. "Phillipa!" she called stretching out her arms.

Bridget watched her two sisters embrace and her heart squeezed tight with emotion. Tina pulled back. "Look at you. I love your hair. That dress is fabulous. What happened to my sister, the librarian?"

"I'm still here," Phillipa said. "A stylist put together some things for my visit to the States."

"Regardless, you look fabulous, but shorts and no shoes are the summertime uniform here. Come visit your niece. She can't wait to see Aunt Pippa," Tina said, and tossed Bridget a glance of concern before she led them inside the house.

Bridget and Phillipa played with their gorgeous niece until dinnertime when Hildie served a superb, filling meal. Between the margaritas, the food and the security of her sisters, Phillipa grew drowsy early in the evening. Tina ushered her to one of the bedrooms and returned to the den with Bridget and Zach.

"She's different than I expected," Tina said. "Stefan said she was stressed, but—" Tina frowned. "What do you think is behind all this?"

"A man," Bridget said as she sipped a glass of ice water.

Tina's eyebrows rose. "What makes you say that?"

"Something Pippa said on the way here."

"What? Who?" Tina demanded.

"I didn't pry. She just seemed too fragile," Bridget said.

Tina sighed. "How did you get that out of her?"

"It was a sideways comment. I was complaining about Stefan and how he doesn't want any of us to date."

"True," Tina said.

"Too true," Zach said from behind the newspaper he was reading.

Tina glanced at her husband and smiled.

"In this case, I was speaking of Ryder," Bridget said.

"Hmm," Tina said.

"So far, he seems like a good guy," Zach said. "If he was willing to punch out that reporter who was after you, he gets my vote."

"It's all about the violence," Tina said, rolling her eyes.

"Protecting a woman is a primitive response in a man. Protectiveness is an important trait."

"I'm sure Stefan will love hearing that opinion," Bridget said wryly.

"Stefan just needs to be reminded about what he would do to protect Eve," Zach said bluntly, then shook his newspaper and appeared to begin to read again.

"She needs a massage," Tina said. "A ride on the water. And perhaps Hildie's double-strength margaritas."

Three days later, the sisters went to Dallas and shopped for dresses. Bridget was distracted. She was late. Not for an appointment. She was late for her period, and she had been, well, exposed to the possibility of becoming pregnant. Although they had used contraception, Bridget wasn't sure if she had landed in the small percentile of women for whom it had failed.

"What do you think?" Tina asked as Phillipa tried on a gown. "I think the cocoa color is perfect on her."

Bridget blinked, looking at Pippa. "Yes, it's beautiful. It really accentuates all your positive attributes."

"Although, a pastel or dark navy would be fabulous, too, don't you think?" Tina said.

"I completely agree," she said and forced herself to pay attention to the rest of the shopping expedition. She rendered her positive opinion to Tina's choice for a dress, but nixed the idea of getting a new gown for herself.

Tina and Phillipa gasped at once. "Are you ill?" Phillipa asked.

"What is wrong?" Tina demanded. "You never turn down the opportunity to get a new designer gown."

Bridget brushed their concerns aside. "It's nothing," she said. "I have a ton of gowns I brought with me that I haven't yet worn. We've already spent enough time shopping. It's not necessary to find a gown for me."

"Enough time shopping," Pippa echoed. "You've often said there's no such thing as too much shopping."

Uncomfortable with her sisters' scrutiny, Bridget shrugged her shoulders. "Okay, I'll admit it. I'm hungry and we might end up with rubber chicken tonight."

Tina giggled and rolled her eyes. "Now we have the real answer. I could use a good meal, too. Crab sounds especially good."

The thought of crab turned Bridget's stomach. "Or even a nice sandwich. You know where we can find a good variety of food, Tina. Where should we go?"

Delighted to give the attention back to her sister, Bridget joined her sisters for a late lunch. Her phone rang during their meal and she excused herself to take the call. "Ryder, talk to me. I swear it feels as if it's been three months since I heard your voice."

He laughed. "Same here. Are you having fun with your sisters?"

"For the most part," she said. "We still haven't figured out what's wrong with Phillipa, but I think it's a man. I'm hoping she'll talk with us. It's always more miserable to suffer by yourself. And whatever your problems are, they seem ten times worse if you don't share. Speaking of worries, how are you and the twins?"

"The only way the twins and I could be better would be if you were around," he said.

Her heart went squishy at his words. "Oh, that's so sweet. They've probably already forgotten me."

"No chance."

"You know, the other day, I was wondering, did you ever think you were going to have children? I know becoming a doctor was important, but did you *ever* think you would start a family?"

"It wasn't a priority," he said. "My career was always number one…. Just a moment," he said and she heard him talking with someone else. Then he came back on the line. "Listen, I need to go soon. Are you okay? I'm hearing something in your voice."

"Oh, no," she said, lying because she knew she didn't have time to discuss her real feelings. "It's just family stuff."

He paused a few seconds. "But you mentioned starting a family. What's on your mind?"

"Nothing," she insisted. "I was just thinking about how you'd been thrust into the position of being a father so quickly. I wondered what your original plans were."

She heard him give a quick response to someone on the other end of the line. "Are you pregnant?"

Shocked at the accuracy of his question, she sucked in a quick breath. Something inside her insisted on denial. She would figure that out later. "Oh, my goodness. How could I be pregnant? You and I are so careful."

"Nothing provides perfect protection except abstinence," he said.

"Oh, that's ridiculous. We're fine. We're perfectly fine," she insisted, her heart racing.

"Thanks for the reassurance," he said. "You and I both have enough going on without adding a baby to the mix."

"So true," she said, but her stomach twisted viciously.

"I have to go. I'll call later."

"Ciao," she said and stared blindly at her cell phone. What if she *was* pregnant? It was clear that Ryder didn't want another baby. How would she handle this? Would she have to do it all alone? Panic raced through her. She broke into a cold sweat. She shuddered at the possibility of dealing with her family's disapproval and interference.

"Bridget," her sister Tina said, breaking her out of her reverie. "The food's been here for several minutes. What's wrong with you today? You seem totally distracted."

Bridget took a breath and pulled herself together, forcing a big smile. "Oh, Tina, you know how I am. If I've got more than one and a half things on my mind, I'm distracted. I'm still thinking about the babies and the medical program for Chantaine. I need that sandwich. Thank you for coming to get me," she said and marched back to the table, praying her sister wouldn't ask any more questions.

That night, Bridget and her sisters dressed at her suite at the hotel. She felt as if she were on automatic. A green dress. Green was a good color for her. Mineral powder, subtle eyes, bold, red lips. She didn't feel bold, but she needed to be confident. She needed to be someone bigger than her current self because her current self was feeling confused and vulnerable. Lord, she hoped it was late PMS.

She gave her sister Phillipa a hug. "You look fabulous."

"You overstate," Phillipa said. "You always have."

"Not this time. Look at how gorgeous you look," she said, pointing to the full-length mirror.

Tina stepped into the room from the bathroom. "What are you two arguing about?"

"I told Phillipa she looked fabulous and gorgeous and she said I'm exaggerating and I said I'm not," Bridget said.

Tina walked to Phillipa and put her hands tenderly on her cheeks. "For once, Bridget understated."

Phillipa closed her eyes and squeezed them tight as if she were fighting tears. "You two are being so kind. I know all of this is because you're worried about me."

"Well, it's true we're worried about you," Bridget said.

"Bridget," Tina said with a chiding expression.

"It's true. It's also true that I wouldn't include fabulous and gorgeous in the same sentence if I didn't truly believe it," Bridget said.

Phillipa's lips twitched. "You make a good point. The real you leaks out after a short time."

Bridget lifted her hand. "What did I say?"

Tina sighed. "We just want you to be okay. You're our baby," she said, stroking Phillipa's hair.

"I'm not a baby. I'm a grown-up. I can manage my life. I just need a little recalibration."

"And you can get that here," Tina said.

Phillipa smiled. Tina's cell phone rang and she picked up. "It's Zachary."

Moments later, Zachary arrived in a limo driven by security. The three princesses and Zach rode to the charity ball. As they stepped outside the limo, they were greeted by flashing cameras and reporters.

"Welcome to Dallas's premier Charity Ball, Your Highnesses. To what do we owe the honor of your presence tonight?" a reporter asked.

Just lucky, I guess, Bridget thought, but managed to swallow the comment.

"I live just outside of Fort Worth with my husband and daughter, and I've been so happy to receive visits from both my sisters, Bridget and Phillipa," Tina said.

"Your sister Bridget has been in town for over a month. There have been rumors about her and one of our doctors—"

"We're here tonight to celebrate the charity of the people of Texas, which is so much bigger than rumors, don't you agree?" Tina asked. "It was lovely to meet you."

They moved on to the next reporter, and Tina's responses reminded Bridget why her sister had done such a superlative job representing Chantaine.

"She's so good," Bridget muttered.

"Times two," Phillipa said.

"If only she could be in two places at once," Bridget said with a sigh.

"You're doing pretty well," Pippa said.

"My time is limited," Bridget said. "I don't have Tina's endurance."

"Maybe, this once, you underestimate yourself," her sister said.

"I think not, but I appreciate your kindness. On to our rubber chicken," she whispered and was thrilled she could make Phillipa laugh.

"What are you two talking about?" Tina demanded.

"You don't want to know," Bridget said.

Tina shot her a curt micro-look before she plastered a serene expression on her face. Zach escorted the group inside to their table at the front of the room. They made small talk with the others seated at their table. Soon enough, announcements and presentations began. Bridget was stunned when Nic LaFitte stepped forward to receive an award of recognition. The Devereaux had a long-standing grudge against the Lafittes. Nic's father had caused a humiliating scandal for the royal family.

"What is *he* doing here?" she whispered to Tina.

"Zach says he's a huge contributor here. Everyone loves him," Tina said distastefully.

"They clearly don't know him," she said and nudged Phillipa. "Why can't we escape him?" she whispered. "Maybe it's because he's the devil and that means he can be everywhere."

When Phillipa didn't respond, Bridget glanced at her face and saw that her sister had turned white as a sheet.

Chapter Eleven

"I'm not feeling well," Phillipa said. "Please excuse me."

"Do you want me to go with you?" Bridget asked, her stomach twisting in concern for her sister.

"No, no. I just need a little air," Phillipa said as she slowly rose and lifted her lips in a forced smile. "I'll be back in a little bit."

Bridget watched her sister move through the perimeter of the room as surreptitiously as possible and felt worried.

"Where is she going?" Tina asked in a whisper.

"The powder room," Bridget said. "She says she needs some air."

Tina frowned and glanced at Nic LaFitte as he left the stage. "Do you think this has anything to do with LaFitte?"

"I can't imagine that it would. I mean, none of us

would get involved with a LaFitte. Not even the most rebellious of us and Pippa is nowhere near the most rebellious."

Tina nodded and Bridget paid half attention to the speaker, more attention to her watch. "I'm going to check on Pippa," she whispered.

"I'll go with you," Tina said, and stood just after she did.

Bridget tried to be discreet just as Phillipa had been, but she noticed several heads turning in her direction. She immediately searched for the first ladies' room and didn't find Phillipa there. "Where is she?" she muttered to herself.

"I'm starting to get a bad feeling about LaFitte," Tina said as they left the room.

"I can't believe Pippa would be that foolish. She's extremely intelligent and quite practical," Bridget said as she scoured the lobby for her sister.

"I wonder if she went outside," Tina said.

"It's possible. She said she needed some air," Bridget said, then spotted a coat closet and pointed toward it. "You don't think she would be there, do you? It's the last place I would look in this hot, humid weather and the door is closed."

Tina glanced in the same direction and shrugged. "I don't think so, but we may as well check."

Bridget led the way to the door and stopped just outside, pressing her ear closer to listen. Hearing nothing, she cracked the door open.

"This is insanity," Phillipa said. "It will never work."

"Why not?" a male voice demanded. "If I want you and you want me, what is most important?"

"Want is a temporary emotion," Phillipa said. "There are more important things than temporary emotions."

"If that's true, then why are you here with me?" he asked.

Tina gasped and the sound traveled through the door like a thunderclap. Seconds later, Phillipa and Nic LaFitte appeared in the doorway.

"Get away from my sister," Bridget said.

"That's for her to say, not you," LaFitte said.

"You're just using her," Tina said. "You only want her because she can redeem your terrible family name."

"Not everyone finds my family name reprehensible. Some even respect it," he said.

"That's respect you've bought with money," Tina said. "Leave Phillipa alone. You can never be good enough for her. If you have any compassion, you'll at least protect her reputation by leaving now."

LaFitte tightened his jaw. "I'll leave, but Phillipa will make the ultimate decision about the future of our relationship." He glanced behind him and met Phillipa's shocked, pale face. "Ciao, darling. Call me when you get some courage. Some things are meant to be," he said and strode away.

"Oh, darling," Bridget said and immediately went to Phillipa and took her in her arms.

Tina soon followed. "Oh, you poor thing. The LaFittes are so evil. It's clear he intends to trick you."

Phillipa's face crumpled. "He was so kind to me," she whispered.

"Of course he was," Tina said. "He's a snake like the rest of his family. And you're too sweet to know the difference."

"Are you saying he couldn't possibly be attracted to me just because I'm me?" Phillipa asked, her voice filled with desperation.

Bridget felt her heart shatter at the pain in her sister's voice. "Of course not," she said. "You're an amazing, beautiful and wonderful girl. You're a precious gem and you must be protected from anyone who doesn't deserve you."

"And no LaFitte would *ever* deserve you," Tina said.

Moments later, out of consideration for Phillipa, they left the event. Bridget and Tina fought over where Phillipa should spend the night. Bridget eventually won. "She shouldn't have to ride an extra hour back to the ranch tonight," Bridget said. "I have plenty of room in my suite. Along with the makings of margaritas or any other toddy she may require tonight."

"But Zach and I could protect her from any unwanted advances from LaFitte," Tina said.

"His advances weren't unwanted," Phillipa whispered. "I was attracted to him and wished he would contact me. I finally gave in and sent a message to him. He met me and that was how it all started."

Tina sucked in a sharp breath, then silence fell in the limousine. Zach tipped back a glass of bourbon.

"Well, I'm glad you came to your senses," Tina said.

Bridget gave Phillipa a hug. "We don't need to talk or think about this anymore tonight. You've already had enough stress tonight. You're due some rest. You can come to my room and fall asleep all snug and safe in your bed. You can think about LaFitte tomorrow if necessary. Tonight it's not necessary."

"You sound like that Scarlett O'Hara in the American film *Gone with the Wind*," Tina said.

"In this case, she offered a nice bit of wisdom," Bridget countered.

"Please don't argue," Phillipa said.

"We're not," Bridget said, giving Tina a strong glance. "Tina and I agree, don't we?"

Tina took a quick breath. "Yes, we do. I think we all need some extra rest tonight. In fact, I think Zach and I will stay overnight at your hotel."

"What?" Zach asked.

"Yes," Tina said decisively. "We can stay overnight at Bridget's hotel in a separate suite, of course. I'm sure Hildie won't mind keeping the baby."

"Yes, but—"

"In the morning, we can wake up and all have brunch together," she said brightly.

"And if Phillipa sleeps in, then Mom and Dad can enjoy a night away from their little darling and Phillipa can visit you at the ranch later."

Tina frowned, but nodded.

Moments later, they exited the limo into the hotel and Bridget and Phillipa took the lift to the penthouse. "Thank you," Phillipa said after they entered the elevator.

Bridget took her sister's hand. "We all need a break every now and then. If your sister won't give it to you, then who *will* give it to you?"

"Yes, but Tina clearly hates Nic," Bridget said in a shaky voice.

"All of us hate the LaFitte family. Part of it is not

logical. After all, if Father had married the woman who married LaFitte, none of us would exist. Maybe we don't like to lose. Plus there's the matter of the LaFitte who killed one of our great-uncles." Bridget sighed. "And, after all the bad they did to us, they're so bloody wealthy and successful. That's enough of a reason to hate them."

"His mother is dying," Phillipa said.

Bridget glanced at her sister. "Really. How?"

"Cancer. It's been a terribly grueling experience. She's currently near the end."

Bridget took a deep breath. "I don't wish that on anyone."

"Neither do I," Phillipa said as the elevator dinged their arrival to the penthouse.

Bridget clasped her sister's hand. "You must promise me that you won't think about this anymore tonight. You need to take a break from it. It's hurting you. More important, you can't fix it tonight."

Phillipa squeezed her hand in return. "I may not agree with a lot of what you've said, but it's true that I can't fix all of this tonight. I should just go to bed and try to sleep."

Bridget nodded. "And get a massage in the morning. I'll keep Tina away."

"You're usually nagging me to take on more palace duties. When did you become my fairy protector?" Phillipa asked.

"Oh, well, I'll nag again soon enough. Enjoy the respite," Bridget said.

The next morning, Bridget did just as she'd promised and arranged for a soothing massage for her younger sister. Tina would only be put off so long before she was knocking on the door of Bridget's suite. Bridget opened the door. "We're sipping lime water and relaxing on the balcony. Would you like to join us?" she asked. "And whatever you do, don't hound her and don't bring up LaFitte. I've got her nice and relaxed after her massage."

Tina nodded in agreement. "We'll take her out on Zach's new boat."

"But don't try to matchmake," Bridget said.

Tina frowned. "You don't think a male distraction would help?" she whispered.

"No," Bridget said emphatically. "Pippa has fallen hard for LaFitte. She needs to get over him before she moves on to the next."

"You seem to have enormous insight on this matter. Surprising," Tina said, lifting her eyebrow in a suspicious manner.

Bridget feigned an airy sigh. "Underestimated again. When will it end?"

After her sisters left, Bridget returned several calls. As soon as she finished, though, the quiet settled over her like a heavy blanket. She still hadn't started her period yet. Tempted to wear a disguise and buy an early pregnancy test from a drugstore, she put it off. She never knew who was watching and who might discuss her purchase with the paparazzi. Perhaps by tomorrow…

Her cell phone rang and she saw Ryder's return number on her screen. He was the one person to whom she hadn't made a return call. Her heart hammered with nerves as she took the call. "Hello, Ryder," she said.

"Damn good to hear your voice. I was starting to

wonder if you'd disappeared or headed to Chantaine or Italy without letting me know," he said.

"I wouldn't do that," she said. "I've just been tied up with my sisters. How are my boys?"

"Your boys are screaming to see you. Even Suzanne says they miss you. Come over for the weekend," he said.

Her heart jumped again and she began to pace. On the one hand, she was desperate to see Ryder again. On the other hand, she was distracted by the possibility that she could be pregnant. Ryder had been much more intuitive about her worries than she would have ever expected.

He made a buzzing sound. "Time's up. Because you didn't say no, that must mean yes. I'll pick you up around five," he said.

"Wait," she said breathlessly. "Let Raoul bring me. That way he can go through his security protocol and I won't be hassled by him or my brother. Hopefully," she added in a low voice.

"Good," Ryder said. "The twins have a trick they want to show you. See you soon," he said.

"Trick?" she echoed, but he'd already disconnected the call.

Anticipation zinged through her and she giggled. Her mood felt as if it had lifted into the stratosphere. Amazing that he had that effect on her so quickly. Frightening, really, if she thought about it too deeply, so she wouldn't.

A few hours later, she tried to ignore the lecture Raoul was giving her about how she was taking risks and how she should stay away from windows.

"Your Highness, do you understand what I'm saying?" Raoul asked.

"Absolutely," she said.

"You haven't been listening to a word I've said," he said.

"That's not true. I've listened to at least every third word you've said. I'm not reckless, but I won't let my position steal my joy. You never know how long you'll have that opportunity. There's so much drudgery you have to grab the joy."

Silence followed. "That's remarkably deep, Your Highness," he said. "But after protecting you for five years, I'm not surprised. You hide your depth well," he said, glancing at her through the rearview mirror.

Bridget felt a twist in her chest at her guard's revelation. "Thank you, Raoul. You deserve sainthood for being my guard."

"You are not as bad as you profess," he said. "But stay away from windows and call me before you walk outside the house."

She laughed as he pulled the car to the curb of Ryder's home. "Way to slide in those instructions," she said and opened her door before he could. "Ciao."

Before she arrived on the porch, the door flung open and Ryder greeted her, sweeping her inside. "Your men are waiting for you," he said and pulled her into his arms.

He felt so strong and wonderful and alive. She felt as if she'd come home. She was safe and more whole than she'd ever dreamed possible. He picked her up and spun her around and she couldn't help laughing.

"You act like you haven't seen me in a year," she said, squeezing his strong shoulders.

"It has been a year," he said and searched her face. "Right?"

A shriek sounded just a few steps away.

Bridget glanced at the floor and saw the twins scooting toward her and Ryder. "Oh, bloody hell," she said, panicked. "They're moving! We have to stop them."

Ryder roared with laughter. "That was my first response, too," he said and squeezed her shoulders. "But crawling is next. After that, standing. Then walking."

Bridget stared, torn between exultation and cold fear, and shook her head. "What are you going to do?"

"Cope," he said. "Manage them, if such a thing is possible. The good news is they get worn out a lot faster," he said.

Tyler stopped at Bridget's feet and gurgled.

Her heart twisted so tightly that she could hardly breathe. "Oh, you darling," she said and bent down to pick up the baby. She groaned. "You've gained weight. Is that possible?"

Ryder picked up Travis and extended him toward Bridget. She gave the baby a kiss and cooed at him. He cooed at her in return and her chest expanded, filling her with an overwhelming sense of love and emotion. "Oh, you darlings. I've missed both of you."

"Both?" Ryder asked.

"All three. Especially you," she said and sank onto the sofa with the baby on her lap. "The last few days have been full of drama. Poor Phillipa has been seduced by one of our family enemies. She's such an innocent. I know he's taken advantage of her, but I'm hoping she'll regain her sense."

"Who's this enemy? I thought you Devereaux were peaceful and moderate," he said, joining her on the sofa.

"We are for the most part," she said. "But the LaFittes have been bad news for our family. One of them murdered my great-uncle. And one seduced my father's bride away from him," she said.

"I can understand the first, but the second, not so much. You wouldn't have been born if your father had married a different woman," he said.

"True," she said. "But the LaFittes are still on our don't list. No discussion," she said.

"What about me?" he asked in a rough voice. "Am I on your don't list?"

Her breath hitched in the back of her throat. "Probably, but that hasn't stopped me, has it?"

His lips lifted in a lazy half grin. "Guess not. I ordered Italian for dinner. Bought red wine on the way home."

"Sounds great, but I'm all about water these days. I'm on a new diet that favors lemon and lime water. It's supposed to cleanse the toxins. Do you have any limes?"

Ryder blinked. "Limes?"

"No problem. Filtered water is good."

"So, red wine is out?" he asked.

"Just during my lime phase," she said with a smile.

They watched the twins scoot around the den until they wore themselves out. Ryder rocked Tyler and she rocked Travis. It took only moments before Travis was drooling on her shoulder. She met Ryder's gaze and he gave a slight nod and they carried the babies up to their cribs.

Seconds later, they walked downstairs and shared a

late meal. Although Italian fare didn't appeal to her at the moment, Bridget pushed the food around her plate to make it look as if she'd eaten it. Later, she took her plate into the kitchen and pushed the contents into the trash can.

Did this mean she was pregnant? she wondered. She loved Italian food. If she hated it, now what did it mean? Her stomach twisted into a knot, but she took a deep breath and returned to the den. "Delicious dinner," she said and sat down beside him.

"You didn't eat everything. It must not have been that delicious," he said, sliding his arm over her shoulder.

"I had a late lunch and I'm watching my girlish figure," she said with a smile.

"I'll take care of that second job. I have no problem watching your girlish figure," he said, sliding his lips along her neck.

She laughed, exulting in his caress. Turning toward him, she lifted her mouth to his. "Kiss me," she said.

"Is that an order?"

"Kinda," she said.

He gave a low, dirty chuckle and did as she commanded.

The next morning, Ryder awakened early. Bridget's back was pressed against him. His hand was curled around her bare waist. Her skin was butter soft against his palm. It was a good morning. The best kind of morning. Bridget was with him.

He couldn't remember a time when he'd been more at peace. Something primitive inside him drove him to keep her with him. He started to understand why men kidnapped their women and kept them in luxurious captivity. Which was crazy. When had he ever felt this need for a woman? When had a woman ever filled up all his emptiness and need?

Bridget wiggled against him, then suddenly raced out of bed to the master bath. A couple moments later, she returned, carefully crawling into the bed and inching herself toward him.

Several things clicked through his brain. His gut twisted. "Bridget," he murmured against her ear.

"Yes," she whispered.

"Are you pregnant?"

Silence passed. Way too long. His heart sank. *Another baby?* He couldn't imagine it. How in the world—

"I don't know," she finally said. "I'm late."

A half dozen emotions sliced through him. He couldn't speak.

"How late?" he finally managed.

"A week and a half," she said, still not turning to look at him.

"We should do a test," he said.

"No," she said. "I can't take a test, and you can't do it for me. The press is watching me even more than usual now. I want to know as much as you do, but a few more days may give us the answer without any exposure to the press," she said and finally turned toward him.

"You're late. No red wine. Why didn't you tell me?"

Her eyes clouded with turmoil. "Our relationship is still new. We haven't made any sort of promises to each other."

His heart pounded against his chest. The thought of another baby scared the crap out of him. His brother's babies had become his own. The baby he shared with Bridget would be his to protect as well.

"If you're pregnant, you need to start taking prenatal vitamins as soon as possible. You need to get on a regimen—"

"And if I'm not, I can go back to my red wine–swilling, unhealthy ways," she said.

He bit the inside of his lip to keep from laughing. "I still think you should let me do a test."

She shook her head. "Three more days. I'll live healthy until then."

He searched her face. "I would protect you if you're pregnant with my child, Bridget. I would marry you. I would protect our child."

Her eyes still swam with emotion, some of which he couldn't read. "That's good to know," she said and tucked her head under his chin. "Can we talk about something else until then?"

Ryder spent the weekend secluded in happiness with Bridget. They shared the care of the twins, took the boys for a stroll in the neighborhood despite Raoul's protests and spent their nights together, his body wrapped around hers, her body wrapped around his.

He returned to work Monday wondering if she was pregnant, wishing he could keep her with him. He met with Dr. Hutt.

"Dr. Robinson is still having financial problems due to his family. It's distracting him from his duties," Dr. Hutt said.

Ryder immediately felt defensive. "We need to look

for a solution instead of immediately booting him out of the program."

"I agree," Hutt said, surprising Ryder with his response.

"What about your princess friend?" he asked, leaning back in his chair. "Wouldn't this be a perfect solution? She gives him a bonus scholarship, he takes a tour of her country. Win, win."

"Are you serious?" Ryder asked.

"Yes," he said. "You and I must manage residents from all eco-social backgrounds. Not everyone is from your background. Not everyone is from mine."

For the first time in months, he felt a measure of hope. Maybe, just maybe Hutt could see past his privileged upbringing. "Are you sure you shouldn't push him harder?" he asked. "Maybe he just needs to work more."

His colleague frowned. "He's already working hard. Harder than I ever did," he said.

Ryder was stunned. He'd never known Hutt was capable of such insight. "When did this change happen?"

"The last time you and I met, I went home and couldn't sleep. For several nights. Dr. Walters not only kicked my butt, he also *encouraged* you. He wasn't one man to the residents. He stepped into their shoes and gave them what they needed. As advisers, we have to do the same."

Ryder shook his head. "When in hell did you become a reasonable man?"

His colleague laughed. "It's amazing the kind of perspective a wife can offer when you choose to talk to her."

"Your wife did this?" Ryder asked.

Hutt shrugged. "Professionally speaking, of course, she didn't," he said.

Ryder felt a change click through him and extended his hand to Dr. Hutt. "Give my best to your wife," he said.

"And give my best to your princess," Hutt said.

One day later, Bridget called him. He was in surgery, so he checked his messages. "Meet me today. Name the time," she said. "I have good news."

His day was crazy, but he managed to meet her at a quiet cocktail bar after work.

"Rough day?" she asked as she sipped a martini.

He felt a crazy surge of disappointment. The last couple of days, he'd secretly begun to like the idea of having a baby with Bridget. "You're not pregnant."

"I'm not," she said and lifted her glass to his. She smiled in relief. "Cheers."

"Cheers," he said. "And damn."

She blinked. "Damn?"

"Maybe I could have forced you into a shotgun marriage if you were pregnant."

She laughed and took another sip of her martini. "I wouldn't want a shotgun wedding for you or me," she said.

"I don't know," he said. "I think we could have made the best of it."

She sucked in a deep breath and glanced away. "Perhaps, but now we don't have to," she said with a shaky smile. She bit her lip. "My other news is that another medical center has stepped forward to participate in our program."

Surprised, Ryder searched her gaze. "Really?"

"We finally have doctors willing to come to Chantaine," she said, relief crossing her face. "I followed your advice and found experts willing to visit Chantaine and give training. And this medical center is willing to offer our scholarship and package to their residents. So far, two have signed up for our program. They weren't our first choice, but Stefan is confident this arrangement will be in the best interest of the country."

"Wow," Ryder said. "What a coincidence. Today Dr. Hutt and I agreed to send one of our residents to Chantaine. He's a talented generalist, but he has financial issues you can solve. Still interested?"

"Of course," she said. "I shouldn't say we're desperate, but we're definitely open. We're also going to need a new director for Chantaine's Health Center, but that's clearly a work in progress."

"I guess this means you're headed for Chantaine… or Italy," he said, his gut tightening into a square knot.

"Not right away, but very soon," she said. "I'll go back with Phillipa."

Chapter Twelve

Ryder returned home well after 9:00 p.m. after meeting Bridget for cocktails and dinner. He had arranged for Suzanne to stay late to watch the twins, but Marshall greeted him.

Marshall handed him a beer. "Hey, big guy. Congratulate me. Suzanne and I got married this weekend in Vegas. I sent her home because she was tired out. I kept her pretty busy this weekend," he added with a wink.

Stunned for the third time today, Ryder stared at Marshall. "What?"

"Suzanne and I got married. Don't worry, she's determined to still be your nanny even though I told her she could be a lady of leisure."

Ryder accepted the beer and took a sip. "Oh, Lord help me."

"That's not quite a congrats, but I'll take it," Marshall

said, giving Ryder a fist bump. "You look kinda strange, big guy. What's up?"

Ryder shook his head and sank onto his couch. "Just a crazy day. Are you sure Suzanne is still going to take care of the twins?"

Marshall sat on the other side of the couch. "Yeah. She's determined. You know she can't have babies, right? That's why her husband left her. His stupidity, my good luck."

"Bridget mentioned something about it," Ryder said, his mind falling back a few days to when her pregnancy had still been a possibility. And now she would be leaving soon. He knew the twins would miss her.

"Yeah, I told her there's more than one way to crack that nut. Getting a baby. We'll check out the IVF stuff, then we'll look into our adoption options. She was surprised I would be open to that. She's an amazing woman. I would do anything for her," Marshall said.

"Why didn't you tell me you were going to do this?" Ryder demanded.

"You'd already warned me away from Suzanne, but I wanted to get to know her. It took some work to get her to go out with me, but I knew she was the one for me. She's the first really good woman I've met and I knew I didn't want to let her go."

Ryder felt a twist of envy that Marshall had been able to overcome the obstacles that might have kept him and Suzanne apart. "Congratulations," he said, extending his hand.

Marshall nodded and smiled. "Still can't believe I was able to talk her into eloping. Of course, now is the hard part, but with her, I don't think it's gonna be that hard."

"She's a strong woman. If anyone can keep you in line, she's the one," Ryder said.

"Yeah, speaking of women, what's up with your princess?"

Ryder's gut tightened again. "I think she's headed back to Chantaine soon."

Marshall's eyebrows lifted in surprise. "Whoa. I thought you two—"

"Temporary," Ryder said. "For Pete's sake, she's a princess, and I've got my hands full with the boys and my position at the hospital."

"Hmm," Marshall said. "I could have sworn you two had it going on. Shame you couldn't work it out. Sorry, bud," he said and thumped Ryder on the shoulder. "Hope you don't mind, but my *wife* is waiting for me at home."

"Okay, okay," Ryder said with a faint smile. "Just make sure she gets enough sleep to take care of the boys."

Marshall just gave a dirty laugh and walked out the door.

Ryder stared into the distance and felt more alone than ever. For the most part, he hadn't minded being alone. In the past, it had meant he had to take care of only himself. All that had changed when his brother had died and Ryder had taken on the twins. Now it was just him and the twins.

An image of Bridget floated through his mind and he got an itchy, unsettled feeling inside him. Trying to dismiss it, he went to the kitchen and glanced through the mail for the day, but that itchy feeling didn't go away.

Ryder rubbed at his gut, but it didn't do any good. A sense of dread that started in his stomach climbed to the back of his throat.

Ryder swore under his breath. He'd fallen for the woman. Worse yet, he'd begun to rely on her. He, who relied on no one but himself. Shaking his head, he called himself ten kinds of fools. A princess? Putting his trust in anyone was dangerous, but a princess. Talk about impossible situations.

He ground his teeth. She was leaving. He needed to get used to the idea immediately. He needed to cut every thought of her from his mind.

Bridget felt ripped apart at the prospect of leaving Ryder and the boys, but she couldn't stall any longer. She'd completed her assignment and it was time for her to return to Chantaine before she took her long-delayed gap year in Italy. Somehow, she couldn't work up the same kind of excitement she'd felt during the last two years about finally taking a break.

She didn't know which upset her most: leaving Ryder and the twins or the fact that Ryder had ignored all of her calls. Desperate to make arrangements to see him one last time, she took matters into her own hands, went to the hospital and parked herself in his office when his assistant was away from her desk. She wasn't going through any gatekeepers this time.

After forty-five minutes of waiting, she saw Ryder finally open his office door. He looked at her and his expression registered shock, then all emotion seemed to vanish from his face. "Hello, Bridget. Sorry, I don't have time to visit."

His remoteness stabbed her. "I understand. I just didn't want to leave without seeing you and the twins again."

"Why? We won't be a part of your life anymore. There's no need to pretend we were anything more than a phase."

She dropped her jaw, surprised at his evaluation of the time they'd shared. "A phase?" she repeated in disbelief. "Is that all I was to you? A phase?"

Ryder gave a bitter laugh. "There's no need for drama. Both of us knew this was coming. It just came a little sooner than expected. I appreciate everything you did to help the twins. You provided a needed diversion for all three of us."

"A diversion," she said, feeling herself begin to shake.

"Don't get so upset. We knew from the beginning that there was no future to our relationship. I sure as hell am not the right man to be a princess's husband and you're not the type of woman to put up with a doctor's demanding schedule."

She felt as if he'd slapped her. He made her sound like she was a selfish, high-maintenance shrew. She bit the inside of her lip. "I had no idea you thought so little of me." She swallowed over the lump in her throat. "You really had me fooled. I've spent the last few days searching for ways to continue to see you and be with you. I realize it would be the ultimate long-distance relationship, but I couldn't bear the idea of not being in your life. I fell for both you and the boys." Her voice broke and she looked away, shaking her head. "At least, I fell for who I thought you were. I thought you felt the same way, but clearly I was—"

"No," he said, gripping her shoulders. She looked up and saw in his eyes that he was as tortured as she was. "No, you weren't wrong. I fell for you, too, much more than I intended. I've spent the last days telling myself to forget you. I know that's impossible, but I have to try."

Her eyes filled with tears. "I don't want you to forget me. I don't want you to speak about us in the past tense. You—you've become so important to me."

He winced as if in pain. "But it can't work. Our lives are just too different. We need to make it easy for each other to get used to the facts. The fact is you have to return to your country. You have responsibilities there. I have mine here."

She tried hard to hang on to her composure, but she couldn't. It hurt too much. She dropped her forehead against his chest. "This is so hard," she said, feeling tears streak down her face.

"It is," he said, sliding his hand through her hair and holding her close.

"Promise me you won't forget me," she said and lifted her gaze to look at him. "Give me that much."

"Never," he promised. "Never," he said and lowered his mouth to hers for a kiss. Their last kiss.

Ryder couldn't remember a time when he had felt like his guts had been ripped out and put through a grinder. Every waking moment, he was aware of the breathtaking pain. He tried, but couldn't block the sight of Bridget's tears from his mind. The way she'd felt in his arms. He would never feel that again. He would never feel that sense of unexpected joy just by seeing her smile or hearing her tease him.

Swearing under his breath as he arrived home, he ripped open the top few buttons of his shirt. Not only was he in mental hell, but the hot Dallas weather seemed to be determined to put him in physical hell, too.

"Hey, big guy," Marshall said as he held one of the twins while Suzanne changed the diaper of the other. "You don't look too good. Did you lose someone on the table today?"

One of the babies squealed at the sight of him. The sound gave Ryder a slight lift. He walked over and gave each baby a hug.

"No, I didn't lose a patient. Just got some things on my mind. Sorry I'm late. Tomorrow should be better."

He saw Marshall lift his eyebrows. "Hey, Suzy Q, how about I help you take the boys upstairs for a while. Ryder and I can drink a beer and watch a couple innings of a ball game. Are you okay with that?"

"Sure," she said. "I'll play some music and read to them."

Marshall gave his wife a firm kiss, then carried both boys upstairs.

A moment later, his friend returned. Ryder had already gotten two beers out of the fridge. "I don't want to talk about it," he muttered as he sank onto the couch.

"Okay," Marshall said and used the remote to turn on the TV. The Dallas team was losing again. Marshall swore. "They just can't pull it together."

"They need a different pitcher," Ryder said.

"They need a different everything," Marshall said.

Silence passed. "Suzanne tells me your princess stopped by today to give the boys some gifts before she returns to Champagne or wherever the hell she lives."

His gut twisted. Tomorrow. "It's Chantaine," he said.

"Whatever," Marshall said. "Suzanne said she held it together with the babies but fell apart on the front porch."

Ryder narrowed his eyes against another stab of emotion and took a quick breath. "It sucks all around."

"Hmm. Seems like a lot of unnecessary torture to me," Marshall said.

Ryder shot his friend a hard glance. "Unnecessary?" he asked.

"Well, yeah, if y'all are that miserable without each other, then stay together."

Impatience rippled through him. "Okay, Mr. Relationship Expert, exactly how would we do that?"

"Ask her to marry you. Ask her to stay," he said and took a sip of his beer. "Nice play," he said, nodding toward the screen.

Ignoring Marshall's comment on the game, Ryder set down his beer. "How in hell can I do that? She's a princess from another country and she works for her country. I work eighteen hours a day and I have twin boys. No woman in her right mind would agree to that kind of life. She deserves better."

"I take it to mean you didn't have the guts to ask her what she would want," he said.

Anger roared through him. "Guts? Who are you talking to about guts? Guts is what it takes to let her go."

"Hmm," Marshall said. "You know, Suzanne and I are gonna have a baby."

"She's pregnant already?" Ryder asked.

"No. We don't know *how* we're going to have a baby. We just know we will. I told you about this the other day, but you probably weren't listening. There are lots of ways to have a baby these days. IVF, surrogacy, adoption in the States, overseas…" He nodded. "Yep, they're putting in the second-string pitcher. Let's see what happens now."

"What's your point?" Ryder demanded.

"There's more than one way to crack a nut," he said. "There's more than one solution to a problem. You could ask Bridget to move here. You could commute for a while. Just because you commute for a while doesn't mean you'll have to do it forever. Hell, didn't you say her country needed some doctors? If you really wanted to, you could move to Champagne and be a doctor there."

"Chantaine," Ryder corrected, mentally dismissing Marshall's suggestions in one fell swoop.

"Well, my man, you're going to have to make some career changes anyway," Marshall said. "Those babies are little now, but when they get older they're going to need to have their daddy around more than an hour or two every day. You're gonna have to figure out what kind of father you want to be, and I'm guessing it's nothing like the father you had."

Ryder mused over that for a long moment. He'd been fighting change ever since his brother had died. Although he'd done his best with the twins, he'd clung to what was most familiar to him, and that was his career. Outside of the hospital, he'd felt completely out of control. For a time, Bridget had made the new responsibility he'd faced feel a little lighter. She'd even made it fun.

He wondered how she would have responded if he'd asked her to stay. If he'd asked her to marry him. His heart hammered at the ridiculous possibility. The very idea of it was ludicrous. Even more ridiculous was the idea of his quitting his position, uprooting the twins and moving across the world for a completely different life with the woman who had made him fall in love with her. She hadn't asked for that because she hadn't wanted it. Ryder scowled at Marshall. The man was just stirring up a bunch of craziness because he'd found and married the woman of his dreams.

"At least, we can be miserable together," Bridget said to Phillipa, adjusting her dark, oversized sunglasses as she and her sister strode through the airport. She planned on keeping these sunglasses on her face night and day, inside and outside except when she was in her private quarters. No amount of cosmetics concealed the gutted agony in her eyes.

"It would have been nice to have the private jet," Phillipa said.

"So true, but Stefan always gets first rights to the jet. Plus, it's supposed to be much less expensive to travel commercial on the long-haul flights. At least we'll be together in first class. Hopefully they'll have a distracting movie. Although with my luck, it will be one of those dreadful tales with an unhappy ending from that American author. What's his name?"

"Robert James Waller," Phillipa said. "I've never liked sad movies. I know that some people say crying is cleansing, but I hate it."

"Me, too," Bridget said.

"I don't mean to upset you, but did you ever even ask Dr. McCall if he wanted you to stay?"

Bridget's stomach twisted. "He said our future was

impossible. He didn't even want to discuss the possibility of our seeing each other after this trip back to Chantaine." She felt her throat tighten with emotion and took a tiny breath. "No hope," she said.

Pippa reached over to take her hand. "I'm so sorry. You seemed so different once you met him. I'd thought he might be the one."

Her heart stretching and tightening, Bridget squeezed her sister's hand. "I'm lucky to have such a sweet sister."

"Your Highness," Raoul said, stepping to Bridget's side. "I apologize for the interruption, but Dr. McCall has arrived at the airport. He wishes to speak to you. I must warn you that you don't have much ti—"

Shocked, thrilled, afraid to hope, she felt her breath lodge somewhere between her lungs and throat. "I will speak to him," she managed in a whisper that sounded hoarse to her own ears.

Seconds that felt like eons later, Ryder stood in front of her.

"Hi," he said, meeting her gaze dead-on.

Her heart was hammering so fast that she could hardly breathe. "Hi. What brings you here?"

He took a deep breath and cocked his head to one side. "You mentioned that your country needs a new medical director. I wondered if you thought I could handle the job?"

Stunned and confused, she shook her head. "Excuse me? Are you asking for the position?"

He paused a half beat, then nodded. "Yeah, I guess I am."

Torn between throwing herself in his arms and trying to keep her head from spinning, she bit her lip. "Would you like me to talk to Stefan? I'm sure he would be thrilled."

"That's good. How would you feel about it?" he asked. "How would you feel about the twins and me coming to Chantaine?"

Bridget was so light-headed that she feared she might faint. She grabbed the back of a chair. "I would be beyond thrilled."

"Thrilled enough to marry me?"

She gasped, unable to register his question. "Excuse me?"

He moved toward her and took her hands in his. "I love you. I want my future with you. I want my children's future with you. I know it's fast, but will you—"

"Yes," she said, her eyes filling with tears of joy. Her heart was overflowing. "Yes, yes and yes."

Ryder took her into his arms and she hugged him tightly. The secret dream of having a man love her just for herself had just come true.

Five months later, Bridget stood in front of Ryder in the chapel of the oldest church in Chantaine and pinched herself. Her sisters dabbed at tears with handkerchiefs. Her brother Stefan beamed his approval. He was so thrilled one of his siblings had finally made a marriage that would benefit Chantaine. With Ryder as the newly appointed medical director of Chantaine, there was no shortage of residents clamoring to come to their country. Her sister-in-law Eve gave her an encouraging nod. The twins ran along the side aisle like the wild rascals they were. Her youngest brother and Raoul chased after them. Bridget had reached a new level of terror when the boys had started pulling up, and worse, walking. Not one day passed, however, when she didn't thank God for Ryder and the boys.

The priest led them in their vows. Ryder's voice was clear and strong. His gaze was resolute. She knew she could count on this man for the rest of her life. Surprisingly enough, she knew he could count on her, too. Ryder's love had triggered something hidden deep inside her, something she'd hoped she possessed, but it had never surfaced. With Ryder in her life, she didn't mind her royal duties, yet she could say no to Stefan when necessary.

Even with all the sacrifices and changes Ryder had made, he seemed happier and more relaxed. At the same time, he saw many opportunities for improvement and expansion in Chantaine's health program. She still couldn't believe how everything had worked out. Every day, she grew closer to Ryder and fell more deeply in love with him. She counted her blessings that she would spend the rest of her life with him and the twins. Despite her best efforts, though, he refused to reveal his honeymoon plans. As long as it didn't involve the desert, and it did involve just the two of them, she would be happy.

With the twins squealing in delight, the priest appeared to smother a chuckle. "I now pronounce you husband and wife. You may kiss your bride," he said.

Ryder took her face in his hands as if it were the most precious thing in the world and lowered his mouth to hers. She threw her hands around his neck and kissed him with all her heart.

Distantly, she heard the sound of laughter and

applause. She pulled back and turned to the many witnesses seated in the chapel, glancing toward the twins.

Ryder's mind must have been moving in the same direction. "Tyler," he called. "Travis. Come here right now."

The twins turned suddenly solemn, but made their way to the front of the church. Dressed in pale blue short suits, both boys lifted their arms toward her and Ryder. Heedless of her designer wedding dress, she scooped up Tyler while Ryder picked up Travis.

"Ladies and gentlemen, may God bless this happy union."

As the group in the church applauded again, Ryder leaned toward her and kissed her again. "I'm taking you to Italy, Your Highness. Tomorrow."

* * * * *

CROWN PRINCE'S CHOSEN BRIDE

KANDY SHEPHERD

To Cathleen Ross,
in gratitude for your friendship!

CHAPTER ONE

USING AN OLD-FASHIONED wooden spoon and her favourite vintage-style ceramic bowl, Gemma Harper beat the batter for the cake she was baking to mark the end of her six months' self-imposed exile from dating.

Fittingly, the cake was a mixture of sweet and sour—a rich white chocolate mud cake, flavoured with the sharp contrast of lemon and lime. For Gemma, the six months had been sweet with the absence of relationship angst and tempered by sour moments of loneliness. But she'd come out of it stronger, wiser, determined to break the cycle of choosing the wrong type of man. *The heartbreaking type.*

From now on things would be different, she reminded herself as she gave the batter a particularly vigorous stir. She would not let a handsome face and a set of broad shoulders blind her to character flaws that spelled ultimate doom to happiness. She would curb the impulsiveness that had seen her diving headlong into relationships because she thought she was in love with someone she, in fact, did not really know.

And she was going to be much, *much* tougher. Less forgiving. No more giving 'one last chance' and then another to a cheating, lying heartbreaker, unworthy of her, whose false promises she'd believed.

She was twenty-eight and she wanted to get married and have kids before too many more years sped by.

'No more Ms Bad Judge of Men,' she said out loud.

It was okay to talk to herself. She was alone in the large industrial kitchen at the converted warehouse in inner-city Alexandria, the Sydney suburb that was headquarters to her successful party planning business. Party Queens be-

longed to her and to her two business partners, Andie New-
man and Eliza Dunne. The food was Gemma's domain,
Andie was the creative genius and Eliza the business brain.

After several years working as a chef and then as a food
editor on magazines, in Party Queens Gemma had found
her dream job. Going into partnership with Andie and
Eliza was the best decision she'd ever made. And throwing herself headlong into work had been the best thing she
could have done to keep her mind off men. She would do
anything to keep this business thriving.

Gemma poured the batter into a high, round pan and
carefully placed it into a slow oven, where it would cook
for one and a half hours. Then she would cover it with coconut frosting and garnish it with fine curls of candied
lemon and lime peel. Not only would the cake be a treat
for her and her partners to share this afternoon, in celebration of the end of her man-free six months, it was also
a trial run for a client's wedding cake.

Carefully, she settled the cake in the centre of the oven
and gently closed the oven door.

She turned back to face the island countertop, to find
she was no longer alone. A tall, broad-shouldered man
stood just inside the door. She gasped, and her hand—en-
cased in a hot-pink oven mitt—went to her heart.

'Who are you and how the heck did you get in here?'
she asked, her voice high with sudden panic.

Even through her shock she registered that the intruder
was very handsome, with a lean face and light brown
hair. *Just her type.* No. *No longer her type*—not after six
months of talking herself out of that kind of very good-
looking man. Especially if he was a burglar—or worse.

She snatched up a wooden spoon in self-defence. Drips
of cake batter slid down her arm, but she scarcely noticed.

The man put up his hands as if to ward off her spoon.
'Tristan Marco. I have a meeting this morning with Eliza

Dunne. She called to tell me she was caught in traffic and gave me the pass code for the door.'

The stranger seemed about her age and spoke with a posh English accent laced with a trace of something else. Something she couldn't quite place. French? German? He didn't look Australian. Something about his biscuit-coloured linen trousers, fine cream cotton shirt and stylish shoes seemed sartorially European.

'You can put down your weapon,' he said, amusement rippling through his voice.

Gemma blushed as she lowered the wooden spoon. What good would a spoon have been against a man taller than six foot? She took a deep breath in an attempt to get her heart rate back to somewhere near normal. 'You gave me quite a shock, walking in on me like that. Why didn't you press the buzzer?'

He walked further into the room so he stood opposite the island counter that separated them. This close she noticed vivid blue eyes framed by dark brows, smooth olive skin, perfect teeth.

'I'm sorry to have frightened you,' he said in that intriguing accent and with an expressive shrug of his broad shoulders. 'Ms Dunne did not tell me anyone else would be here.'

Gemma took off her oven mitts, used one to surreptitiously wipe the batter dribbles from her arm and placed them on the countertop.

'I wasn't frightened. It's just that I'm on my own here and—' *now wasn't* that *a dumb thing to say to a stranger?* '—Eliza will be here very soon.'

'Yes, she said she would not be long,' he said. His smile was both charming and reassuring. 'I'm looking forward to meeting her. We have only spoken on the phone.'

He was gorgeous. Gemma refused to let the dangerous little fluttering of awareness take hold. She had just spent six months talking herself out of any kind of instant attraction. She was not going to make those old mistakes again.

'Can I help you in the meantime?' Gemma asked. 'I'm Gemma Harper—one of Eliza's business partners.'

To be polite, she moved around the countertop to be nearer to him. Realising she was still in her white chef's apron, she went to untie it, then stopped. Might that look as if she was *undressing* in front of this stranger?

She gave herself a mental shake. *Of course it wouldn't.* Had six months without a date made her start thinking like an adolescent? Still, there was no real need to take the apron off.

She offered him her hand in a businesslike gesture that she hoped negated the pink oven mitts and the wielding of the wooden spoon. He took it in his own firm, warm grip for just the right amount of time.

'So you are also a Party Queen?' he asked. The hint of a smile lifted the corners of his mouth.

'Yes, I'm the food director,' she said, wishing not for the first time that they had chosen a more staid name for the business. It had all started as a bit of a lark, but now, eighteen months after they had launched, they were one of the most popular and successful party planning businesses in Sydney. And still being teased about being Party Queens.

'Did you…did you want to see Eliza about booking a party?' she asked cautiously. To her knowledge, the steadfastly single Eliza wasn't dating anyone. But his visit to their headquarters might be personal. Lucky Eliza, if that was the case.

'Yes, I've been planning a reception with her.'

'A reception? You mean a wedding reception?'

The good ones were always taken. She banished the flickering disappointment the thought aroused. This guy was a stranger and a client. His marital status should be of no concern to her. Yet she had to admit there was something about him she found very attractive beyond the obvious appeal of his good looks. Perhaps because he seemed somehow…different.

'No. Not a wedding.' His face seemed to darken. 'When I get married, it will not be *me* arranging the festivities.'

Of course it wouldn't. In her experience it was always the bride. It sometimes took the grooms a while to realise that.

'So, if not a wedding reception, what kind of reception?'

'Perhaps "reception" is not the right word. My English…' He shrugged again.

She did like broad shoulders on a man.

'Your English sounds perfect to me,' she said, her curiosity aroused. 'Do you mean a business reception?'

'Yes and no. I have been speaking to Eliza about holding a party for me to meet Australians connected by business to my family. It is to be held on Friday evening.'

It clicked. 'Of course!' she exclaimed. 'The cocktail party at the Parkview Hotel on Friday night.' It was now Monday, and everything was on track for the upscale event.

'That is correct,' he said.

'I manage the food aspect of our business. We're using the hotel's excellent catering team. I've worked with them on devising the menu. I think you'll be very happy with the food.'

'It all looked in order to me,' he said. 'I believe I am in capable hands.'

Everything fell into place. Tristan Marco was their mystery client. Mysterious because his event had been organised from a distance, by phone and email, in a hurry, and by someone for whom Eliza had been unable to check credit details. The client had solved that problem by paying the entire quoted price upfront. A very substantial price for a no-expenses-spared party at a high-end venue. She,

Eliza and Andie had spent quite some time speculating on what the client would be like.

'You are in the best possible hands with our company,' she reassured him.

He looked at her intently, his blue eyes narrowed. 'Did I speak with you?' he said. 'I am sure I would have remembered your voice.'

She certainly would have remembered *his*.

Gemma shook her head. 'Eliza is our business director. She does most of our client liaison. You are not what we—' She clapped her hand to her mouth. *Put a zip on it, Gemma.*

'Not what you what?' he asked with a quizzical expression.

'Not…not what we expected,' she said. Her voice trailed away, and she looked down in the direction of his well-polished Italian shoes.

'What *did* you expect?'

She sighed and met his gaze full on. There was no getting out of this. She really needed to curb her tendency to blurt things out without thinking. That was why she worked with the food and Eliza and Andie with the clients.

'Well, we expected someone older. Someone not so tall. Someone heavier. Someone perhaps even…bald. With a twirling black moustache. Maybe…maybe someone like Hercule Poirot. You know…the detective in the Agatha Christie movies?'

Someone not so devastatingly handsome.

Thank heaven, he laughed. 'So are you disappointed in what you see?' He stood, arms outspread, as if welcoming her inspection.

Gemma felt suddenly breathless at the intensity of his gaze, at her compulsion to take up his unspoken offer to admire his tall, obviously well-muscled body, his lean, handsome face with those incredibly blue eyes, the full sensual mouth with the top lip slightly narrower then the lower, the way his short brown hair kicked up at the front in a cowlick.

'Not at all,' she said, scarcely able to choke out the words. *Disappointed was* not *the word that sprang to mind.*

'I am glad to hear that,' he said very seriously, his gaze not leaving hers. 'You did not know me, but I knew *exactly* what to expect from Party Queens.'

'You…you did?' she stuttered.

'Party Queens was recommended to me by my friend Jake Marlowe. He told me that each of the three partners was beautiful, talented and very smart.'

'He…he did?' she said, her vocabulary seeming to have escaped her.

Billionaire Jake Marlowe was the business partner of Andie's husband, Dominic. He'd been best man at their wedding two Christmases ago. Who knew he'd taken such an interest in them?

'On the basis of my meeting with you, I can see Jake did not mislead me,' Tristan said.

His formal way of speaking and his charming smile made the compliment sound sincere when it might have sounded sleazy. *Had he even made a slight bow as he spoke?*

She willed herself not to blush again but without success. 'Thank you,' was all she could manage to say.

'Jake spoke very highly of your business,' Tristan said. 'He told me there was no better party-planning company in Sydney.'

'That was kind of him. It's always gratifying to get such good feedback.'

'I did not even talk with another company,' Tristan said with that charming smile.

'Wow! I mean…that's wonderful. I…we're flattered. We won't let you down, I promise you. The hotel is a perfect venue. It overlooks Hyde Park, it's high end, elegant and it prides itself on its exemplary service. I don't think I've ever seen so much marble and glamour in one place.'

She knew she was speaking too fast, but she couldn't seem to help it.

'Yes. The first thing I did was inspect it when I arrived in Sydney. You chose well.' He paused. 'I myself would prefer something more informal, but protocol dictates the event must be formal.'

'The protocol of your family business?' she asked, not quite sure she'd got it right.

He nodded. 'That is correct. It must be upheld even when I am in another country.'

'You're a visitor to Australia?' Another piece of the puzzle fell into place. The phone calls had all come from Queensland, the state to the north of New South Wales. Where Jake Marlowe lived, she now realised.

'Yes,' he said.

She still couldn't place the accent, and it annoyed her. Gemma had studied French, German and Italian—not that she'd had much chance to practise them—and thought she had a good ear.

'What kind of business does your family run?' she asked.

That was another thing the Party Queens had wondered about as they'd discussed their mystery client. *He was still a mystery.*

Tristan was still too bemused by the vision of this cute redhead wearing bright pink oven mitts and wielding a wooden spoon as a weapon to think straight. He had to consider his reply and try not to be distracted by the smear of flour down her right cheek that seemed to point to her beautiful full mouth. While he'd been speaking with her, he'd had to fight the urge to lean across and gently wipe it off.

Should he tell her the truth? Or give the same evasive replies he'd given to others during his incognito trip to Sydney? He'd been here four days, and no one had recognised him...

Visiting Australia had been on his list to do before he turned thirty and had to return home to step up his involvement in 'the business'. He'd spent some time in Queensland with Jake. But for the past few days in Sydney, he had enjoyed his anonymity, relished being just Tristan. No expectations. No explanations. Just a guy nearing thirty, being himself, being independent, having fun. It was a novelty for him to be an everyday guy. Even when he'd been at university in England, the other students had soon sussed him out.

He would have to tell Party Queens the truth about himself and the nature of his reception sooner or later, though. *Let it be later.*

Gemma Harper was lovely—really lovely—with her deep auburn hair, heart-shaped face and the shapely curves that the professional-looking white apron did nothing to disguise. He wanted to enjoy talking with her still cloaked in the anonymity of being just plain Tristan. When she found out his true identity, her attitude would change. It always did.

'Finance. Trade. That kind of thing,' he replied.

'I see,' she said.

He could tell by the slight downturn of her mouth that although she'd made the right polite response, she found his family business dull. More the domain of the portly, bald gentleman she'd imagined him to be. Who could blame her? But he didn't want this delightful woman to find *him* dull.

He looked at the evidence of her cooking on the countertop, smelled something delicious wafting from the oven.

'And chocolate,' he added. 'The world's best chocolate.'

Now her beautiful brown eyes lit up with interest. *He'd played the right card.*

'Chocolate? You're talking about my favourite food group. So you're from Switzerland?'

He shook his head.

'Belgium? France?' she tried.

'Close,' he said. 'My country is Montovia. A small principality that is not far from those countries.'

She paused, her head tilted to one side. 'You're talking about Montovian chocolate?'

'You know it?' he asked, surprised. His country was known more for its financial services and as a tax haven than for its chocolate and cheese—undoubtedly excellent as they were.

She smiled, revealing delightful dimples in each cheek. He caught his breath. *This Party Queen really was a beauty.*

'Of course I do,' she said. 'Montovian chocolate is sublime. Not easy to get here, but I discovered it when I visited Europe. Nibbled on it, that is. I was a backpacker, and it's too expensive to have much more than a nibble. It's… Well, it's the gold standard of chocolate.'

'I would say the platinum standard,' he said, pleased at her reaction.

'Gold. Platinum. It's just marvellous stuff,' she said. 'Are you a *chocolatier*?'

'No,' he said. 'I am more on the…executive side of the business.' That wasn't stretching the truth too far.

'Is that why you're here in Sydney? The reason for your party? Promoting Montovian chocolate?'

'Among other things,' he said. He didn't want to dig himself in too deep with deception.

She nodded. 'Confidential stuff you can't really talk about?'

'That's right,' he said. He didn't actually like to lie. Evade—*yes*. Lie—*no*.

'Don't worry—you'd be surprised at what secrets we have to keep in the party business,' she said. 'We have to be discreet.'

She put her index finger to her lips. He noticed she didn't wear any rings on either hand.

'But the main reason I am in Sydney is for a vacation,' he said, with 100 per cent truthfulness.

'Really? Who would want a vacation from Montovian chocolate? I don't think I'd ever leave home if I lived in Montovia,' she said with another big smile. 'I'm joking, of course,' she hastened to add. 'No matter how much you love your job, a break is always good.'

'Sydney is a marvellous place for a vacation. I am enjoying it here very much,' he said.

And enjoying it even more since he'd met her. Sydney was a city full of beautiful women, but there was something about Gemma Harper that had instantly appealed to him. Her open, friendly manner, the laughter in her eyes, those dimples, the way she'd tried so unsuccessfully to look ferocious as she'd waved that wooden spoon. She was too pretty to ever look scary. Yet according to his friend Jake, all three of the partners were formidably smart businesswomen. Gemma interested him.

'March is the best time here,' she said. 'It's the start of autumn down-under. Still hot, but not too hot. The sea is warm and perfect for swimming. The school holidays are over. The restaurants are not crowded. I hope you're enjoying our lovely city.' She laughed. 'I sound like I'm spouting a travel brochure, don't I? But, seriously, you're lucky to be here at this time of year.'

The harbourside city was everything Tristan had hoped it would be. But he realised now there was one thing missing from his full enjoyment of Sydney—female company.

The life he'd chosen—correction, the life he had had chosen *for* him—meant he often felt lonely.

'You are the lucky one—to live in such a beautiful city on such a magnificent harbour,' he said.

'True. Sydney *is* great, and I love living here,' she said. 'But I'm sure Montovia must be, too. When I think of your chocolate, I picture snow-capped mountains and lakes. Am I right?'

'Yes,' he said. He wanted to tell her more about his home but feared he might trip himself up with an untruth. His experience of life in Montovia was very different from what a tourist might find.

'That was a lucky guess, then,' she said. 'I must confess I don't know anything about your country except for the chocolate.'

'Not many people outside of Europe do, I've discovered,' he said with a shrug.

And that suited him fine in terms of a laid-back vacation. Here in Sydney, half a world away from home, he hadn't been recognised. He liked it that way.

'But perhaps our chocolate will put us on the map down-under.'

'Perhaps after your trip here it will. I think…'

She paused midsentence, frowned. He could almost see the cogs turning.

'The menu for your reception… We'll need to change the desserts to showcase Montovian chocolate. There's still time. I'll get on to it straight away.' She slapped her hand to her mouth. 'Sorry. I jumped the gun there. I meant if you approve, of course.'

'Of course I approve. It's a very good idea. I should have thought of it myself.' Only devising menus was quite out of the range of his experience.

'Excellent. Let me come up with some fabulous chocolate desserts, and I'll pass them by you for approval.'

He was about to tell her not to bother with the approval process when he stopped himself. *He wanted to see her again.* 'Please do that,' he said.

'Eliza shouldn't be too much longer—the traffic can't be that bad. Can I take you into our waiting area? It's not big, but it's more comfortable than standing around here,' she said.

'I am comfortable here,' he said, not liking the idea of her being in a different room from him. 'I like your kitchen.' All stainless steel and large industrial appliances, it still somehow seemed imbued with her warmth and welcome.

Her eyes widened. They were an unusual shade of brown—the colour of cinnamon—and lit up when she smiled.

'Me, too,' she said. 'I have a cake in the oven, and I want to keep an eye on it.'

He inhaled the citrus-scented air. 'It smells very good.'

She glanced at her watch. 'It's a new recipe I'm trying, but I think it will be delicious. I don't know how long you're planning to meet with Eliza for, but the cake won't be ready for another hour or so. Then it has to cool, and then I—'

'I think our meeting will be brief. I have some more sightseeing to do—I've booked a jet boat on the harbour. Perhaps another time I could sample your cake?' He would make certain there would be another time.

'I can see that a cake wouldn't have the same appeal as a jet boat,' she said, with a smile that showed him she did not take offence. 'What else have you seen of Sydney so far?' she asked.

'The usual tourist spots,' he said. 'I've been to the Opera House, Bondi Beach, climbed the Sydney Harbour Bridge.'

'They're all essential. Though I've never found the courage to do the bridge climb. But there's also a Sydney tourists don't get to see. I recommend—'

'Would you show me the Sydney the tourists don't see? I would very much like your company.'

The lovely food director's eyes widened. She hesitated. 'I...I wonder if—'

He was waiting for her reply, when a slender, dark-haired young woman swept into the room. Tristan silently cursed under his breath in his own language at the interruption. She immediately held out her hand to him.

'You must be Mr Marco? I'm so sorry to have kept you waiting—the traffic was a nightmare. I'm Eliza Dunne.'

For a moment he made no acknowledgment of the newcomer's greeting—and then he remembered. He was using Marco as a surname when it was in fact his second given name. He didn't actually have a surname, as such. Not when he was always known simply as Tristan, Crown Prince of Montovia.

CHAPTER TWO

GEMMA CLOSED HER eyes in sheer relief at Eliza's well-timed entrance. *What a lucky escape.* Despite all her resolve not to act on impulse when it came to men, she'd been just about to agree to show Tristan around Sydney.

And that would have been a big mistake.

First, Party Queens had a rule of staff not dating clients. The fact that Andie had broken the rule in spectacular fashion by falling in love with and marrying their billionaire client Dominic Hunt was beside the point. She, Gemma, did not intend to make any exceptions. The business was too important to her for her to make messy mistakes.

But it wasn't just about the company rules. If she'd said yes to Tristan she could have told herself she was simply being hospitable to a foreign visitor—but she would have been lying. And lying to herself about men was a bad habit she was trying to break. She found Tristan way too appealing to pretend that being hospitable was all it would be.

'Thank you for taking care of Mr Marco for me, Gemma,' Eliza said. 'The traffic was crazy—insane.'

'Gemma has looked after me very well,' Tristan said, again with that faint hint of a bow in her direction.

Her heart stepped up a beat at the awareness that shimmered through her.

'She hasn't plied you with cake or muffins or cookies?' asked Eliza with a teasing smile.

'The cake isn't baked yet,' Gemma said. 'But I have cookies and—'

'Perhaps another cake, another time,' Tristan said with a shrug of those broad shoulders, that charming smile. 'And I could give you chocolate in return.'

The shrug. The accent. Those blue, blue eyes. *The Montovian chocolate.*

Yes! her body urged her to shout.

No! urged her common sense.

'Perhaps…' she echoed, the word dwindling away irresolutely.

Thankfully, Eliza diverted Tristan's attention from her as she engaged him in a discussion about final guest numbers for his party.

Gemma was grateful for some breathing space. Some deep breathing to let her get to grips with the pulse-raising presence of this gorgeous man.

'I'll let you guys chat while I check on my cake,' she said as she went back around the countertop.

She slipped into the pink oven mitts and carefully opened the oven door. As she turned the pan around, she inhaled the sweet-sharp aroma of the cake. Over the years she had learned to gauge the progress of her baking by smell. Its scent told her this cake had a way to go. This kind of solid mud cake needed slow, even cooking.

That was what she'd be looking for in a man in future. A slow burn. Not instant flames. No exhilarating infatuation. No hopping into bed too soon. Rather a long, slow getting to know each other before any kind of commitment—physical or otherwise—was made. The old-fashioned word *courtship* sprang to mind.

She'd managed six months on her own. She was in no rush for the next man. There was no urgency. Next time she wanted to get it right.

Still, no matter what she told herself, Gemma was superaware of Tristan's presence in her kitchen. And, even though he seemed engrossed in his conversation with Eliza, the tension in the way he held himself let her know that he was aware of her, too. The knowledge was a secret pleasure she hugged to herself. It was reassuring that she could still attract a hot guy. Even if there was no way she should do anything about it.

She scraped clean her mixing bowl and spoon and put them in the dishwasher while keeping an ear on Tristan and Eliza's conversation about the party on Friday and an eye on Tristan himself. On those broad shoulders tapering to narrow hips, on the long legs she imagined would be lean and hard with muscle.

Catching her eye, he smiled. Her first instinct was to blush, then smile back. For a long moment their gazes held before she reluctantly dragged hers away and went back to the tricky task of finely slicing strips of candied lemon peel.

Okay, she wasn't in dating exile any more. There was no law to say she couldn't flirt just a little. But she had spent six months fine-tuning her antennae to detect potential heartbreak. And there was something about this handsome Montovian that had those antennae waving wildly with a message of caution. They detected a mystery behind his formal way of speaking and courteous good manners. It wasn't what he'd said but what he *hadn't* said.

Then there was the fact Tristan was only here for a few days. To be a good-looking tourist's vacation fling was *not* what she needed in order to launch herself back into the dating pool. She had to be totally on guard, so she wouldn't fall for the first gorgeous guy who strolled into her life.

She'd learned such painful lessons from her relationship with Alistair. It had been love at first sight for both of them—or so she'd thought. Followed by an emotional rollercoaster that had lasted for eighteen months. Too blinded by desire, love—whatever that turbulent mix of emotions had been—she'd only seen the Alistair she'd wanted to see. She had missed all the cues that would have alerted her he wasn't what he'd sworn he was.

She'd heard the rumours before she'd started to date

him. But he'd assured her that he'd kicked his cocaine habit—*and* his reputation as a player. When time after time he'd lapsed, she'd always forgiven him, given him the one more chance he'd begged for. And then another. After all, she'd loved him and he'd loved her—hadn't he?

Then had come the final hurt and humiliation of finding him in the bathroom at a party with a so-called 'mutual friend'. Doing *her* as well as the drugs. Gemma doubted she'd ever be able to scour that image from her eyes.

After that there'd been no more chances, no more Alistair. She'd spent the last six months trying to sort out why she always seemed to fall for the wrong type of man. Her dating history was littered with misfires—though none as heart-wrenchingly painful as Alistair's betrayal.

On her first day back in the dating world she wasn't going to backtrack. Tristan was still a mystery man. He had perhaps not been completely honest about himself and was on vacation from a faraway country. How many more strikes against him could there be?

But, oh, he was handsome.

Eliza had suggested that Tristan follow her into her office. But he turned towards Gemma. 'I would like to speak to Gemma again first, please,' he said, with unmistakable authority.

Eliza sent Gemma a narrow-eyed, speculative glance. 'Sure,' she said to Tristan. 'My office is just around the corner. I'll wait for you there.'

Gemma could hear the sound of her own heart beating in the sudden silence of the room as Eliza left. Her mouth went dry as Tristan came closer to face her over the countertop.

His gaze was very direct. 'So, Gemma, you did not get a chance to answer me—will you show me your home town?'

It took every bit of resolve for her not to run around

to the other side of the countertop and babble, *Of course. How about we start right now?*

Instead she wiped her suddenly clammy hands down the sides of her apron. Took a deep breath to steady her voice. 'I'm sorry, Tristan. But I…I can't.'

He looked taken aback. She got the distinct impression he wasn't used to anyone saying *no* to him.

He frowned. 'You are sure?'

'It wouldn't be…appropriate,' she said.

'Because I am a client?' he asked, his gaze direct on hers.

She shifted from foot to foot, clad in the chef's clogs she wore in the kitchen. 'That's right,' she said. 'I'm sorry, but it's company policy.'

Just for a moment, did disappointment cloud those blue eyes? 'That is a shame. As I said, I would very much enjoy your company.'

'I…well, I would enjoy yours, too. But…uh…rules are rules.'

Such rules *could* be broken—as Andie had proved. But Gemma was determined to stick to her resolve, even if it was already tinged with regret.

His mouth twisted. 'I know all about rules that have to be followed whether one likes it or not,' he said with an edge to his voice. 'I don't like it, but I understand.'

What did he mean by that? Gemma wasn't sure if he was referring to the Party Queens rules or a different set of rules that might apply to him. She sensed there might be a lot she didn't understand about him. And now would never get a chance to.

'Thank you,' she said. 'I'll email the amended dessert menu to you.'

'Dessert menu?'

'Using Montovian chocolate for your party,' she prompted.

'Of course,' he said. 'I will look forward to it. I am sorry I will not be seeing more of Sydney with you.'

'I...I'm sorry, too.' But she would not toss away all that hard work she'd done on her insecurities.

'Now I must let you get back to work while I speak with Eliza,' he said, in what sounded very much like dismissal.

Gemma refused to admire his back view as he left the kitchen. *She liked a nice butt on a man.* For better or for worse, that ship had sailed. And she felt good about her decision. She really did.

But she was on edge as she prepared the coconut frosting by melting white chocolate and beating it with coconut cream. She kept glancing up, in case Tristan came back into the room. Was so distracted she grated the edge of her finger as well as the fine slivers of lemon and lime peel that would give the frosting its bite. But a half-hour later, when his meeting with Eliza concluded, he only briefly acknowledged her as he passed by the doorway to her kitchen.

She gripped her hands so tightly her fingernails cut into her hands. The sudden feeling of loss was totally irrational. She would *not* run after him to say she'd changed her mind.

An hour later, as Gemma was finishing her work on the cake, Eliza popped her head around the door.

'Cake ready?' she asked. 'The smell of it has been driving me crazy.'

'Nearly ready. I've been playing with the candied peel on top and tidying up the frosting,' Gemma said. 'Come and have a look. I think it will be perfect for the Sanderson wedding.'

'Magnificent,' Eliza said. She sneaked a quick taste of the leftover frosting from the bowl. 'Mmm...coconut. Nice touch. You really are a genius when it comes to food.'

Gemma knew her mouth had turned downwards. 'Just not such a genius when it comes to guys.'

Eliza patted her on the shoulder. 'Come on—you've done so well with your sabbatical. Aren't we going to celebrate your freedom to date—I mean to date *wisely*—with this cake?'

Both Gemma and Andie had been totally supportive during her man break. Had proved themselves again and again to be good friends as well as business partners.

Gemma nodded. 'I know...' she said, unable to stop the catch in her voice. It was the right thing to have turned down Tristan's invitation, but that didn't stop a lingering sense of regret, of wondering *what might have been.*

'What's brought on this fit of the gloomies?' Eliza asked. 'Oh, wait—don't tell me. The handsome mystery man—Tristan Marco. He's just your type, isn't he? As soon as I saw him, I thought—'

Gemma put up her hand to stop her. 'In looks, yes, I can't deny that. He's really hot.' She forced a smile. 'Our guesses about him were *so* far off the mark, weren't they?'

'He's about as far away from short, bald and middle-aged as he could be,' Eliza agreed. 'I had to stop myself staring at him for fear he'd think I was incredibly bad mannered.'

'You can imagine how shocked I was when he told me *he* was our client for the Friday night party. But I don't think he told me everything. There's still a lot of the mystery man about him.'

'What do you mean, *still* too much mystery? What did you talk about here in your kitchen?'

Gemma filled Eliza in on her conversation with Tristan, leaving out his invitation for her to show him around Sydney. Eliza would only remind her that dating clients was a no-no. And, besides, she didn't want to talk about it—she'd made her decision.

Eliza nodded. 'He told me much the same thing—although he was quite evasive about the final list of guests.

But what the heck? It's his party, and he can invite anyone he wants to it as long as he sticks with the number we
quoted on. We're ahead financially, so it's all good to me.'

'That reminds me,' Gemma said. 'I have to amend the
desserts for Friday to include Montovian chocolate. And
he needs to approve them.'

'You can discuss the menu change with him on Wednesday.'

Gemma stopped, the blunt palette knife she'd used to
apply the frosting still in her hand. 'Wednesday? Why
Wednesday?'

'Tristan is on vacation in Sydney. He's asked me to book
a private yacht cruise around the harbour on Wednesday.
And to organise an elegant, romantic lunch for two to be
taken on board.'

A romantic lunch for two?

Gemma let go of the palette knife so it landed with a
clatter on the stainless steel benchtop, using the distraction to gather her thoughts. So she'd been right to distrust
mystery man Tristan. He'd asked her to show him around
Sydney. And at the same time he was making plans for
a romantic tryst with another woman on a luxury yacht.

Thank heaven she'd said *no*.

Or had she misread him? Had his interest only been in
her knowledge of local hotspots? After a six-month sabbatical, maybe her dating skills were so rusty she'd mistaken his meaning.

Still, she couldn't help feeling annoyed. Not so much at
Tristan but at herself, for having let down her guard even
if only momentarily. If she'd glimpsed that look of interest in *his* eyes, he would have seen it in *hers*.

'Which boat did you book?' she asked Eliza.

The cooking facilities on the charter yachts available
in Sydney Harbour ranged from a basic galley to a full-
sized luxury kitchen.

'Because it will be midweek, I managed to get the *Argus* on short notice.'

'Wow! Well done. He should love that.'

'He did. I showed him a choice of boats online, but the *Argus* was the winner hands down.'

'His date should be really impressed,' Gemma said, fighting off an urge to sound snarky.

'I think that was the idea—the lucky lady.'

The *Argus* was a replica of a sixty-foot vintage wooden motor yacht from the nineteen-twenties and the ultimate in luxury. Its hourly hire rate was a mind-boggling amount of dollars. To book it for just two people was a total extravagance. Party Queens had organised a corporate client's event for thirty people on the boat at the start of summer. It was classy, high-tech and had a fully equipped kitchen. Tristan must *really* want to impress his date.

'So I'm guessing if lunch is on the *Argus* we won't be on a tight budget.'

'He told me to "spend what it takes",' said Eliza with a delighted smile. The more dollars for Party Queens, the happier Eliza was.

Gemma gritted her teeth and forced herself to think of Tristan purely as a client, not as an attractive man who'd caught her eye. It would be better if she still thought of him as bald with a pot belly. 'It's short notice, but of course we can do it. Any restrictions on the menu?'

Planning party menus could involve dealing with an overwhelming array of food allergies and intolerances.

'None that he mentioned,' said Eliza.

'That makes things easier.' Gemma thought out loud. 'An elegant on-board lunch for two…I'm thinking seafood—fresh and light. A meal we can prep ahead and our chef can finish off on board. We'll book the waiter today.'

'"Romantic" is the keyword, remember? And he wants the best French champagne—which, of course, I'll organise.' Eliza had an interest in wine as well as in spread-sheets.

'I wonder who his guest is?' Gemma said, hoping she wouldn't betray her personal interest to Eliza.

'Again, he didn't say,' Eliza said.

Gemma couldn't help a stab of envy towards Tristan's date, for whom he was making such an effort to be *romantic*. But he was a client. And she was a professional. If he wanted romantic, she'd give him romantic. In spades.

'But tell me—why will *I* be meeting with Tristan on Wednesday?'

'He wants you to be on board for the duration—to make sure everything is perfect. His words, not mine.'

'What? A lunch for two with a chef and a waiter doesn't need a supervisor, as well. You know how carefully we vet the people who work for us. They can be trusted to deliver the Party Queens' promise.'

Eliza put up her hands in a placatory gesture. 'Relax. I know that. I know the yacht comes with skipper and crew. But Tristan asked for you to be on board, too. He wants you to make sure everything goes well.'

'No!' Gemma said and realised her protest sounded over-the-top. 'I…I mean there's no need for me to be there at all. I'll go over everything with the chef and the waiter to make sure the presentation and service is faultless.'

Eliza shook her head. 'Not good enough. Tristan Marco has specifically requested your presence on board.'

Gemma knew the bottom line was always important to Eliza. She'd made sure their business was a success financially. With a sinking heart Gemma realised there would be no getting out of this. And Eliza was only too quick to confirm that.

'You know how lucrative his party on Friday is for us, Gemma. Tristan is an important client. You really have to do this. Whether you like it or not.'

CHAPTER THREE

ON WEDNESDAY MORNING Gemma made her way along the harbourside walk on the northern shore of Sydney Harbour. Milson's Point and the Art Deco North Sydney Swimming Pool were behind her as she headed towards the wharf at Lavender Bay, where she was to join the *Argus*. As she walked she realised why she felt so out of sorts— she was jealous of Tristan's unknown date. And put out that he had replaced her so quickly.

It wasn't that she was jealous of the other woman's cruise on a magnificent yacht on beautiful Sydney Harbour. Or the superb meal she would be served, thanks to the skill of the Party Queens team. No. What Gemma envied her most for was the pleasure of Tristan's company.

Gemma seethed with a most unprofessional indignation at the thought of having to dance attendance on the couple's romantic rendezvous. There was no justification for her feelings—Tristan had asked to spend time with her and she had turned him down. In fact, her feelings were more than a touch irrational. But still she didn't like the idea of seeing Tristan with another woman.

She did not want to do this.

Why had he insisted on her presence on board? This was a romantic lunch for *two*, for heaven's sake. There was only so much for her to do for a simple three-course meal. She would have too much time to observe Tristan being charming to his date. *And, oh, how charming the man could be.*

If she was forced to watch him kiss that other woman, she might just have to jump off board and brave the sharks and jellyfish to swim to shore.

Suck it up, Gemma, you turned him down.

She forced herself to remember that she was the director of her own company, looking after an important client. To convince herself that there were worse things to do than twiddle her thumbs in the lap of luxury on one of the most beautiful harbours in the world on a perfect sunny day. And to remind herself to paste a convincing smile on her face as she did everything in her power to make her client's day a success.

As she rounded the boardwalk past Luna Park fun fair, she picked up her pace when she noticed the *Argus* had already docked at Lavender Bay. The charter company called it a 'gentleman's cruiser', and the wooden boat's vintage lines made it stand out on a harbour dotted with slick, modern watercraft. She didn't know much about boats, but she liked this one—it looked fabulous, and it had a very well-fitted-out kitchen that was a dream to work in.

The Lavender Bay wharf was on the western side of the Sydney Harbour Bridge, virtually in its shadow, with a view right through to the gleaming white sails of the Opera House on the eastern side. The water was unbelievably blue to match the blue sky. The air was tangy with salt. How could she stay down on a day like this? *She would make the most of it.*

Gemma got her smile ready as she reached the historic old dock. She expected that a crew member would greet her and help her on board. But her heart missed a beat when she saw it was Tristan who stood there. Tristan... in white linen trousers and a white shirt open at the neck to reveal a glimpse of muscular chest, sleeves rolled back to show strong, sinewy forearms. Tristan looking tanned and unbelievably handsome, those blue eyes putting the sky to shame. Her heart seemed almost literally to leap into her throat.

She had never been more attracted to a man.

'Let me help you,' he said in his deep, accented voice as he extended a hand to help her across the gangplank.

She looked at his hand for a long moment, not sure what her reaction would be at actually touching him. But she knew she would need help to get across because she felt suddenly shaky and weak at the knees. She swallowed hard against a painful swell of regret.

What an idiot she'd been to say no *to him.*

Gemma looked as lovely as he remembered, Tristan thought as he held out his hand to her. Even lovelier— which he hadn't thought possible. Her auburn hair fell to her shoulders, glinting copper and gold in the sunlight. Her narrow deep blue cut-off pants and blue-and-white-striped top accentuated her curves in a subtle way he appreciated. But her smile was tentative, and she had hesitated before taking his hand and accepting his help to come on board.

'Gemma, it is so good to see you,' he said while his heart beat a tattoo of exultation that she had come—and he sent out a prayer that she would forgive him for insisting in such an autocratic manner on her presence.

She had her rules—he had his. His rules decreed that spending time with a girl like Gemma could lead nowhere. But he hadn't been able to stop thinking about her. So her rules had had to be bent.

'The Party Queens motto is No Job Too Big or Too Small,' Gemma said as she stepped on board. 'This…this is a very small job.'

He realised he was holding her hand for longer than would be considered polite. That her eyes were flickering away from the intensity of his gaze. But he didn't want to let go of her hand.

'Small…but important.' Incredibly important to him as the clock ticked relentlessly away on his last days of freedom.

She abruptly released her hand from his. Her lush mouth tightened. 'Is it? Then I hope you'll be happy with the menu.'

'Your chef and waiter are already in the kitchen,' he said. 'You have created a superb lunch for us.'

'And your guest for lunch? Is she—?'

At that moment a crew member approached to tell him they were ready to cast off from the dock and start their cruise around the harbour.

Tristan thanked him and turned to Gemma. 'I'm very much looking forward to this,' he said. *To getting to know her.*

'You couldn't have a better day for exploring the harbour,' she said with a wave of her hand that encompassed the impossibly blue waters, the boats trailing frothy white wakes behind them, the blue sky unmarred by clouds.

'The weather is perfect,' he said. 'Did Party Queens organise that for me, too?'

It was a feeble attempt at humour and he knew it. Gemma seemed to know it, too.

But her delightful dimples flirted in her cheeks as she replied, 'We may have cast a good weather spell or two.'

He raised his eyebrows. 'So you have supernatural powers? The Party Queens continue to surprise me.'

'I'd be careful who you're calling a witch,' she said with a deepening of the dimples. 'Andie and Eliza might not like it.'

A witch? She had bewitched him, all right. He had never felt such an instant attraction to a woman. Especially one so deeply unsuitable.

'And you?' In his country's mythology the most powerful witches had red hair and green eyes. This bewitching Australian had eyes the colour of cinnamon—warm and enticing. 'Are *you* a witch, Gemma Harper?' he asked slowly.

She met his gaze directly as they stood facing each other on the deck, the dock now behind them. 'I like to think I'm a witch in the kitchen—or it could be that I just have a highly developed intuition for food. But if you want to think I conjured up these blue skies, go right ahead. All part of the service.'

'So there is no limit to your talents?' he said.

'You're darn right about that,' she said with an upward tilt of her chin.

For a long moment their eyes met. Her heart-shaped face, so new to him, seemed already familiar—possibly because she had not been out of his thoughts since the moment they'd met. He ached to lift his hand and trace the freckles scattered across the bridge of her nose with his finger, then explore the contours of her mouth, her top lip with its perfect, plump bow. *He ached to kiss her.*

But there could be no kissing. Not with this girl, who had captured his interest within seconds of meeting her. Not when there were rules and strictures guiding the way he spent his life. When there were new levels of responsibility he had to step up to when he returned home. He was on a deadline—everything would change when he turned thirty, in three months' time. These next few days in Sydney were the last during which he could call his time his own.

His life had been very different before the accident that had killed his brother. Before the *spare* had suddenly become the *heir*. His carefree and some might even say hedonistic life as the second son had been abruptly curtailed.

There had been unsuitable girlfriends—forbidden to him now. He had taken risks on the racing-car circuit and on horseback, had scaled the mountains that towered over Montovia. Now everything he did came under scrutiny. The Crown took priority over everything. Duty had always governed part of his life. Now it was to be his all.

But he had demanded to be allowed to take this vacation—insisted on this last freedom before he had to buckle
under to duty. To responsibility. For the love of his country.

His fascination with Gemma Harper was nowhere on
the approved official agenda...

'I'm trying to imagine what other feats of magic you
can perform,' he said, attempting to come to terms with
the potent spell she had cast on him. The allure of her lush
mouth. The warmth of her eyes. The inexplicable longing
for her that had led him to planning this day.

He should not be thinking this way about a commoner.

She bit her lip, took a step back from him. 'My magic
trick is to make sure your lunch date goes smoothly. But
I don't need a fairy's wand for that.' Her dimples disappeared. 'I want everything to be to your satisfaction. Are
you happy with the *Argus*?'

Her voice was suddenly stilted, as if she had extracted
the laughter and levity from it. *Back to business* was the
message. And she was right. A business arrangement. That
was all there should be between them.

'It's a very handsome boat,' he said. He was used to
millionaire's toys. Took this level of luxury for granted.
But that didn't stop him appreciating it. And he couldn't
put a price on the spectacular view. 'I'm very happy with
it for this purpose.'

'Good. The *Argus* is my favourite of any of the boats
we've worked on,' she said. 'I love its wonderful Art Deco
style. It's from another era of graciousness.'

'Would you like me to show you around?' he said.

If she said yes, he would make only a cursory inspection of the luxury bedrooms, the grand stateroom. He did
not want her to get the wrong idea. Or to torture himself
with thoughts of what could never be.

She shook her head. 'No need. I'm familiar with the

layout,' she said. 'We held a corporate party here earlier in the spring. I'd like to catch up with my staff now.'

'Your waiter has already set up for lunch on the deck.'

'I'd like to see how it looks,' she said.

She had a large tan leather bag slung over her shoulder. 'Let me take your bag for you,' he said.

'Thank you, but I'm fine,' she said, clutching on to the strap.

'I insist,' he said. The habits of courtliness and chivalry towards women had been bred into him.

She shrugged. 'Okay.' Reluctantly, she handed it to him.

The weight of her bag surprised him, and he pretended to stagger on the deck. 'What have you got in here? An arsenal of wooden spoons?'

Her eyes widened, and she laughed. 'Of course not.'

'So I don't need to seek out my armour?'

It was tempting to tell her about the suits of medieval armour in the castle he called home. As a boy he'd thought everyone had genuine armour to play with—it hadn't been until he was older that he'd become aware of his uniquely privileged existence. Privileged and restricted.

But he couldn't reveal his identity to her yet. He wanted another day of just being plain Tristan. Just a guy getting to know a girl.

'Of course you don't need armour. Besides, I wasn't actually going to *hit* you with that wooden spoon, you know.'

'You had me worried back in that kitchen,' he teased. He was getting used to speaking English again, relaxing into the flow of words.

'I don't believe that for a second,' she said. 'You're so much bigger than me, and—'

'And what?'

'I…I trusted that you wouldn't hurt me.'

He had to clear his throat. 'I would never hurt you,' he said. And yet he wasn't being honest with her. Inadvertently, he *could* hurt her. But it would not be by intent. *This was just one day.*

'So what's really in the bag?' he asked.

'It's only bits and pieces of my favourite kitchen equipment—just in case I might need them.'

'Just in case the chef can't do his job?' he asked.

'You *did* want me here to supervise,' she said, her laughter gone as he reminded her of why she thought she was on board. 'And supervise I need to. Please. I have to see where we will be serving lunch.'

There was a formal dining area inside the cabin, but Tristan was glad Party Queens had chosen to serve lunch at an informal area with the best view at the fore of the boat. Under shelter from the sun and protected from the breeze. The very professional waiter had already set an elegant table with linen mats, large white plates and gleaming silver.

Gemma nodded in approval when she saw it. Then straightened a piece of cutlery into perfect alignment with another without seeming to be aware she was doing it.

'Our staff have done their usual good job,' she said. 'We'll drop anchor at Store Beach at lunchtime. That will be very *romantic.*'

She stressed the final word with a tight twist of her lips that surprised him.

'I don't know where Store Beach is, but I'm looking forward to seeing it,' he said.

'It's near Manly, which is a beachside suburb—the start of our wonderful northern beaches. Store Beach is a secluded beach accessible only from the water. I'm sure you and your...uh...*date* will like it.' She glanced at her watch. 'In the meantime, it's only ten o'clock. We can set up for morning tea or coffee now, if you'd like?'

'Coffee would be good,' he said. Sydney had surprised

him in many ways—not least of which was with its excellent European-style coffee.

Gemma gave the table setting another tweak and then stepped away from it. 'All that's now lacking is your guest. Are we picking her up from another wharf, or is she already on board?'

'She's already on board,' he said.

'Oh…' she said. 'Is she—?' She turned to look towards the passageway that led to the living area and bedrooms.

'She's not down there,' he said.

'Then where—?'

He sought the correct words. 'She…she's right here,' he said.

'I don't see anyone.' She frowned. 'I don't get it.'

He cleared his throat. '*You* are my guest for lunch, Gemma.'

She stilled. For a long moment she didn't say anything. Tristan shifted from foot to foot. He couldn't tell if she was pleased or annoyed.

'*Me?*' she said finally, in a voice laced with disbelief.

'You said there was a rule about you not spending time outside of work with clients. So I arranged to have time with you while you were officially at work.'

Her shoulders were held hunched and high. 'You…you tricked me. I don't like being tricked.'

'You could call it that—and I apologise for the deception. But there didn't seem to be another way. I had to see you again, Gemma.'

She took a deep intake of breath. 'Why didn't you just ask me?'

'Would you have said "yes"?'

She bowed her head. 'Perhaps not.'

'I will ask you now. Will you be my guest for lunch on board the *Argus*?'

She looked down at the deck.

He reached out his hand and tilted her chin upwards so she faced him. 'Please?'

He could see the emotions dancing across her face. Astonishment. A hint of anger. And could that be relief?

Her shoulders relaxed, and her dimples made a brief appearance in the smoothness of her cheeks. 'I guess as you have me trapped on board I have no choice but to say "yes".'

'Trapped? I don't wish you to feel trapped...' He didn't want to seem arrogant and domineering—job descriptions that came with the role of crown prince. His brother had fulfilled them impeccably. They sat uncomfortably with Tristan. 'Gemma, if this is unacceptable to you, I'll ask the captain to turn back to Lavender Bay. You can get off. Is that what you want?'

She shook her head. 'No. That's not what I want. I...I want to be here with you. In fact, I can't tell you how happy I am there's no other woman. I might have been tempted to throw her overboard.'

Her peal of laughter that followed was delightful, and it made him smile in response.

'Surely you wouldn't do that?'

She looked up at him, her eyes dancing with new confidence. 'You might be surprised at what I'm capable of,' she murmured. 'You don't know me at all, Tristan.'

'I hope to remedy that today,' he said.

Already he knew that this single day he'd permitted himself to share with her would not be enough. He had to anchor his feet to the deck so he didn't swing her into his arms. He must truly be bewitched. Because he couldn't remember when he'd last felt such anticipation at the thought of spending time with a woman.

'Welcome aboard, Gemma,' he said—and had to stop himself from sweeping into a courtly bow.

CHAPTER FOUR

GEMMA COULDN'T STOP SMILING—in relief, anticipation and a slowly bubbling excitement. After all that angst, *she* was Tristan's chosen date for the romantic lunch. *She* was the one he'd gone to so much effort and expense to impress. The thought made her heart skitter with wonder and more than a touch of awe.

She'd joked about casting spells, but *something* had happened back there in her kitchen—some kind of connection between her and Tristan that was quite out of the ordinary. It seemed he had felt it, too. She ignored the warning of the insistent twitching of her antennae. This magical feeling was *not* just warm and fuzzy lust born from Tristan's incredible physical appeal and the fact that she was coming out of a six-month man drought.

Oh, on a sensual level she wanted him, all right—her knees were still shaky just from the touch of his hand gripping hers as he'd helped her across the gangplank. But she didn't want Tristan just as a gorgeous male body to satisfy physical hunger. *It was something so much deeper than that.* Which was all kinds of crazy when he was only going to be around for a short time. And was still as much of a mystery to her as he had been the day they'd met.

For her, this was something more than just physical attraction. But what about him? Was this just a prelude to seduction? Was he a handsome guy with all the right words—spoken in the most charming of accents—looking for a no-strings holiday fling?

She tried to think of all those 'right' reasons for staying away from Tristan but couldn't remember one of them. By tricking her into this lunch with him, he had taken the decision out of her hands. But there was no need to get carried away. This was no big deal. *It was only lunch.* It would be up to her to say *no* if this was a net cast to snare her into a one-night stand.

She reached up and kissed him lightly on the cheek in an effort to make it casual. 'Thank you.'

She was rewarded by the relief in his smile. 'It is absolutely my pleasure,' he said.

'Does Eliza know?' she asked. *Had her friend been in on this deception?*

Tristan shook his head. 'I didn't tell her why I wanted you on board. I sense she's quite protective of you. I didn't want anything to prevent you from coming today.'

Of course Eliza was protective of her. Andie, too. Her friends had been there to pick up the pieces after the Alistair fallout. Eliza had seemed impressed with Tristan, though—impressed with him as a client...maybe not so impressed with him as a candidate for Gemma's first foray back into the dating world. He was still in many ways their Mr Mystery. *But she could find out more about him today.*

'I did protest that I wasn't really needed,' she said, still secretly delighted at the way things had turned out. 'Not when there are a chef and a waiter and a crew on the boat.'

'I'm sure the bonus I added to the Party Queens fee guaranteed your presence on board. She's a shrewd businesswoman, your partner.'

'Yes, she is,' Gemma agreed. No wonder Eliza hadn't objected to Gemma's time being so wastefully spent. How glad she was now that Eliza had insisted she go. But she felt as though the tables had been turned on her, and she wasn't quite sure where she stood.

She looked up at Tristan. Her heart flipped over at how handsome he was, with the sea breeze ruffling his hair, his eyes such a vivid blue against his tan. He looked totally at home on this multi-million-dollar boat, seemingly not impressed by the luxury that surrounded them. She wondered what kind of world he came from. One where money was not in short supply, she guessed.

'I...I'm so pleased about this...this turn of events,' she said. 'Thrilled, in fact. But how do we manage it? I...I feel a bit like Cinderella. One minute I'm in the kitchen, the next minute I'm at the ball.'

He seemed amused by her flight of fancy, and he smiled. What was it about his smile that appealed so much? His perfect teeth? The warmth in his eyes? The way his face creased into lines of good humour?

'I guess you could see it like that...' he said.

'And if I'm Cinderella...I guess *you're* the prince.'

His smile froze, and tension suddenly edged his voice. 'What...what do you mean?'

Gemma felt a sudden chill that was not a sea breeze. It perplexed her. 'Cinderella... The ball... The prince... The pumpkin transformed into a carriage... You know...' she said, gesturing with her hands. 'Don't you have the story of Cinderella in your country?'

'Uh...of course,' he said with an obvious relief that puzzled her. 'Those old fairytales originally came from Europe.'

So she'd unwittingly said the wrong thing? Maybe he thought she had expectations of something more than a day on the harbour. Of getting her claws into him. She really was out of practice. At dating. At flirting. Simply talking with a man who attracted her.

'I meant... Well, I meant that Cinderella meets the prince and you...well, you're as handsome as any fairytale prince and... Never mind.'

She glanced down at her white sneakers, tied with jaunty blue laces. Maybe this wasn't the time to be making a joke about a glass slipper.

Tristan nodded thoughtfully. 'Of course. And I found Cinderella in her kitchen…'

She felt uncomfortable about carrying this any further. He seemed to be making too much effort to join in the story. His English was excellent, but maybe he'd missed the nuances of the analogy. Maybe he had trouble with her Australian accent.

'Yes. And talking of kitchens, I need to talk to the chef and—' She made to turn back towards the door that led inside the cabin.

Tristan reached out and put his hand on her arm to stop her.

'You don't need to do anything but enjoy yourself,' he said, his tone now anything but uncertain. 'I've spoken to your staff. They know that you are my honoured guest.'

He dropped his hand from her arm so she could turn back to face him. 'You said that? You called me your "honoured guest"?' There was something about his formal way of speaking that really appealed to her. His words made her want to preen with pleasure.

'I did—and they seemed pleased,' he said.

Party Queens had a policy of only hiring staff they personally liked. The freelance chef on board today was a guy she'd worked with in her restaurant days. But it was the Australian way to be irreverent… She suspected she might be teased about this sudden switch from staff to guest. Especially having lunch in the company of such an exceptionally good-looking man.

'They were pleased I'm out of their hair?' she asked.

'Pleased for *you*. They obviously hold their boss in high regard.'

'That's nice,' she said, nodding.

Hospitality could be a tense business at times, what with deadlines and temperamental clients and badly behaving guests. It was good to have it affirmed that the staff respected her.

'What about lunch?' she said, indicating the direction of the kitchen. 'The—?'

Tristan waved her objections away. 'Relax, Gemma.' A smile hovered at the corners of his mouth. As if he were only too aware of how difficult she found it to give up control of her job. 'I'm the host. You are my guest. Forget about what's going on in the kitchen. Just enjoy being the guest—not the party planner.'

'This might take some getting used to,' she said with a rueful smile. 'But thank you, yes.'

'Good,' he said.

'I'm not sure of one thing,' she said. 'Do you still want me as your tour guide? If that's the case, I need to be pointing out some sights to you.'

She turned from him, took a few steps to the railing and looked out, the breeze lifting her hair from her face.

'On the right—oh, hang on…don't we say "starboard" on a boat? To *starboard* are the Finger Wharves at Walsh Bay. The configuration is like a hand—you know, with each wharf a finger. The wharves are home to the Sydney Theatre Company. It's a real experience to go to the theatre there and—'

'Stop!'

She turned, to see Tristan with his hand held up in a halt sign. His hands were attractive, large with long elegant fingers. Yes, nice hands were an asset on a man, too. She wondered how they would feel—

She could not go there.

Gemma knew she'd been chattering on too much about the wharves. Gabbling, in fact. But she suddenly felt…*nervous* in Tristan's presence. And chatter had always been her way of distancing herself from an awkward situation.

She spluttered to a halt. 'You don't want to know about

the wharves? Okay, on the left-hand side—I mean the *port* side—is Luna Park and…'

Tristan lowered his hand. Moved closer to her. So close they were just kissing distance apart. She tried not to look at his mouth. That full lower lip…the upper lip slightly narrower. *A sensual mouth was another definite asset in a man.* So was his ability to kiss.

She flushed and put her hand to her forehead. Why was she letting her thoughts run riot on what Tristan would be like to kiss? She took a step back, only to feel the railing press into her back. It was a little scary that she was thinking this way about a man she barely knew.

'There's no need for you to act like a tour guide,' he said. 'The first day I got here I took a guided tour of the harbour.'

'But you asked me to show you the insider's Sydney. The Wharf Theatre is a favourite place of mine and—'

'That was just a ploy,' he said.

Gemma caught her breath. 'A ploy?'

'I had to see you again. I thought there was more chance of you agreeing to show me around than if I straight out asked you to dinner.'

'Oh,' she said, momentarily lost for words. 'Or…or lunch on the harbour?'

Her heart started to thud so hard she thought surely he must hear it—even over the faint thrumming of the boat's motor, the sound of people calling out to each other on the cruiser that was passing them, the squawk of the seagulls wheeling over the harbour wall, where a fisherman had gutted his catch.

'That is correct,' Tristan said.

'So…so you had to find another way?' To think that all the time she'd spent thinking about *him*, he'd been thinking about *her*.

For the first time Gemma detected a crack in Tristan's self-assured confidence. His hands were thrust deep into the pockets of his white trousers. 'I…I had to see if you were as…as wonderful as I remembered,' he said, and his accent was more pronounced.

She loved the way he rolled his r*'s.* Without that accent, without the underlying note of sincerity, his words might have sounded sleazy. But they didn't. They sent a shiver of awareness and anticipation up her spine.

'And…and are you disappointed?'

She wished now that she'd worn something less utilitarian than a T-shirt—even though it was a very smart, fitted T-shirt, with elbow-length sleeves—and sneakers. They were work clothes. Not 'lunching with a hot guy' clothes. Still, if she'd had to dress with the thought of impressing Tristan, she might still be back at her apartment, with the contents of her wardrobe scattered all over the bed.

'Not at all,' he said.

He didn't need to say the words. The appreciation in his eyes said it all. Her hand went to her heart to steady its out-of-control thud.

'Me neither. I mean, I'm not disappointed in *you.*' *Aargh, could she sound any dumber?* 'I thought you were pretty wonderful, too. I… I regretted that I knocked back your request for me to show you around. But…but I had my reasons.'

His dark eyebrows rose. 'Reasons? Not just the company rules?'

'Those, too. When we first started the business, we initiated a "no dating the clients" rule. It made sense.'

'Yet I believe your business partner Andie married a client, so that rule cannot be set in concrete.'

'How did you know that?' She answered her own question, 'Of course—Jake Marlowe.' The best friend of the groom. 'You're right. But Andie was the exception.' Up until now there had been no client who had made *Gemma* want to bend the rules.

'And the other reasons?'

'Personal. I…I came out of a bad relationship more… more than a little wounded.'

'I'm sorry to hear that.' His eyes searched her face. 'And now?'

She took a deep breath. Finally she had that heartbeat under control. 'I've got myself sorted,' she said, not wanting to give any further explanation.

'You don't wear a ring. I assumed you were single.' He paused. '*Are* you single?'

Gemma was a bit taken aback by the directness of his question. 'Very single,' she said. Did that sound too enthusiastic? As if she were making certain he knew she was available?

Gemma curled her hands into fists. She had to stop second guessing everything she said. Tristan had thought she was wonderful in her apron, all flushed from the heat of the oven and without a scrap of make-up. She had to be herself. Not try and please a man by somehow attempting to be what he wanted her to be. She'd learned that from her mother—and it was difficult to unlearn.

Her birth father had died before she was born and her mother, Aileen, had brought Gemma up on her own until she was six. Then her mother had met Dennis.

He had never wanted children but had grudgingly accepted Gemma as part of a package deal when he'd married Aileen. Her mother had trained Gemma to be grateful to her stepfather for having taken her on. To keep him happy by always being a sweet little girl, by forgiving his moody behaviour, his lack of real affection.

Gemma had become not necessarily a *people* pleaser but a man pleaser. She believed that was why she'd put up with Alistair's bad behaviour for so long. It was a habit she was determined to break.

She decided to take charge of the conversation. 'What about you, Tristan? Are you single, too?'

He nodded. 'Yes.'

'Have you ever been married?'

'No,' he said. 'I…I haven't met the right woman. And you?'

'Same. I haven't met the right man.' Boy, had she met some wrong ones. But those days were past. *No more heartbreakers.*

The swell from a passing ferry made her rock unsteadily on her feet as she swayed with the sudden motion of the boat.

Tristan caught her elbow to steady her. 'You okay?' he said.

The action brought him close to her. So close she could feel the strength in his body, smell the fresh scent of him that hinted at sage and woodlands and the mountain country he came from. There was something so *different* about him—almost a sense of *other.* It intrigued her, excited her.

'F-fine, thank you,' she stuttered.

His grip, though momentary, had been firm and warm on her arm, and her reaction to the contact disconcerted her. She found herself trembling a little. Those warning antennae waved so wildly she felt light-headed. She shouldn't be feeling this intense attraction to someone she knew so little about. *It was against her every resolve.*

She took another steadying breath, as deep as she could without looking too obvious. The *Argus* had left the Harbour Bridge behind. 'We're on home territory for me now,' she said, in a determinedly conversational tone. 'Come over to this side and I'll show you.'

'You live around here?' he said as he followed her.

'See over there?' She waved to encompass the park that stretched to the water under the massive supports for the bridge overhead, the double row of small shops, the terraced houses, the multi-million-dollar apartments that sat at the edge of the water. 'You can just see the red-tiled roof of my humble apartment block.'

Tristan walked over to the railing, leaned his elbows on the top, looked straight ahead. Gemma stood beside him, very aware that their shoulders were almost nudging.

'Sydney does not disappoint me,' he said finally.

'I'm glad to hear that,' she said. 'What made you come here on your vacation?'

He shrugged. 'Australia is a place I always wanted to see. So far from Europe. Like the last frontier.'

Again, Gemma sensed he was leaving out more than he was saying. Her self-protection antennae were waving furiously. She had finetuned them in those six months of sabbatical, so determined not to fall into old traps, make old mistakes. Would he share more with her by the end of the day?

'I think you need to travel west of Sydney to see actual last-frontier territory,' she said. 'No kangaroos hopping around the place here.'

'I would like to see kangaroos that aren't in a zoo,' he said. He turned to face her. 'Living in Sydney must be like living in a resort,' he said.

Gemma tried to see the city she'd lived in all her life through his eyes. It wasn't that she took the beauty of the harbour for granted—it was just that she saw it every day. 'I hadn't thought about it like that but, yes, I see what you mean,' she said. Although she'd worked too hard ever to think she was enjoying a resort lifestyle.

'Do you like living here?' he said.

'Of course,' she said. 'Though I haven't actually lived anywhere else to compare. Sometimes I think I'd like to try a new life in another country. If Party Queens hadn't been such a success, I might have looked for a job as a chef in France. But in the meantime Sydney suits me.'

'I envy you in some ways,' he said. 'Your freedom. The lack of stifling tradition.'

She wondered at the note of yearning in his voice.

'There's a lot more to Sydney than these areas, of course,' she said. 'The Blue Mountains are worth seeing.' She stopped herself from offering to show them to him. He didn't want a tour guide. She didn't want to get too involved. *This was just lunch.*

'I would like to see more, but I go back home on Monday afternoon. With the party on Friday, there is not much time.'

'That's a shame,' she said, keeping her voice light and neutral. She knew this—*Tristan*—was only for today... an interlude. But she already had the feeling that a day, a week, a month wouldn't ever be enough time with him.

'I have responsibilities I must return to.' His tone of voice indicated that he might not be 100 per cent happy about that.

'With your family's corporation? Maybe you could consider opening an Australian branch of the business here,' she said.

He looked ahead of him, and she realised he was purposely not meeting her eyes. 'I'm afraid that is not possible—delightful as the thought might be.'

He turned away from the railing and went over to where he had put down her bag. Again, he pretended it was too heavy to carry, though she could see that with his muscles it must be effortless for him.

'Let's stash your bag somewhere safe and see about that coffee.'

'You don't want to see more sights?'

He paused, her bag held by his side. 'Haven't I made it clear, Gemma? Forgive my English if I haven't. I've seen a lot of sights in the time I've been in Australia. In the days I have left the only sight I want to see more of is *you.*'

CHAPTER FIVE

TRISTAN SAT OPPOSITE Gemma at a round table inside the cabin. After his second cup of coffee—strong and black—he leaned back in his chair and sighed his satisfaction.

'Excellent coffee, thank you,' he said. Of all the good coffee he'd enjoyed in Australia, he rated this the highest.

Gemma looked pleased. 'We're very fussy about coffee at Party Queens—single origin, fair trade, the best.'

'It shows,' Tristan said.

He liked Party Queens' meticulous attention to detail. It was one of the reasons he felt confident that his reception on Friday would be everything he wanted it to be—although for reasons of security he hadn't shared with them the real nature of the gathering.

'Not true,' Tristan muttered under his breath in his own language. He could have told Eliza by now. The reason he was holding back on the full facts was that he wanted to delay telling Gemma the truth about himself for as long as possible. Things would not be the same once his anonymity was gone.

'I'm glad you like the coffee. How about the food?' she asked.

Her forehead was pleated with the trace of a frown, and he realised she was anxious about his opinion.

'Excellent,' he pronounced. Truth be told, he'd scarcely noticed it. Who would be interested in food when he could feast his eyes on the beautiful woman in front of him?

To please her, he gave his full attention to the superbly arranged fruit platter that included some of the ripe mangoes he had come to enjoy in Queensland. There was also a selection of bite-sized cookies—both savoury, with cheese, and sweet, studded with nuts—arranged on the bottom tier of a silver stand. On the top tier were small square cakes covered in dark chocolate and an extravagant coating of shredded coconut.

'It all looks very good,' he said.

'I know there's more food than we can possibly eat, but we knew nothing about your lunch date and her tastes in food,' Gemma said.

'In that case I hope you chose food *you* liked,' he said.

'As a matter of fact, I did,' she said, with a delightful display of dimples.

'What is this cake with the coconut?' he asked.

'You haven't seen a lamington before?'

He shook his head.

'If Australia had a national cake it would be the lamington,' she said. 'They say it was created in honour of Lord Lamington, a nineteenth-century governor.'

'So this cake has illustrious beginnings?'

'You could call it a grand start for a humble little cake. In this case they are perhaps more illustrious, as I made them using the finest Montovian chocolate.'

'A Montovian embellishment of an Australian tradition?'

'I suspect our traditions are mere babies compared to yours,' she said with another flash of dimples. 'Would you like to try one?'

Tristan bit into a lamington. 'Delicious.'

Truth be told, he preferred lighter food. He had to sit through so many official dinners, with course after rich course, that he ate healthily when he had the choice. The mangoes were more to his taste. But he would not hurt her feelings by telling her so.

Gemma looked longingly at the rest of the cakes. 'I have the world's sweetest tooth—which is a problem in this job. I have to restrict myself to just little tastes of what we cook, or I'd be the size of a house.'

'You're in very good shape,' he said.

She had a fabulous body. Slim, yet with alluring curves. He found it almost impossible to keep his eyes from straying to it. He would have liked to say more about how attractive he found her, but it would not be appropriate. *Not yet...perhaps not ever.*

She flushed high on her cheekbones. 'Thank you. I wasn't fishing for a compliment.'

'I know that,' he said.

The mere fact that she was so unassuming about her beauty made him want to shower her with compliments. To praise the cuteness of her freckles, her sensational curves. To admit to the way he found himself wanting to make her smile just to see her dimples.

There was so much he found pleasing about her. But he was not in a position to express his interest. Gemma wasn't a vacation-fling kind of girl—he'd realised that the moment he met her. And that was all he could ever offer her.

It was getting more difficult by the minute to keep that at the top of his mind.

'I'll try just half a lamington and then some fruit,' she said.

She sliced one into halves with a knife and slowly nibbled on one half with an expression of bliss, her eyes half closed. As she licked a stray shred of coconut from her lovely bow-shaped top lip, she tilted back her head and gave a little moan of pleasure.

Tristan shifted in his seat, gripped the edge of the table so hard it hurt. It was impossible for his thoughts not to stray to speculation about her appetite for other pleasures, to how she would react to his mouth on hers, his touch...

There was still a small strand of coconut at the corner

of her mouth. He ached to lean across the table, taste the chocolate on her lips, lick away that stray piece of coconut.

She looked at him through eyes still half narrowed with sensual appreciation. 'The Montovian chocolate makes that the best lamington I've ever tasted.'

She should *always* have chocolate from Montovia.

Tristan cleared his throat. He had to keep their conversation going to distract himself. In his hedonistic past he had been immune to the seduction techniques of worldly, sophisticated temptresses, who knew exactly what they were doing as they tried to snare a prince. Yet the unconscious provocation of this lovely girl eating a piece of cake was making him fall apart.

'I believe you're a trained chef?' he said. 'Tell me how that happened.'

'How I became a chef? Do you really need to know that?'

'I know very little about you. I need to know everything.'

'Oh,' she said, delightfully disconcerted, the flush deepening on her creamy skin. 'If that's what you want…'

'It is what I want,' he said, unable to keep the huskiness from his voice. There was so much more he wanted from her, but it was impossible for him to admit to the desire she was arousing in him.

'Okay,' she said. 'I was always interested in food. My mother wasn't really into cooking and was delighted to let me take over the kitchen whenever I wanted.' She helped herself to some grapes, snipping them from the bunch with a tiny pair of silver scissors.

'So you decided to make a career of it?' It wouldn't be an easy life, he imagined. Hard physical work, as well as particular skills required and—

He completely lost his train of thought. Instead he

watched, spellbound, as Gemma popped the fat, purple grapes one by one into her luscious mouth.

Inwardly, he groaned. *This was almost unbearable.*

'Actually, I was all set to be a nutritionist,' she said, seemingly unaware of the torment she was putting him through by the simple act of eating some fruit. 'I started a degree at the University of Newcastle, which is north of Sydney. I stayed up there during the vacations and—'

'Why was that? I went to university in England but came home for at least part of every vacation.'

He'd loved the freedom of living in another country, but home had always been a draw card for him—the security and continuity of the castle, the knowledge of his place in the hierarchy of his country. His parents, who were father and mother to him before they were king and queen.

Gemma pulled a face—which, far from contorting her features, made her look cute. *Had she cast a spell on him?*

'Your home might have been more…welcoming than mine,' she said.

A shadow darkened her warm brown eyes at what was obviously an unpleasant memory. It made him sad for her. His memories of childhood and adolescence were happy. Life at the castle as the 'spare' had been fun—he had had a freedom never granted to his brother. A freedom sorely lost to him now—except for this trip. There had always been some tension between his father and mother, but it had been kept distanced from him. It hadn't been until he'd grown up that he'd discovered the cause of that tension— and why both his parents were so unhappy.

'You were not welcome in your own home?' he asked.

'My mother was always welcoming. My stepfather less so.'

'Was he…abusive?' Tristan tensed, and his hands tightened into fists at the thought of anyone hurting her.

She shook her head. The sunshine slanting in through

the windows picked up amber highlights and copper glints in her hair as it fell around her face. He wanted to reach out and stroke it, see if it felt as fiery as it looked.

'Nothing like that,' she said. 'And he wasn't unkind—just indifferent. He didn't want children, but he fell in love with my mother when I was a little kid and I came as part of the package deal.'

'A "package deal"? That seems a harsh way to describe a child.'

Again he felt a surge of protectiveness for her. It was a feeling new to him—this desire to enfold her in safety and shield her from any harm the world might hurl at her. A girl he had known for only a matter of days...

Her shrug of one slender shoulder was obviously an effort to appear nonchalant about an old hurt, but it was not completely successful. 'He couldn't have one without the other. Apparently he wanted my mother badly—she's very beautiful.'

'As is her daughter.' He searched her face. It was disconcerting, the way she seemed to grow lovelier by the minute.

'Thank you.' She flushed again. 'My mother always told me I had to be grateful to my stepfather for looking after us. *Huh.* Even when I was little I looked after myself. But I did my best to please him—to make my mother happy.' She wrinkled her neat, straight nose. 'Why am I telling you all this? I'm sure you must find it boring.'

'You could never be boring, Gemma,' he said. 'I know that about you already.'

It was true. Whether or not she'd cast some kind of witch's spell over him, he found everything about her fascinating. He wanted nothing more than to find out all about her. Just for today, the rest of his life was on hold. It was just him and Gemma, alone in the curious intimacy of a boat in the middle of Sydney Harbour. Like a regular, everyday date of the kind that would not be possible for him once he was back home.

'Are you sure you want to hear more of my ordinary little story?' she asked, her head tilted to one side.

'Nothing could interest me more.'

She could read out loud the list of ingredients from one of her recipes and he'd hang on every word, watching the expressions flit across her face, her dimples peeking in and out. Although so far there didn't appear to be a lot to smile about in her story.

The good-looking dark-haired waiter came to clear their coffee cups and plates. Gemma looked up and smiled at him as she asked him to leave the fruit. Tristan felt a surge of jealousy—until he realised the waiter was more likely to be interested in *him* rather than *her*. Gemma thanked him and praised the chef.

After the waiter had left, she leaned across the table to Tristan. Her voice was lowered to barely above a whisper. 'It feels weird, having people I know serve me,' she said. 'My instinct is to jump up and help. I'm used to being on the other side of the kitchen door.'

Tristan had been used to people serving him since he was a baby. An army of staff catered to the royal family's every need. He'd long ago got used to the presence of servants in the room—so much that they'd become almost invisible. When he went back he would have a hand-picked private staff of his own to help him assume his new responsibilities as crown prince.

The downside was that there was very little privacy. Since his brother had died every aspect of his life had been under constant, intense scrutiny.

Gemma returned to her story. 'Inevitably, when I was a teenager I clashed with my stepfather. It made my mother unhappy. I was glad to leave home for uni—and I never went back except for fleeting visits.'

'And your father?'

'You mean my birth father?'

'Yes.'

'He died before I was born.' Her voice betrayed no emotion. It was as if she were speaking about a stranger.

'That was a tragedy.'

'For my mother, yes. She was a ski instructor in the French resort of Val d'Isère, taking a gap year. My father was English—also a ski instructor. They fell madly in love, she got pregnant, they got married and soon after he got killed in an avalanche.'

'I'm sorry—that's a terrible story.'

Skiing was one of the risky sports he loved, along with mountaineering and skydiving. The castle staff was doing everything it could to wean him off those adrenaline-pumping pastimes. He knew he had to acquiesce. The continuity of the royal family was paramount. His country had lost one heir to an accident and could not afford to lose him, too.

But he railed against being cosseted. Hated having his independence and choice taken away from him. Sometimes the price of becoming king in future seemed unbearably high. But duty overruled everything. Tragedy had forced fate's hand. He accepted his inheritance and everything that went with it—no matter the cost to him. *He was now the crown prince*.

Gemma made a dismissive gesture with her hands. 'I didn't know my father, so of course I never missed him. But he was the love of my mother's life. She was devastated. Then his posh parents arrived at the resort, looked down their noses at my mother, questioned the legality of my parents' marriage—it *was* totally legit, by the way— and paid her to forget she was ever married and to never make a claim on them. They even tried to bar her from the funeral back in England.' Her voice rose with indignation.

'You sound angry,' he said. But what her father's parents had done was something *his* parents had done when he and his brother were younger. They would have paid any amount of money to rid the family of an unsuitable woman. Someone who might reflect badly on the throne. A commoner. *Someone like Gemma.*

His parents' actions had slammed home the fact that marriage for a Montovian prince had nothing to do with love or passion. It was about tradition and duty and strategic alliance. When he had discovered the deep hypocrisy of his parents' relationship, his cynicism about the institution of marriage—or at least how it existed in Montovia—had been born.

That cynicism had only been reinforced by his brother's marriage to the daughter of a duke. The castle had trumpeted it as a 'love match'. Indeed, Carl had been grateful to have found such a pretty, vivacious bride as Sylvie. Only after the splendid wedding in the cathedral had she revealed her true self—venal and avaricious and greedy for the wealth and status that came with being a Montovian princess. She'd cared more for extravagant jewellery than she had for his brother.

Consequently, Tristan had avoided marriage and any attempts to get him to the altar.

He schooled his face to appear neutral, not to give Gemma any indication of what he was thinking. Her flushed face made it very clear that she would *not* be sympathetic to those kind of regal machinations.

'You're darn right. I get angry on behalf of my poor mother—young and grieving,' she said. 'She wanted to throw the money in their faces, but she was carrying me. She swallowed her pride and took the money—for my sake. I was born in London, then she brought me home to Sydney. She said her biggest revenge for their treatment of her was that they never knew they had a grandchild.'

Tristan frowned. He was part of a royal family with a lineage that stretched back hundreds of years. Blood meant everything. 'How did you feel about that?'

Gemma toyed with the remainder of the grapes. He noticed her hands were nicked with little scars and her nails were cut short and unpolished. There were risks in everything—even cooking.

'Of course, I've always felt curious about my English family,' she said. 'I look nothing like my mother or her side of the family. When I was having disagreements with my stepfather, I'd dream of running away to find my other family. I know who they are. But out of loyalty to my mother I've never made any attempt to contact my Clifford relatives.'

'So your name is really Gemma Clifford?'

She shook her head. 'My stepfather adopted me. Legally I bear his name. And that's okay. For all his faults, he gave me a home and supported me.'

'Until you went to university in Newcastle?'

'Whatever his other faults, he's not mean. He kept on paying me an allowance. But I wanted to be independent—free of him and of having to pretend to be someone I was not simply to please him. I talked my way into a part-time kitchen hand's job at the best restaurant in the area. As luck would have it, the head chef was an incredibly talented young guy. He became a culinary superstar in Europe in the years that followed. Somehow he saw talent in me and offered me an apprenticeship as a chef. I didn't hesitate to ditch my degree and accept—much to my parents' horror. But it was what I really wanted to do.'

'Have you ever regretted it?'

'Not for a minute.'

'It seems a big jump from chef to co-owning Party Queens,' Tristan said.

Gemma offered the remaining grapes to him. When he

refused, she popped some more into her mouth. He waited for her to finish them.

'It's a roundabout story. When my boss left for grander culinary pastures, his replacement wasn't so encouraging of me. I left the Newcastle restaurant and went back to Sydney.'

'To work in restaurants?'

'Yes—some very good ones. But it's still a very male-dominated industry. Most of the top chefs are men. Females like me only too often get relegated to being pastry chefs and are passed over for promotion. I got sick of the bullying in the kitchen. The sexist behaviour. I got the opportunity to work on a glossy women's magazine as an assistant to the food editor and grabbed it. In time I became a food editor myself, and my career took off.'

'That still doesn't explain Party Queens,' he said. 'Seems to me there's a gap there.' He'd trained as a lawyer. He was used to seeing what was missing from an argument, what lay beneath a story.

She leaned across the table and rested on her elbows. 'Are you interviewing me?' Her words were playful, but her eyes were serious.

'Of course not. I'm just interested. You're very successful. I want to know how you got there.'

'I've worked hard—be in no doubt about that. But luck plays a part in it, too.'

'It always does,' he said.

Lucky he had walked in on her in her kitchen. Lucky he'd been born into a royal family. And yet there were days when he resented that lucky accident of birth. Like right here, right now, spending time with this woman, knowing that he could not take this attraction, which to his intense gratification appeared to be mutual, *anywhere*. Because duty to his country required sacrificing his own desires.

'There's bad luck too, of course,' Gemma went on.

'Andie was lifestyle editor on the magazine—she'd trained as an interior designer. Eliza was on the publishing side. We became friends. Then the magazine closed without warning and we were all suddenly without a job.'

'That must have been a blow,' he said. He had never actually worked for an employer, apart from his time as a conscript in the Montovian military. His 'job prospects'— short of an exceedingly unlikely revolution—were assured for life.

Again, Gemma shrugged one slender shoulder. 'It happens in publishing. We rolled with it.'

'I can see that,' he said. He realised how resilient she was. And independent. She got more appealing by the minute.

'People asked us to organise parties for them while we were looking for other jobs—between us we had all the skills. The party bookings grew, and we began to see we had a viable business. That's how Party Queens was born. We never dreamed it would become as successful as it has.'

'I'm impressed. With you and with your business. With all this.' He indicated the *Argus*, the harbour, the meal.

'We aim to please,' she said with that bewitching smile.

He could imagine only too well how she might please him and he her.

But he was not here in Sydney to make impossible promises to a girl next door like Gemma. Nor did he want to seduce her with lies just for momentary physical thrills.

Or to put his own heart at any kind of risk.

This could be for only one day.

CHAPTER SIX

GEMMA COULDN'T REMEMBER when she'd last felt so at ease with a man. So utterly comfortable in his presence. Had she *ever* before felt like this?

But she didn't want to question the *why* of it. Just to enjoy his company while she had the chance.

After she'd polished off all the grapes, she and Tristan had moved back out onto the deck. He hadn't eaten much—no more cake and just some mango. She'd got the impression he was very disciplined in his eating habits—and probably everything else. But getting to know Tristan was still very much a guessing game.

The *Argus* had left the inner harbour behind and set course north for Manly and their lunchtime destination of Store Beach. The sun had moved around since they'd gone inside for coffee, and the crew had moved two vintage steamer-style wooden deckchairs into the shade, positioned to take advantage of the view.

She adjusted the cushions, which were printed with anchor motifs, and settled down into one of them. Tristan was to her right, with a small table between them. But as soon as she'd sat down, she moved to get up again.

'My hat,' she explained. 'I need to get it from my bag. Even though we're in the shade, I could get burned.'

Immediately, Tristan was on his feet. 'Let me get it for you,' he said, ushering her to sit back down.

'There's no need. Please… I can do it,' she protested.

'I insist,' he said in a tone that brooked no further resistance.

Gemma went to protest again, then realised that would sound ungracious. *She wasn't used to being cared for by a man.* 'Thank you,' she conceded. 'It's right at the top of the bag.'

'Next to the rolling pins?' he said.

'But no wooden spoons,' she said with a smile.

Not only would Alistair not have dreamed of fetching her hat for her, he would have demanded she get him a beer while she was up. *Good manners were very appealing in a man.*

Tristan held himself with a mix of upright bearing and athletic grace as he headed back into the cabin. Gemma lay back and watched him through her sunglasses. His back view was every bit as pleasing as his front. Broad shoulders tapered to a wide back and then narrow hips. *There could be no doubt that a good butt was also an asset in a man.*

He looked effortlessly classy in the white linen trousers and the loose white shirt. They were so perfectly cut she wondered if they'd been tailored to fit him. Could you get men's casual clothes made to measure? She knew you could have suits bespoke. Anything was possible if you had enough money, she supposed.

He returned with her hat—a favourite white panama. She reached out to take it from him, but he came to the side of her chair and bent down to put it on her head. His face was very close. She could almost imagine he was bending down to kiss her. If he did, she wouldn't stop him. No…she might even kiss him first. She was thankful her sunglasses masked her eyes, so her expression didn't give her away.

'Nice hat,' he said as he placed it on her head. As he tugged it into place, his hands strayed lightly over her hair, her ears, her throat—just the merest touch, but it was enough to set her trembling.

She forced her voice to sound steady—not to betray how excitingly unnerving she found his nearness. 'I've had this hat for years, and I would be greatly distressed if I lost it.'

Again she caught his scent. She remembered how years

ago in high school she'd dated a perfectly nice boy who'd had everything going for him, but she hadn't liked the way he'd smelled. Not that he'd been unclean or unwashed— it was just his natural scent that had turned her off. But Tristan's fresh scent sent her nerve endings into a flurry of awareness.

Was there *anything* about Tristan she didn't find appealing?

His underlying mystery, that sense of him holding back still had her guard up—but perhaps that mystery was part of his appeal. And it was in her power to find out what made Tristan tick. *Just ask him, Gemma.*

There were many points of interest she could draw his attention to on their way to Manly. But she would not waste time on further guidebook lectures. *The only sight I want to see more of is you,* he'd said.

Did he have any idea of how good those words made her feel?

Her self-esteem had taken a terrible battering from Alistair. Six months had not been enough to fix it fully. Just hours in Tristan's company had her feeling better about herself than she had for a long time. The insistent twitching of her antennae told her that his charming words might be calculated to disarm and seduce. But her deeper instincts sensed sincerity—though for what purpose she was still at a loss.

Enjoy the moment, she told herself, *because that's all you've got with him.*

After Tristan had settled into his deckchair, she turned to him, slipped off her sunglasses. 'Your interview technique is so good you know quite a lot about me. Now it's my turn to discover Tristan.'

He gestured with his hands to indicate emptiness. 'There is not much I can tell you,' he said.

Did he mean that literally?

For all the instant intimacy of the situation, she still sensed those secrets. Her antennae waved gently, to remind her to be wary of men who were not what they seemed.

'Ask me questions—I will see if I can answer them,' he said.

As in, he would see if he was *able* to answer her questions? Or *allowed* to answer them? Or he just plain didn't *want* to answer them?

She chose her first question with care. 'What language do you speak in Montovia?' she asked. 'French? German? I think I can detect both in your accent.'

'We speak Montovian—our own language,' he said. 'We are a small country and it is influenced by the other European countries that surround us.'

'Say something to me in Montovian,' she said. 'I'm interested in languages.'

'I've been told it is not an attractive language, so I am warning you,' he said. 'Even to my ears it sounds quite harsh.'

He turned to her and spoke a few sentences as he gazed into her eyes. She tried to ignore the way his proximity made her heart race.

'I didn't understand a word of that, but your language is not unattractive.' And neither was his voice—deep, masculine, arresting. 'What did you actually say to me?'

'You really want to know?'

'Yes.'

'I said that the beauty of this magnificent harbour could not compare to the beauty of the woman sitting beside me.'

Spoken by anyone else, the words might have sounded corny, over the top. But spoken with Tristan's accent they were swoon worthy.

'Oh,' she said, again lost for words. She felt herself blush—that was the problem with being a creamy-skinned redhead...there was no hiding her reactions. 'Seriously?'

He smiled. 'You'll never know, will you? Unless you learn Montovian—and no one outside of my country learns Montovian.'

'Why not?'

'Because it is only spoken in Montovia. I also speak German, French, Italian and Spanish,' he said.

'I'm seriously impressed,' she said. 'I studied French and Italian at school. Then German at night school before I went to Europe on a backpackers' bus tour. But I never use those languages here, and I fear I've lost what skills I had.'

'You'd pick them up again in the right environment. I was out of the habit of speaking English, but I'm getting better at it every day.' His eyes narrowed in that intense way he had of looking at her, as if he were seeking answers—to what, she didn't know. 'Especially talking to you, Gemma'.

'You've inspired me to study some more so that—'

Only just in time she caught herself from saying, *So that next time I'll surprise you by speaking fluent French.* She was surprised at the sharp twist of pain at the reminder that there would be no next time for her and Tristan.

She finished her sentence, hoping he hadn't noticed the pause. 'So that my skills don't just dwindle away. Did you learn English at school?'

'Yes. I also had a tutor. My parents felt it was essential we spoke good English.'

'"We"? You have brothers and sisters?'

Tristan stared out to sea. 'I have a younger sister. I… I had an older brother. He…he died when his helicopter came down in the mountains a year ago.'

Gemma wasn't sure what to say that wouldn't be a cliché. 'I…I'm so sorry to hear that,' was the best she could manage.

His jaw tightened. 'It was…terrible. His wife and their little boy were with him. My family will never get over it.'

Gemma was too shocked to speak. She went to reach out and put her hand on his arm but decided against it, not sure how welcome her touch would be in this moment of remembered tragedy.

'I carry the loss of my brother with me in my heart. There is not a day that I do not think of him.'

'I'm so sorry,' she said again. She wished she could give him comfort. But they were still essentially strangers.

He took a deep breath. 'But enough of sadness,' he said. He turned to her. 'I don't want to talk about tragic things, Gemma.'

There was a bleakness in his eyes, and his face seemed shadowed. She was an only child. She couldn't imagine how it would feel to lose a sibling—*and* his sibling's family. 'No,' she agreed.

How lucky she'd been in her life not to have suffered tragedy. The loss of her birth father hadn't really touched her, though she suspected her mother still secretly grieved. Gemma *had* had her share of heartbreak, though. She had genuinely loved Alistair, and the way their relationship had ended had scarred her—perhaps irredeemably. It would be difficult to trust again.

A silence fell between them that Gemma didn't know quite how to fill. 'Tell me more about Montovia,' she said eventually. 'Are there magnificent old buildings? Do you have lots of winter sports? Do you have a national costume?'

'Yes to all of that. Montovia is very beautiful and traditional. It has many medieval buildings. There is also a modern administrative capital, where the banks and financial services are situated.'

'And the chocolate?'

'The so-important chocolate? It is made in a charming old factory building near the lake, which is a tourist attraction in its own right.'

I'd love to go there some day.

Her words hung unspoken in the air between them. Never could she utter them. He was a tourist—just passing through before he went back to his own life. And she was a woman guarding her heart against falling for someone impossible.

'That sounds delightful,' she said.

'There is a wonderful chocolate shop and tea room near my home. I used to love to go there when I was a child. So…so did my brother and sister.'

Gemma wondered about his sister, but didn't want to ask. 'Where do you live?' she said instead.

He took another deep breath. It seemed to Gemma that he needed to steady himself against unhappy thoughts. His brother must be entwined in Tristan's every childhood memory.

'I live in the old capital of Montovia—which is also called Montovia.'

'That could get confusing, couldn't it?'

'Everyone knows it. The town of Montovia grew up around the medieval castle and the cathedral and sits on the edge of a lake.'

Gemma sat forward in her chair. 'A castle? You live near a *castle*?'

'But of course. Montovia is ruled by a hereditary monarchy.'

'You mean a king and a queen?'

'Yes.'

'I wasn't expecting that. I assumed Montovia would be a republic—a democracy.'

'It is… We have a hereditary monarchy, but also a representative democracy with an elected parliament—and a legal system, of course.'

'So the king and queen are figureheads?'

He shook his head. 'They are rulers, with the power to dissolve parliament. Although that has never happened.'

'Castles and kings and queens—it sounds like something out of a fairytale.' She was too polite to say it sounded feudalistic. Not when he sounded so passionate, defending a way of life that didn't seem of this century.

'On the contrary, it is very real. Our country is prosperous. Montovians are very patriotic. Each of our subjects—I...uh...I mean the people...would fight to the death to protect their way of life. We have compulsory military service to ensure we are ready in case they should ever have to.'

'You mean conscription?'

'Yes. For all males aged eighteen. Women can volunteer, and many do.'

She shuddered. 'I don't think I would want to do that.'

'They would probably welcome someone like you as a cook.'

He smiled. Was he teasing her?

'But I'd still have to do the military training. I've seen what soldiers have to do—running with big packs on their back, obstacle courses, weapons...' Her voice dwindled away at the sheer horror of even contemplating it.

'Sign up even as a cook and you'd have to do the training. And no wooden spoons as weapons.'

'You'll never let me forget that, will you?'

'Never,' he said, his smile widening into a grin.

Until he went on his way and never gave this girl in Sydney another thought.

Why were they even talking about this? She was unlikely to visit Montovia, let alone sign up for its military.

'Did you serve?' she asked.

'Of course. My time in the army was one of the best times of my life.'

Oh, yes. She could imagine him in uniform. With his

broad shoulders and athletic build. That must be where his bearing came from. Tristan in uniform would be even hotter than Tristan in casual clothes. Or Tristan without any—

Don't go there, Gemma.

But her curiosity about Montovia was piqued. When she went home this evening, she would look up the country and its customs on the internet.

'Did you actually have to go to battle?' she asked.

'I spent time with the peacekeeping forces in eastern Europe. My brother went to Africa. It was good for us to see outside our own protected world.'

'You know, I wasn't really aware that such kingdoms as Montovia still existed.'

'Our royal family has ruled for centuries,' he said— rather stiffly, she thought. 'The people love the royal family of Montovia.'

'Do *you*?' she asked. 'You're not harbouring any secret republican leanings?'

His eyebrows rose, and he looked affronted. 'Never. I am utterly loyal to the king and queen. My country would not be Montovia without the royal family and our customs and traditions.'

Gemma was silent for a long moment. 'It's all so outside of my experience. As a child I led an everyday suburban existence in a middle-class suburb of Sydney. You grew up in a town with a medieval castle ruled by a king and queen. What…what different lives we must lead.'

He steepled his fingers together. 'Yes. Very different.'

Tristan was glad of the interruption when the waiter brought out a tray with the cool drinks they had ordered. *He had to be more careful.* He'd been on tenterhooks while chatting with Gemma for fear that he would inadvertently reveal the truth about himself and his family. There had been a few minor slip-ups, but nothing that couldn't be excused as a mistake with his English.

He drank iced tea as Gemma sipped on diet cola. It was too early for anything stronger.

The longer he maintained this deception, the harder it would become to confess to it. But did that really matter? After the party on Friday night he wouldn't need to be in any further contact with Party Queens. Or with Gemma.

He could leave the reveal until she found out for herself—when he appeared at his party wearing his ceremonial sash and medals. No doubt she would be shocked, would maybe despise him for lying to her. Her opinion should not matter—he would never see her again after the party.

But her opinion of him did matter. *It mattered very much.*

Just now there had been an opportunity for him to explain his role in the royal family of Montovia—but he had not been able to bring himself to take it. He was still hanging on fiercely to the novelty of being just Tristan in Gemma's eyes.

'I haven't finished my interrogation yet,' she said, a playful smile lifting the corners of her mouth.

He liked it that she was unaware of his wealth and status. It must be obvious to her that he was rich. But she seemed more interested in *him* than in what he had. It was refreshing.

'You said you went to university in England?' she asked.

'To Cambridge—to study European law.'

Her finely arched auburn brows rose. 'You're a lawyer?'

'I don't actually practise as a lawyer. I have always worked for…for my family's business. A knowledge of European law is necessary.'

For trade. For treaties. For the delicate negotiations required by a small country that relied in some measure on the goodwill of surrounding countries—but never took that goodwill for granted.

'Is it your father's business?'

'Yes. And it was my grandparents' before that.' Back and back and back, in an unbroken chain of Montovia's hereditary monarchy. It had been set to continue in his brother's hands—not his.

Tristan knew he could not avoid talking about his brother, much as it still hurt. There'd been an extravagance of public mourning for his brother's death—and the death of his little son, whose birth had placed a second male between Tristan and the throne. But with all the concern about his unexpected succession to the position of crown prince, Tristan hadn't really been able to mourn the loss of Carl, his brother and best friend. Not Carl the crown prince. And his sweet little nephew. This trip away had been part of that grieving process. Being with Gemma was helping.

'My brother played a senior role in the...the business. I now have to step up to take his role.'

'And you're not one hundred per cent happy about that, are you?'

'I never anticipated I would have to do it. The job is not my choice.'

Not only had he loved his brother, he had also admired the way Carl had handled the role of crown prince. Tristan had never resented not being the heir. He had never been sure if he had an unquestioning allegiance to the old ways in order not to challenge the archaic rules that restricted the royal family's existence even in the twenty-first century. One onerous rule in particular...

'Will it bring more responsibility?' Gemma asked. 'Will you be more involved in the chocolate side of things?'

For a moment he wasn't sure what she meant. Then he

remembered how he had deliberately implied that chocolate was part of his family's business.

'More the finance and managerial side,' he said. And everything else it took to rule the country.

'I'm sure you will rise to the challenge and do a wonderful job,' she said.

He frowned. 'Why do you say that, Gemma, when we scarcely know each other?'

Her eyes widened. 'Even in this short time I'm convinced of your integrity,' she said. 'I believe you will want to honour your brother's memory by doing the best job you can.'

His integrity. Short of downright lying, he had been nothing but evasive about who he was from the moment they'd met. How would she react when she found out the truth?

The longer he left it, the worse it would be.

He turned to face her. 'Gemma, I—'

Gemma suddenly got up from her deckchair, clutching her hat to her head against a sudden gust of wind. 'We're passing across the Heads.'

'The Heads?'

'It's the entrance from the ocean to Sydney Harbour, guarded by two big headlands—North Head and South Head. But, being exposed to the Pacific Ocean, the sea can get rough here, so prepare for a rocky ride ahead.'

CHAPTER SEVEN

Tristan had planned with military precision in order to make this day with Gemma happen. But one important detail had escaped his plan.

He cursed his inattention with a blast of favourite curse words. Both relatively sheltered when they'd been conscripted to the military, he and his brother had expanded their vocabulary of new and interesting words with great glee. He had never lost the skill.

Gemma was standing beside him at the bow of the *Argus*. 'Do I detect some choice swearing in Montovian?' she asked with a teasing smile.

'Yes,' he said, still furious with himself.

'Can you translate for me?'

'No,' he said.

'Or tell me what it was all about?'

Exasperated, he waved his hand to encompass the view. 'Look at this place—Store Beach...even more perfect than you said it would be.'

'And there's a problem with that?'

The *Argus* had dropped anchor some one hundred metres from shore. The beach was more what he would call a bay, with a sheltered, curving stretch of golden sand. Eucalypt trees and other indigenous plants grew right down to where the sand started. The water rippled through shades of azure to wash up on the beach in a lacy white froth. The air was tangy with salt and the sharp scent of the eucalypts. It took no stretch of the imagination to feel as if they were on a remote island somewhere far away.

'Not a problem with the beach,' he said. 'It's difficult to believe such a pristine spot could be so close to a major city.'

'That's why we chose Store Beach for your lunch date,' she said. 'And, being midweek, we've got it all to ourselves. So what's the problem?'

'It's hot, the water looks awesome, I want to swim. But I didn't think to bring a swimsuit—or order one for you.'

Her eyebrows rose. 'For me? *Order* a swimsuit for me?'

'Of course. You would not have known to bring one as you thought you would be working. There is a concierge at my hotel—I should have asked her to purchase a choice of swimsuits for you.'

Gemma's brows drew together in a frown. 'Are you serious?'

'But of course.'

'You are, aren't you?' Her voice was underscored with incredulity.

'Is there something wrong with that?'

'Nothing *wrong*, I guess. But it's not the kind of thing an Australian guy would do, that's for sure. None that *I* know, anyway.'

Tristan realised he might sound arrogant, but went ahead anyway. 'It is the kind of thing I would do, and I am annoyed that I did not do so.'

She tilted her head to one side, observing him as if he were an object of curiosity. 'How would you have known my size?'

'I have observed your figure.' He couldn't help but cast an appreciative eye over the curves of her breasts and hips, her trim waist. 'I would have made a very good estimate.'

Immediately, he suspected he might have said the wrong thing. Again he muttered a Montovian curse. Under stress—and the way she was looking at him *was* making him stressed—he found his English wasn't turning out quite the way he wanted it to.

Thankfully, after a stunned silence on her part, Gemma erupted into a peal of delightful laughter. 'Okay…I'm flattered you've made such a close observation of my figure.'

'It's not that I…I didn't mean—'

Her voice was warm with laughter. 'I think I know what you mean.'

'I did not say something…inappropriate?'

'You kinda did—but let's put it down to culture clash.'

'You do not think me…bad mannered? Rude?'

Crass. That was the word he was seeking. It was at the tip of his tongue. He had a master's degree in law from a leading English university. Why were his English language skills deserting him?

It was *her.*

Gemma.

Since the moment she'd come at him with her wooden spoon and pink oven mitts she'd had him—what was the word?—*discombobulated.* He was proud he had found the correct, very difficult English word, but why didn't he feel confident about pronouncing it correctly? The way she made him feel had him disconcerted, disorientated, behaving in ways he knew he should not.

But the way she was smiling up at him, with her dimples and humour in her brown eyes, made him feel something else altogether. *Something that was forbidden for him to feel for a commoner.*

She stretched up on her toes to kiss him lightly on the cheek, as she had done when she'd boarded the boat. This time her lips lingered longer, and she was so close he inhaled her heady scent of vanilla and lemon and a hint of chocolate, felt the warmth of her body. He put his hand to his cheek, where he had felt the soft tenderness of her lips, and held it there for a moment too long.

'I don't think you're at all rude,' she said. 'I think you're charming and funny and generous…and I…I…'

For a long moment her gaze held his, and the flush high on her cheekbones deepened. Tristan held his breath, on tenterhooks over what she might say next. But she took a step back, took a deep, steadying breath—which made her breasts rise enticingly under her snug-fitting top—and said something altogether different from what he'd hoped she might say.

'And I can solve your swimsuit problem for you,' she said.

'You can?'

'First the problem of a swimsuit for me. That impossibly big bag of mine also contains a swimsuit and towel. The North Sydney Olympic Pool is on the way from Lavender Bay wharf to my apartment in Kirribilli. I intended to swim there on my way home—as I often do.'

'That's excellent—so you at least can dive in and swim.'

'So can you.'

'But I—'

'I understand if you don't want to go in salt water in your smart white trousers. Or…or in your underwear.'

Her voice had faltered when she'd mentioned his underwear. A sudden image of her in *her* underwear flashed through his mind—lovely Gemma, swimming in lacy sheer bra and panties, her auburn hair streaming behind her in the water…

He had to clear his throat to speak. 'So what do you suggest?'

'In a closet in the stateroom is a selection of brand-new swimwear for both men and women. Choose a swimsuit and the cost of it will be added to the boat hire invoice.'

'Perfect,' he said. 'You get everything right, don't you, Party Queen Gemma?'

Her expression dimmed. 'Perhaps not everything. But I'll claim this one.'

'Shall we go swimming?' he asked. 'I saw a swimming

platform aft on the boat.' His skin prickled with heat. He should have worn shorts and a T-shirt instead of trying to impress Gemma in his bespoke Italian sportswear. 'I can't wait to get into that water.'

'Me, too. I can't think of anything I would rather do on a beautiful day like this.'

Tristan could think of a number of things he'd like to do with *her* on a beautiful day like this. All of which involved them wearing very few clothes—if any at all.

Gemma changed quickly and went back out onto the deck, near the swimming platform at the back. Tristan had gone into the stateroom to choose a swimsuit and change. She felt inexplicably shy as she waited for him. Although she swam often, she never felt 100 per cent comfortable in a swimsuit. The occupational hazard of a career filled with tempting food made her always think she needed to lose a few pounds to look her best in Lycra.

Her swimsuit was a modest navy racer-back one-piece, with contrast panels of aqua and white down the sides. More practical than glamorous. Not, in fact, the slightest bit seductive. Which was probably as well...

The door from the stateroom opened and Tristan headed towards her. Tristan had confessed to 'observing' her body. She smiled at the thought of his flustered yet flattering words. She straightened her shoulders and sucked in her tummy. And then immediately sucked in a breath as well at the sight of him. He'd looked good in his clothes, but without them—well, *nearly* without them—he was breathtaking in his masculinity.

Wearing stylish swim shorts in a tiny dark-blue-and-purple check and nothing else, he strode towards her with athletic grace and a complete lack of self-consciousness. *He was gorgeous.* Those broad shoulders, the defined muscles of his chest and arms, the classic six-pack belly and long, leanly muscled legs were in perfect proportion. He didn't have much body hair—just a dusting in the right places, set off against smooth golden skin.

He smiled his appreciation of *her* in a swimsuit. His smile and those vivid blue eyes, his handsome, handsome face and the warmth of his expression directed at her, all made her knees so wobbly she had to hold on to the deck railing for support. Her antennae didn't just wave frantically—they set off tiny, shrill alarms.

She realised she was holding her breath, and it came out as a gasp she had to disguise as a cough.

'Are you okay?' Tristan asked.

'F-fine,' she said as soon as she was able to recover her voice. As fine as a red-blooded woman *could* be when faced with a vision of such masculine perfection and trying to pretend she wasn't affected.

The crew had left a stack of red-and-white-striped beach towels in a basket on the deck. Tristan picked one up and handed it to her. 'Your swimsuit is very smart,' he said.

The open admiration in his eyes when he looked at her made her decide she had no cause for concern about what he thought of her shape.

She had to clear her throat. 'So...so is yours.'

Tristan picked up a towel for himself and slung it around his neck. As he did so, Gemma noticed something that marred all that physical perfection—a long, reddish scar that stretched along the top of his shoulder.

Tristan must have noticed the line of her gaze. 'You have observed my battle wound?'

She frowned. 'I thought you said you didn't go to war?'

'I mean my battle wound from the polo field. I came off one of my ponies and smashed my collarbone.'

She wanted to lean over and stroke it but didn't. 'Ouch. That must have hurt.'

'Yes. It did,' he said with understatement.

She didn't know if it was Tristan's way or just the way he spoke English. She wondered how different he might be if she were able to converse with him in fluent Montovian.

'I have a titanium plate and eight pins in it.'

'And your pony?' Gemma wasn't much of a horseback rider, but she knew that what was called a polo 'pony' was actually a very expensive and highly trained thoroughbred horse. Polo was a sport for the very wealthy.

'He was not hurt, thank heaven—he is my favourite pony. We have won many chukkas together.'

'Can you still play polo?'

'I hope to be able to play in the Montovian team this summer.'

She could imagine Tristan in the very tight white breeches and high black boots of a polo player, fearlessly ducking and weaving in perfect unison with a magnificent horse.

'You play polo for your country?'

'I have that honour, yes,' he said.

Again she got that feeling of *otherness*. Not only did he and she come from different countries and cultures, it seemed Tristan came from a different side of the tracks, as well. The posh, extremely wealthy side. Her stepfather was hardly poor, but he was not wealthy in the way she suspected Tristan was wealthy. Dennis was an orthodontist, with several lucrative practices. She could thank him for her perfectly aligned teeth and comfortable middle-class upbringing.

As a single mother, I could never have given you this life, her mother had used to say, reinforcing her instructions for Gemma always to be grateful and acquiescent. *Why couldn't you have married someone who didn't always make me feel in the way?* Gemma had wanted to shout back. But she had loved her mother too much to rebel.

Running a string of polo ponies, hiring a luxury yacht

on Sydney Harbour for just two people, the upcoming no-expenses-spared function on Friday night all seemed to speak of a very healthy income. If she thought about it, Tristan had actually *bought* her company on the boat today—and it had been a very expensive purchase.

But she didn't care about any of that.

She liked Tristan—*really* liked him—and he was far and away the most attractive man she had ever met. It was a waste of time to worry when she just wanted to enjoy his company.

She reached into her outsize bag for her high-protection sunscreen. 'You go in the water. I still have to put on some sun protection,' she said to Tristan.

'I'll wait for you,' he said.

Aware of Tristan's intense gaze, she felt self-conscious smoothing cream over her arms and legs, then twisting and turning to get to the spot on her back she could never quite reach. 'Australia is probably not the best climate for me,' she said. 'I burn, I blister, I freckle...'

'I think your pale skin is lovely,' he said. 'Don't try to tan it.'

'Thank you,' she said. It wasn't a compliment she heard often in a country obsessed with tanning.

'Let me help,' said Tristan. He grabbed the tube of sunscreen before she could protest. 'Turn around.'

She tensed as she heard him fling the towel from around his neck, squeeze cream from the tube. Then relaxed as she felt his hands on her back, slowly massaging in the cream with strong, sure fingers, smoothing it across her shoulders and down her arms in firm, sweeping motions.

The sensation of his hands on her body was utter bliss—she felt as if she was melting under his touch. When his hands slid down her back, they traced the sides of her breasts, and her nipples tightened. His breath fanned her hair, warm and intimate. She closed her eyes and gave herself over to sensation. *To Tristan.*

Her breathing quickened as her body responded to him, and from behind her she heard his breath grow ragged. He rested his hands on her waist. She twisted around, her skin slick with cream, and found herself in the circle of his arms.

For a long, silent moment she looked up into his face—already familiar, dangerously appealing. She knew he would see in her eyes the same mix of yearning and desire and wariness she saw in his: the same longing for something she knew was unwise. She swayed towards him as he lowered his head and splayed her hands against his bare, hard chest, his warm skin. She sighed as his lips touched hers in the lightest of caresses, pressed her mouth against his as she returned his kiss.

He murmured against her mouth. 'Gemma, I—'

Then another voice intruded. 'Gemma, I need to get your opinion on the plating of the yellow-tail kingfish *carpaccio.* Do you want— Oh. *Sorry.* I didn't realise I was interrupting—'

Gemma broke away from Tristan's kiss. Glared over his shoulder to her chef, who had his hands up in surrender as he backed away.

'No need. I'll sort the *carpaccio* out for myself.'

But he had a big grin plastered on his face, and she knew the team at Party Queens would find out very soon that Gemma had been caught kissing the client. She muttered a curse in English—one she was sure Tristan would understand. *She wanted to keep Tristan to herself.*

Tristan's arms remained firmly around her, and she didn't really want to leave them. But when he pulled her towards him again, she resisted. 'It's as well our chef came along,' she said. 'We shouldn't really be starting something we can't continue, should we?'

Tristan cleared his throat, but his voice was husky when he replied. 'You are right—we should not. But that does not stop me wanting to kiss you.'

She took a step back. 'Me neither. I mean I want to kiss *you*, too. But…but you're only here a few days and I—'

I'm in danger of falling for you, even though I hardly know you and I have to protect myself from the kind of pain that could derail me.

'I understand. It would be best for both of us.' He sounded as if he spoke through gritted teeth.

Disappointment flooded through her but also relief that he hadn't pressed for more. After the world of promise in that brief, tender kiss, she might have been tempted to ignore those frantically waving antennae and throw away every self-protective measure and resolve she had made in that lonely six months.

'Yes,' was all she could murmur from a suddenly choked throat.

'What I really need is to get into that cold water,' he said.

'You mean…like a cold shower?'

'Yes,' he said, more grimly than she had heard him speak before.

'Me, too,' she said.

He held out his hand. 'Are you coming with me?'

CHAPTER EIGHT

As TRISTAN SWAM alongside Gemma, seeing her pale limbs and the auburn hair floating around her shoulders reminded him of the Montovian myths of water nymphs. Legend had it that these other-world temptresses in human form inhabited the furthest reaches of the vast lakes of Montovia. They were young, exquisite and shunned human contact.

If a man were to come across such a nymph, he would instantly become besotted, bewitched, obsessed by her. His beautiful nymph would entice him to make love to her until he was too exhausted to swim and he'd drown—still in her embrace—in the deepest, coldest waters. The rare man who survived and found his way home would go mad with grief and spend the rest of his life hunting the shores of the lakes in a desperate effort to find his nymph again.

Montovians were a deeply superstitious people—even the most well educated and sophisticated of them. Tristan shrugged off those ancient myths, but in a small part of his soul they lived on despite his efforts to deny them.

Gemma swam ahead of him with effortless, graceful strokes, ducking beneath the water, turning and twisting her body around. How did he describe how she seemed in the water? *Joyous.* That was the word. She was quite literally in her element, playing in the water like some... well, like a nymph enchantress.

She turned back to face him, her hair slicked back off her face, revealing her fine bone structure, the scattering of freckles across the bridge of her nose. She trod water until he caught up with her.

'Isn't the water wonderful?' she said. 'I would have hated you if I'd had to stay in the kitchen while you cavorted in the sea with that other woman—uh, that other woman who didn't actually exist.'

'You would have "hated" me?' he asked.

'Of course not. I…I… You…'

Again he got the sense that she had struggled with the urge to say something significant—and then changed her mind.

'I'm very thankful to you for making this day happen. It…it's perfect.'

'I also am grateful that you are here with me,' he replied. 'It is a day I will not forget.'

How could he forget Gemma? He would bookmark this time with her in his mind to revisit it in the lonely, difficult days he would face on his return to Montovia.

A great lump of frustration and regret seemed to choke him as he railed against the fate that had led him to this woman when duty dictated he was not able to follow up on the feelings she aroused in him. When he'd been second in line to the throne, he had protested against the age-old rules governing marriage in Montovia. Now he was crown prince, that avenue had been closed to him.

Not for the first time he wished his brother had not gone up in his helicopter that day.

'Do you want to swim to shore?' she asked. 'C'mon— I'll race you.'

She took off in an elegant but powerful freestyle stroke. Tristan was fit and strong, but he had to make an effort to keep up with her.

They reached the beach with her a few strokes ahead. He followed her as they waded through the shallows to the sand, unable to keep his eyes off her. Her sporty swimsuit showed she meant business when she swam. At the same time it clung to every curve and showcased the smooth expanse of her back, her shapely behind, her slender strong legs.

Gemma Harper was a woman who got even more attractive the better he knew her. *And he wanted her.*

She stopped for him to catch up. Her eyes narrowed. 'I hope you didn't let me win on purpose in some chivalrous gesture?'

'No. You are a fast swimmer. It was a fair race.'

He was very competitive in the sports he played. Being bested by a woman was something new, and he respected her skill. But how could a Montovian, raised in a country where the snow-fed lakes were cold even in midsummer, compete with someone who'd grown up in a beachside city like Sydney?

'I used to race at school—but that was a long time ago. Now I swim for fun and exercise. And relaxation.' She looked at him as if she knew very well that he was not used to being beaten. 'You'd probably beat me at skiing.'

'I'm sure you'd challenge me,' he said. 'Weren't both your parents ski instructors?'

'Yes, but I've only ever skied in Australia and New Zealand. Skiing in Europe is on my wish list—if I ever get enough time away from Party Queens to get there, that is.'

Tristan uttered something non-committal in reply instead of the invitation he wished he could make. There was nothing he would like better than to take her skiing with him. Show her the family chalet, share his favourite runs on his favourite mountains, help her unwind après-ski in front of a seductively warm log fire... But next winter, and the chance of sharing it with Gemma, seemed far, far away.

The sand was warm underfoot as he walked along the beach with her, close enough for their shoulders to nudge against each other occasionally. Her skin was cool and smooth against his and he found it difficult to concentrate on anything but her, difficult to clear his mind of how much he wanted her—and could not have her.

He forced himself to look around him. She'd brought him to an idyllic spot. The vegetation that grew up to the sand was full of birdlife. He saw flashes of multi-coloured parrots as they flew through the trees, heard birdsong he couldn't identify.

'How could you say Sydney is not like living in a resort when a place like this is on your doorstep?' he asked.

'I guess you *would* feel like you were on vacation if you lived around here,' she said. She waved her hand at the southern end of the beach. 'Manly, which seems more like a town than a suburb, is just around the bay. You can hire a two-man kayak there and paddle around to here with a picnic. It would be fun to do that sometime.'

But not with him. He would be far away in Montovia, doing his duty, honouring his family and his country. No longer master of his own life. 'That would be fun,' he echoed. He could not bear the thought of her kayaking to this beach with another man.

She sat down on the sand, hugging her knees to her chest. He sat down next to her, his legs stretched out ahead. The sun was warm on his back, but a slight breeze kept him cool.

'Did you wonder why this beach is called Store Beach?' she asked.

'Not really. But I think you are going to tell me.'

'How did you get to know me so quickly?' she asked, her head tilted to one side in the manner he already found endearing.

'Just observant, I guess,' he said. *And because he was so attracted to her.* He wanted to know every little thing about her.

'There must be a tour guide inside me, fighting to get out,' she joked.

'Set her free to tell me all about the beach,' he said. This sea nymph had bewitched him so thoroughly that sitting on a beach listening to the sound of her voice seemed like heaven.

'If you insist,' she said with a sideways smile. 'Behind us, up top, is an isolation hospital known as the Quarantine Station. Stores for the station were landed here. For the early settlers from Europe it was an arduous trip of many months by sailing ship. By the time some of them got here, they had come down with contagious illnesses like smallpox. They were kept here—away from the rest of Sydney. Some got better…many died.'

Tristan shuddered. 'That's a gruesome topic for a sunny day.'

'The Quarantine Station closed after one hundred and fifty years. They hold ghost tours there at night. I went on one—it was really spooky.'

Her story reminded Tristan of what a very long way away from home he was. Even a straightforward flight was twenty-two hours. Any kind of relationship would be difficult to maintain from this distance—even if it were permitted.

'If I had time I would like to go on the ghost tour, but I fear that will not be possible,' he said.

Had he been here as tourist Tristan Marco, executive of a nebulous company that might or might not produce chocolate, he would have added, *Next time I'll do the ghost tour with you.* But he could not in all fairness talk about 'next time' or 'tomorrow.' Not with a woman to whom he couldn't offer any kind of relationship beyond a no-strings fling because she had not been born into the 'right' type of family.

'We should be heading back to the boat for lunch,' she said. 'I'm looking forward to being a guest for the awesome menu I planned. Swimming always makes me hungry.'

He stood up and offered her his hand to help her. She hesitated, then took it and he pulled her to her feet. She stood very close to him. Tristan took a step to bring her even closer. Her hair was still damp from the sea and fell in tendrils around her face. He smoothed a wayward strand from her cheek and tucked it around her ear. He heard her quick intake of breath at his touch before she went very still.

She looked up at him without saying a word. Laughter danced in her eyes and lifted the corners of her lovely mouth. He kept his hand on her shoulder, and she swayed towards him in what he took as an invitation. There was nothing he wanted more than to kiss her. He could not resist a second longer.

He kissed her—first on her adorable dimples, one after the other, as he had longed to do from the get go. Then on her mouth—her exquisitely sensual mouth that felt as wonderful as it looked, warm and welcoming under his. With a little murmur that sent excitement shooting through him, she parted her lips. He deepened the kiss. She tasted of chocolate and salt and her own sweet taste. Her skin was cool and silky against his, her curves pressed enticingly against his body.

All the time he was kissing her Tristan, knew he was doing so under false pretences. He was not used to deception, had always prided himself on his honesty. He wanted more—wanted more than kisses—from this beautiful woman he held in his arms. But he could not deceive her any longer about who he really was—and what the truth meant to them.

Tristan was kissing her—seriously kissing her—and it was even more wonderful than Gemma had anticipated. She had wanted him, wanted *this*, from the time she had first seen him in her kitchen. Her heart thudded in double-quick time, and pleasure thrummed through her body.

But she was shocked at how quickly the kiss turned from something tender into something so passionate that it ignited in her an urgent hunger to be closer to him. Close, closer…as close as she could be.

She had never felt this wondrous sense of connection and certainty. That time was somehow standing still. That she was meant to be here with him. That this was the start of something life-changing.

They explored with lips and tongues. Her thoughts, dazed with desire, started to race in a direction she had not let them until now. *Could* there be a tomorrow for her and Tristan? Why had she thought it so impossible? He wasn't flying back to the moon, after all. Long distance could work. Differences could be overcome.

Stray thoughts flew around her brain, barely coherent, in between the waves of pleasure pulsing through her body.

Tristan gently bit her bottom lip. She let out a little sound of pleasure that was almost a whimper.

He broke away from the kiss, chest heaving as he gasped for breath. She realised he was as shocked as she was at the passion that had erupted between them. Shocked and…and shaken.

Gemma wound her arms around his neck, not wanting him to stop but glad they were on a public beach so that there would be no temptation to sink down on the sand together and go further than kisses. She gave her frantic antennae their marching orders. This. To be with him. It was all she wanted.

'Tristan…' she breathed. 'I feel like I'm in some wonderful dream. I…I don't want this day to end.'

Then she froze as she saw the dismay in his eyes, felt the tension in his body, heard his low groan. She unwound her arms from around his neck, crossed them in front of her chest. She bit her lip to stop her mouth from trembling. Had she totally misread the situation?

'You might not think that when you hear what I have to say to you.' The hoarse words rushed out as if they'd been dammed up inside him and he could not hold on to them any longer.

She couldn't find the words to reply.

'Gemma. We have to talk.'

Did any conversation *ever* go well when it started like that? Why did those four words, grouped together in that way, sound so ominous?

'I'm listening,' she said.

'I have not been completely honest with you.'

Gemma's heart sank to the level of the sand beneath her bare feet. Here it came. He was married. He had a girlfriend back home. Or good old *I'm not looking for commitment.*

Those antennae were now flopped over her forehead, weary and defeated from trying to save her from her own self-defeating behaviour.

She braced herself in readiness.

A pulse throbbed under the smooth olive skin at his temple. 'My family business I told you about…?'

'Yes?' she said, puzzled at the direction he was taking.

'It isn't so much a *business* as such…'

Her stomach clenched. The wealth. The mystery. Her sense that he was being evasive. 'You mean it's a…a criminal enterprise? Like the mafia or—?'

He looked so shocked she would have laughed at his expression if she'd had the slightest inclination to laugh. Or even to smile.

'No. Not that. You've got it completely wrong.'

She swallowed against a suddenly dry throat. 'Are you…are you a spy? From your country's intelligence service? If so, I don't know what you're doing with me. I don't know anything. I—'

The shock on his face told her she'd got that wrong, too.

'No, Gemma, nothing like that.'

He paused, as if gathering the strength to speak, and then his words came out in a rush.

'My family is the royal family of Montovia. My parents are the king and queen.'

CHAPTER NINE

GEMMA FELT AS if all the breath had been knocked out of her by a blow to the chest. She stared at him in total disbelief. 'You're kidding me, right?'

'I'm afraid I am not. King Gerard and Queen Truda of Montovia are my parents.'

'And...and you?'

'I am the crown prince—heir to the throne.'

Gemma felt suddenly light-headed and had to take in a few short, shallow breaths to steady herself. Strangely, she didn't doubt him. Those blue eyes burned with sincerity and a desperate appeal for her to believe him.

'A...a prince? A real-life prince? You?'

That little hint of a bow she'd thought she'd detected previously now manifested itself in a full-on bow to her. A formal bow—from a prince who wore swim shorts and had bare feet covered in sand.

'And...and your family business is—?'

'Ruling the country...as we have done for centuries.'

It fitted. Beyond all belief, it fitted. All the little discrepancies in what he'd said fell into place.

'So...what is a prince doing with a party planner?' Hurt shafted her that she'd been so willingly made a fool of. 'Slumming it?'

Despite all her resolutions, she'd slid back into her old ways. Back at the dating starting gates, she'd bolted straight for the same mistake. She'd fallen for a good-looking man who had lied to her from the beginning about who he was. Lied big-time.

She backed away from him on the sand. Stared at him as if he were a total stranger, her hands balled by her sides.

Her disappointment made her want to lash out at him in the most primitive way. But she would not be so uncivilised.

Her voice was cold with suppressed fury, and when she spoke it was as if her words had frozen into shards of ice to stab and wound him. 'You've lied to me from the get go. About who you are—what you are. You lied to get me onto the boat. I don't like liars.'

And she didn't want to hear any more lies.

Frantically, she looked around her. Impenetrable bushland behind her. A long ocean swim to Manly in front of her. And she in a swimsuit and bare feet.

Tristan put out a hand. 'Gemma. I—'

She raised both hands to ward him off. 'Don't touch me,' she spat.

Tristan's face contorted with an emotion she couldn't at first identify. Anger? Anger at *her*?

No—anger at himself.

'Don't say that, Gemma. I…I liked you so much. You did not know who I was. I wanted to get to know you as Tristan, not as Crown Prince Tristan. It was perhaps wrong of me.'

'Isn't honesty one of the customs of your country? Or are princes exempt from telling the truth?'

His jaw clenched. 'Of course not. I'm furious at myself for not telling you the truth earlier. I am truly sorry. But I had to see you again—and I saw no way around it. If you had known the truth, would you have relaxed around me?'

She crossed her arms firmly against her chest. But the sincerity of his words was trickling through her hostility, slowly dripping on the fire of her anger.

'Perhaps not,' said. She would have been freaking out, uncertain of how to behave in front of royalty. As she was now.

'Please. Forgive me. Believe the sincerity of my motives.'

The appeal in his blue eyes seemed genuine. *Or was she kidding herself?* How she wanted to believe him.

'So...no more lies? You promise every word you say to me from now on will be the truth?'

'Yes,' he said.

'Is there any truth in what you've told me about you? About your country? You really *are* a prince?'

'I am Tristan, Crown Prince of Montovia.'

'Prince Tristan...' She slowly breathed out the words, scarcely able to comprehend the truth of it. *Of all the impossible men, she'd had to go and fall for a prince.*

'And everything else you told me?'

'All true.'

'Your brother?'

The pain in his eyes let her know that what he'd told her about his brother's death was only too true.

'Carl was crown prince, heir to the throne, and he trained for it from the day he was born. I was the second in line.'

'The heir and the spare?' she said.

'As the "spare," I had a lot more freedom to live life the way I wanted to. I rebelled against the rules that governed the way we perform our royal duties. Then everything changed.'

'Because of the accident? You said it's your brother's job you are stepping up to in the "family business," didn't you? The job of becoming the next king?'

'That is correct.'

Gemma put her hands to her temples to try and contain the explosion of thoughts. 'This is surreal. I'm talking to a *prince*, here. A guy who's one day going to be king of a country and have absolute power over the lives of millions people.'

'Not so many millions—we are a small country.'

She put down her hands so she could face him. 'But still... You're a prince. One day you'll be a king.'

'When you put it like that, it sounds surreal to me, too. To be the king was always my brother's role.'

Her thoughts still reeled. 'You don't just live *near* the castle, do you?'

'The castle has been home to the royal family for many hundreds of years.'

'And you probably *own* the town of Montovia—and the chocolate shop with the tea room where you went as a little boy?'

'Yes,' he said. 'It has always been so.'

'What about the chocolate?'

'Every business in Montovia is, strictly speaking, our business. But businesses are, of course, owned by individuals. They pay taxes for the privilege. The chocolate has been made by the same family for many years.'

'Was your little nephew a prince, too?'

'He...little Rudolph...*was* a prince. As son of the crown prince, he was next in line to the throne. He was only two when he died with his mother and father.'

'Truly...truly a tragedy for your family.'

'For our country, too. My brother would have been a fine ruler.'

She shook her head, maintained her distance from him. 'It's a lot to take in. How were you allowed to come to Australia on your own if you're the heir? After what happened to your brother?'

'I insisted that I be allowed this time on my own before I take up my new duties. Duties that will, once I return, consume my life.'

'You're a very important person,' she said slowly.

'In Montovia, yes.'

'I would have thought you would be surrounded by bodyguards.'

Tristan looked out to sea and pointed to where a small white cruiser was anchored. 'You might not have noticed, but the *Argus* was discreetly followed by that boat. My two Montovian bodyguards are on it. My parents insisted on me being under their surveillance twenty-four hours a day while I was in a foreign country.'

'You mean there are two guys there who watch you all the time? Did they see us kissing?' She felt nauseous at the thought of being observed for the entire time—both on the boat and on the beach.

'Most likely. I am so used to eyes being on me I do not think about it.'

'You didn't think you could have trusted me with the truth?'

'I did not know you,' he said simply. 'Now I do.'

Their lives were unimaginably different. Not just their country and their culture. He was *royalty*, for heaven's sake.

'I don't have to call you your royal highness, do I?' She couldn't help the edge to her voice.

'To you I am always Tristan.'

'And my curtsying skills aren't up to scratch.'

Pain tightened his face. 'This is why I went incognito. You are already treating me differently now you know I am a prince. Next thing you'll be backing away from me when you leave the room.'

'Technically we're on a beach, but I get your drift. I'm meant to back away from you across the sand?'

'Not now. But when—' he crossed himself rapidly '—when, God forbid, my father passes and I become king, then—'

'I'd have to walk backwards from your presence.'

'Yes. Only in public, of course.'

'This is…this is kind of incomprehensible.' It was all so unbelievable, and yet she found herself believing it. And no matter how she tried, she could not switch off her attraction to him.

A shadow crossed over his face. 'I know,' he said. 'And…and it gets worse.'

'How can it get worse than having to back away out of the presence of a guy my own age? A guy I've made friends with? Sort of friends—considering I don't generally make pals of people who lie to me.'

'Only "friends", Gemma?' he said, his brows lifted above saddened eyes. 'I think we both know it could be so much more than that.'

Tristan stepped forward to close the gap between them. This time she didn't back away. He traced her face lightly with his fingers, across her cheekbones, down her nose, around her lips. She had the disconcerting feeling he was storing up the sight of her face to remember her.

'Yes,' she admitted. 'I…I think I knew that from the get go.'

It was difficult to speak because of the little shivers of pleasure coursing through her at his touch.

'I did also,' he said. 'I have never felt this way. It was… *instant* for me. That was why I had to see you again—no matter what I had to do to have you with me.'

'I told you I could cast spells,' she said with a shaky smile. 'Seriously, I felt it too. Which is why I resisted you. Whether you're a prince or just a regular guy, I don't trust the "instant" thing.'

'The *coup de foudre*? I did not believe it could happen either—certainly not to me.'

She frowned. 'I'm not sure what you mean?'

'The bolt of lightning. The instant attraction out of nowhere. I have had girlfriends, of course, but never before have I felt this…this intensity so quickly.'

She *had* felt it before—which was why she distrusted it. Why did it feel so different this time?

It was him. *Tristan*. He was quite unlike anyone she had ever met.

She braced her feet in the sand. 'So how does it get worse?'

'First I must apologise, Gemma, for luring you onto the boat.'

'Apologise? There's no need for that. I'm having a wonderful day…enjoying being with you. We could do it again tomorrow—I have vacation days due to me. Or I could take you to see kangaroos…maybe even a koala.'

'You would want that?'

'We could try and make this work.' She tried to tone down the desperation in her voice, but she felt he was slipping away from her. 'We live on different sides of the world—not different planets. Though I'm not so sure about how to handle the prince thing. That's assuming you want to date me?' She laughed—a nervous, shaky laugh that came out as more of a squeak. 'I feel more like Cinderella than ever…'

Her voice trailed away as she read the bleak expression in his eyes. This was not going well.

'Gemma, you are so special to me already. Of course I would like to date you—if it were possible. But before you plan to spend more time with me you need to hear this first,' he said. 'To know why I had no right to trick you. You said you would never hate me, but—'

'So tell me,' she said. 'Rip the sticking plaster off in one go.'

'I am not free to choose my own wife. The heir to the throne of Montovia must marry a woman of noble blood. It is forbidden for him to marry a commoner.'

His words hit her like blows. 'A…a "commoner"? I'm not so sure I like being called a commoner. And we're not talking marriage—we hardly know each other.'

'Gemma, if the way I feel about you was allowed to develop, it would get serious. *Very* serious.'

He spoke with such conviction she could not help but find his words thrilling. The dangerous, impossible kind of thrilling.

'I…I see,' she said. Until now she hadn't thought beyond today. 'I believe it would get serious for me, too.' *If she allowed herself to get involved.*

'But it could not lead to marriage for us. Marriage for a crown prince is not about love. It is about tradition. My brother's death changed everything. Brought with it an urgency to prepare me for the duties that face me. As crown prince I am expected to marry. I must announce my engagement on my thirtieth birthday. A suitable wife has been chosen for me.'

'An arranged marriage? Surely not in this day and age?'

'There is no compulsion for me to marry her. She has been deemed "suitable" if I cannot find an aristocratic wife on my own. And my time is running out.'

Pain seared through her at the thought of him with another woman. But one day together, a few kisses, gave her no claim on him.

'When do you turn thirty?'

'On the eighteenth of June.'

She forced her voice to sound even, impartial. 'Three months. Will you go through with it? Marry a stranger?'

'Gemma, I have been brought up believing that my first duty is to my country—above my own desires. As second in line to the throne I might have tried to defy it. I even told my family I would not marry if I could not choose my own bride. But as crown prince, stepping into the shoes of my revered brother, who married the daughter of a duke when he was twenty-six and had a son by the time he was twenty-eight, I have no choice but to marry.'

'But not…never…to someone like me…' Her voice

trailed away as the full impact of what he was saying hit her. She looked down to where she scuffed the sand with her bare toes. She had humiliated herself by suggesting a long-distance relationship.

Tristan placed a gentle finger under her chin so she had to look up at him. 'I am sorry, Gemma. That is the way it has always been in Montovia. Much as I would wish it otherwise.' His mouth twisted bitterly. 'Until I met you I was prepared to accept my fate with grace. Now it will be that much harder.'

'Aren't princess brides a bit short on the ground these days?'

'To be from an aristocratic family is all that is required—she does not need to be actual royalty. In the past it was about political alliances and dowries…'

Nausea brewed deep in the pit of her stomach. Why hadn't he told her this before he'd kissed her? Before she'd let herself start to spin dreams? Dreams as fragile as her finest meringue and as easily smashed.

Sincere as he appeared now, Tristan had deceived her. She would never have allowed herself to let down her guard if she'd known all this.

Like Alistair, he had presented himself as a person different from what he really was. And she, despite all best intentions, had let down her guard and exposed her heart. Tristan had started something he knew he could not continue with. That had been dishonest and unfair.

She could not let him know how much he had hurt her. Had to carry away from this some remaining shreds of dignity. For all his apologies, for all his blue blood, he was no better than any other man who had lied to her.

'I'm sorry, too, Tristan,' she said. 'I…I also felt the *coupe de foudre*. But it was just…physical.' She shrugged in a show of nonchalance. 'We've done nothing to regret. Just…just a few kisses.'

What were a few kisses to a prince? He probably had gorgeous women by the hundred, lining up in the hope of a kiss from him.

'Those kisses meant something to me, Gemma,' he said, his mouth a tight line.

She could not deny his mouth possessing hers had felt both tender and exciting. But… 'The fact is, we've spent not even a day in each other's company. I'm sure we'll both get over it and just remember a…a lovely time on the harbour.'

The breeze that had teased the drying tendrils of her hair had dropped, and the sun beat down hot on her bare shoulders. Yet she started to shiver.

'We should be getting back to the boat,' she said.

She turned and splashed into the water before he could see the tears of disappointment and loss that threatened. She swam her hardest to get to the boat first, not knowing or caring if Tristan was behind her.

Tristan stood on the shore and watched Gemma swim away from him in a froth of white water, her pale arms slicing through the water, her vigorous kicks making very clear her intention to get as far away from him as quickly as possible.

He picked up a piece of driftwood and threw it into the bush with such force that a flock of parrots soared out of a tree, their raucous cries admonishing him for his lack of control. He cursed loud and long. *He had lost Gemma.*

She was halfway to the boat already. He wished he could cast a wide net into the sea and bring her back to him, but he doubted she wanted more of his deceitful company.

In Montovian mythology, when a cunning hunter tried to capture a water nymph and keep her for himself, he'd drag back his net to find it contained not the beautiful woman he coveted but a huge, angry catfish, with rows of razor-sharp teeth, that would set upon him.

The water nymphs held all the cards.

An hour later Gemma had showered and dressed and was sitting opposite Tristan at the stylishly laid table on the sheltered deck of the *Argus*. She pushed the poached lobster salad around her plate with her fork. Usually she felt ravenous after a swim, but her appetite had completely deserted her.

Tristan was just going through the motions of eating, too. His eyes had dulled to a flat shade of blue, and there were lines of strain around his mouth she hadn't noticed before. All the easy camaraderie between them had disintegrated into stilted politeness.

Yet she couldn't bring herself to be angry with him. He seemed as miserable as she was. Even through the depths of her shock and disappointment she knew he had only deceived her because he'd liked her and wanted her to like him for himself. Neither of them had expected the intensity of feeling that had resulted.

She still found it difficult to get her head around his real identity. For heaven's sake, she was having lunch with a *prince*. A prince from a kingdom still run on medieval rules. He was royalty—she was a commoner. *Deemed not worthy of him.* Gemma had grown up in an egalitarian society. The inequality of it grated. She did not believe herself to be *less*.

She made another attempt to eat, but felt self-conscious as she raised her fork to her mouth. Did Tristan's bodyguards have a long-distance lens trained on her?

She slid her plate away from her, pushed her chair back and got up from the table.

'I'm sorry, Tristan, I can't do this.'

With his impeccable manners, he immediately got up,

too. 'You don't like the food?' he said. But his eyes told
her he knew exactly what she meant.

'You. Me. What could have been. What can never be.
Remember what I said about the sticking plaster?'

'You don't want to prolong the pain,' he said slowly.

Of course he understood. In spite of their differences
in status and language and upbringing, he already *got* her.

This was heartbreaking. He was a real-life Prince
Charming who wanted her but couldn't have her—not in
any honourable way. And she, as Cinderella, had to return
to her place in the kitchen.

'I'm going to ask the skipper to take me to the wharf at
Manly and drop me off.'

'How will you get home?'

'Bus. Ferry. Taxi. Please don't worry about me. I'm very
good at looking after myself.'

She turned away from him and carried with her the
stricken expression on his face to haunt her dreams.

CHAPTER TEN

GEMMA STRUGGLED TO hear what Andie was saying to her over the rise and fall of chatter, the clink of glasses, the odd burst of laughter—the soundtrack to another successful Party Queens function. The Friday night cocktail party at the swish Parkview Hotel was in full swing—the reception being held to mark the official visit of Tristan, crown prince of Montovia, to Sydney.

Gemma had explained to her business partners what had happened on the *Argus* and had excluded herself from any further dealings with him. Tristan had finalised the guest list with Eliza on Thursday.

Tristan's guests included business leaders with connections to the Montovian finance industry, the importers and top retailers of the principality's fine chocolate and cheese, senior politicians—both state and federal—even the governor of the state.

If she didn't have to be here to ensure that the food service went as it should for such an important function, she wouldn't have attended.

Her antennae twitched. Okay, so she was lying to herself. How could she resist the chance to see him again? On a strictly 'look, don't touch' basis. Because no matter how often she told herself that she'd had a lucky escape to get out after only a day, before she got emotionally attached, she hadn't been able to stop thinking about him.

Not that it had been an issue. Tristan was being the ideal host and was much in demand from his guests. He hadn't come anywhere near her, either, since the initial formal briefing between Party Queens and its client. She shouldn't have felt hurt, but she did—a deep, private ache to see that after all that angst on the *Argus* it seemed he'd been able to put her behind him so easily.

The secret of his identity was now well and truly out. There was nothing the media loved more than the idea of a handsome young European prince visiting Australia. Especially when he was reported to be 'one of the world's most eligible bachelors.' She knew there were photographers swarming outside the hotel to catch the money shot of Prince Charming.

'What did you say, Andie?' she asked her friend again.

Tall, blonde Andie leaned closer. 'I said you're being very brave. Eliza and I are both proud of you. It must be difficult for you, seeing him like this.'

'Yeah. It is. I'm determined to stay away from him. After all it was only one day—it meant nothing.' One day that had quite possibly been one of the happiest days of her life—until that conversation on Store Beach. 'No big deal, really—unless I make it a big deal.'

'He lied to you. Just remember that,' said Andie.

'But he—' It was on the tip of her tongue to defend Tristan by saying he hadn't out-and-out lied, just skirted around the truth. But it was the same thing. Lying by omission. And she wasn't going to fall back into bad old ways by making excuses for a man who had misled her.

But she couldn't help being aware of Tristan. Just knowing he was here had her on edge. He was on the other side of the room, talking to two older men. He looked every inch the prince in an immaculately tailored tuxedo worn with a blue, gold-edged sash across his chest. Heaven knew what the rows of medals pinned to his shoulder signified— but there were a lot of them. He was the handsome prince from all the fairytales she had loved when she was a kid.

Never had that sense of *other* been stronger.

'Don't worry,' said Andie. 'Eliza and I are going to make darn sure you're never alone with him.'

'Good,' said Gemma, though her craven heart *longed* to be alone with him.

'You didn't do all that work on yourself over six months to throw it away on an impossible crush. What would Dr B think?'

The good thing about having worked on a women's magazine was that the staff had had access to the magazine's agony aunt. Still did. 'Dr B' was a practising clinical psychologist and—pushed along by her friends—Gemma had trooped along to her rooms for a series of consultations. In return for a staff discount, she hadn't minded seeing her heavily disguised questions appearing on the agony aunt's advice page in her new magazine.

Dear Dr B,
I keep falling for love rats who turn out to be not what they said they were—yet I put up with their bad behaviour. How can I break this pattern?

It was Dr B who had helped Gemma identify how her unbalanced relationship with her stepfather had given her an excessive need for approval from men. It was Dr B who had showed her how to develop her own instincts, trust her antennae. And given her coping strategies for when it all got too hard.

'I can deal with this,' she said to Andie. 'You just watch me.'

'While you watch Tristan?'

Gemma started guiltily. 'Is it that obvious? He's just so *gorgeous*, Andie.'

'That he is,' said Andie. 'But he's not for you. If you start to weaken, just think of all that stuff you dug up on the internet about Montovia's Playboy Prince.'

'How could I forget it?'

Gemma sighed. She'd been shocked to the core at discovering his reputation. Yet couldn't reconcile it with the Tristan she knew.

Was she just kidding herself?

She must not slide back into bad old habits. People had warned her about Alistair, but she'd wanted to believe his denials about drugs and other women. Until she'd been proved wrong in the most shockingly painful way.

Andie glanced at her watch. 'I need to call Dominic and check on Hugo,' she said. 'He had a sniffle today and I want to make sure he's okay.'

'As if he *wouldn't* be okay in the care of the world's most doting dad,' Gemma said.

Andie and Dominic's son, Hugo, was fifteen months old now, and the cutest, most endearing little boy. Andie often brought him into the Party Queens office, and Gemma doted on him. One day she wanted a child of her own. She was twenty-eight. That was yet another reason not to waste time on men who were Mr Impossible—or Crown Prince Impossible.

'Where's Eliza?' Andie asked. 'I don't want to leave you by yourself in case that predatory prince swoops on you.'

'No need for name-calling,' said Gemma, though Andie's choice of words made her smile. 'Eliza is over there, talking with the best man at your wedding, Jake Marlowe. He's a good friend of Tristan's.'

'So I believe… Dominic is pleased Jake's in town.'

'From the look of it, I don't know that Eliza would welcome the interruption. She seems to be getting on *very* well with Jake. You go and make your phone call. I'm quite okay here without a minder, I assure you. I'm a big girl.'

Gemma shooed Andie off. She needed to check with the hotel liaison representative about the service at the bar. She thought they could do with another barman on board. For this kind of exclusive party no guest should be left waiting for a drink.

But before she could do so a bodyguard of a different kind materialised by her shoulder. She recognised him immediately as one of the men who had been discreetly shadowing Tristan. She shuddered at the thought that he'd been spying on her and Tristan as they'd kissed on the beach.

'Miss Harper, His Royal Highness the Crown Prince Tristan would like a word with you in the meeting room annexe through that door.' He spoke English, with a coarser version of Tristan's accent.

She looked around. Tristan was nowhere to be seen. From the tone of this burly guy's voice, she didn't dare refuse the request.

Neither did she want to.

Tristan paced the length of the small breakout room and paced back again. Where was Gemma? Would she refuse to see him?

He had noticed her as soon as he'd got to the hotel. Among a crowd of glittering guests she had stood out in the elegant simplicity of a deep blue fitted dress that emphasised her curves and her creamy skin. Her hair was pulled up and away from her face to tumble to her shoulders at the back. She was lovelier than ever.

He had to see her.

He was taking a risk, stepping away from the party like this. His idyllic period of anonymity was over. He was the crown prince once more, with all the unwanted attention that warranted.

The local press seemed particularly voracious. And who knew if one of his invited guests might be feeding some website or other with gossipy Prince Charming titbits? That was one of the nicknames the media had given him. They would particularly be looking out for any shot of him with a woman. They would then speculate about her and make her life hell. That girl could not be Gemma. She did not deserve that.

And then she was there, just footsteps away from him. Her high heels brought her closer to his level. The guard left discreetly, closing the door behind him and leaving Tristan alone with her. Could lightning strike twice in the same place? For he felt again that *coup de foudre*—that instant sensation that this was *his woman*.

His heart gave a physical leap at the expression on her face—pure, unmitigated joy at seeing him. For a moment he thought—hoped—she might fling herself into his arms. Where he would gladly welcome her.

Then the shutters came down, and her expression became one of polite, professional interest.

'You wanted to see me? Is it about the canapés? Or the—?'

'I wanted to see you. Alone. Without all the circus around us. I miss you, Gemma. I haven't been able to stop thinking about you.'

Her face softened. 'There isn't a moment since I left the *Argus* that I haven't thought about *you*.'

Those words, uttered in her sweet, melodious voice, were music to his ears.

He took a step towards her, but she put up her hand in a halt sign.

'But nothing has changed, has it? I'm a commoner and you're a prince. Worse, the Playboy Prince, so it appears.'

Her face crumpled, and he saw what an effort it was for her to maintain her composure.

'I…I didn't think you were like that…the way the press portrayed you.'

The Playboy Prince—how he hated that label. Would he ever escape the reputation earned in those few years of rebellion?

'So you've dug up the dirt on me from the internet?' he said gruffly.

She would only have had to type *Playboy Prince* into a search engine and his name would come up with multiple entries.

'Is it true? All the girlfriends? The parties? The racing cars and speedboats?'

There was a catch in her voice that tore at him.

He gritted his teeth. 'Some of it, yes. But don't believe all you read. My prowess with women is greatly exaggerated.'

'You're never photographed twice with the same woman on your arm—princesses, heiresses, movie stars. All beautiful. All glamorous.'

'And none special.'

No one like Gemma.

'Is that true? I…I don't know what to believe.' Her dress was tied with a bow at the waistline, and she was pleating the fabric of its tail without seeming to realise she was doing so.

'I got a lot of attention as a prince. Opportunities for fun were offered, and I took them. There were not the restraints on me that there were on my brother.'

'If I'd been willing, would I have been just another conquest to you? A Sydney fling?'

'No. Never. You are special to me, Gemma.'

'That sounds like something the Playboy Prince might say. As another ploy.'

There was a cynical twist to her mouth he didn't like.

'Not to you, Gemma. Do not underestimate me.'

She was not convinced.

He cursed under his breath. He wanted her to think well of him. Not as some spoiled, privileged young royal. Which he had shown all the signs of being for some time.

'There was a reason for the way I behaved then,' he

said. 'I was mad about an English girl I'd met at university. She was my first serious girlfriend. But my parents made it clear they did not approve.'

'Because she was a commoner?'

'Yes. If she'd been from a noble family they would have welcomed her. She was attractive, intelligent, talented. My parents—and the crown advisers—were worried that it might get serious. They couldn't allow that to happen. They spoke to her family. No doubt money changed hands. She transferred to a different university. I was angry and upset. She refused to talk to me. I realised then what it meant to have my choice of life partner restricted by ancient decrees.'

'So you rebelled?'

'Not straight away. I still believed in the greater good of the throne. Then I discovered the truth behind my parents' marriage. The hypocrisy. It was an arranged marriage— my father is older than my mother. He has a long-time mistress. My mother discreetly takes lovers.' He remembered how gutted he'd felt at the discovery.

'What a shock that must have been.'

'These days they live separate lives except for state occasions. And yet they were determined to force me along the same unhappy path—for no reason I could see. I was young and hot-headed. I vowed if I couldn't marry the girl I wanted then I wouldn't marry at all.'

She sagged with obvious relief. 'That's understandable.'

'So you believe me?'

Slowly, she nodded. 'In my heart I didn't want to believe the person I was reading about was the person I had found so different, so...*wonderful*.'

'I was unhappy then. I was totally disillusioned. I looked at the marriages in my family. All were shams. Even my brother's marriage was as cynical an arrangement as any other Montovian royal marriage.'

'And now?'

She looked up at him with those warm brown eyes. Up close he saw they had golden flecks in them.

'It is all about duty. Duty before personal desire. All the heroes in our culture put duty first. They sacrifice love to go to war or to make a strategic marriage. That now is my role. Happiness does not come into the equation for me.'

'What would make you happy, Tristan?'

'Right now? To be alone with my beautiful Party Queen. To be allowed to explore what…what we feel for each other. Like an everyday guy and his girl. That would make me happy.' He shrugged. 'But it cannot be.'

There was no such thing as happiness in marriage for Montovian royalty.

This sea nymph had totally bewitched him. He had not been able to stop thinking about her. Coming up with one scheme after another that would let him have her in his life and explore if she might be the one who would finally make him want to marry—and discarding each as utterly impossible.

'I…I would like that, too,' she said. 'To be with you, I mean.'

He took both her hands in his and pulled her to him. She sighed—he could not tell if it was in relief or surrender—and relaxed against him. He put his arms around her and held her close. She laid her head on his shoulder, and he dropped a kiss on her sweetly scented hair.

Then he released her and stepped back. 'We cannot risk being compromised if someone comes in,' he explained. 'The last thing we want is press speculation.'

'I…I didn't realise that your life was under such scrutiny,' she said.

'That is why I wanted to be incognito. We could not have had that day together otherwise. I do not regret keeping the truth from you, Gemma. I do not regret that day. Although I am sorry if I hurt you.'

She had abandoned the obsessive pleating of the bow on her dress. But her hands fluttered nervously. Looking into her face, he now understood what it meant to say that someone had her heart in her eyes.

She felt it, too. That inexplicable compulsion, that connection. His feelings for Gemma might be the most genuine emotions he had ever experienced. Not *love* at first sight. He didn't believe that could happen so quickly. But something powerful and intense. Something so much more than physical attraction.

'We…we could have another day…together,' she said cautiously, as if she were testing his reaction.

'What do you mean?'

'We could have *two* days. I'm offering you that chance. You don't leave until Monday morning. All day Saturday and Sunday stretch out before us.'

She was tempting him almost beyond endurance. 'You would want us to spend the weekend together knowing it could never be more than that? Not because I don't *want* it to be more, but because it would never be allowed?'

'Yes. I do want that. I…I ache to be with you. I don't want to spend a lifetime regretting that I didn't take a chance to be with you. I keep trying to talk sense to myself—tell myself that I hardly know you; that you're leaving. But at some deep, elemental level I feel I *do* know you.' She shook her head. 'I'm not explaining this very well, am I?'

'I understand you very well—for it is how I also feel. But I do not want to hurt you, Gemma.'

'And I certainly don't want to get hurt,' she said. 'Or hurt *you*, for that matter. But I don't want to be riddled with regret.'

'Remember in three months' time I must announce my

engagement to a suitable bride. I cannot even offer to take you as my mistress—that would insult both you and the woman who will become my wife. I will not cheat on her. I will *not* have a marriage like that of my parents.'

'I understand that. Understand and admire you for your honesty and…and moral stance. I'm offering you this time with me, Tristan, with no strings attached. No expectations. Just you and me together. As we will never be allowed to be again.'

He was silent for a moment too long. Common sense, royal protocol—all said he should say no. If the press found out it would be a disaster for her, uncomfortable for him. The Playboy Prince label would be revived. While such a reputation could be laughed off, even admired, for the second or third in line to the throne, it was deeply inappropriate for the crown prince and future king.

Gemma looked up at him. She couldn't mask the longing in her eyes—an emotion Tristan knew must be reflected in his own. Her lovely, lush mouth trembled.

'I should go,' she said in a low, broken voice. 'People will notice we've left the room. There might be talk that the prince is too friendly with the party planner. It…it could get awkward.'

She went to turn away from him.

Everything in Tristan that spoke of duty and denial and loyalty to his country urged him to let her walk away.

But something even stronger urged him not to lose his one chance to be with this woman with whom he felt such a powerful connection. If he didn't say something to stop her, he knew he would never see her again.

He couldn't bear to let her go—no matter the consequences.

Tristan held out his hand to her.

'Stay with me, Gemma,' he said. 'I accept your invitation to spend this time together.'

CHAPTER ELEVEN

NEXT MORNING, in the grey light of dawn, Tristan turned to Gemma, who was at the wheel of her car. 'Where exactly are you taking me?'

'We're heading west to my grandmother's house in the Megalong Valley in the Blue Mountains. She died a few years ago, and she left her cottage to me and my two cousins. We use it as a weekender and for vacations.'

'Is it private?'

'Utterly private. Just what we want.'

He and Gemma had plotted his escape from the hotel in a furtive whispered conversation the previous night, before they had each left the annexe room separately to mingle with his guests. There had been no further contact with each other until this morning.

While it was still dark, she had driven to his hotel in the city and parked her car a distance away. He had evaded his bodyguards and, with his face covered by a hoodie, had met her without incident. They had both laughed in exhilaration as she'd gunned the engine and then floored the accelerator in a squeal of tyres.

'The valley is secluded and rural—less than two hundred people live there,' Gemma said. 'You might as well be ten hours away from Sydney as two. The cottage itself is on forty acres of garden, pasture and untamed bushland. We can be as secluded as we want to be.'

She glanced quickly at him, and he thrilled at the promise in her eyes. This was a relaxed Gemma, who had pulled down all the barriers she'd put up against him. She was warm, giving—and his without reservation for thirty-six hours.

'Just you and me,' he said, his voice husky.

'Yes,' she said, her voice laced with promise. 'Do you think there's any chance your goons—sorry, your body-guards—could find us?'

'I was careful. I left my laptop in my suite and I've switched off my smartphone so it can't be tracked. But I did leave a note to tell them I had gone of my own free will on a final vacation and would be back late Sunday night. The last thing we want them to think is that I've been kid-napped and start a search.'

'Is kidnapping an issue for you?' Her grip visibly tight-ened on the steering wheel.

'It is an issue for anyone with wealth. The royal chil-dren are always very well guarded.'

'I'm not putting you at risk, am I? I...I couldn't bear it if I—'

'Here, the risk is minimal. Please do not concern your-self with that. We are more at risk from the media. But I checked that no one was lurking about at my hotel.'

'Can you imagine the headlines if they did find us? *Playboy Prince in Secluded Love Nest with Sydney Party Planner.*'

Tristan rather liked the concept of a love nest. 'They would most likely call you a *sexy* party planner.'

Gemma made a snort of disgust, then laughed. 'I'll own sexy. Or how about: *Playboy Prince Makes Aussie Con-quest*? They'll want to get the local angle in, I'm sure.'

'You could also be *Mystery Redhead*?' he suggested.

He found he could joke about the headlines the press might make about his life—there had been enough of them in the past. Now he was crown prince he did not want to feature in any more. He appreciated the effort Gemma was making to preserve their privacy.

They made up more outrageous headlines as Gemma drove along the freeway until Sydney was behind them.

'Are you going to unleash your inner tour guide and tell me about the Blue Mountains?' Tristan asked as the road started to climb.

'How did you know I was waiting for my cue?' she said.

'Please, go ahead and tell me all I need to know—plus *more* than I need to know,' he said.

'Now that I've been invited…' she said, with a delightful peal of laughter.

Tristan longed to show her Montovia some day—and pushed aside the melancholy thought that that was never likely to happen. He had thirty-six hours with her stretching ahead of him—bonus hours he had not thought possible. He would focus his thoughts on how he could make them special for her.

'They're called the Blue Mountains because they seem to have a blue haze over them from a distance, caused by the eucalypt oil from the trees,' she said.

'I didn't know that,' he said.

'Don't think of them as mountains like Montovian mountains. Australia is really old, geologically, and the mountains would have been underwater for millions of years. They're quite flat on top but very rugged. There are some charming small towns up there, and it's quite a tourist destination.'

It wasn't that he found what she was saying boring. On the contrary, visiting Australia had long been on his 'to do' list. But Tristan found himself getting drowsy.

For the last three nights he had slept badly, kept awake by thoughts of Gemma and how much he wanted her to be part of his life. Now she was next to him and they were together. Not for long enough, but it was more than he could have dreamed of. For the moment he was content. To drift off to the sound of her voice was a particular kind of joy…

When he awoke, Gemma was skilfully negotiating her car down a series of hairpin bends on a narrow road where the Australian bush grew right to the sides.

'You've woken just in time for our descent into the valley,' she said. 'Hold on—it's quite a twisty ride.'

The road wound through verdant rainforest and huge towering indigenous trees before emerging onto the valley floor. Tristan caught his breath in awe at the sight of a wall of rugged sandstone mountains, tinged red with the morning sun.

'It's magnificent, isn't it?' she said. 'You should see it after heavy rain, when there are waterfalls cascading down.'

The landscape alternated harshness with lush pastures dotted with black and white cattle. There was only the occasional farmhouse.

'Do you wonder why I'm driving so slowly?' Gemma asked.

'Because it's a narrow road?' he ventured.

'Because—ah, here they are. Look!'

A group of kangaroos bounded parallel to the road. Tristan wished he had a camera. His smartphone was switched off, and he didn't dare risk switching it back on.

'You have to be careful in the mornings and evenings not to hit them as they cross the road.' She braked gently. 'Like that—right in front of the car.'

One after the other the kangaroos jumped over a low spot in the fence and crossed the road. Halfway across, the largest one stopped and looked at him.

'He is as curious about me as I am about him,' Tristan whispered, not wanting to scare the creature. 'I really feel like I am in Australia now.'

'I promised you kangaroos in the wild, and I've delivered,' Gemma said with justifiable triumph.

While he could promise her nothing.

* * *

As Gemma showed Tristan around the three-bedroom, one-bathroom cottage, she wondered what he really thought of it. He was, after all, used to living in a castle. The royal castle of Montovia was splendid—as befitted the prosperous principality.

Her internet research had showed her a medieval masterpiece clinging to the side of a mountain and overlooking a huge lake ringed by more snow-topped mountains. Her research had not shown her the private rooms where the family lived, but even if they were only half as extravagant as the public spaces Tristan had grown up in, they would be of almost unimaginable splendour.

And then there was a summer palace, at the other end of the lake. And royal apartments in Paris and Florence.

No doubt wherever he lived, he was waited on hand and foot by servants.

But she would not be intimidated. She was proud of her grandma's house—she and her cousins would probably always call it that, even though it was now their names on the deed of ownership.

She loved how it had been built all those years ago by her grandfather's family, to make the most of the gun-barrel views of the escarpment. To a prince it must seem very humble. But Gemma would never apologise for it.

Tristan stood on the wide deck her grandfather had added to the original cottage. It looked east, to the wall of the escarpment lit by the morning sun, and it was utterly private. No one could see them either from the neighbouring property or from the road.

Tristan put his arm around her to draw her close, and she snuggled in next to him. No more pretence that what they felt was mere friendship. She'd known when she'd invited him to spend his final weekend with her what it would lead to—and it was what she wanted.

Tristan looked at the view for a long time before he spoke. 'It's awe-inspiring to see this ancient landscape all around. And to be able to retreat to this charming house.'

She should have known that Tristan would not look down his princely nose at her beloved cottage.

'I've always loved it here. My grandmother knew what the situation was with my stepfather and made sure I was always welcome whenever I wanted. Sometimes I felt it was more a home than my house in Sydney.'

He turned to look back through the French doors and into the house, with its polished wooden floors and simple furnishings in shades of white.

'Was it like this when your grandmother had it? I think not.'

'Good guess. I loved my grandma, but not so much her taste in decorating. When I inherited with my cousins Jane and John—they're twins—I asked Andie to show us what to do with it to bring it into the twenty-first century. Not only did she suggest stripping it back to the essentials and painting everything we could white, but she used the house as a makeover feature for the magazine. We got lots of free help in return for having the house photographed. We put in a new kitchen and remodelled the bathroom, and now it's just how we want it.'

'The canny Party Queens wave their magic wands again?'

'You could put it like that.'

He pulled her into his arms. 'You're an amazing woman, Gemma Harper. One of many talents.'

'Thank you, Your Highness. And to think we're only just getting to know each other...I have many hidden talents you have yet to discover.'

'I've been keeping *my* talents hidden, too,' he said. 'But for no longer.'

He traced the outline of her mouth with his finger, the

light pressure tantalising in its unexpected sensuality. Her mouth swelled under his touch, and she ached for him to kiss her there. Instead he pressed kisses along the line of her jaw and down to the sensitive hollows of her throat. She closed her eyes, the better to appreciate the sensation. How could something so simple ignite such pleasure?

She tilted back her head for more, but he teased her by planting feather-light kisses on her eyelids, one by one, and then her nose.

'Kiss me properly,' she begged, pressing her aching mouth to his.

He laughed deep in his throat, then deepened the kiss into something harder and infinitely more demanding. She wound her arms around his neck to pull him closer, craving more. Her antennae thrummed softly—not in warning but in approval. She wanted him. She needed him. He was hers. Not forever, she knew that. But for *now*.

This was the first time she had walked into a less-than-ideal relationship with her eyes wide open. It was her choice. With Tristan she had not been coerced or tricked. She just hoped that when the time came she would be able to summon the inner strength to let him go without damage to her heart and soul—and not spend a lifetime in futile longing for him.

But she would not think of that now. Her mind was better occupied with the pleasure of Tristan's mouth, his tongue, his hands skimming her breasts, her hips.

He broke away from the kiss so he could undo the buttons of her shirt. She trembled with pleasure when his fingers touched bare skin. He knew exactly what he was doing, and she thrilled to it.

'I haven't shown you around outside,' she said breathlessly. 'There are horses. I know you like horses. More kangaroos maybe...'

Oh! He'd pulled her shirt open with his teeth. Desire,

fierce and insistent, throbbed through her. She slid his T-shirt over his head, gasped her appreciation of his hard, muscular chest.

He tilted her head back to meet his blue eyes, now dark with passion. 'How many times do I have to tell you? The only sight I'm interested in is you. *All of you.*'

CHAPTER TWELVE

THE SUNLIGHT STREAMING through the bedroom window told Gemma she had slept for several hours and that it must be heading towards noon. She reached out her hand to find the bed empty beside her, the sheets cooling.

But his lingering scent on the pillow—on *her*—was proof Tristan had been there with her. So were the delicious aches in her muscles, her body boneless with satisfaction. She stretched out her naked limbs, luxuriating in the memories of their lovemaking. Was it the fact he was a prince or simply because he was the most wonderful man she had ever met that made Tristan such an awesome lover?

She wouldn't question it. Tristan was Tristan, and she had never been gladder that she'd made the impulsive decision to take what she could of him—despite the pain she knew lay ahead when they would have to say goodbye.

Better thirty-six hours with this man than a lifetime with someone less perfect for her.

Her tummy rumbled to let her know the hour for breakfast was long past and that she'd had very little to eat the night before.

The aroma of freshly brewed coffee wafted to her nostrils, and she could hear noises coming from the kitchen. She sat up immediately—now fully awake. Tristan must be starving, too. How could she have slept and neglected him? *How could she have wasted precious time with him by sleeping?*

She leapt out of bed and burrowed in the top drawer of the chest of drawers, pulled out a silk wrap patterned with splashes of pink and orange and slipped it on. She'd given the wrap to her grandmother on her last birthday and kept it in memory of her.

She rushed out to the kitchen to find Tristan standing in front of the open fridge, wearing just a pair of blue boxer shorts. Her heart skipped a beat at the sight. Could a man be more perfectly formed?

He saw her and smiled a slow smile. The smile was just for her, and memories of their passionate, tender lovemaking came rushing back. The smile told her his memories of her were as happy. They were so good together. He was a generous lover, anticipating her needs, taking her to heights of pleasure she had not dreamed existed. She in turn revelled in pleasing him.

All this she could see in his smile. He opened his arms, and she went straight to them, sighing with pleasure as he pulled her close and slid his hands under the wrap. His chest was warm and hard, and she thrilled at the power of his body. He hadn't shaved, and the overnight growth of his beard was pleasantly rough against her cheek.

For a long moment they stood there, wrapped in each other's arms. She rested her head against his shoulder, felt the steady thud of his heartbeat, breathed in the male scent of him—already so familiar—and knew there was nowhere else she would rather be.

'You should have woken me,' she murmured.

'You looked so peaceful I did not have the heart,' he said. 'After all, you drove all the way here. And I only woke half an hour ago.'

'I…I don't want to waste time sleeping when I could be with you.'

'Which is why I was going to wake you with coffee.'

'A good plan,' she said.

'Hold still,' he said as he wiped under her eye with his finger.

'Panda eyes?' She hadn't removed her mascara the night before in the excitement of planning their escape.

'Just a smear of black,' he said. 'It's good now.'

She found it a curiously intimate gesture—something perhaps only long-time couples did. It was difficult to believe she had only met him on Monday. And would be losing him by the next Monday.

'You've been busy, by the look of it,' she said.

The table was set for a meal. She noticed he had set the forks and spoons face down, as she'd seen in France. The coffee machine hissed steam, and there were coffee mugs on the countertop.

'I hope you don't mind.'

'Of course not. The kitchen is designed for people to help themselves. No one stands on ceremony up here. It's not just me and my cousins who visit. We let friends use it, too.'

'I went outside and picked fresh peaches. The tree is covered in them.'

'You picked tomatoes, too, I see.'

Her grandmother's vegetable garden had been her pride and joy, and Gemma was determined to keep it going.

'Are you hungry?'

'Yes!'

'We could have breakfast, or we could have lunch. Whatever you choose.'

'Maybe brunch? You're going to *cook*?'

'Don't look so surprised.'

'I didn't imagine a prince could cook—or would even know his way around a kitchen.'

'You forget—this prince spent time in the army, where his title did not earn him any privileges. I also studied at university in England, where I shared a kitchen with other students. I chose not to have my own apartment. I wanted to enjoy the student experience like anyone else.'

'What about doing the dishes?' she teased.

'But of course,' he replied in all seriousness. 'Although I cannot say I enjoy that task.'

She pressed a quick kiss to his mouth—his beautiful, sensual mouth which she had now thoroughly explored. He tasted of fresh, ripe peach. 'Relax. The rule in this kitchen is that whoever cooks doesn't have to do the dishes.'

'That is a good rule,' he said in his formal way.

She could not resist another kiss, and then squealed when he held her close and turned it into something deeper, bending her back over his arm in dramatic exaggeration. She laughed as he swooped her back upright.

He seemed so blessedly normal. And yet last night he had worn the ceremonial sash and insignia indicating his exalted place in a hereditary monarchy that stretched back hundreds of years. He'd hobnobbed with the highest strata of Sydney society with aplomb. It was mind-blowing.

'The fridge and pantry are well stocked,' she said. 'It's a long way up the mountain if we run out of something.'

'I have already examined them. Would you like scrambled eggs and bacon with tomatoes? And whole-wheat toast?'

'That sounds like a great idea. It makes a pleasant change for someone to cook for me.'

'You deserve to be cherished,' he said with a possessive arm still around her. 'If only—'

'No "if onlys",' she said with a sudden hitch to her voice. 'We'll go crazy if we go there.'

To be cherished by him was an impossible dream…

She was speared by a sudden shaft of jealousy over his arranged bride. Did that well-born woman have any idea how fortunate she was? Or *was* she so fortunate? To be married to a man in a loveless marriage for political expediency might not make for a happy life. As it appeared had been the case for Tristan's parents.

'So—what to do after brunch?' she asked. 'There are horses on the property that we're permitted to ride. Of course they're not of the same calibre as your polo ponies, but—'

'I do not care what we do, so long as I am with you.'

'Perhaps we could save the horses for tomorrow?' she said. 'Why don't we walk down to the river and I'll show you some of my favourite places? We can swim, if you'd like.'

'I didn't pack my swim shorts.'

'There's no need for swimsuits,' she said. 'The river is on our property, and it's completely private.'

A slow smile spread across his face, and her body tingled in response. Swimming at the river this afternoon might be quite the most exciting it had ever been. She decided to pack a picnic to take with them, so they could stay there for as long as they wanted.

Gemma woke during the night to find Tristan standing by the bedroom window. The only light came from a full moon that sat above the enormous eucalypts that bounded the garden. It seemed every star in the universe twinkled in the dark canopy of the sky.

He was naked, and his body, silvered by the moonlight, looked like a masterpiece carved in marble by a sculptor expert in the depiction of the perfect male form.

Gemma slid out of bed. She was naked, too, and she slid her arms around him from behind, resting her cheek on his back. He might look like silvered marble but he felt warm, and firm, and very much a real man.

'You okay?' she murmured.

He enfolded her hands with his where they rested on his chest.

'I am imagining a different life,' he said, his voice low and husky. 'A life where I am a lawyer, or a businessman working in Sydney. I live in a water-front apartment in Manly with my beautiful party-planner wife.'

She couldn't help an exclamation and was glad he couldn't see her face.

'You know her, of course,' he said, squeezing her hand. 'She and I live a resort life, and she swims every day in the sea. We cross the harbour by ferry to get to work, and I dream of the day I can have my own yacht. On some weekends we come up here, just the two of us, and ride horses together and plan for the day that we...that we—' His voice broke.

He turned to face her. In the dim light of the moon his face was in shadow, but she could see the anguish that contorted his face.

'Gemma, I want it so much.' His voice was hoarse and ragged.

'It...it sounds like a wonderful life,' she said, her own voice less than steady. 'But it's a fantasy. As much a fantasy as that party planner living with you as a princess in a fairytale castle. We...we will only get hurt if we let ourselves imagine it could actually happen.'

'There is...I could abdicate my role as crown prince.'

For a long moment Gemma was too shocked to say anything. 'You say that, but you know you could never step down from your future on the throne. Duty. Honour. Responsibility to the country you love. They're ingrained in you. You couldn't live with that decision. Besides, I wouldn't let you.'

'Sometimes that responsibility feels like a burden. I was not born to it, like my brother.'

'But you *will* rise to it.'

He cradled her face in his hands, looked deep into her eyes, traced the corner of her mouth with his thumb. 'Gemma, you must know how I feel about you—that I am falling in lo—'

'No.' She put her hand over his mouth to stop him. 'Don't go there,' she said. 'You can't say the *L* word until you can follow it with a proposal. And we know that's not going to happen. Not for us. Not for a prince and a party planner. I…I feel it, too. But I couldn't bear it if we put words to it. It would make our parting so much more painful than…than it's already going to be.'

She reached up and pulled his head down to hers, kissed him with all the passion and feeling she could bring to the kiss. Felt her tears rolling down her cheeks.

'This. This is all we can have.'

Tristan held Gemma close as she slept, her head nestled in his shoulder. He breathed in her sweet scent. Already he felt that even blindfolded he would recognise her by her scent.

His physical connection with this special woman was like nothing he had ever experienced. Their bodies were in sync, as though they had made love for a lifetime. He couldn't label what they shared as *sex*—this was truly making *love*.

Being together all day, cooking companionably—even doing the dishes—had brought a sense of intimacy that was new to him. Was this what a *real* marriage could be like? As opposed to the rigid, hypocritical structure of a royal marriage?

What he felt with Gemma was a heady mix of physical pleasure and simple joy in her company. Was that how marriage should be?

There was no role model for a happy marriage in his family. His parents with their separate lives… His brother's loveless union… And from what he remembered of his grandparents, his grandmother had spent more time on the committees of her charitable organisations than she had with his grandfather. Except, of course, when duty called.

Duty. Why did he have to give up his chance of love for *duty*?

Because he didn't have a choice.

He had never felt for another woman what he felt for Gemma. Doubted he ever would. She was right—for self-protection neither of them could put a label on what they felt for each other—but he knew what it was.

She gave a throaty little murmur as she snuggled closer. He dropped a kiss on her bare shoulder.

The full impact of what he would miss out on, what he had to give up for duty, hit him with the impact of a sledgehammer.

Feeling as he did for Gemma, how could he even contemplate becoming betrothed to another woman in three months' time? He could taste the bitterness in his mouth. Another loveless, miserable royal marriage for Montovia.

He stayed awake for hours, his thoughts on an endless loop that always seemed to end with the Montovian concept of honour—sacrificing love for duty—before he eventually slept.

When Tristan awoke it was to find Gemma dropping little kisses over his face and murmuring that breakfast was ready. He had other ideas, and consequently it was midmorning before they got out of bed.

They rode the horses back down to the river. He was pleased at how competent Gemma was in the saddle. Despite their differences in social status, they had a lot in common, liked doing the same things, felt comfortable with each other. *If only...*

He felt a desperate urgency as their remaining time together ticked on—a need to landmark each moment. Their last swim. Their last meal together. The last time they'd share those humble domestic duties.

He was used to being brave, to denying his feelings, but he found this to be a kind of torture.

Gemma had *not* been trained in self-denial. But she was brave up until they'd made love for the last time.

'I can't bear knowing we will never be together like this again,' she said, her voice breaking. 'Knowing that I will never actually see you again, except in the pages of a magazine or on a screen.'

She crumpled into sobs, and there was no consoling her. How could he comfort her when he felt as if his heart was being wrenched out of him and pummelled into oblivion?

Tristan tilted her chin up so he could gaze deep into her eyes, reddened from where she'd tried to scrub away her tears. Her lovely mouth trembled. It was a particular agony to know he was the cause of her pain.

He smoothed her hair, bedraggled and damp with tears, from her face. 'Gemma, I am sorry. I should not have pursued you when I knew this could be the only end for us.'

She cleared her voice of tears. Traced his face with her fingers in a gesture he knew with gut-wrenching certainty was a farewell.

'No. Never say that,' she said. 'I don't regret one moment I've spent with you. I wish it could be different for us. But we went into this with our eyes open. And now... and now I know what it *should* be like between a man and a woman. I had no idea, you see, that it could be like this.'

'Neither did I,' he choked out. Nor what an intolerable burden duty to his beloved country could become.

'So no beating ourselves up,' she said.

But for all her brave words he had to take the wheel of her car and drive back to Sydney. She was too distressed to be safe.

Only too quickly he pulled up the car near his hotel and killed the engine. The unbearable moment of final farewell was upon them.

He gave her the smartphone he had bought to use in Australia so they could easily stay in touch. 'Keep it charged,' he said.

'I won't use it, you know,' she said, not meeting his eyes. 'We have to make a clean break. I'll go crazy otherwise.'

'If that's what you want,' he said, scarcely able to choke out the words with their stabbing finality. But he stuffed the phone into her bag anyway.

'It's the only way,' she said, her voice muffled as she hid her face against his shoulder. 'But…but I'll never forget you and…and I hope you have a good life.'

All the anger and ambivalence he felt towards his role as heir to the throne threatened to overwhelm him. 'Gemma, I want you to know how much I—'

She pushed him away. 'Just go now, Tristan. Please.'

He wanted to be able to say there could be more for them, but he knew he could not. Instead he pulled the hoodie up over his face, got out of the car and walked back to his life as crown prince without looking back.

CHAPTER THIRTEEN

Ten weeks later

GEMMA SAT ON the bed in a guest room at the grand gated Georgian house belonging to her newly discovered English grandparents. She was a long way from home, here in the countryside near Dorchester, in the county of Dorset in the south-west of England.

In her less-than-steady hand she held the smartphone Tristan had insisted on leaving with her on the last day she'd seen him. It was only afterwards that she'd realised why. If she needed to get in touch with him she doubted the castle staff would put through a call to the crown prince from some unknown Australian girl.

The phone had been charging for the last hour.

She had never used it—rather had kept to her resolve never to contact him. That had not been easy in the sad black weeks that had followed the moment when he had stumbled from her car and had not looked back. But she had congratulated herself on how well she had come through the heartbreak of having her prince in her life for such a short time before she'd had to let him go.

The only time she had broken down was when she had flicked through a gossip magazine to be suddenly confronted by an article about the crown prince of Montovia's upcoming birthday celebrations. It had included photos of Tristan taken at the Sydney reception, looking impossibly handsome. A wave of longing for him had hit her with such intensity she'd doubled over with the pain of it.

Would contacting him now mean tearing the scab off a wound better left to heal?

When she thought about her time with him in Sydney—
she refused to think of it as a fling—it had begun to take
on the qualities of a fondly remembered dream. After this
length of time she might reasonably have expected to start
dating again. Only she hadn't.

'Don't go thinking of him as your once-in-a-lifetime
love,' Andie had warned.

'I never said he was,' Gemma had retorted. 'Just that he
could have been if things had been different.'

Now, might she have been given another chance with
Tristan?

Gemma put down the phone, then picked it up again.
Stared at it as if it might give her the answer. Should she
or shouldn't she call him?

She longed to tell Tristan about her meeting with the
Cliffords. But would he be interested in what she had to
say? Would he want to talk to her after all this time? *Would
he even remember her?*

She risked humiliation, that was for sure. By now he
might be engaged to some princess or a duchess—that girl
in Sydney a distant memory.

But might she always regret it if she didn't share with
Tristan the unexpected revelation that had come from her
decision to seek out her birth father's family?

Just do it, Gemma.

With trembling fingers she switched on the phone and
the screen lit up. So the service was still connected. It was
meant to be. She *would* call.

But then she was astounded to find a series of recent
missed calls and texts of escalating urgency flashing up
on the screen. All from Tristan. All asking her to contact
him as soon as possible.

Why?

It made it easy to hit Call rather than have to take the
actual step of punching out his number.

He answered almost straightaway. Her heart jolted so hard at the sound of his voice she lost *her* voice. She tried to say hi, but only a strangled gasp came out.

'Gemma? Is that you?'

'Yes,' she finally managed to squeak out.

'Where *are* you?' he demanded, as if it had been hours rather than months since they'd last spoken. 'I've called the Party Queens office. I've called both Andie and Eliza, who will not tell me where you are. Are you at the cottage? Are you okay?'

Gemma closed her eyes, the better to relish the sound of his voice, his accent. 'I'm in Dorset.'

She wondered where he was—in some palatial room in his medieval castle? It was difficult to get her head around the thought.

There was a muffled exclamation in Montovian. 'Dorset, England?'

She nodded. Realised that of course he couldn't see her. 'Yes.'

'So close. And I didn't know. What are you doing there?'

'Staying with my grandparents.'

'They…they are not alive. I don't understand…'

She could almost see his frown in his words.

'My birth father's parents.'

'The Clifford family?'

He'd remembered the name. 'Yes.'

What else did he remember? She hadn't forgotten a moment of their time together. Sometimes she revisited it in dreams. Dreams from which she awoke to an overwhelming sense of loss and yearning for a man she'd believed she would never see again—or hear.

'The people who paid your mother off? But they are not known to you…'

She realised she was gripping the phone so tensely her fingers hurt. 'They are now. I came to find them. After all your talk of your birthright and heritage, I wanted to know about mine. I told my mother I could no longer deny my need to know just because my stepfather felt threatened that she'd been married before.'

Her time with Tristan had made her want to take charge of her life and what was important to her.

'Those people—did they welcome you?'

'It seems I look very much like my father,' she said. In fact her grandmother had nearly fainted when Gemma had introduced herself.

'They were kind?'

The concern in his voice made her think Tristan still felt something for her.

'Very kind. It's a long story. One I'd like to share with you, Tristan.' She held her breath, waiting for his answer.

'I would like to hear it. And there is something important I have to tell you.'

'Is that why you were calling me?'

'Yes. I wanted to fly to Australia to see you.'

'You were going to fly all that way? But it's only two weeks until your birthday party.'

'I want to see you. Can you to come to Montovia?'

For a long moment she was too shocked to reply. 'Well, yes, I would like to see Montovia,' she finally choked out. *Tristan.* She just wanted to see Tristan. Here, there, Australia—she didn't care where. 'When?'

'Tomorrow.'

Excitement or trepidation? Which did she feel more? 'I'll look up flights.'

'I will send a private jet,' he said, without hesitation.

Of course he would.

'And a limousine to pick you up from where you are in Dorset.'

'There's no need. I have a rental car...I can drive—'

'I will send the car.'

When she'd flown to England from Australia she'd had no intention of contacting Tristan. Certainly not of visiting Montovia. The meeting with her grandparents had changed everything.

It wasn't until after she had disconnected the phone that she realised she hadn't asked Tristan what was so important that he'd left all those messages.

The next day the limousine arrived exactly on time and took her to Bristol airport. She was whisked through security and then onto the tarmac.

It wasn't until she began to climb the steps to board the plane that she started to feel nervous. *What the heck was she doing here?*

She'd been determined to take charge of her own life after so many years of acquiescing to men, but then with one word from Tristan—actually, two words: *private* and *jet*—she'd rolled over and gone passive again.

Then he was there, and thoughts of anything else were crowded out of her mind.

Tristan.

He stood at the top of the steps, towering over her. Tall, broad-shouldered, wearing an immaculately tailored business suit in deepest charcoal with a narrow grey tie. His hair was cut much shorter—almost military in style. When she'd last seen him he hadn't shaved for two days and had been wearing blue jeans and a T-shirt. The time before that he'd been wearing nothing at all.

He looked the same, but not the same.

And it was the *not the same* that had her feet seemingly stuck to the steps and her mouth unable to form words of greeting.

He was every bit as handsome as she remembered. But this Tristan appeared older, more serious. A man of wealth and stratospheric status—greeting her on board a private jet that was to fly her to his castle. While she was still very much just Gemma from Sydney.

Gemma looked the same as Tristan had remembered—her hair copper bright, her heart-shaped face pretty, her lovely body discreetly shown off in deep pink trousers and a white jacket. As he watched her, he thought his heart would burst with an explosion of emotion.

He had never lost faith that he would see her again. That faith had paid off now, after all those dark hours between the moment he had said goodbye to her in Sydney and this moment, when he would say hello to her again. Hours during which he had honoured her request not to contact her. Hours when he had worked with all the driven frenzy of the Montovian fisherman searching for his water nymph to find a way they could be together.

But Gemma stood frozen, as though she were uncertain whether to step up or back down. There wasn't a dimple in sight.

Was it fear of flying? Or fear of *him*?

He hadn't said he'd be on the jet to meet her—he'd had to reschedule two meetings with his father and the inner circle of court advisers to make the flight. He hadn't wanted to make a promise he might not have been able to keep. Perhaps she was too shocked at his presence to speak.

He cursed under his breath. Why hadn't he thought to radio through to the chauffeur?

Because he'd been too damn excited at the thought of seeing her so soon to follow through on detail.

Now he wanted to bound down those steps, sweep her into his arms and carry her on board. The dazed look in her cinnamon-coloured eyes made him decide to be more circumspect. What had he expected? That she would fall back into his arms when, for all she knew, the situation hadn't changed between them and he still could not offer her anything more than a tryst?

Tristan urged himself to be patient. He took a step down to her, his arms outstretched in welcome. 'Gemma. I can't believe you're in Europe.'

For a long moment she looked up at him, searching his face. He smiled, unable to hide his joy and relief at seeing her again.

At last her lovely mouth tilted upwards and those longed-for dimples flirted once more in her cheeks. Finally she closed the remaining steps between them.

'Tristan. I can't believe it's you. I… I thought I would never see you again. Your smile…it's still the same.'

That puzzled him. Of course his smile was still the same. Probably a lot warmer and wider than any smile on his face since he'd last seen her. But all he could think about was Gemma. Back in his arms where she belonged.

He held her close for a long moment measured by the beating of her heart against him. He breathed in her essence, her scent heart-rendingly familiar.

Gratitude that everything had worked out surged through him. He didn't know how she had come to be just an hour's flight away from him, but he didn't question it. The need to kiss her was too strong—questions and answers could come later.

He dipped his head to claim her mouth. She kissed him back, at first uncertainly and then with enthusiasm.

'Tristan…' she murmured in that throaty, familiar way.

At last. Now everything was going to be as he wanted it.

CHAPTER FOURTEEN

GEMMA HAD ONLY ever seen the inside of a private jet in movies. Was this a taste of the luxury in which Tristan lived? If so, she guessed it was her first look at his life in Montovia. The armchair-like reclining seats, the sofas, the bathrooms... All slick and sleek, in leather, crystal and finest wool upholstery. The royal Montovian coat of arms—an eagle holding a sword in its beak—was embroidered on the fabrics and etched into crystal glasses. No wonder Tristan had not been overly impressed with the *Argus*—it must have seemed everyday to him.

Once they were in the air the attendant, in a uniform that also bore the royal coat of arms, served a light lunch, but Gemma was too tightly wound to eat. Tristan didn't eat much either. She wanted to tell him her news but didn't know how to introduce the topic. They sat in adjoining seats—close, but not intimate. She wasn't yet ready for intimate.

She was grateful when he asked outright. 'So, tell me about your meeting with your new grandparents.'

'They're not new—I mean they've been there all the time, but they didn't know I existed, of course.'

'They honestly had never checked up on your mother over the years?'

The words spilled out of her. 'Their shock at meeting me appeared genuine. The dimples did it, I think; my grandmother has them too. Eliza had joked that the Cliffords would probably want a DNA test, but they scarcely looked at my birth certificate. They loved their son very much. I think they see me as some kind of unexpected gift. And I... Well, I like them a lot.'

'It must have been exciting for you to finally find out about your father,' he said. 'Did it fill a gap for you?'

'A gap I didn't really know was there,' she said. 'You know I had only ever seen one photo of my father? The Cliffordses' house is full of them. He was very handsome. Apparently, he was somewhat of an endearing bad boy, who dropped out of Oxford and was living as a ski bum when he met my mother. His parents were hoping he'd get it out of his system and come back to the fold, but then he…he died. The revelation that he was married came as a huge shock to them.'

'What about the way they treated your mother?'

'I'm not making any excuses for them. I still think it was despicable. But apparently there's some serious money in the family, and there had been gold-diggers after him before. I told them my mother had no idea about any of that. She was clueless about English class distinctions.'

'For your sake, I am glad it's worked out for you…'

Gemma could sense the unspoken question at the end of his sentence. 'But you want to know why I decided to share my adventure with you.'

'Yes,' he said. 'I know you turned on the smartphone I left you because you decided to get in touch with me. I can only suppose it was because of your meeting with your new family.'

'You're right. But before I tell you I want to ask you something.' She felt her cheeks flush warm. 'It's your birthday in two weeks' time. I…I saw in a magazine that you have a big party planned. Are you…are you engaged to be married? To the girl your parents chose for you? Or anyone else?'

'No,' he said, without hesitation.

She could not help her audible sigh of relief.

Tristan met her gaze. 'What about you? Is there another man in your life?'

'There has been no one since…since you.'

'Good,' he said fiercely, his relief also apparent.

Seeing Tristan again told her why she had felt no interest in dating other men. Their attraction was as strong, as compelling, as overwhelming as it had ever been.

'Before I tell you what happened at my grandparents' house, let me say I come to you with no expectations,' she said. 'I realise when it comes down to it we…well, we've only known each other a week, but—'

Tristan made a sound of impatience that definitely involved Montovian cursing. 'A *week*? I feel I have known you a lifetime, Gemma. I know all I need to know about you.'

He planted a swift kiss on her mouth—enough to thrill her and leave her wanting more. She would have liked to turn to him, pull his head back to hers—but not before she'd had her say.

'You might want to know this, as well,' she said. 'You're speaking to a person who is, in the words of her newly discovered grandmother, "very well bred".'

Tristan frowned. 'I'm not sure what you mean.'

It had taken her a while to get her head around what she'd learned. Now she felt confident of reciting the story, but still her words came out in a rush. As if she still didn't quite believe it.

'It seems that on my grandmother's side I am eighth cousin to Prince William, the Duke of Cambridge, through a common distant ancestor, King George II, and also connected by blood to the Danish royal family. One of the connections was "on the wrong side of the blanket", but apparently that doesn't matter as far as genealogy is concerned.'

'But…but this is astonishing.'

She couldn't blame Tristan for his shocked expression;

she was sure her grandparents had seen the same look on her face.

'I thought so, too,' she said. 'In fact I couldn't believe it could possibly be true. But they showed me the family tree—to which I am now going to be added, on the short little branch that used to end with my father.'

Tristan shook his head in disbelief. 'After all I have done—'

'What do you mean? What have you done?'

'It is not important,' he said with a slight shake of his head. 'Not now.'

The way he'd said that had made it sound as though it *was* important. She would have to ask him about it at another time. Right now she was more concerned at the impact of her own news.

'I…I wanted to ask you if that connection is strong enough for… Well, strong enough to make things between us not so impossible as when I was just a commoner. Not that I'm not a commoner still, really. But as far as bloodlines are concerned—that's what my grandmother calls them—I…I have more of a pedigree than I could ever have imagined.'

He nodded thoughtfully. 'Forgive me, Gemma. This is a lot to take in.'

A chill ran up her spine. Was she too late? 'I'd hoped it might make a difference to…to us. That is if there *is* an "us".'

His dark brows rose, as if she had said something ridiculous. 'As far as I am concerned there was an "us" from the moment you tried to attack me with that wooden spoon.'

She smiled at the reminder. 'You are never, ever going to let me forget that, are you?'

'Not for the rest of our lives,' he said.

She could see it took an effort for him to keep his voice steady.

'Gemma, I've been utterly miserable without you.'

It was still there between them—she could see it in his eyes, hoped he saw it in hers. The attraction that was so much more than physical. If it no longer had to be denied because of the discovery of her heritage, where might it go from here?

Like champagne bubbles bubbling to the top of a glass, excitement fizzed through her.

'Me...me too. Though I've tried very hard to deny it. Kept congratulating myself on how well I'd got over you. I had no hope, you see. I didn't know—none of us did— that the requisite noble blood was flowing in my veins.'

'Stay with me in Montovia, Gemma. Be my guest of honour at the party. Let me woo you as a prince *can* woo the eighth cousin of a prince of this country.'

Again that word *surreal* flashed through her mind. Perhaps this was all meant to be. Maybe she and Tristan were part of some greater plan. Who knew? And Party Queens could manage without her. She hadn't taken a break since the business had started.

'Yes, Tristan,' she said. 'Show me Montovia. I couldn't think of anything better than spending the next few weeks with you.'

She hugged his intention to 'woo' her—what a delightfully old-fashioned word—to herself like something very precious. Then she wound her arms around his neck and kissed him.

By the time the jet started its descent into Montovia, and the private airfield that served the castle, she and Tristan were more than ready to go further than kisses. She felt they were right back where they'd left off in her grandmother's cottage. He might be a prince, but more than that he was the man she wanted—wanted more than ever.

And they had two weeks together.

She couldn't remember when she'd felt happier.

Gemma caught her breath in admiration as, on Tristan's command to the pilot, the jet swooped low over the town of old Montovia. In the soft light of late afternoon it looked almost too beautiful to be real.

The medieval castle, with its elaborate towers and turrets, clung to the side of a forest-covered mountain with the ancient town nestled below. The town itself was set on the shore of a lake that stretched as far as she could see, to end in the reflections of another snow-capped mountain range. A medieval cathedral dominated the town with its height and grandeur.

'You can see from here how strategically they built the castle, with the mountains behind, the lake in front, the steep winding road, the town walls,' said Tristan, from where he sat beside her. 'The mountains form a natural barricade and fortification—it would be an exceptional army that could scale them. Especially considering there's snow and ice on the passes most months of the year.'

He kept his hand on her shoulder as he showed her what to look for out of the window. Gemma loved the way he seemed to want to reassure himself she was there, with a touch, a quick kiss, a smile. It was like some kind of wonderful dream that she was here with him after those months of misery. And all because she'd followed up on her curiosity about her father.

'It's good to see you taking your turn as tour guide,' she said. 'There's so much I want to know.'

'Happy to oblige,' he said with his charming smile. 'I love Montovia, and I want you to love it, too.'

For just two weeks? She didn't dare let herself think there could be more...

She reached out to smooth his cowlick back into place— that unruly piece of hair that refused to stay put. It was a small imperfection. He was still beautiful in the way of a virile man.

That inner excitement continued to bubble. Not because of castles and lakes and mountains. But because of Tristan. *She loved him.* No longer did she need to deny it—to herself or anyone else. She loved him—and there was no longer any roadblock on a possible future together.

'The castle was originally a fortress, built in the eleventh century on the ruins of a Roman *castellum*,' he said. 'It was added to over the centuries to become what it is now. The south extension was built not as a fortress but to showcase the wealth and power of the royal family.'

Gemma laughed. 'You know, I didn't see all that strategy stuff at all. I only saw how beautiful the setting is, how picturesque the town, with those charming old houses built around the square. Even from here I can see all the flower boxes and hanging baskets. Do you realise how enchanting cobbled streets are to Australian eyes? And it looks like there's a market being held in the town square today.'

'The farmers from the surrounding cantons bring in their goods, and there's other household stuff for sale, too—wooden carvings, metalwork, pottery. We have a beautiful Christmas market in December.'

'I can't wait to see more of the countryside. And to walk around the town. Am I allowed to? Are you? What about your bodyguards?'

'We are as safe as we will ever be in our own town. We come and go freely. Here the royal family are loved, and strangers are rare except for tourists.'

'Do you mean strangers are not welcome?' A tiny pinprick was threatening to leak the happiness from her bubble.

'Are you asking will you be welcome?'

'I might be wondering about it,' she said, quaking a little. 'What will you tell your family about me?'

'They know all about the beautiful girl I met in Sydney. They know I flew to England to get her today. You will be their guest.'

That surprised her. Why would he have told anyone about his interlude with an unsuitable commoner? And wouldn't she be staying with *him*, not his family?

'Will I be seen as an interloper?'

'You are with me—that automatically makes you not a stranger.'

She noticed a new arrogance to Tristan. He was crown prince of this country. Was he really still the Tristan she had fallen for in Sydney? Or someone else altogether?

'I'm glad to hear that,' she said. She paused. 'There's another thing. A girly thing. I'm worried about my clothes. When I left Sydney I didn't pack for a castle. I've only got two day dresses with me. And nothing in the slightest bit formal. I wasn't expecting to travel.' She looked down at what she was wearing. 'Already this white jacket is looking less than its best. What will your parents think of me?'

Being taken home to meet a boyfriend's parents was traumatic at best. When they were a king and queen, the expectation level went off the scale.

'You are beautiful, Gemma. My mother and father are looking forward to meeting you. They will not even notice your clothes. You look fine in what you are wearing.'

Hmm. *They lived in a castle.* She very much doubted casual clothes would be the order of the day. In Dorset she'd felt totally underdressed even in her newly found grandparents' elegant house. At least she'd managed to pop into Dorchester and buy a dress, simply cut in navy linen.

'I have so many questions. When will I meet your parents? Will…will we be allowed to stay together? Do I—?'

'First, you are invited to dinner tonight, to meet my parents and my sister. Second, you will stay in one of the castle's guest apartments.'

Again there was that imperious tone.

'By myself?'

Her alarm must have shown on her face.

'Don't worry, it is not far from mine.'

'Your apartment?'

'We each have our independent quarters. I am still in the apartment I was given when I turned eighteen. The crown prince's much grander apartment will be mine when its refurbishment is complete. I wanted my new home to be completely different. I could not live there with sad memories of when the rooms were Carl's.'

'Of course…' Her words trailed away.

She shouldn't be surprised that she and Tristan wouldn't be allowed to share a room. Another pinprick pierced that lovely bubble. She hadn't anticipated being left on her own. And she very much feared she would be totally out of her depth.

CHAPTER FIFTEEN

TRISTAN WANTED TO have Gemma to himself for a little longer before he had to introduce her to his family. He also wanted to warn his parents and his sister not to say anything about the work he'd done on what he had privately termed 'Project Water Nymph' in the months since he'd been parted from Gemma.

He sensed in her a reticence he had not expected—he'd been surprised when she'd reminded him she'd only known him for a week. There was no such reticence on his part—he had no doubt that he wanted her in his life. But instinct now told him she might feel pressured if she knew of the efforts he'd gone to in order to instigate change.

Not that he regretted the time he'd spent on the project—it had all been to the good in more ways than one. But news of her noble connections had removed some of that pressure. So long as no one inadvertently said something to her. He wanted her to have more time here before he told her what he'd been doing while she'd been tracking down her English connections.

'Let me show you my favourite part of the castle before I take you to your rooms,' he said. 'It is very old and very simple—not like the rooms where we spend most of our time. I find it peaceful. It is where I go to think.'

'I'd love that,' she said, with what seemed like genuine interest.

'This part of the castle is open to the public in the summer, but not until next month,' he said. 'We will have it to ourselves today.'

He thought she would appreciate the most ancient part of the castle, and he was not disappointed. She exclaimed her amazement at all his favourite places as he led her along the external pathways and stone corridors that hugged the walls of the castle, high above the town.

'This is the remains of the most heavily barricaded fortress,' he explained. 'See the slits in the walls through which arrows were fired? Those arched lookouts came much later.'

Gemma leaned her elbows on the sill of the lookout. 'What a magnificent view across the lake to the mountains! It sounds clichéd, but everywhere I look in your country I see a postcard.'

With her hair burnished by the late-afternoon sun, and framed by the medieval arch, Gemma herself looked like a beautiful picture. To have her here in his home was something he'd thought he'd never see. He wanted to keep her here more than he'd ever wanted anything. This image of Gemma on her first day in Montovia would remain in his mind forever.

He slipped his arms around her from behind. She leaned back against his chest. For a long time they looked at the view in a companionable silence. He was the first to break it. 'To me this has the same kind of natural grandeur as the view from the deck of your grandmother's cottage,' he said.

'You're right,' she said. 'Very different, but awe-inspiring in the same way.'

'I wish we could stay here much longer, but I need to take you to your rooms now so that you can have some time to freshen up before dinner.'

And so that he'd have time to prepare his family for his change in strategy.

If this was a guest apartment, Gemma could only imagine what the royal family's apartments were like. It comprised a suite of elegantly decorated rooms in what she thought was an antique French style. Andie would know exactly how to describe it.

Gemma swallowed hard against a sudden lump in her throat. Andie and Party Queens and Sydney and her everyday life seemed far, far away. She was here purely for Tristan. Without his reassuring presence she felt totally lost and more than a tad terrified. What if she made a fool of herself? It might reflect badly on Tristan, and she *so* didn't want to let him down. She might have been born with noble blood in her veins, but she had been raised as just an ordinary girl in the suburbs.

She remembered the times in Sydney when she had thought about Tristan being *other*. Here, in this grand castle, surrounded by all the trappings of his life, she might as well be on a different planet for all she related to it. Here, *she* was *other*.

A maid had been sent to help her unpack her one pitifully small suitcase. She started to speak to her in Montovian, but at Gemma's lack of response switched to English. The more Gemma heard Montovian spoken, the less comprehensible it seemed. How could she let herself daydream about a future with Tristan in a country where she couldn't even speak the language?

She stood awkwardly by while the maid shook out her hastily packed clothes and woefully minimal toiletries and packed them away in the armoire. Knowing how to deal with servants was totally outside of her experience.

The maid asked Gemma what she wanted to wear to dinner, and when Gemma pointed out the high-street navy dress, she took it away to steam the creases out. By the time Gemma had showered in the superb marble bathroom—thankfully full of luxurious bath products—her dress was back in the bedroom, looking 100 per cent better than it had.

Did you tip the maids? She would have to ask Tristan.

There was so much she needed to ask him, but she didn't want to appear so ignorant he might regret inviting her here.

Her antennae gave a feeble wave, to remind her that Tristan had fallen for her the way she was. He wouldn't expect her to be any different. She would suppress her tremors of terror, watch and learn and ask questions when necessary.

She dressed in the navy sheath dress and the one pair of high-heeled shoes she'd brought with her, a neutral bronze. The outfit had looked fine in an English village, but here it looked drab—the bed was better dressed than she was, with its elegant quilted toile bedcover.

Then she remembered the exquisite pearl necklace her new grandmother had insisted on giving her from her personal jewellery collection. The strand was long, the pearls large and lustrous. It lifted the dress 100 per cent.

As she applied more make-up than she usually would Gemma felt her spirits rise. Darn it, she had royal blood of her own—even if much diluted. She would *not* let herself be intimidated. Despite their own personal problems, the king and queen had raised a wonderful person like Tristan. How could they *not* be nice people?

When Tristan, dressed in a different immaculate dark business suit, came to escort her to dinner, he told her she looked perfect and she more than half believed him.

Feeling more secure with Tristan by her side, Gemma tried not to gawk at the splendour of the family's dining room, with its ornate ceilings and gold trimmings, its finely veined white marble and the crystal chandeliers that hung over the endless dining table. Or at the antique silk-upholstered furniture and priceless china and silver. And these were the private rooms—not the staterooms.

Tristan had grown up with all this as his birthright.
How would she ever fit in? Even though he hadn't actu-

ally come out and said it, she knew she was on trial here. Now there was no legal impediment to them having a future together, it was up to her to prove she *could* fit in.

Tristan's parents were seated in an adjoining sitting room in large upholstered chairs—not thrones, thank heaven. His blonde mother, the queen, was attractive and ageless—Gemma suspected some expert work on her face—and was exquisitely groomed. She wore a couture dress and jacket, and outsize diamonds flashed at her ears, throat and wrists. His father had dark greying hair and a moustache, a severe face and was wearing an immaculately tailored dark suit.

Tristan had said they dressed informally for dinner.

Thank heaven she'd changed out of the cotton trousers and the jacket grubby at the cuffs.

Ordinary parents would have risen to greet them. Royal parents obviously did not. Why hadn't Tristan briefed her on what was expected of her? What might be second nature to him was frighteningly alien to her.

Prompted perhaps by some collective memory shared with her noble ancestors, Gemma swept into a deep curtsy and murmured, 'Your Majesties.'

It was the curtsy with which she'd started and ended every ballet class for years when she'd been a kid. She didn't know if it was a suitable curtsy for royalty, but it seemed to do the trick. Tristan beamed, and his mother and father smiled. Gemma almost toppled over in her relief.

'Thank you, my dear,' said his mother as she rose from her chair. 'Welcome.' She had Tristan's blue eyes, faded to a less vivid shade.

The father seemed much less forbidding when he smiled. 'You've come a long way to reach us. Montovia makes you welcome.'

Tristan took her hand in a subtle declaration that they

were a couple, but Gemma doubted his parents needed it. She suspected his mother's shrewd gaze missed nothing.

When Tristan's sister joined them—petite, dark-haired Natalia—Gemma sensed she might have a potential friend at the castle.

'Tristan mentioned you might need to buy some new clothes?' Natalia said. 'I'd love to take you shopping. And of course you'll need something formal for Tristan's party next week.'

Royals no doubt needed to excel at small talk, and any awkwardness was soon dispelled as they sat down at the table. If she hadn't already been in love with Tristan, Gemma would have fallen in love with him all over again as he effortlessly included her in every conversation.

He seemed pleased when she managed a coherent exchange in French with his mother and another in German with his father.

'I needed to fill all my spare time after you left Sydney so I wouldn't mope,' she whispered to him. 'I found some intensive language classes.'

'What do you think about learning Montovian?' he asked.

'I shall have to, won't I?' she said. 'But who will teach me?'

There was a delicious undercurrent running between her and Tristan. She knew why she was here in his country—to see if she would like living in Montovia. But it was a formality, really. If she wanted to be with him, here she would have to stay. Nothing had been declared between them, so there was still that thrilling element of anticipation—that the best was yet to come.

'*I* will teach you, of course,' he said, bringing his head very close to hers so their conversation remained private.

'It seems like a very difficult language. I might need a lot of attention.'

'If attention is what you need, attention is what you shall get,' he said in an undertone. 'Just let me know where I need to focus.'

'I think you might already know where I need attention,' she said.

'Lessons should start tonight, then,' he said, and his eyes narrowed in the way she found incredibly sensuous.

'I *do* like lessons from you,' she murmured. 'All sorts of lessons.'

'I shall come to your room tonight, so we can start straight away,' he said.

She sat up straighter in her antique brocade dining chair. 'Really?'

'You didn't think I was going to let you stay all by yourself in this great rattling castle?'

'I did wonder,' she said.

'I have yearned to be alone with you for close on three months. Protocol might put us in different rooms. That doesn't mean we have to stay there.'

The soup course was served. But Gemma felt so taut with anticipation at the thought of being alone—completely alone—with Tristan she lost her appetite and just pushed the soup around in her bowl.

It was the first of four courses; each course was delicious, if a tad uninspired and on the stodgy side. Gemma wondered who directed the cook, and wondered, if she were to end up staying in Montovia, if she might be able to improve the standard of the menus without treading on any toes.

The thought took her to a sudden realisation—one she had not had time to consider. She knew the only way she would be staying in Montovia was if she and Tristan committed to something permanent.

Finding out the truth about her father's family had precipitated their reunion with such breakneck speed, putting their relationship on a different footing, that she hadn't had time to think about the implications.

If she and Tristan… If she stayed in Montovia she would have to give up Party Queens. In fact she supposed she would have to give up any concept of having her own life. Though there was actually no reason why she couldn't be involved with the business remotely.

She had spent much of the last year working to be herself—not the version of herself that others expected her to be. Without her work, without her friends, without identification with her own nationality, would she be able to cope?

Would being with Tristan be enough?

She needed to talk to Tristan about that.

CHAPTER SIXTEEN

BUT SHE DIDN'T actually have much time alone with Tristan. The next day his parents insisted on taking them to lunch at their mountain chalet, more than an hour and a half's drive away from the castle. The honour was so great there was no way she could suggest she would rather be alone with Tristan.

The chalet was comparatively humble. More like a very large, rustic farmhouse, with gingerbread wood carving and window boxes planted with red geraniums. A hearty meal was served to them by staff dressed in traditional costume—full dirndl skirts for the women and leather shorts and embroidered braces for the men.

'Is this the real Montovia?' she asked Tristan. 'Because if it is, I find it delightful.'

'It is the traditional Montovia,' he said. 'The farmers here still bring their cattle up to these higher pastures in the summer. In winter it is snowed in. People still spend the entire winter in the mountains. Of course, this is a skiing area, and the roads are cleared.'

Would she spend a winter skiing here? Perhaps all her winters?

That evening was taken up with his cousin and his girlfriend joining them for the family dinner. They were very pleasant, but Gemma was surprised at how stilted they were with her. At one point the girlfriend—a doctor about her own age—started to say how grateful she was to Gemma, but her boyfriend cut her off before she could finish the sentence.

Natalia, too, talked about her brother's hard work in

changing some rule or another, before being silenced by a glare from Tristan.

And although they all spoke perfect English, in deference to her, there were occasional bursts of rapid Montovian that left Gemma with the distinct impression that she was being left out of something important. It wasn't a feeling she liked.

She tackled Tristan about it when he came to her room that night.

'Tristan, is there something going on I should know about?'

'What do you mean?' he said, but not before a flash of panic tightened his face.

'I mean, Mr Marco, you made a promise not to lie to me.'

'No one is lying. I mean... *I* am not lying.'

'"No one"?' She couldn't keep the hurt and betrayal from her voice.

'I promise you this is not bad, Gemma.'

'Better tell me, then,' she said, leading him over to the elegant chaise longue, all gilt-edged and spindly legged, but surprisingly comfortable.

Tristan sank down next to her. He should have known his family would let the secret slip. No way did he want Gemma to feel excluded—not when the project had been all about including her.

'Have I told you about the myth of the Montovian water nymph?' he asked.

'No, but it sounds intriguing.'

Tristan filled her in on the myth. He told her how he saw her as *his* sea nymph, with her pale limbs and floating hair enticing him in the water of Sydney Harbour.

'When I got back to Montovia, I was like the fisherman who escaped his nymph's deadly embrace but went mad without her and spent his remaining years searching the lake for her.'

Gemma took his hand. 'I was flailing around by myself, too, equally as miserable.'

He dropped a kiss on her sweet mouth. 'This fisherman did not give up easily. I searched the castle archives through royal decrees and declarations to find the origin of the rule that kept us apart. Along the way I found my purpose.'

'I'm not sure what you mean.' she said.

'Remember, I've been rebelling against this rule since my Playboy Prince days? But I began to realise I'd gone about it the wrong way—perhaps a hangover from being the "spare". I'd been waiting for *someone else* to change the rules.'

He gave an unconsciously arrogant toss of his head.

'So I decided *I* was the crown prince. *I* was the lawyer. *I* was the person who was going to bring the royal family of Montovia kicking and screaming into the twenty-first century. All motivated by the fact I wanted the right to choose my own bride, no matter her status or birth.'

'So this was about *me*?'

'Yes. Other royal families allow marriage to commoners. Why not ours?'

'Be careful who you're calling a commoner,' she said. 'Now I know why I disliked the term so much. My noble blood was protesting.'

Tristan laughed. He loved her gift of lightening up a situation. It would stand her in good stead, living in a society like Montovia's.

'I practically lived in the archives—burrowing down through centuries of documents. My research eventually found that the rule could be changed by royal decree,' he said. 'In other words, it was in the power of the king—my father—to implement a change.'

'You must have been angry he hadn't already done so.'

'I was at first. Then I realised my father genuinely believed he was bound by law. Fact is, he has suffered from its restrictions more than anyone. He has loved his mistress since they were teenagers. She would have been his first choice of bride.'

Gemma slowly shook her head. 'That's so sad. Sad for your father, sad for his mistress and tragic for your mother.'

'It is all that. Until recently I hadn't realised my father's relationship with his mistress stretched back that far. They genuinely love each other. Which made me all the more determined to change the ruling—not just for my sake but for future generations of our family.'

'How did you go about it?'

'I recruited some allies. My sister Natalia who—at the age of twenty-six—has already refused offers of marriage from six eligible, castle-approved suitors.'

'"Suitors". That's such an old-fashioned word,' she mused.

'There is nothing modern about life in the royal castle of Montovia, I can assure you. But things are changing.'

'And you like being that agent of change?'

'I believe my brother would have preserved the old ways. I want to be a different kind of king for my country.'

'That's what you meant by finding your purpose.' She put her hand gently on his cheek, her eyes warm with approval. 'I'm proud of you.'

'Thank you,' he said. 'You met my next recruit tonight—my cousin, who is in love with that lovely doctor he met during their time in the military. Then my mother came on board. She suggested we recruit my father's mistress. It is too late for them, but they want to see change.'

'Your father must have felt outnumbered.'

'Eventually he agreed to give us a fair hearing. We presented a united front. Put forward a considered argument. And we won. The king agreed to issue a new decree.'

'And you did all that—'

'So I could be with my sea nymph.'

For a long, still moment he searched her face, delighted in her slow smile.

'A lesser man might have given up,' she said.

'A lesser man wouldn't have had you to win. If I hadn't met you and been shown a glimpse of what life could be like, I would have given in to what tradition demanded.'

'Instead you came to terms with the role you were forced to step up to, and now Montovia will get a better ruler when the time comes.'

'All that.'

'I wish I'd known what you were doing,' she said.

'To get our hopes up and for them to come to nothing would have been a form of torture. I called you as soon as I got the verdict from the king.'

She frowned. 'What about your arranged bride? Where did she fit into this?'

'I discovered she did not want our marriage any more than I did. She was being pressured by her ambitious father. He was given sufficient reparation that he will not cause trouble.'

'So why didn't you tell me all this when I told you about my grandparents?'

'I did not want you to feel pressured by what I had done. My feelings for you have been serious from the start. I realised you'd need time to get used to the idea.'

She reached up and put her hand on his face. 'Isn't it already serious between us?'

He took her hand and pressed a kiss into her palm. 'I mean committed. It would be a very different life for you in Montovia. You will have to be sure it is what you want.'

'Yes,' she said slowly.

Tristan felt like the fisherman with his net. He wanted to secure Gemma to live with him in his country. But he knew, like the water nymph, she had to make that decision to swim to shore by herself.

CHAPTER SEVENTEEN

ON FRIDAY MORNING Tristan's sister, Natalia, took Gemma shopping to St Pierre, the city that was the modern financial and administrative capital of Montovia.

Gemma would rather have gone with Tristan, but he had asked Natalia to take her, telling them to charge anything she wanted to the royal family's account. No matter the cost.

St Pierre was an intriguing mix of medieval and modern, but Gemma didn't get a chance to look around.

'You can see the city another time,' Natalia said. 'Montovians dress more formally than you're probably used to. The royal family even more so. You need a whole new wardrobe. Montovians expect a princess to look the part.'

'*You* certainly do,' said Gemma admiringly.

Natalia dressed superbly. Gemma hoped she would be able to help her choose what she needed to fit in and do the right thing by Tristan. She suspected the white jacket might never get an airing again.

Natalia looked at her a little oddly. 'I wasn't talking about me. I was talking about you, when you become crown princess.'

Gemma was too stunned to speak for a moment. 'Me? Crown princess?'

'When you and Tristan marry you will become crown princess. Hadn't you given that a thought?'

Natalia spoke as though it were a done deed that Gemma and Tristan would marry.

'It might sound incredibly stupid of me, but no.'

In the space of just a few days she'd been whisked away by private jet and landed in a life she'd never known existed outside the pages of glossy magazines. She hadn't thought any further than being with the man she loved.

Natalia continued. 'You will become Gemma, crown princess of Montovia—the second highest ranking woman in the land after the queen—and you will have all the privileges and obligations that come with that title.'

Gemma's mouth went suddenly dry and her heart started thudding out of control. How could she, a girl from suburban Sydney, become a princess? She found the thought terrifying.

'It's all happened so incredibly quickly,' she said to Natalia. 'All I've focused on is Tristan—him stepping up to the role of crown prince and making it his own. I...I never thought about what it meant for me.'

Panic seemed to grasp her stomach and squeeze it hard. She took some deep breaths to try and steady herself but felt the blood draining from her face.

Natalia had the same shrewd blue eyes as her mother, the queen. 'Come on, let's get you a coffee before we start shopping. But you need to talk about this to Tristan.'

'Yes...' Gemma said, still dazed by the thought. *They had not talked nearly enough.*

Natalie regarded her from the other side of the table in the cafe she had steered Gemma to. She pushed across a plate of knotted sugar cookies. 'Eat one of these.'

Gemma felt a little better after eating the cookie. It seemed it was a traditional Montovian treat. She must get the recipe...

'The most important thing we've got to get sorted is a show-stopping formal gown for next Saturday night,' said Natalie. 'Tristan's birthday is a real milestone for him. My brother has changed the way royal marriages have worked for centuries so you two can be together. All eyes will be on you. We've got to have you looking the part.'

Again, terror gripped Gemma. But Natalia put a comforting hand on her arm.

'There are many who are thankful to you for being a catalyst for change. Me included.'

'That's reassuring,' said Gemma. Although it wasn't. Not really. What about those who *didn't* welcome change—and blamed her for it?

'The more you look like a princess, the more you'll be treated like one,' said Natalia.

Natalia took her into the kind of boutiques where price tags didn't exist. The clothes she chose for Gemma—from big-name designers, formal, sophisticated—emphasised the impression that she was hurtling headfirst into a life she'd never anticipated and was totally unprepared for.

She had to talk to Tristan.

But by the time she got back to the castle, sat through another formal dinner with his family—this time feeling more confident, in a deceptively simple black lace dress and her pearls—she was utterly exhausted.

She tried to force her eyes to stay open and wait for Tristan, but she fell fast asleep in the vast antique-style bed before he arrived.

During the night she became aware of him sleeping beside her, with a possessive arm around her waist, but when she woke in the morning he was gone. And she felt groggy and disorientated from a horrible dream.

In it, she had been clad only in the gauzy French bra and panties Natalia had helped her buy. Faceless soldiers had been dragging her towards a huge, grotesquely carved throne while she shouted that she wasn't dressed yet.

CHAPTER EIGHTEEN

BEING CROWN PRINCE brought with it duties Tristan could not escape. He hated leaving Gemma alone for the morning, but the series of business meetings with his father and the Crown's most senior advisers could not be avoided.

Gemma had still been asleep when he'd left her room. He'd watched her as she'd slept, an arm flung over her head to where her bright hair spilled over the pillow. Her lovely mouth had twitched and her eyelids fluttered, and he'd smiled and wondered what she was dreaming about. He'd felt an overwhelming rush of wonder and gratitude that she was there with him.

Like that fisherman, desperately hunting for his water nymph, the dream of being reunited with Gemma was what had kept him going through those months in the gloomy castle archives. He saw the discovery of her noble blood as confirmation by the fates that making her his bride was meant to be.

He'd gently kissed her and reluctantly left the room.

All throughout the first meeting he'd worried about her being on her own but had felt happier after he'd been able to talk to her on the phone. She'd reassured him that she was dying to explore the old town and had asked him for directions to his childhood favourite chocolate shop and tea room. He'd arranged for his driver to take her down and back. They'd confirmed that she'd meet him back at the castle for lunch.

But now it was lunchtime, and she wasn't in the rose garden, where he'd arranged to meet her. She wasn't answering her phone. His driver confirmed that he had brought her back to the castle. Had she gone back to her room for a nap?

He knocked on the door to her guest apartment. No answer. He pushed it open, fully expecting to find her stretched out on the bed. If so, he would revise his plans so that he could join her on the bed and *then* go out to lunch.

But the bed was empty, the apartment still and quiet. There was a lingering trace of her perfume, but no Gemma. *Where was she?*

A wave of guilt washed over him because he didn't know. He shouldn't have left her on her own. He'd grown up in the labyrinth of the castle. But Gemma was totally unfamiliar with it. She might actually have got lost. Be wandering somewhere, terrified. He regretted now that he'd teased her, telling her that some of the rooms were reputed to be haunted.

As he was planning where to start looking for her, a maid came into the room with a pile of fresh towels in her arms. She dipped a curtsy. Asked if he was looking for his Australian guest. She had just seen Miss Harper in the kitchen garden…

Tristan found Gemma standing facing the view of the lake, the well-tended gardens that supplied fruit and vegetables for the castle behind her. Her shoulders were bowed and she presented a picture of defeat and misery.

What the heck was wrong?

'Gemma?' he called. 'Are you okay?'

As he reached her she turned to face him. He gasped. All colour had drained from her face, so that her freckles stood out in stark contrast, her eyes were red rimmed and even her hair seemed to have lost its sheen. She was dressed elegantly, in linen trousers and a silk top, but somehow the look was dishevelled.

He reached out to her but she stepped back and he let his arms fall by his sides. 'What's happened?'

'I…I can't do this, Tristan.' Her voice was thick and broken.

'Can't do what? I don't know what you mean.'

She waved to encompass the castle and its extensive grounds. 'This. The castle. The life. It's so different. It's so *other*.' She paused. 'That's why I came here.' She indicated the vegetable garden, with its orderly plantings. 'Here it is familiar; here I feel at home. I…I pulled a few weeds from those carrots. I hope you don't mind?'

He wasn't exactly sure what she meant by 'other', but her misery at feeling as if she didn't fit in emanated from her, loud and clear.

'I'm sorry, Gemma. I didn't know you were feeling like this. I shouldn't have left you on your own.'

Her chin tilted upwards. 'I don't need a nursemaid, Tristan. I can look after myself.'

'You're in a foreign country, and you need a guide. Like you were *my* guide when I was in your home country.'

She took a deep, shuddering breath. 'I need so much more than a guide to be able to fit in here,' she said. 'I…I was so glad to be here with you—so excited that we could be together when we thought we never could.'

Was so glad?

'Me, too. Nothing has made me happier,' he said.

'But I didn't think about what it would mean to be a *princess*. A princess worthy of you. I'm a Party Queen— not a real queen in waiting. You need more than…than me…for Montovia.'

'Let me be the judge of that,' he said. 'What's brought this on, Gemma? Has someone scared you?'

Who could feel so threatened by the change of order they might have tried to drive her away? When he found who it was, heads would roll.

Gemma sniffed. 'It started with Natalia, she—'

His sister? He was surprised that she would cause trouble. 'I thought you liked her, that she was helping you?'

'I do. She was. But—'

He listened as she recounted what had happened the day before in St Pierre.

'I felt so…ignorant,' Gemma concluded. 'It hadn't even entered my head that I would be crown princess. And I have no idea of what might be expected of me.'

Mentally, Tristan slammed his hand against the side of his head. Why look for someone to blame when it was himself he should be blaming? He had not prepared her for what was ahead. Because she'd made such a good impression on his family, he had made assumptions he shouldn't have. Once she had swept into that magnificent curtsy, once he had seen the respect with which she interacted with his parents, he'd been guilty of assuming she would be okay.

His gut twisted painfully when he thought about how unhappy she was. And she hadn't felt able to talk to him. The man who loved her.

Tristan spoke through gritted teeth. 'My fault. I should have prepared you. Made it very clear to everyone that—'

'That I'm wearing my princess learner plates?' she said with another sniffle.

He was an intelligent, well-educated man who'd thought he knew this woman. Yet he'd had no idea of what she'd gone through since he'd dumped her into his world and expected her to be able to negotiate it without a map of any kind.

'What else?'

'The maid. I asked her to help me with a few phrases in Montovian, so I could surprise you. She told me her language was so difficult no outsider could ever learn to speak it. Then she rattled off a string of words that of course I

didn't understand and had no chance of repeating. I felt…
I felt helpless and inadequate. If I can't learn the language,
how can I possibly be taken seriously?'

'She loses her job today,' he said, with all the autocracy
a crown prince could muster.

Gemma shook her head. 'Don't do that. She was well-
meaning. She was the wrong person to ask for help. I
should have asked—'

'*Me*. Why didn't you?'

'I…I didn't want to bother you,' she whispered. 'You
have so much on your plate with your new role. I…I'm
used to being independent.' She looked down at her feet,
in their smart new Italian walking shoes.

'I'm sorry, Gemma. I've let you down. I can't tell you
how gutted I am that you are so unhappy.'

She looked up at him, but her eyes were guarded. 'I
was okay until Natalia mentioned something this morning
about when I become queen. She was only talking about
the kind of jewellery I'd need, but I freaked. Becoming
crown princess is scary enough. But *queen*!'

Now Tristan gritted his teeth. He'd let duty rule him
again—to his own personal cost. Those meetings this
morning should have been postponed. He might have lost
Gemma. Might still lose her if he didn't look after her better. And that would be unendurable.

'Anything else to tell me?'

She twisted the edge of her top between her fingers.
'The old man in the chocolate shop. He—'

'He said something inappropriate?' He found it hard to
reconcile that with his memories of the kindly man.

'On the contrary. He told me what a dear little boy you
were, and how he was looking forward to treating *our* children when we brought them in for chocolate.'

'And that was a problem?' Tristan was puzzled at the
way Gemma had taken offence at those genial words.

'Don't you see? *Children*. We've never talked about children. We haven't talked about our future at all. I feel totally unprepared for all this. All I know is that we want to be together. But is it enough?'

He did not hesitate. 'Yes. I have no doubt of that.'

She paused for so long dread crept its way into his heart.

'I...I'm not sure it is. You can do better than me. And I fear that if I try to be someone I'm not—like I spent so much of my life doing—I will lose myself and no longer be the person you fell in love with. You've grown up in this royal life. It's all so shockingly different for me—and more than a little scary. I don't want to make your life a misery because I'm unhappy. Do you understand that?'

'I will do anything in my power to make you happy.' His voice was gruff.

'I've been thinking maybe your ancestors had it right. When your new spouse comes from the same background and understands your way of life, surely that must be an advantage?'

'No,' he said stiffly. 'Any advantage is outweighed by the massive *dis*advantage of a lack of love in such a marriage.'

'I'm not so sure,' she said. 'Tristan, I need time to think this through.'

Tristan balled his hands into fists. He was not going to beg. She knew how he felt—how certain he had always been about her. But perhaps he had been wrong. After all the royal feathers he had ruffled, the conventions he had overturned, maybe Gemma did not have the strength and courage required to be his wife and a royal princess.

'Of course,' he said.

He bowed stiffly in her direction, turned on his heel and strode away from her.

Gemma watched Tristan walk away with that mix of military bearing and athletic grace she found so attractive. It struck her how resolute he looked, in the set of his shoulders, the strength of his stride.

He was walking out of her life.

Her hand went to her heart at the sudden shaft of pain. What a massive mistake she had just made.

He must think she didn't care. And that couldn't be further from how she felt.

The truth hit her with a force that left her breathless. This wasn't about her not understanding the conventions of being a princess, being nervous of making the wrong kind of curtsy. It was about her fearing that she wasn't good enough for Tristan. Deep down, she was terrified he would discover her inadequacies and no longer want her. This was all about her being afraid of getting hurt. She had behaved like a spineless wimp. A spineless, *stupid* wimp.

Through all the time she'd shared with Tristan, fragmented as it had been, he had been unequivocal about what he felt for her. He had tricked her onto the *Argus* because he had been so taken with her. He had confessed to a *coup de foudre.* He had left her with his phone because he had wanted to stay in touch. *He had changed the law of his country so they could be together.*

It was *she* who had resisted him from the get go—she who had backed off. *She* who had insisted they break all contact. If he hadn't left those messages on the phone, would she have even found the courage to call him?

And now the man who was truly her once-in-a-lifetime love had left her. He was already out of sight.

She had to catch him—had to explain, had to beg for another chance. To prove to him she would be the best of all possible princesses for him.

But he was already gone.

She ran after him. Became hopelessly confused as she hit one dead end after the other. Clawed against a bolted gate in her frustration. Then she remembered the ancient walkway he had taken her to on that first afternoon. The place where he went to think.

She peered up at the battlement walls. Noted the slits through which his ancestors had shot their arrows. Noticed the steps that wound towards the walkway. And picked up her speed.

He was there. Standing in the same arched lookout where she'd stood, admiring that magnificent view of the lake. His hands were clasped behind his back, and he was very still.

It struck her how solitary he seemed in his dark business suit. How *lonely*. Tristan was considered one of the most eligible young men in the world. Handsome, charming, intelligent and kind. Yet all he wanted was her. And she had let him down.

She swore under her breath, realised she'd picked up a Montovian curse word. And that it hadn't been as quiet as she'd thought.

He whipped around. Unguarded, she saw despair on his face—and an anger he wasn't able to mask. Anger at *her*.

'Gemma. How did you find me here?'

What if he wouldn't forgive her?

'I followed my heart,' she said simply.

Without a word Tristan took the few steps to reach her and folded her in his arms. She burrowed against his chest and shuddered her deep, heartfelt relief. *This was where she belonged.*

Then she pulled back from his arms so she could look up into his face. 'Tristan, I'm so sorry. I panicked. Was afraid I'd let you down. I lost sight of what counts—us being together.'

'You can *learn* to be a princess. All the help you need is here. From me. From my sister…my mother. The people who only wish you happiness.'

'I can see that now. You stepped up to be crown prince. I can step up to be crown princess. *I can do it.* But, Tristan, I love you so much and—'

He put his hand over her mouth to silence her. 'Wait. Don't you remember when we were at your grandmother's cottage? You instructed me not to say the L word until I was able to propose.'

'I do remember.' Even then she'd been putting him off. She felt hot colour flush her cheeks. 'When it comes to proposing, is it within the Montovian royal code of conduct for the woman to do the asking?'

'There's nothing I know of that forbids it,' he said.

'Okay, then,' she said. 'I'll do it. Tristan, would you—?'

'Just because you *can* propose, it doesn't mean I want you to. This proposal is mine.'

'I'm willing to cede proposing rights to you,' she said. She spread out her hands in mock defeat.

He took them both in his, looked down into her face. Her heart turned over at the expression in the blue eyes that had so captivated her from the beginning.

'Gemma, I love you. I love you more than you can imagine. 'Will you be my wife, my princess, my queen? Will you marry me, Gemma?'

'Oh, yes, Tristan. *Yes* to wife. *Yes* to princess. *Yes* to queen. There is nothing I want more than to marry you and love you for the rest of my life.'

Tristan kissed her long and sweetly, and she clung to him. How could she ever have thought she could exist without him?

'There's one more thing,' he said.

He reached into his inner pocket and drew out a small velvet box.

She tilted her head to one side. 'I thought…'

'You thought what?'

'Natalia implied that part of the deal at the crown

prince's birthday is that he publicly slips the ring on his betrothed's finger.'

'It has always been the custom. But I'm the Prince of Change, remember? I *had* intended to follow the traditional way. Now I realise that proposing to you in front of an audience of strangers would be too overwhelming for you—and too impersonal. This is a private moment— *our* moment.'

He opened the box and took out an enormous, multicarat cushion-cut diamond ring. She gasped at its splendour.

'I ordered the ring as soon as my father agreed to change the rule about royals marrying outside the nobility. I never gave up hope that you would wear it.'

He picked up her left hand. She noticed his hand was less than steady as he slid the ring onto her third finger.

'I love you, Gemma Harper—soon to be Gemma, crown princess of Montovia.'

'More importantly, soon to be your wife,' she said.

She held up her hand, twisting and turning it so they could admire how the diamond caught the light.

'It's magnificent, and I shall never take it off,' she said. She paused. 'Natalia said it was customary to propose with the prince's grandmother's ring?'

'That's been the custom, yes,' he said. 'But I wanted to start our own tradition, with a ring that has significance only to us. Your ring. Our life. Our way of ruling the country when the time comes.'

'Already I see how I can take my place by your side.'

'*Playboy Prince Meets His Match*?' he said, his voice husky with happiness.

'*Mystery Redhead Finds Her Once-in-a-Lifetime Love...*' she murmured as she lifted her face for his kiss.

CHAPTER NINETEEN

As GEMMA SWEPT into the castle ballroom on Tristan's arm, she remembered what Natalia had told her. 'The more you look like a princess, the more you'll be treated like one.'

She knew she looked her best. But was it *princess* best?

The exquisite ballgown in shades of palest pink hugged her shape in a tight bodice, then flared out into tiers of filmy skirts bound with pink silk ribbon. Tiny crystals sewn randomly onto the dress gleamed in the light of the magnificent chandeliers under which guests were assembled to celebrate the crown prince's thirtieth birthday.

The dress was the most beautiful she had ever imagined wearing. She loved the way it swished around her as she walked. Where in Sydney would she wear such a gown? Back home she might devise the *menu* for a grand party like this—she certainly wouldn't be the crown prince's guest of honour. What was that old upstairs/downstairs thing? Through her engagement to Tristan—still unofficial—she had been rapidly elevated to the very top stair.

The dress was modest, its bodice topped with sheer silk chiffon and sleeves. Natalia had advised her that a princess of Montovia was expected to dress stylishly yet modestly. She must never attract attention for the wrong reasons, be the focus of critical press or be seen to reflect badly on the throne.

So many rules to remember. Would she ever be able to relax again?

'You are the most beautiful woman in the room,' Tristan murmured in her ear. 'There will be much envy when I announce you as my chosen bride.'

'As long as I'm the most beautiful woman in your eyes,' she murmured back.

'You will always be that,' he said.

The thing was, she believed him. She felt beautiful when she was with him—whether she was wearing a ball-gown or an apron.

Yet even knowing she looked like a princess in the glorious gown, with her hair upswept and diamonds bor-rowed from the queen—*she had borrowed jewellery from a queen!*—she still felt her stomach fall to somewhere near the level of her silver stilettoes when she looked into the room. So many people, so many strange faces, so much priceless jewellery.

So many critical eyes on her.

Would they see her as an interloper?

Immediately Tristan stepped closer. 'You're feeling in-timidated, aren't you?'

She swallowed hard against a suddenly dry throat. 'Maybe,' she admitted.

In this glittering room, full of glittering people, she didn't know a soul except for Tristan and his family. And she was hardly on a first-name basis with the king and queen.

'Soon these faces will become familiar,' Tristan said. 'Yes, there are courtiers and officials and friends of my parents. But many of these guests are my personal friends—from school, the military, from university. They are so looking forward to meeting you.'

'That's good to hear,' she said, grateful for his consid-eration. Still, it was unnerving.

Thank heaven she hadn't been subjected to a formal receiving line. That would come at their formal engage-ment party, when she'd have the right to stand by Tristan's side as his fiancée. This was supposedly a more informal affair. With everyone wearing ballgowns and diamonds. Did Montovians actually *ever* do informal?

'Let me introduce you to someone I think you will like very much,' Tristan said.

He led her to a tall, thin, grey-haired man and his plump, cheery-faced wife. He introduced the couple as Henry and Anneke Blair.

'Henry was my English tutor,' Tristan said.

'And it was a privilege to teach you, Your Highness,' Henry said.

'Your English is perfect,' said Gemma.

'I was born and bred in Surrey, in the UK,' said Henry, with a smile that did not mock her mistake.

'Until he came to Montovia to climb mountains and fell in love with a local girl,' said his wife. 'Now he speaks perfect Montovian, too.'

Henry beamed down affectionately at his wife. So an outsider *could* fit in.

'Gemma is keen to learn Montovian,' said Tristan. 'We were hoping—'

'That I could tutor your lovely fiancée?' said Henry. He smiled at Gemma—a kind, understanding smile. 'It would be my pleasure.'

'And I would like very much to share with you the customs and history of the Montovian people,' said Anneke. 'Sometimes a woman's point of view is required.'

Gemma felt an immense sense of relief. She couldn't hope to fit in here, to gain the people's respect, if she couldn't speak the language and understand their customs. 'I would like lessons every day, please,' she said. 'I want to be fluent as soon as possible. And to understand the way Montovian society works.'

Tristan's smile told her she had said exactly the right thing.

Tristan had been right, Gemma thought an hour later. Already some of the faces in the crowd of birthday celebration guests were familiar. More importantly, she sensed a swell of goodwill towards her. Even among the older guests—whom she might have expected would want to adhere to the old ways—there was a sense that they cared for Tristan and wanted him to be happy. After so much tragedy in the royal family, it seemed the Montovians were hungry for a story with a happy ending and an excuse for gaiety and celebration.

She stood beside Tristan on a podium as he delivered a charming and witty speech about how he had fallen so hard for an Australian girl, he had worked to have the law changed so they could be together, only to find that she was of noble birth after all.

The audience obviously understood his reference to water nymphs better than she did, judging by the laughter. It was even more widespread when he repeated his speech in Montovian. She vowed that by the time his thirty-first birthday came around she would understand his language enough to participate.

She noticed the king had his head close to a tall, middle-aged woman, chatting to her with that air of familiarity only long-time couples had, and realised she must be his mistress. Elsewhere, the queen looked anxious in the company of a much younger dark-haired man. Even from where she stood, Gemma realised the man had a roving eye.

How many unhappy royal marriages had resulted from the old rules?

Then Tristan angled his body towards her as he spoke. 'It is the custom that if a crown prince of Montovia has not married by the age of thirty he is obliged to announce his engagement on the night of his birthday celebration. In fact, as you know, he is supposed to propose to his future bride in front of his assembled guests. I have once again broken with tradition. To me, marriage is about more than tradition and alliances. It is about love and a shared life and bringing children up out of the spotlight. I felt my future wife deserved to hear me ask for her hand in marriage in private.'

In a daze, Gemma realised she was not the only person in the room to blink away tears. Only now did she realise the full depth of what Tristan had achieved in this conservative society in order to ensure they could spend their lives together.

He took her hand in his and turned them back so they both faced the guests. The chandeliers picked up the facets in her diamond ring so it glinted into tiny shards of rainbow.

'May I present to you, my family and friends, my chosen bride: Gemma Harper-Clifford—future crown princess of Montovia.'

There was wild applause from an audience she suspected were usually rather more staid.

Her fiancé murmured to her. 'And, more importantly, my wife and the companion of my heart.'

'*Crown Prince Makes Future Bride Shed Tears of Joy…*' she whispered back, holding tightly to his hand, wanting never to let it go.

EPILOGUE

Three months later

IF TRISTAN HAD had his way, he would have married Gemma in the side chapel of the cathedral the day after he'd proposed to her.

However, his parents had invoked their roles as king and queen to insist that some traditions were sacrosanct and he would break them at his peril.

His mother had actually made mention of the medieval torture room in the dungeon—still intact and fully operational—should her son imagine he could elope or in any other way evade the grand wedding that was expected of him. And Tristan hadn't been 100 per cent certain she was joking.

A royal wedding on the scale that was planned for the joining in holy matrimony of Tristan, crown prince of Montovia, and Gemma Harper-Clifford, formerly of Sydney, Australia, would usually be expected to be a year in the planning.

Tristan had negotiated with all his diplomatic skills and open chequebook to bring down the planning time to three months.

But he had been so impatient with all the rigmarole required to get a wedding of this scale and calibre off the ground that Gemma had quietly taken it all away from him. She'd proceeded to organise the whole thing with remarkable efficiency and grace.

'I am a Party Queen, remember?' she'd said, flushed with a return of her old confidence. 'This is what I *do*. Only may I say it's a heck of a lot easier when the groom's family own both the cathedral where the service is to take place *and* the castle where the reception is to be held. Not to mention having a limitless budget.'

Now he stood at the high altar of the cathedral, dressed in the full ceremonial military uniform of his Montovian regiment, its deep blue tunic adorned with gold braid and fringed epaulettes. Across his chest he wore the gold-trimmed blue sash of the royal family and the heavy rows of medals and insignia of the crown prince.

Beside him stood his friend Jake Marlowe as his best man, two of his male cousins and an old school friend.

Tristan peered towards the entrance to the cathedral, impatient for a glimpse of his bride. She'd also invoked tradition and moved into his parents' apartment for the final three days before the day of their wedding. He had no idea what her dress—ordered on a trip to Paris she'd made with Natalia—would look like.

Seemed she'd also embraced the tradition of being ten minutes late for the ceremony...

Then he heard the joyous sound of ceremonial trumpets heralding the arrival of the bride, and his heart leapt. He was surprised it didn't set his medals jangling.

A tiny flower girl was the first to skip her way down the seemingly endless aisle, scattering white rose petals along the red carpet. Then Gemma's bridesmaids—his sister, Princess Natalia, Party Queens Andie and Eliza and Gemma's cousin Jane—each in gowns of a different pastel shade, glided down.

The trumpets sounded again, and the huge cathedral organ played the traditional wedding march. At last Gemma, flanked by her mother on one side and her Clifford grandfather on the other—both of whom were going to 'give her away'—started her slow, graceful glide down the aisle towards him.

Tristan didn't see the king and queen in the front pew,

nor the hundreds of guests who packed the cathedral, even though the pews were filled with family, friends and invited dignitaries from around the world, right down to the castle servants in the back rows. And the breathtaking flower arrangements might not have existed as far as Tristan was concerned.

All he saw was Gemma.

Her face was covered by a soft, lace-edged veil that fell to her waist at the front and at the back to the floor, to join the elaborate train that stretched for metres behind her, which was attended by six little girls from the cathedral school. Her full-skirted, long-sleeved dress was both magnificent and modest, as was appropriate for a Montovian bride. She wore the diamond tiara worn by all royal brides, and looked every inch the crown princess.

As she got closer he could see her face through the haze of the veil, and he caught his breath at how beautiful she was. Diamonds flashed at her ears—the king and queen's gift to her. And on her wrist was his gift to her—a diamond-studded platinum bracelet, from which hung a tiny platinum version of the wooden spoon she had wielded at their first meeting.

His bride.

The bride he had chosen and changed centuries of tradition for so he could ensure she would become his wife.

Tristan. There he was, waiting for her at the high altar, with the archbishop and the two bishops who would perform the ceremony behind her. She thought her heart would stop when she saw how handsome he looked in his ceremonial uniform. And the love and happiness that made his blue eyes shine bright was for her and only her. It was a particular kind of joy to recognise it.

She had never felt more privileged. Not because she was marrying into a royal family, but because she was joining her life with the man she loved. The *coup de foudre* of love at first sight for the mysterious Mr Marco had had undreamed-of repercussions.

She felt buoyed by goodwill and admiration for the way she was handling her new role in the royal family. And she was surrounded by all the people she loved and who loved her.

There was a gasp from the congregation when she made her vows in fluent Montovian. When Tristan slid the gold band onto her ring finger, and she and the man she adored were pronounced husband and wife, she thought her heart would burst from happiness.

After the service they walked down the aisle as a new royal couple to the joyful pealing of the cathedral bells. They came out onto the top of the steps of the cathedral to a volley of royal cannons being fired—which, Gemma could not help thinking, was something she had never encountered at a wedding before. And might not again until their own children got married.

Below them the town square was packed with thousands of well-wishers, who cheered and threw their hats in the air. *Their subjects.* It might take a while for an egalitarian girl from Australia to truly grasp the fact that she had *subjects*, but Tristan would help her with all the adjustments she would make in the years to come. With Tristan by her side, she could face anything.

Tension was building in the crowd below them and in the guests who had spilled out of the cathedral behind them. The first royal kiss of the newly wed prince and his princess was what they wanted.

She looked up at Tristan, saw his beloved face smiling down at her. They kissed.

The crowd erupted, and she was almost blinded by the lights from a multitude of camera flashes. They kissed again, to the almost hysterical delight of the crowd. A third kiss and she was almost deafened by the roar of approval.

Tristan had warned her that lip-readers would be planted in the audience, to see what they might say to each other in this moment. Why not write the headlines for them?

'*Prince Weds Party Planner*?' Tristan whispered.

'*And They Live Happily Ever After...*' she murmured as, together with her husband, she turned to wave to the crowd.

* * * * *